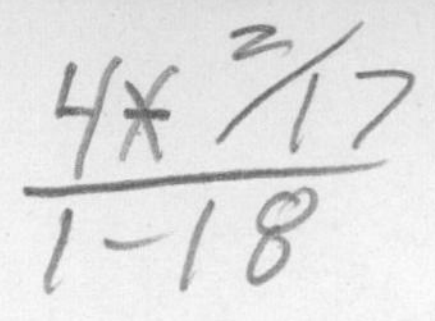

Third You Die

Books by Scott Sherman

SECOND YOU SIN

THIRD YOU DIE

Published by Kensington Publishing Corporation

Third You Die

SCOTT SHERMAN

KENSINGTON BOOKS
www.kensingtonbooks.com

KENSINGTON BOOKS are published by

Kensington Publishing Corp.
119 West 40th Street
New York, NY 10018

All Kensington titles, imprints, and distributed lines are available at special quantity discounts for bulk purchases for sales promotion, premiums, fund-raising, educational or institutional use.

Special book excerpts or customized printings can also be created to fit specific needs. For details, write or phone the office of the Kensington Special Sales Manager: Kensington Publishing Corp., 119 West 40th Street, New York, NY 10018. Attn. Special Sales Department. Phone: 1-800-221-2647.

ISBN-13: 978-0-7582-6652-1
ISBN-10: 0-7582-6652-9

First Kensington Trade Paperback Printing: October 2012
10 9 8 7 6 5 4 3 2 1

Printed in the United States of America

This book is for my mother, the fabled and fabulous "Terry T."

I keep waiting to write a book that's a little less raunchy to dedicate to her, but, since she survived reading the first two in the Kevin Connor series, I think she can handle this one, too.

My mother is a passionate writer and speaker. Growing up, we took family vacations in Florida. While the other mothers gossiped and ordered drinks by the pool, mine sat at an umbrella-shielded table with a manual typewriter, crafting an epistolary journal through letters to family and friends. She has a gift for language that is natural and charmingly creative—she employs humor and wordplay to make persuasive arguments and spin endlessly entertaining stories about everyday life.

She inspired every good thing in me, not the least of which is my love of reading and writing. Thanks, Mom, I love you forever.

Acknowledgments

Thank you for joining Kevin and me for his third outing. Let's hope he survives.

This was the first book I wrote as a single father, and it wasn't always easy. Okay, like everything else in my life in those transition months, it was staggeringly tough. Many thanks to my friends and family who stood by during this difficult period, especially to my sons, Sasha and David, who had to deal not only with divided dads, but with a dad who was divided. They say great art comes from great pain, but don't get your hopes up. Smile.

Much love to my literary agent, Matthew Carnicelli, and my editor at Kensington, John Scognamiglio. Thanks, guys, for helping Kevin come back.

PS: As with *Second You Sin,* there's a theme in the chapter titles to this book—can you figure it out? Send in your correct answer to the link on the home page at www.firstyoufall.com. On February 1, 2013, I'll pick a correct response at random. If you're right, you'll have your choice between a signed copy of *Third You Die* or the chance to have your name in print as a victim in my next book. Or, if you say something nice about the book, maybe both.

I always planned on the Kevin Connor books as being a trilogy. I'm glad to say that if they end with *Third You Die,* I think it's a satisfying send-off. However, weeks after sending off the manuscript, I thought, "What if . . . ?" I realized there may be more places to take Kevin, Tony, Freddy, and Rafi yet.

One of the things a mystery series writer has to juggle is keeping the aspects of your characters that readers enjoy while not letting them get stagnant. To my mind, too many series become dull when the protagonist and his or her circumstances are the same from book one to book twenty.

At the end of this book, I hope you agree that the Kevin here has grown a lot from the boy you met in *First You Fall.*

What do you think? Do you want to see more of his evolution, or shall we leave him now? I can't say much more without giving away what my beloved River Song from *Doctor Who* would warn are "spoilers, darling, spoilers." (PS: If you're a *Doctor Who* fan, you'll find a loving reference somewhere in this book. An Easter egg just for you!)

If you would like to see more of Kevin, please help spread the word. While I might like to write another in the series, and you might like to read it, my publisher would like to sell it. So, tell your friends, tell your neighbors, leave positive reviews on bookselling sites, and if all else fails, wouldn't you like a second copy of *Third You Die* for, I don't know, swatting flies or propping open doors?

Please join me on Twitter @ScottWrites, as, apparently, my entire self-worth as a human being is determined by the number of "followers" I have. Who knew?

Or check out my blog at www.scottshermanonline.com for the most current links to other social networks, as well as my thoughts on the mundane to the . . . less mundane.

Thanks for reading and for your support.

1

Perfect Fit

Listening to them bicker, interrupt, and compete among themselves for who had the most outrageous story, I couldn't decide which of the sex workers annoyed me most: the busty dominatrix in her black leather halter, too-tight read-my-lips matching slacks, and spiked, knee-high boots; the spray-tanned gay porn actor wearing a muscle-clinging T-shirt and painted-on jeans; or the plushie in the purple dinosaur costume who got off dressing as one of America's most beloved childhood icons.

"When men come before me," the dominatrix said haughtily, her imperious tone implying that not only they but we didn't deserve her time, "I give them something they can't get anywhere else. The feeling they are totally taken care of, that they no longer have to be 'in charge.' I give them the release that can only be achieved with true obedience. I give them the freedom of abandoning control and letting someone else—"

"You give them a spanking and they give you a few hundred bucks," the porn star interrupted. "You're a kitten with a whip, honey. Not a cross between Mother Teresa and Sigmund Freud. You need to stop taking this shit so seriously."

The dominatrix gave him a withering look that probably sent the submissives who hired her into quivering ecstasy. Her plain features knotted into a mask of extreme displeasure, thin lips and baggy eyes narrowing with practiced precision. "I wouldn't expect someone like *you* to understand," she sniffed. While I imagined that some women in her line of work role-played their arrogance, Mistress Vesper's bitchiness was no act. Well, I suppose there was something to be said for finding work that suited you.

"Someone like *me?*" The porn star, Brock Peters, was pretty butch, but I had a feeling that after a half hour of hearing Mistress Vesper's pretentious characterizations of her "art," he was about to go *Real Housewives* on her. The prodigious muscles in his shoulders rippled with tension. "You mean someone who has sex with guys for money? Someone like, I don't know, *you?*" He pointed his strong chin at her and pursed his mouth.

"As I've tried to explain," Mistress Vesper sighed, "what I do goes beyond the merely physical. When I'm with a man, I give him the release that only comes with pain, with the abandonment of the ego and the embrace of the id, the ultimate satisfaction of surrender, of . . ."

I stopped listening. This time, it wasn't my ADHD making me zone out. Rather, it was my need to find some way to rein this discussion in, to make it productive and interesting. After all, it was my job.

Up until six months ago, I'd have been on their end of the panel. A full-time professional call boy, I earned my living fulfilling the sexual needs and fantasies of a varied and well-to-do clientele.

It wasn't work I was ashamed of or regretted. I made tons of money, I had a good time, and I was always safe and sensible. Like Mistress Vesper, although hopefully with less smugness and self-aggrandizement, I'd like to think I was a valuable outlet for men who genuinely needed professional companionship.

Still, I knew it wasn't a long-term career. Sooner or later, my looks or luck would run out. I'd seen enough boys wear out their welcome in the business to know a forced retirement from hustling is never pretty.

Problem was, I wasn't qualified to do much else. Although I'm no dummy, my attention deficit disorder made completing college really hard for me. So hard, in fact, I dropped out year one.

At the time, I hadn't even been diagnosed. I just thought I was stupid and lazy. It was a potential-client-turned-friend, Allen Harrington, who realized the ditziness that everyone else attributed to my being blond was more likely a treatable disorder. He referred me to an appropriate doctor, and for the first time in my life, the mental haze through which I wandered parted enough for me to get stuff done. It was revelatory.

Now, liberal doses of Adderall make it a lot easier for me to focus and succeed. Someday, I tell myself, I'll go back to school for my degree. But you know how it goes—"someday" is a moving target, and so far I haven't hit it.

Allen did me another kindness. Before his death (his murder, actually, which I, ironically enough, was instrumental in solving) he left me a sizable inheritance for tuition when I was ready to resume my studies.

I have plenty of other uses for that money, but, out of respect for Allen's wishes, and as a promise to myself, I'm letting it sit and gather interest. *Someday,* I tell myself.

I tell Allen, too, if he's listening.

My world changed half a year ago when my mother appeared as a guest on *That's Yvonne,* a morning talk show named after its host. At the time, Yvonne was America's third most popular female celebrity. A sexy and spirited Latina, she enjoyed a carefully crafted public persona that was warm, caring, generous, and just risqué enough to titillate without being offensive. She was a saucier Oprah.

Then, in a disastrous meeting that rivaled that of the *Titanic*'s introduction to the inglorious iceberg, the beloved daytime diva crossed paths with my mother.

Shortly afterward, Yvonne's career sank lower than the luxury liner had.

Like most of my stories, it's a long one, but I'll try to give you the ADHD version. A boy I used to have a crush on in high school, Andrew Miller, was working as a producer on Yvonne's show. He booked my mother as a guest, partly as a way to see me again. Turned out, he'd known about my interest in him and was ready to follow up.

Had I known back then, I'd have been on him like pasties on Lady Gaga. Unfortunately, his timing was bad. By the time he contrived our reunion, the last thing I needed was another guy to juggle. Which was too bad, because Andrew was still hotness on legs. Long, muscled legs, that carried him with the confident grace of the natural-born athlete he was. Legs that even under loose khakis revealed rippling thighs you couldn't but imagine nude as you . . .

Okay, I'm getting off track here.

Focus, Kevin, focus.

So, my mom was talking with Yvonne when the hostess revealed herself as a homophobic, anti-Semitic bitch. Unknown to both of them, the conversation was being videotaped. When Yvonne threatened to sue my mother for making her bald (I told you it was a long story), Andrew, who had long suffered under Yvonne's imperious rule, leaked the video online. That was pretty much it for the woman formerly known as "The Darling of Daytime."

When the producers of *That's Yvonne* sacked her, they needed a new talker to take her place. By this time, the online video of her meltdown had achieved over five million views. Who better to replace Yvonne than the Long Island hausfrau who took her down? By then, my mother had appeared on *Good Morning America,* the David Letterman show, and even on *60 Minutes*. It turned out her brash tell-it-like-it-is style, lack of personal boundaries, and borderline vulgarity that so embarrassed me growing up made her a natural for TV. Audiences found her a genuinely likable character—easy to relate to and impossible to look away from.

Of course, people stare at car crashes, too.

My mother made it part of the deal that Andrew be promoted to head producer and, thus, her TV career was born. The show, named after her, was now *Sophie's Voice*. (Apparently, I was the only person in the world who thought a pun based on a book about the Holocaust was in bad taste.)

Four months after going on air, *Sophie's Voice* was an undeniable hit. No one could say how long the ride would last (remember Ricki Lake?) but, for now, my mother and everyone else involved in the show was riding high.

"I've always known I was a star," my mother told me calmly in her office, as her staff whooped and hollered after the show's first month's shockingly high ratings hinted that her fame was possibly more than a passing fad. "I'm just glad everyone else figured it out, too."

"The only saving grace about your mother's newfound notoriety," my long-suffering father told me on the phone later that day, with his trademark blend of pessimistic optimism, "is that she was *already* impossible to live with. It's not like she could get any worse. Plus, this *fakakte* TV show keeps her out of the house. So, that's good."

Meanwhile, the show was an opportunity for me, too. I'd been getting away with calling myself a "consultant" for the past few years, but I knew I'd eventually need a "real" job. When Andrew approached me about working on my mother's show, I was initially reluctant. For one thing, the idea of spending that much time with my mother, in a high-pressure environment, was about as appealing as a colonoscopy, only with more crap involved. It's not that I don't love her—I do—it's just she drives me crazy.

For another, I didn't have any experience in television. What would I *do?*

Luckily, this time Andrew got it right. His idea was to make me the coordinator of casting. This meant it was my job to help choose and screen the guests that appeared on the show.

I might have never worked in TV before, but years of being a call boy had taught me how to quickly size up people, figure out if they were crazy or not, and how to bring out their best.

Those skills proved right in line with those needed to pick the kinds of guests who'd "pop" on a daytime talk show. I had a knack for getting inside the heads of potential interviewees. I could help them find their most interesting story and focus them on how to tell it. I could also craft the questions for my mother to ask and help the producers with setups that would wring the most drama from the guest's appearance.

Part of what made me successful at getting people to open up to me was my personality, but part was my appearance. I'm not the handsomest guy in the world, but what I am is *cute*. Short, boyish, with floppy blond hair and a button nose, I'm unthreatening and look trustworthy, the archetypal All-American boy next door. That image supported me for years as a hustler; now it worked for me as an interviewer.

Hey, you gotta play the hand you're dealt.

Plus, no longer making my living in an illegal profession *definitely* made things easier with Tony Rinaldi, the cop who recently graduated from being my semi-boyfriend to full-time lover. He'd been tolerant of my work, but I knew he didn't approve. Plus, now that we were kind of raising a kid together, it was even more complicated. So, *Sophie's Voice,* while not without its challenges, was proving to be a good thing.

Of course, we'd see how things went after today's taping. This was a pretty far-out panel. It had the potential of being an episode that would keep people talking for days, or the kind of train wreck that would have people switching to the Food Network as fast as their remotes could carry them.

I was about to find out.

2

Afterparty

"Come on, ladies," my mother yelled as she strode onstage, shouting to be heard over the raucous cries of her studio audience. "Let's be real for a minute. We all like to get a little . . . wild . . . in the bedroom every once in a while, don't we?"

The audience hooted their agreement as I struggled not to imagine what my mother might have done in the bedroom that would qualify as "wild."

Must. Turn. Off. Brain.

"All right," my mother said, settling into the easy chair from which she hosted the show. She dropped her voice to a conspiratorial whisper. "Maybe not *all* of us. Let's face it, I'm pretty sure the wildest thing I've ever done in the bedroom was wear my rollers to sleep."

The audience exploded in laughter.

"What can I say? I'm a nice Jewish girl from Long Island. But, you know what? It takes all kinds. And today, we have a panel of playful and proud entrepreneurs who've figured out how to turn their kinks into cash. Or, as we like to call it, fetishes for fun and profit!"

More whooping from the suburban housewives in the stands. They knew my mother was about to give them a PG-13 glimpse into a world they'd previously experienced only through the genius of Sidney Sheldon and Judith Krantz.

It was also a world in which I've done a lot more than read about it. When things got serious between me and Tony, I'd made a deal with him: I wouldn't give up working as a paid escort, but I'd only do "non-insertive" sex work. That meant no blow jobs, no fucking. I had to get creative.

So, I wound up specializing in guys who had more . . . elaborate fantasies. I acted out all kinds of doctor/patient, naughty schoolboy and look-but-don't-touch scenes. I had sessions with a john who wanted me to pelt him with pies while dressed like a clown and got paid $500 from another who just wanted to smell my wet hair. It wasn't a bad gig.

I also enjoyed it beyond the financial rewards. I felt like I was doing these guys a real service. What got them off didn't hurt anyone but them. And not physically, either—I'm talking about the emotional pain that accompanies sexual drives that don't fit the "norm." When one of my clients got into a relationship, there was always a tension for him—does he dare tell his partner the truth about what he wants? Or is it wiser to play it safe and not risk the rejection that might accompany telling your lover that you want him to dress up like Captain America and throw his shield at your balls?

It's a terrible thing to be ashamed of your own sexuality.

What my mother was about to expose her audience to was tame in comparison to some of the things I'd done.

"First, we'll hear from a woman who gets paid hundreds of dollars from men who want her to spank them!" my mother continued. The audience's cheers went even wilder when my mother mock-whispered, "although, those of us who are married probably would be more than happy to do it for free when our husbands forget to take out the garbage for the fifth time in a row, right, ladies?

"Then, we meet a gay man who didn't have the courage to come out until he found out he could get paid for it—and now he's one of the adult film industry's biggest stars. And let me tell you, ladies, I got a look at this guy backstage as he was getting dressed for the show, and I can see why he's so 'big,' in the business, if you know what I mean." Her wink made the comment more adorable than lewd.

"Last, but not least, we'll be introducing you to the world of plushophiles, people who get their jollies from dressing like stuffed animals. At least, I *hope* we'll be introducing you to that world. Because, if you're already into that kind of thing, what are you doing here? There's a Build-A-Bear Workshop not two blocks away!"

More laughter. I'd suggested that line and was happy to hear it go over so well.

"Then, we'll bring 'em all together and see how they get along. Is there harmony among those who walk on the saucy side of the street, or is business the dirtiest game of all? Stay tuned, and we'll be back with our wildest show yet!"

The APPLAUSE sign lit up, but it wasn't needed. As always, my mom had the crowd in the palm of her hand.

I just hoped she could keep it there.

"Well, my boy," Andrew Miller said in a mock-authoritative tone, "once again, you done me proud."

We were standing in the back of the studio as the crowd rose to cheer the departing panel of perverts who'd entertained them for the past forty minutes. The show had gone great. My mother kept the conversation just racy enough to be entertaining without it becoming threatening. She found the humor in every kink, but was never demeaning. The guests seemed to genuinely enjoy talking with her. The last segment, where they all came out together, was raunchy, raucous, and, in the end, good-natured. The highlight was when Mistress Vesper spanked the gay porn star Brock Peters to demonstrate her craft.

"Now I know why I like guys," he proclaimed, and the audience screamed with delighted shock. My mother suggested the mistress might have more success with the plushie, but he couldn't feel anything through his thick purple dinosaur suit.

Andrew threw his arm around my shoulders. "That's going to be one for the archives. Honestly, Kevin," he said, pulling me closer, "I can't think of anyone else who could have put together such a great panel. Or gotten more out of them." He punctuated his praise with an extra little squeeze.

I was too aware of the heat coming off his body. His ridged

oblique muscles pressed against me—I could feel their definition through my shirt and his. He must be ridiculously shredded. I felt myself tingling in places I shouldn't be tingling.

I loved Tony, but I was only human.

"Thanks," I said, twisting my body away and turning as if I wanted to face him. Actually, I just wanted to put some distance between us. "I'm relieved. They were a pretty . . . colorful bunch in the pre-interview. Things got a little heated."

Andrew's eyes swept me from head to toe. "What's wrong with getting a little hot?"

When we reunited six months ago, Andrew came on like a house on fire, and I had to hose him down. He'd behaved himself since then, but there was still an undercurrent of flirtatiousness. One which I kind of enjoyed. As long as it didn't sweep me out to sea, that is.

Speaking of which, we were about to be swamped by the flood of audience members leaving the theater. They gathered their things, noisily discussing how much fun they'd had.

"Let's go backstage," I suggested, "and bid our guests a fond good-bye. Shall we?"

"You got it," Andrew agreed. "But I'm not getting too close to the plushie. Did you notice the stains on his fur?"

I gave a little shudder. "Maybe you can handle Mistress Vesper."

"I'd rather handle that Brock Peters. He looks even better in real life than on my TV."

"You watch his movies?"

"Watch them? I own the boxed set."

I smacked him on the shoulder. "You are the biggest horn dog."

"Guilty." Andrew shrugged. "Plus, Peters came with a few other guys from his studio. Half the cast of *Star Whores—The Phantom Penis* are here."

"And me without my autograph book," I told him with a grin. I batted my eyes coquettishly. "Whatever will I do?"

"Come on," Andrew said, swatting my butt. "I'm sure we'll find something they can sign."

* * *

On the way backstage with Andrew, a production assistant stopped me with a question about the next day's show.

"Go on," I told Andrew. "I'll catch up with you later." I answered the PA's queries and headed to say my good-byes.

My parting exchanges with both Mistress Vesper and the plushie went quickly. I didn't see Andrew in either room. Maybe he'd finished quickly.

Mistress Vesper gave me a firm handshake. She extended an invitation for me to feel free to give her a call if I was a "bad boy" who needed some punishment. I promised to keep her in mind.

Plushie tried to hug me good-bye, but I avoided it with a playful high five. I'm not a germaphobe, but I imagined the places that fake fur had been and doubted it was easy to clean. I could practically see the salmonella and Ebola crawling all over it. I beat a hasty retreat and wiped the palm of my hand on my pants.

My last stop was to the small room we'd set up for Brock Peters, but it was empty. I must have missed him. No great loss. I was walking out when I heard voices and laughter coming from down the hall. It sounded like a party. The only thing in that direction was a large space we sometimes used for full staff meetings.

Just then, another PA came out of it with an armful of empty pizza boxes. I gave her a quizzical look.

"It's the gay porn guys," she said, anticipating my question. "There's a whole gaggle of them. Bigger than the entourage that arrived with Beyoncé. When Andrew saw they were overflowing the space we'd given them, he invited them to use the conference room."

She looked at the cardboard boxes she was schlepping to the trash. "He sprang for 'catering,' too. You should check it out. It's a good time."

On my way to the conference room, I noticed a gross smell. I sniffed and followed it to Oliver Armstrong, our maintenance worker. As I got closer, the odor got worse, almost overpowering.

Oliver was a good worker, but a bit of a weirdo, with an Asperger's-like discomfort around people. I was one of the few guys here he could look in the eyes. He also seemed a little slow. I was glad we were able to employ him, but I sometimes worried about him.

Had he not been showering lately? The stench emanating from him was gag-inducing. Rotten eggs mixed with body odor covered in sour milk. It barely smelled human. My eyes watered.

I dreaded having this conversation with him. It was hard enough for him to feel comfortable around people, and now one of the few he trusted had to confront him. But someone had to let him know this kind of hygiene wasn't acceptable in the workplace.

"Oliver," I began, "I hate to tell you this, but . . ."

Oliver held up a silver canister he'd been carrying by his side. "It's not me," he said. He moved the container closer to me, and sure enough the smell strengthened.

"My lord," I said, waving at him to hold the canister away. "What is that crap?"

"Some kind of chemical." He pointed to the label. "Ethanethiol."

"What is it?" I asked. "Some kind of insecticide?" I hoped not. It might get rid of the roaches, but it'd likely send the staff scurrying, too.

Oliver shuffled nervously. He hadn't been doing anything wrong, but just this level of human interaction was hard for him. "Naw, it's the gas company. They installed it in the main system in the basement. It's part of the alarm system. If there's a gas leak, some of this stuff gets out, too."

"So we die of the stench before the gas kills us?" I asked.

Oliver smiled. It was nice to see he could get a joke. "Actually, it's to save us. Gas is odorless. If it leaks, we wouldn't know till it was too late. But they said if we do have a breakdown, this stuff will be released into the line. Gets everyone out of the building real quick-like."

"Yeah," I agreed. "That makes sense. There'd be no missing that smell."

"And that's what it smells like *inside* the bottle," Oliver said.

"I was there when they poured some into the alarm system. I thought I'd hurl."

"You throwing that away?" I asked.

"No, the gas people said we have to save it. I'm bringing it into the storeroom. I'm gonna put it into a trash bag, then another, and throw them both into a sealed storage box I have in there. That should be enough to keep the smell from leaking out."

"I hope so," I said. "But you have to work there every day. If that's not enough, let me know. We'll find somewhere else to store it."

Oliver looked genuinely touched that I cared enough to offer my help. "You got it, man," he said, smiling despite the stench.

Two smiles from Oliver in one conversation. I felt like I'd won the jackpot.

I reached the conference room. The PA with the pizza boxes wasn't exaggerating. The room was filled with about fifty people, all talking excitedly. About ten were staffers with the show; the others must have arrived with Brock. If so, they'd have to catch up with him later. I wasn't surprised to see his attention monopolized by Andrew. The two stood closerthanthis in a far corner of the room, their body language engaged and flirtatious.

Everyone else appeared to be either friends of Brock's or coworkers. A mix of pretty boys, handsome men, and the less physically favored who bankrolled the operation. It was one of the latter who approached me first.

"Well, hello," he drawled, stretching out the greeting like a lizard uncoils his tongue. It wasn't the only reptilian thing about him. High cheekbones drew your attention to his badly capped teeth. His skin was pulled unnaturally tight, and his eyes were slanted and narrowed to barely functional slits by what I'd guess were at least a handful of overambitious face-lifts.

Had it not been for all the tinkering, he might have been handsome. Underneath it all, you could see the bone structure of a movie star from the 1950s. But too much plastic surgery, too many tanning beds, and his predatory smile combined to give him the friendly appeal of a hungry crocodile.

He regarded me with the same top-to-bottom appraisal Andrew had earlier, but this one was decidedly creepier, accompanied by lip smacks and a quiet whistle of approval at the end. I'd been a professional sex worker for years, but never felt dirtier than I did under this slimy bastard's spectacularly unsubtle review.

Had I been the ingénue of a Jane Austen novel, I would have slapped him at this point. Instead, I gave him my phoniest smile. (Actually, I'm not sure about that metaphor. I've never read any Jane Austen except for *Pride and Prejudice and Zombies,* where I'm pretty sure the guy who updated it might have taken some dramatic license.)

"Tell me," Lizard Man asked, "why is a perfect specimen like you not working for me?"

"For one reason: I already have a job," I answered, pointing to my ID badge. "I help coordinate the show."

"This," he said, cupping my chin, "is a face that belongs in front of the camera, not behind it." He craned his neck to peer over my shoulder. "Speaking of behinds . . ."

I stepped back.

"I didn't get your name," I said.

The crocodile reached into the pocket of his expensive silk blazer. He extracted a pricey-looking pewter business card holder that he flicked open through some hidden mechanism. A single card automatically slid forward. It was like a magic trick meant to astound the easily impressed. I was reminded of an entertainer at a children's party and wondered if my new acquaintance liked his boys on the younger side.

"Mason Jarre," he announced, as I took his card. It was heavy and expensively embossed. He pronounced his last name "Jar-Ray," as if from the French. His heavy Brooklyn accent spoke otherwise.

"I'm the owner of SwordFight Productions. Brock Peters is *exclusive* with us."

Your mother must be so proud, I wanted to say. "Well, we really enjoyed having him on today's show. Thanks for sharing."

"I'm serious about the offer." He ignored my attempt to shift the conversation. "You have the face of an angel and a body built for sin. I could make you a star." He ran his tongue, which thankfully wasn't forked, over his lower lip.

I kept smiling, but in my head I was thinking of running after Oliver to get some of that ethanethiol. That'd empty the room. I'd already had enough of these people. "I don't want to be a star. But thanks."

Mason reached out and took my hand. He curled his fingers around mine, in a gesture that forced me to more tightly cup his business card. "*Everyone* wants to be a star, angel." He looked past me. "But don't take my word for it."

He turned to the younger man who had come up from behind and now stood at Mason's left. "This is one of my finest directors, Kristen LaNue."

Kristen looked like a younger, Hispanic version of Mason. Undamaged by age, or, more accurately, by excessive efforts to fight it, Kristen was genuinely attractive. He had Mason's long, angular features, but with pretty green eyes and smooth, unblemished skin. He had a trendy buzz cut that flattered his well-shaped head and a neatly trimmed goatee that called attention to his full, sensuous lips. I'd guess he was about twenty years younger than Mason, which would put him in the mid-thirties.

Had I opened a door to find him there in my call boy days, I'd have been thankful to find someone that attractive. Since I worked partly for tips, I'd also have appreciated his obviously expensive clothing. He wore a Ralph Lauren Black Label denim bomber over the same line's V-neck tee. I'd been drooling over them at Bloomingdale's a few days ago—the jacket went for an impressive $3,000. Even the T-shirt was north of a Benjamin.

I couldn't tell what kind of jeans he wore, but they looked damn good on him. Tapered enough to highlight his strong thighs, but not obnoxiously tight, they rode low on his narrow hips. My guess was they didn't come from the Gap. Neither did his boots, which I pegged as Maison Martin Margiela, adding at least another grand to his outfit.

Apparently, directing dirty movies was a more lucrative job than I realized. I might need to reassess my career choice.

"I can always count on you to find the prettiest boy in the room," Kristen said to Mason. The comment was gratuitous, but Kristen pulled it off with more charm than his mentor. He extended his hand and gave me a firm shake, holding on for a second or two too long. We exchanged introductions.

His voice was sexy, too. Lightly but noticeably accented.

"I was just telling Kevin," Mason said, "he should drop in for an interview. I'd love to see how he comes across on tape. I bet he'd light the camera on fire."

Kristen leaned into me. "You'll have to excuse him," he said with a wink. "He's always recruiting. Although"—he arched his eyebrows suggestively—"he's not wrong. I hope you don't mind my saying this, but you're an extraordinarily good-looking young man. Very much the whole Abercrombie thing going on. Have you modeled?"

I shook my head. "I'm flattered, but I'm really not interested."

Kristen shrugged. "Well, don't dismiss it out of hand. You'd be surprised how much you can make and the doors it can open. You know, sex is a natural and healthy part of life. You're a beautiful boy, and beauty is one of the few gifts you can share that gives back more than you give. Getting paid for making love doesn't make you a whore."

Having actually *been* a whore, I wanted to laugh. I had no problem exchanging sex for money. I just didn't want it recorded.

You never knew when you might want to run for president.

"Thanks," I said, starting to make my exit.

"Kevin." Kristen hadn't raised his voice, but it still froze me in my tracks. He had a natural authority I'd wager served him well in his job. I could see him commanding a chaotic film set. "Promise me you'll think about it. I take my art very seriously. I think you'll be proud to have worked with me."

His "art." A pornographer with pretensions. I couldn't decide if it was sweet or obnoxious.

At least I never called my sex work "physical therapy."

3

The Road to Temptation

After bidding the politest possible good-byes to Mason and Kristen, I decided to get out of there. I was halfway to the door when I bumped into a strikingly pretty young man.

"Sorry," I said.

He wasn't my type at all, but I couldn't help but be impressed. Blond hair in an almost eighties shag, parted down the middle. Bright blue eyes framed by girlishly long eyelashes. Creamy-looking skin that made you want to lick it.

He was of medium build, bigger than me, but still boyish. Slim and well muscled like an Australian lifeguard.

Despite his slight advantage in height, he reminded me of a younger version of myself. He could have been my kid brother.

"No problem," he said quietly. "I'm Brent."

"Kevin," I said, extending my hand. "Nice to meet you." He looked so ill at ease that I smiled to relax him.

He glanced at my hand as if it surprised him there, then took it and pumped with the earnestness of a high school student interviewing for an internship. His eyes searched my face for a sign of something . . . recognition?

"Brent *Havens,*" he clarified.

"Okay," I answered. "Kevin *Connor.*" Maybe we were playing some new game that involved emphasizing your last name.

Brent seemed confused by my obvious mirroring of his inflection, then something else. Relieved?

"I just . . . you don't know who I am?"

"Sorry." I grimaced. "I don't mean to be rude. Should I?"

"No." Brent smiled more comfortably now, revealing perfect teeth and an adorable dimple. "I mean, it's just at these industry things Mason makes me come to, everyone usually knows me. Well, they *think* they know me. They've seen my pictures. Videos." A look of distaste crossed his face. "You really have no idea who I am?"

With his postpubescent good looks and slightly androgynous sexiness, he looked like he could be the star of a Nickelodeon or Disney TV show. But I was long past my days of *Degrassi* and *iCarly*. I grimaced. "Sorry, buddy. I think this is the first time I've ever seen you."

"Then you'd make a really bad detective. Look around you, bro."

He waved around the room, where people had propped or pinned various SwordFight Productions posters. In one, about ten guys stood shirtless with their arms around each other. The two in the middle stood closest to the camera and dominated the group. One was Brock Peters, the model we'd just had on the show.

The other was Brent.

I noticed a few other posters then, as well as some brochures left out by the pizzas. Sure enough, Brent's pretty face appeared on more than half of them. One of the signs was a smiling close-up of him with the headline "The New Face of SwordFight—Our Freshest Catch Yet."

Clearly, Brent was a rising star. Or a risen one.

"I'm kind of glad you didn't know me," Brent said. "I'm tired of those guys who think they do." He crossed his arms defensively across his chest and stuck out his chin at the "Fresh Catch" poster. "They know *him*."

I felt like he was defending himself from a charge I hadn't lobbed.

"I'm glad I met *you* first, then," I said, realizing as I did that it came out a little flirtatious. Which wasn't what I was going for.

At least, not consciously.

"I don't understand how you could be working with Sword-Fight and not have seen me, though." Brent's voice carried a hint of suspicion. I was sure a boy as pretty as he had men lie to him on many an occasion to get close.

"I'm not with Mason," I explained. "I'm with the show."

Brent looked a little confused. Once again I had the weird sense I knew what he was thinking. *Isn't that what Mason does? Make shows?*

"*This* show," I clarified. "The one Brock was on. *Sophie's Voice.*"

Brent's smile returned, as did his relief. Relaxed, he looked even cuter. Younger, too. "Oh my god," he enthused, now exuding a total tween vibe. "I *love* her. You get to *work* with her? That must be *so much* fun." He bounced on his heels with enthusiasm.

Wanting to keep him at ease, I tried to think of something that would convince him to further relax his guard. "I'll tell you a secret, if you promise to keep it to yourself."

Brent's eyebrow rose with the wariness of a boy accustomed to guys trying to make deals with him. I knew the feeling. He hesitated, and then nodded.

I regretted making him anxious again, but knew the payoff would be worth it.

"I do more than just work with her—she's my mom."

"No!"

"Yes!"

Brent gushed some more about my mother and how great it must be to have a "totally cool" mother like her. I let him enjoy the fantasy.

"You're so lucky," he said. "A great mom and a rocking job. You must love your work."

"Don't you?" The life of a porn star was the fantasy of many.

Brent shrugged. "Parts of it." Then, a dirty smile. "Okay, *big* parts of it. It can be a lot of fun. And it's kind of cool to be able to get in to any club or meet any guy. And the money's sweet.

"But . . . look, I'm not stupid. I sought this out. I went after this. I sent my homemade video to Mason because I wanted to be in the movies. I knew what I was getting into. But I didn't expect to always be so . . . on display. Like a piece of meat.

"And they're always wanting you to do *more*. To give the audience something they haven't seen you do before. I mean, I'm only twenty-one, but I'm running out of tricks."

"You're twenty-one?" That was the part that surprised me the most.

Brent laughed. "I know, I look a lot younger. I get that all the time. I bet you do, too."

I nodded.

"You know, I couldn't help but notice . . . ," Brent began.

"We could pass as brothers," I finished.

Brent cracked up. Now that he was past his initial discomfort, he was as winning as a boy gets. He got me laughing, too. We were giggling like two schoolboys when our eyes locked and the mood abruptly changed.

"Listen," Brent said. "You seem like a really nice guy. I don't do this a lot, but would you like to get together sometime? Somewhere else? Like, a date?" A blush like a wildfire raced across his cheeks.

Lord, he was a cutie.

"I would love to," I answered. "But I have a boyfriend."

Brent took a step closer. "I won't tell if you don't."

I cocked my head.

"I know," Brent said. "You're a Good Guy, right? One who doesn't cheat on his man?"

"Guilty as charged. Although, if I did, you'd be number one on the list. You're smart, you're adorable, you're funny—so, why are you single?"

Brent pointed at his poster again. "They all want *him*. They don't even know who I am."

"Who are you?"

"Promise not to tell?"

"Hey, I told you *my* secret," I reminded him.

Brent's expression turned serious. "The truth is . . ." He leaned in closer, his lips to my ear. His breath was hot against my face. "I really *am* your brother. Your parents' secret love child whom they abandoned to be raised by wolves and porno producers." He gave a sensual little nip to my earlobe and stepped back.

"So," he concluded, "it's probably better we don't date. Considering the blood relation and all." He grinned cockily.

I hoped he didn't glance downward. His little flirtation had gotten a rise out of me.

Literally.

I'm only human.

I shoved my hands into my front pockets, trying to make it look casual. "So," I asked, "how do you tell the difference?"

The cocky grin faded. "What do you mean?"

"Between the wolves and the producers?"

Brent laughed again, his musical giggle lighting up the room. "If you're going to reject me, could you stop being so funny and interesting?" he asked politely.

"Believe me, it's not that easy saying no to you. Of course, it'd be easier if you'd tell me who I was saying no to. . . ."

"Right," Brent said. He pitched his voice low. "You actually want to know the real me. It's a nice change."

This time, he extended a hand. "I'm Richard. Everyone calls me Richie, though. From Queens, New York."

I took his hand in mine, this time with none of the earlier formality. I felt like we'd become fast friends. There was an immediate connection between us. I knew there'd be even more of one if I ever told him how I'd been making a living just a few months ago.

"Well, it's nice to meet you, Richie. And, if you're into it, I'd still like to get together for a coffee or something. Maybe we can figure out how you can meet a guy who isn't only interested in 'him.' " I made air quotes with my fingers while nodding toward his poster.

"Actually, I already have. This guy named Charlie. I kind of like him. But the problem is, he's got major issues with my work. He doesn't want me to ever be 'Brent' again. He can't stand the thought of me being with other guys. Especially on film. He really hates it. I keep telling him to separate what I *do* from who I *am*, but I think it's a losing battle."

I thought of my own situation with Tony. He never pressured me to give up my work, but there was a time when I had to change the specifics of what I did to appease him. "Is this Charlie guy worth finding a new line of work?"

"Maybe. But not yet. And since he's getting kind of pushy about it, I'm thinking I'm going to have to break it off with him."

His face seemed to lengthen with sadness. "Which is really too bad, ya know?"

I nodded sympathetically.

" 'Cause I'm kind of sweet on him. But these guys, they go from one extreme to the other. They either want the fantasy, like the old men who offer me fifty thousand a month to live with them and role-play characters from my movies, or they want to kill the fantasy, destroy 'Brent Havens' and everything that goes along with him.

"Besides"—Brent's expression darkened—"it's a lot easier to get into this business than to leave it."

"What do you mean?"

Brent—or should I say Richie now?—dropped his voice again. "Look around you. SwordFight has spent a lot of money promoting me. Making me a 'star.' They could make it hard for me to walk away."

My mind immediately went to organized crime. "What do you mean?"

"It's a dirty business. But I have insurance. I know stuff about them, too. I could blow the lid off SwordFight.

"The stories I could tell could shut them down. Probably put some of them in jail. How they helped me . . ." He didn't finish his sentence as his eyes widened with a new idea.

"Hey, maybe I could do it here. On your mom's show. Get my story out before they have a chance to spin things their way."

I didn't have the heart to tell him *Sophie's Voice* wasn't exactly *60 Minutes*. Plus, something about what he said didn't ring true. I'd have to think about it later, when I wasn't distracted by how damn adorable he was.

"Maybe," I said. "Let's add it to the list of things we can talk about over coffee." I handed him my business card.

He tucked it into the back of his jeans.

"You should have my number, too," he said. He grabbed a pen off a desk pushed against the wall. "Gimme your hand."

Brent wrote his digits on my wrist, dragging it out to keep the physical contact going as long as possible. "Coffee's so boring, though. Sure it wouldn't be more fun to talk after a couple of drinks? Maybe at my place?" He arched his eyebrows suggestively. He finished writing his number and traced over it with his index finger.

I had to admit the boy was good. Too good. I wouldn't trust myself at his place. Even without the alcohol.

His finger running along my wrist felt ridiculously sensual. Why was I so attracted to this kid? He was an undeniably well-put-together specimen, but not my type. Since falling for Tony I really hadn't been particularly interested in *anyone*. Yeah, Andrew was tempting, and there'd always be a place in my heart—and pants—for my BFF Freddy, but Brent had me as hot as Sarah Palin at a gun show.

What was it about him?

Or was it me? Was the fact that he resembled me in so many ways part of the turn-on? Had I just discovered *my* kink? Not domination or plushies but clones?

For now, none of that mattered. Brent was an incorrigible flirt. He was going to keep wagging his tail and humping my leg until he wore me down. It was time to throw some cold water on this puppy.

"Did I mention my boyfriend's a cop?" I asked him. I've found that tends to act like the anti-Viagra on even the most determined suitors. Knowing the guy you're trying to cuckold has a gun is more deflating than a cold shower.

"Coffee it is, then," he said, dropping my hand. "When should we—"

We were interrupted by the trumpeting voice of Mason Jarre. "Would you look at them?" he boomed.

He was walking over with Kristen LaNue at his side. "Magnificent," Kristen whispered. "Like two angels."

"Almost twins," Mason marveled. "Are you thinking what I'm thinking?"

"That we need to get these two together on film?" Kristen asked him.

"I can picture the DVD cover in my head already. *Brotherly Love Two,*" Mason suggested. "Or, *Adventures in Twincest.*" His eyes darted from one of us to the other, back and forth. I was pretty sure he was imagining the climactic scene at that very moment. His voice was thick with excitement. "We can work out the details later."

Mason pissed me off. I'd already made it clear to him I wasn't interested. If there's one thing I hate, it's a guy who won't take no for an answer.

I would have told him off right then and there, but I couldn't think of a way to express my aversion to appearing in porn without sounding like I disapproved of Brent for doing it.

It was Kristen who saved the scene from getting ugly. But then again, he was a director. "Now, don't pressure the boy," he advised Mason. Then, he turned to me. "You have our cards. Think about it, okay? We could at least talk. I promise—we could make it worth your time."

Brent gave me an evil grin. "You really should, Kevin. You know, if we do it on film, it isn't cheating. It's work."

Having made similar distinctions in my own life, I couldn't blame Brent for trying.

"Sure," I said, figuring it was a good time to make my exit. "I'll think about everything. And maybe we *will* get together."

But I said that last part to Kristen, not Brent. For some reason, I had a feeling it'd be better if Kristen and Mason didn't know that Brent and I planned to meet. I'd keep that to myself.

Just like I wouldn't tell Tony about the flirting between me and Brent.

Walking away, it struck me that in the past half hour, more

lies had been told, secrets revealed, and new ones made than I'd have thought possible in such a short time.

It didn't seem like a good basis on which to start a new friendship. Maybe I'd be better off if Brent *didn't* call.

Speaking of which, I'd better not go home with a guy's number scrawled on my arm. Even a guy without Tony's professional investigative training would be suspicious of that. I went to the bathroom to wash it off.

I was about to start scrubbing when I thought, *What the hell?* I took a picture of the number with my iPhone. Who knows? Maybe I'd have a reason to call Brent someday.

A perfectly innocent reason. Yeah, Brent might be delicious, but I had no doubt I'd be able to resist taking a bite.

Does it count as another lie if you only say it to yourself?

4

Best Friends

A month later, I was in my apartment watching the "Kinks for Cash" episode with my best friend, Freddy. It wouldn't air until later that week, but he'd been bugging me about seeing it since he found out Brock Peters was a guest. I got a DVD of the final cut from one of our editors so Freddy would forgive me for what he'd considered an almost unforgivable slight on my part.

It was the night after the taping of the show. Freddy and I went out to dinner, and I told him about meeting Brent Havens and the other weird experiences of the day.

"Wait," Freddy interrupted me. "Let me make sure I understand you. You threw a party for a roomful of gay porn stars and didn't invite me?"

"I didn't exactly throw a—"

"How long has it been that you've hated me?" Freddy asked.

"I don't—"

"Because the only thing I love more than a party is porn, and the only thing I love more than porn is actual sex, and it sounds like you somehow managed to keep me from all three at the same time!"

It was true that Freddy loved sex. I knew that firsthand. We'd started as lovers back in college, but the idea of a committed relationship was about as appealing to Freddy as sunbathing is to a vampire. His idea of monogamy was sleeping with only one guy in the same day. Once he knew your last name, it was a sign the two of you were getting too serious.

So, we became friends. Besties, as the Brits say. There was still a sexual tension between us, but over the years it's faded somewhat. Whether that was due to time or to Tony is hard to say.

It took me a few minutes to convince Freddy there was no "party" and that I had no idea so many of Brock's friends and co-workers would show up. Even so, I admitted, I should have told him that Brock would be on the show.

"If I knew you were a fan, I would have invited you," I explained. "But I had no idea you'd even heard of him."

"Heard of him?" Freddy asked incredulously. "I've done a lot more than *heard* of him. I've *seen* him. I've *studied* him. I've *sullied* myself to him, in all his throbbing muscly goodness."

"So, you like his movies?"

"I'm talking about at the gym. In the steam room. We've gotten it on four or five times there."

"Oh my god," I marveled. "Is there any man in New York you *haven't* slept with?"

If so, it wasn't for lack of trying. Freddy was one of the best-looking guys I've ever known, and that includes men who got paid $2,000 for an hour of their time. A beautifully built African American with perfect features and the piercing eyes of a professional Casanova, Freddy exuded a sexuality that made me believe in the power of pheromones. Men were drawn to him like no one I'd ever met, and Freddy enjoyed his gift to its fullest potential.

"I haven't slept with your husband, darling. At least not yet. So, stop pissing me off before I decide to steal your man, blondie."

"As if," I answered, channeling Alicia Silverstone from *Clueless*.

"Haven't fooled around with Brent Havens, either," Freddy continued. "Although I wouldn't mind. That's one sweet-looking kid. And probably as close to sleeping with you again as I'll ever get."

Huh. Freddy had noticed the similarities, too.

I told him about our awkward flirtation.

"He probably did it just to get on the show," Freddy offered.

"Why," I asked sharply, "would it have to be about *that?* Is it impossible to believe that he found me attractive?"

"Of course not," Freddy said, enjoying this opportunity to yank my chain. "For a man in your late thirties, you've held up remarkably well."

Freddy knew I was twenty-four, the insufferable bitch. "As have you," I countered. "And I don't care what anyone says, I think you look great with that extra weight. There's nothing wrong with a little muffin top."

Despite the fact he knew we were teasing, Freddy couldn't help glancing at his perfectly flat belly.

"Ha!" I said victoriously. "Made you look!"

Freddy decided to ignore my triumph. "I'm just pointing out that Brent Havens sounds like a manipulative little thing who knows how to hook a guy. You said he wanted to get out of the porn business. Maybe he thought that appearing on your mother's show could be the first step to a legitimate career."

"You think he was playing me?"

"I think he's a player. The problem with being a player, though, is you don't always know yourself what's a game and what's real."

"One real thing," I said, "was that the guy who runs his studio, Mason Jarre, was a total sleazebag. He practically raped me with his eyes. He pushed me hard to consider working for him—too hard, if you know what I mean. Wouldn't take no for an answer. I can see why Brent feels like a slab of beef."

"This guy Mason is *forcing* Brent to make movies?"

"No," I answered. "Not exactly."

"So, he wouldn't accept Brent's 'no' when offered, then? When he said he wanted to get out?"

I tried to remember our conversation. "I don't think Brent's asked yet."

"Huh. But you think Mason pressured Brent to work for him in the first place, right? Coerced that innocent-looking sweetie into a life of onscreen debauchery?"

I couldn't say that, either. In fact, I distinctly recalled it differently. "Actually, I think it was the opposite. Now that you bring it up, I don't know that Brent's ever said 'no.' "

"My kind of boy." Freddy grinned. "I don't know, Kev. I've watched some of Brent's work—he seemed to be having a pretty good time. I've seen him in interviews and read articles, too. Feels to me like that kid's doing exactly what he wants to. Not by accident, either. He gets himself where he wants to be. And my feeling is, if he wants to move on to something different, he'll do whatever it takes to make that happen."

"I don't know," I answered. "You didn't meet him like I did. He seemed very sweet. Genuine. Not the Machiavellian figure you're painting."

"Machiowhatnow?" Freddy asked. "What does a Starbucks drink have to do with anything?"

Freddy was what you call street-smart. Let's just leave it at that.

I'd been a psychology major at NYU. Despite my ADHD, what I *did* learn stuck in my head like glue. " 'Machiavellian.' From the sixteenth-century Italian writer and philosopher Niccolò Machiavelli. He wrote about immoral men in a way that seemed to endorse the unethical use of power to get ahead. He's become a symbol for selfishness and greed. Psychologists even have a test called the MACH-IV that measures a person's likeliness to deceive and manipulate others for his personal gain."

"Thanks for the lecture, Doctor IQ. Put simply: Brent's power is his sexuality, right? So, that's what he'd use."

See? Street-smart. Not an insult after all.

Had Brent been planning to use me? Was I really so naïve that I fell for it?

Of course, I hadn't told him I worked for the show until midway through our conversation. On the other hand, maybe he noticed the ID his boss missed and figured it out when I first bumped into him.

Assuming he hadn't planned the whole thing and been the one to bump into *me*.

My head was spinning out of control. I either needed to take more Adderall or get off this train.

Disembark, I decided. What did it even matter? Brent hadn't called me and I hadn't called him. Whatever happened, or might have happened, was behind us.

Except, I felt it wasn't. We'd made a connection. I was sure of it. It didn't feel "over" at all.

So, why hadn't we been in touch?

I knew why *I* hadn't called. Too much temptation.

Why hadn't he?

"There's only one thing I don't get," Freddy said, sounding genuinely puzzled.

I leaned forward. In his own way, Freddy could be very insightful. I felt lost in the dark trying to figure this out. Maybe Freddy would shine just the light I needed.

"Why," he asked, squinting with the effort to understand what could very well be the question that would clear this all up for me, "would Starbucks name their delicious milky coffee treat after some old Italian guy everyone hates?"

Or, maybe not. "That's a 'macchiato,' honey. Not a 'Machiavelli.' "

"I *thought* that sounded wrong," Freddy said, shoving me in the shoulder like I was the one who'd made a mistake. "I just didn't want to embarrass you by correcting you. I'm considerate that way."

The funny thing is that made perfect sense to him. Freddy's self-confidence in the face of even his obvious mistakes was his one perfect defense.

"Yeah," I said, "that's me. Always confusing my caffeinated beverages with reviled Renaissance-era writers. It always pisses off the baristas when I order a grande skinny Michelangelo."

"Not to mention confusing boys who want to get on TV with those who want to get in to your pants," Freddy added. "You know, that's something you might want to look at if you're going to continue working as a casting director."

Damn that Freddy. Maybe he *had* shed some light. I just didn't want to see what it revealed.

* * *

"Well . . ." I began when the DVD was done. We were sitting on the couch in front of my too-big-for-the-room fifty-five-inch TV, and I turned to see his face. "What did you think?"

"It was great. Like one of those jokes you'd hear from old comedians," Freddy said. "A dominatrix, a gay porn star, and a purple dinosaur walk into a bar. Only the bar is really a TV talk show, and the bartender is a Long Island hausfrau who somehow wound up as its host." He stopped.

"That's a decent set-up," I conceded. "But it needs a punch line."

"Yeah, but the only one I can think of involves the reveal that the hausfrau's son turns out to have done more kinky shit than the three guests put together, and I'm afraid if I say it, you're gonna slap me on the head."

I slapped him on the head anyway.

"So very big 'ow,' " Freddy whined, rubbing his close-cut hair. "I hate it when I'm right."

"Lucky for you it hardly ever happens," I said.

"You know, you're not too old for a spanking," Freddy said. Faster than I could react, he reached out and threw an arm around my neck. "Come here, you little . . ."

"Would you cut it out?" I said, laughing.

"What, you think Mistress Vesper is the only gal in town who knows how to treat a bad boy?" He pulled more strongly and I pushed my hands against his chest. Pecs like granite pushed back. I might have felt his nipples swell under my touch, but everything about Freddy was so hard I really couldn't tell.

Entwined as we were, it would have been tough for someone watching to tell if we were embracing or wrestling. We were both breathing hard. From exertion, I told myself. Between that and the grunting we were making a lot of noise.

Which is why we didn't hear the door open.

"Ahem," Tony said, his voice coming with no warning from the doorway. "Am I interrupting something?"

He didn't sound friendly.

5

Home Bodies

"Yeah," Freddy said, still holding me. "Unless you want to join in."

"Love to," Tony said, walking toward us. "What's it going to be? Noogies? Pink bellies?"

"That's too good for the likes of him," Freddy answered. "I was going for a full spanking."

"I'll hold his legs," Tony offered.

For the longest time, I'd worried about letting Freddy and Tony spend time together. My feelings for each of them were too complicated to risk their being in the same room. It was like the threat of matter and antimatter combining.

Once things settled with Tony, though, it became inevitable I'd have to find a way to get them at least comfortable with each other. They were both too important to me to give up one. To my surprise, they got along pretty well. Turns out they actually enjoyed having someone to complain to about me. I didn't mind being the butt of their jokes if it kept peace in the family.

Speaking of butts, mine was saved when Tony's son, Rafi, raced in between his dad's legs. "No 'panking Kebbin!" he ordered. He threw himself on my back, wrapping his arms protectively around my neck.

The message was clear—you'll have to go through me to get to him.

I reached around to give him a reverse hug. "My hero," I said. "How's it going?"

Rafi craned his little head to whisper in my ear. "Were they weally going to 'pank you? 'Cause my daddy says 'panking is wrong."

"Naw, little buddy. They were just funning."

"Good," Rafi said. "I missed you, Kebbin."

"I missed you, too, little buddy." I squeezed tighter. So did he. Which would have been very sweet if his arms weren't crushing my windpipe.

I've said it before and I'll say it again: Love hurts.

Tony saw my face turning red and stepped in to save me. "Hey, Rafman, I'm getting jealous." He sat on a chair across from us and patted his thighs. "Get over here, you."

Rafi abandoned me for the sweeter shores of his daddy's lap, his favorite seat in the house. Mine, too, the little punk.

Freddy took that as an opportunity to make his exit. "Well, I'll leave you to tonight's reenactment of *Two and a Half Men*. Talk later?" he asked me.

"I'll call you tomorrow."

"And you," Freddy said, sinking to his knees to meet Rafi eye-to-eye, "didn't even say hello to me tonight."

"That's 'cause I thought you were gonna 'pank my friend Kebbin," he said, still a little wary.

"Well, do I at least get a good night?" Freddy asked.

Rafi rolled his eyes in a way that looked hysterical on a five-year-old. "Goo' night, Fweddy," he said condescendingly.

Freddy laughed and kissed him on the forehead. "Good night, slugger."

Tony held his hand out for a fist bump. " 'Night, Fred."

Unlike most of my gay friends, Tony didn't hug or kiss other guys for hellos or good-byes. But also unlike them, Tony didn't consider himself gay. He'd been married before we got back together (after a brief fling in high school). The only good thing to come from that union was Rafi (his "real" name, as Tony's Italian heritage might have suggested, was "Raphael," although no one called him that unless they were very cross with him). Tony always maintained the only male he ever had sexual feelings for was me. Much, much more importantly, he also told me I was the only person, of any gender, he'd ever truly loved.

Somehow, we both counted on that being enough to see us through his ongoing process of accepting life as half of a same-sex couple. Because, despite the fact that he'd finally admitted to me that he had a son, and even letting me into the boy's life, part of him still held back.

Which is why, as far as Rafi was concerned, his dad was just my friend. Even worse, Tony had Rafi thinking this was his apartment and I was the roommate. Which meant, on the nights Tony had visitation, I slept on the couch while Tony shared my bedroom with his son.

The activist in me thought this was an unforgivable betrayal of everything in which I believed. An ugly cover-up born of homophobia and self-hatred to which I should never have agreed.

But that political part of me was eclipsed by the simple truth that I'd been in love with Tony Rinaldi since I was fifteen years old, and he was the lanky pony boy two years my senior who lived down the block. He was the sexiest goddamn thing on two legs back then, and he's only gotten better with age. I'd walk on hot coals for Tony, take a bullet, crawl across broken glass, insert whatever cliché you want, I'd do it for this complicated man who held my heart.

I'd even participate in this terrible, soul-crushing, and painful farce in which Tony, the most honorable man I knew, lies to his own son about his love for me.

I knew it hurt Tony, too. It wasn't in his nature to act like this. To mislead his own flesh and blood. I also knew he felt guilty asking me to aid in that deception.

"God, Kevin," he'd said. "He's only five years old. He's my *son*. How can I tell him about this? About us? His mom and I just separated a few months ago. Just give me—give him—some time. Can you do that for me?"

"Of course," I'd told him. "We'll know when the time is right."

The problem was, that time seemed right to me from the start, but Tony didn't seem to find it particularly imminent. Tony had been brought up as hetero as they come. His family, co-workers, and friends were old-school Catholics. For years, he regarded the few months in high school in which we'd fooled around as a bizarre detour from his otherwise straight path.

As far as I knew, he hadn't told anyone about us. It was a Herculean effort for him to admit his feelings even to me. What would it take for him to tell the rest of the world?

In the meantime, we were building a life together on a shaky foundation of half-truths and denial.

I thought of Rafi's arms squeezing the air out of me. I had the terrible feeling that, one way or another, these Rinaldi boys were gonna be the death of me.

Love hurts.

Three hours later, with Tony's tongue halfway down my throat and his hands gripping my denim-covered ass as I straddled him on the couch, I was feeling a lot better.

Rafi had fallen asleep twenty minutes earlier in my bed. His light snores were like a reverse alarm—as long as we heard them, we knew we were safe.

Tony snuck out to help me make up the sofa bed where I'd be sleeping. We got distracted.

"Mmmm," he moaned into my ear. "You feel so fucking good." The growl in his voice almost had me coming in my pants.

I answered him by grinding deeper into his lap. "You like that?"

"Yesss," he hissed. "I wish . . ."

"What?" I licked him from his ear to the base of his neck.

"Aw, man," Tony groaned. He grabbed my hips and pulled me even closer, crushing our absurdly covered erections against each other. "I just . . . I mean . . ." He nodded toward the door of my bedroom. "He's twenty feet away, Kevvy."

He pushed me back. "I can't, babe. Not with him right there. What if he wakes up?"

"We'll hear him," I panted, scooting myself back to where I'd just been. I liked that place. That was my happy place.

Tony put his hands on my shoulders. "Honey, you know how we are when we get going. We wouldn't hear a bomb, let alone a four-year-old ninja in footie pajamas."

"I promise," I said, leaning in for a kiss, "we'll be quiet."

Tony leaned back. "When are we ever quiet?"

He had a point. "We could tie a bell around his neck," I suggested. "Or put up a force field. Have those been invented yet?"

"Sorry, babe. He's only here for two nights. Think you can hold on for that long?"

I grabbed his still steely cock through his dress slacks. "I don't know. Can I? Wouldn't someone notice?"

"Ha, ha," Tony said, not amused. "You really know how to hurt a guy, don't you?" He removed my hand from its perch.

"*Me* hurt a guy?" I asked accusingly. "You're the one trying to kill me with blue balls."

"Poor baby," he said. His hand slid up my thigh toward my aforementioned body parts. "Are they really *blue?* Maybe I should take a look. . . ."

Yes! Score one for the home team.

"If you promise to be quiet," Tony began.

"Like a mouse . . ."

"I mean, really, Kevvy . . ."

"A mute mouse." His hand reached my crotch and rested there. "A mute mouse wearing a gag." He squeezed and I gasped. Quietly.

"I guess we can . . ."

Then the bomb went off.

"Daddy," came a small voice from the bedroom. "I'm tirsty. Can I have some water?"

"Sure, sweetie." Tony tossed me off his lap like I'd suddenly burst into flame. "One minute."

He walked, uncomfortably I'm glad to say, to the kitchen and returned with a half-full plastic kid's tumbler. Just before going into the bedroom, he turned to me with a guilty expression. "I'm sorry," he mouthed.

I nodded. "Me too," I whispered.

"Daddy?" Rafi called.

"Right here, honey."

"Go," I told him.

"He's probably just not used to being here. I'd better lie with him until he falls asleep. I'll try and sneak back out when the coast is clear."

"Don't bother," I said, the words sounding sharper than I intended. I stood and turned my back to him, opening the sofa into a bed. "I mean, I'm beat, too. I'll see you in the morning."

"Kevvy," Tony implored.

"Daddy," Rafi whined.

"Tony," I barked. "Just go. I'm fine. Good night."

"Good night," Tony said, sounding sad. He walked into the bedroom.

"Nite, Kebbin!" Rafi called, happy now that his dad was in sight again.

"Night, little man," I responded.

It was turning into the closing moments of *The Waltons*, only no one was in their right bed.

I was tempted to go in and give Rafi another good night kiss, but I held back. He really was very sweet with me. He'd already taken to throwing his arms around me and saying "I love you, Kebbin," and I always hugged him right back.

I never answered in kind, though. I wasn't quite sure how we all *fit*. I liked Rafi very much. But there was no connection there. I worried about getting too close to him and Tony changing his mind. Leaving me behind for the safer choices. It made me sad.

I lay on the uncomfortable sofa bed. I thought of Tony twenty feet away yet in another world. One where he was a daddy, not another guy's boyfriend. I knew he wasn't sure he'd ever be able to successfully combine the two. Another depressing thought upon which to dwell.

Luckily, I had the pounding pain of my unrelieved and aching testicles to distract me.

Lust hurts.

6

Driven

"He was even better," Andrew whispered to me, although we were behind the closed doors of his glass-walled private office and no one could hear us unless we screamed, "than advertised."

"That's great," I said politely, hoping if I showed the minimal possible interest I'd be spared the grisly details.

It was three days after Tony had left me blue-balled on the couch. The episode of my mom's show that Freddy had sneak-peeked at in my apartment had aired to the world the day before. Grateful for the exposure, and pleased with how he'd come across on screen, Brock Peters called Andrew and invited him out for drinks. They wound up at Brock's place.

"There's this scene in *The Legion of Super Twinks vs. the Beastly Bears of Doom* where Brock hooks his heels behind his ears, which I'd always assumed was done with CGI. Well, it turns out he really can . . ."

I tried not to listen. Tony's next visitation with Rafi wasn't for another few days, and I was hoping he and I could finally finish our lovemaking. I'd have to remember to call him when I got out of here.

"Then, just like he did to Rod Racer in *Buffguy, the Vampire Player,* he flipped me over and . . ."

I also had to call Freddy. He'd left a message that he had gotten together last night with Cody, a guy I'd introduced him to a few months ago. They've been dating on and off since then—the closest Freddy's come to a relationship in, well, ever. I knew Cody was frustrated that they weren't more of a couple, but he was also glad to take what he could get. I thought Cody was a terrific catch, and I hoped Freddy had good news about how things were going.

"All of a sudden, Brock does this thing from *Gone with the Rimmed* where he takes a guy's ass and . . ." Andrew's eyes were gleaming and I swear he was starting to drool.

"Enough!" I said, unable to tune out more of Andrew's endless recap. "What was this—actual sex between the two of you, or the porno version of a Civil War reenactment?"

The light in Andrew's eyes blinked out so quickly that I felt a little guilty for pulling the curtain. "I know, I know," he sighed. "It *was* kind of weird. Brock was nice enough, and, well, you saw, incredibly good-looking. Technically, the sex was great, too. Quite the workout. Very, ah, aerobic.

"But I couldn't separate the real person from the guy in the movies. Everything we did felt like a rerun, even if it was the first time I was actually *in* the scene, as opposed to just watching it.

"What really ruined it for me, though, was the feeling that he was performing. Putting on a show for me. Like he had to be 'Brock Peters' as opposed to a mere ordinary lay.

"The whole thing was a little depressing. Brock seemed so . . . mechanical about it. It makes me look at porn differently. Maybe it's not much fun after all."

I thought about my own time in the sex trade. "You shouldn't generalize," I said. "I'm sure there are some guys in porn who are totally jaded and burnt out, but I'm sure there are others who keep it in perspective. You're a full-time TV producer used to running the show, but it's not like that affects every other aspect of your life. You don't go into the supermarket and tell the manager where to stack the cereal boxes, or rearrange the lighting when you go to a club. There's a difference between what you are and what you do. A healthy person can separate the two." Who had recently told me that?

Andrew looked thoughtful. "You think?"

I know. "Yeah. I hear you talk about Brock, and I figure it's a chicken-and-egg thing. Did years of being in porn make him into a self-centered lover, who's more concerned with technique and dazzling his partner than he is with forming an actual connection? Or, was he a ridiculously handsome, narcissistic stud who got into movies because he *already* saw sex as a 'performance'? One in which he was the star?"

Andrew rested his chin in his hand. He nodded. "Maybe. I don't know. You're right about one thing. It wasn't so much that I felt he was aping his films that bothered me, it was the total lack of interest in, like you said, 'making a connection.' I could have been anyone. He wasn't expecting to 'enjoy' me; he was looking to 'wow' me."

"That's the thing with narcissists. It's all about *them*. Brock wasn't looking for a lover. He's looking for an audience. For attention and applause. And, if my two semesters of psychology at NYU can be trusted, it's a deeply ingrained personality trait. Here's my bet: Porn didn't make him that way; he makes porn because that's the way he is."

Andrew smiled. "I feel kind of . . . relieved. It really bothered me how . . . *detached* Brock seemed. I mean, generally when a guy has his head between my legs, I think he's at least a *little* into me. But not Brock. He reminded me of those guys who demonstrate home appliances at department stores. It's a good show and everything, and at the end you might get a tasty treat, but he's still just going through the paces. I thought maybe I was losing my mojo."

Andrew was still probably one of the ten best-looking guys I've ever met. "You haven't lost a thing," I assured him. "You just happened to spend the night with a guy who wasn't looking for mojo—he was looking for a mirror."

"How did you know he asked me to put one by the bed?" Andrew asked. "Did I tell you that part?"

I'd been speaking metaphorically, but I figured it didn't hurt to leave Andrew guessing. "The magic eye of Kevin," I said, tapping my forehead, "sees all."

In hindsight, I'd wish I did. Then I'd have known to get out of there before disaster came crashing through the door.

* * *

"What," my mother screeched, her voice reaching a frequency I'd have thought capable of breaking windows, "is this *fakakta dreck?*"

This didn't look like it was going to be good. She came crashing into the office like a hurricane, only less concerned with the damage she might be leaving behind. She flapped a paper in her hand wildly. Worst of all, she was using Yiddish, always a bad sign.

Andrew, who was paid by my mother and therefore contractually obligated to placate her, sprang to his feet. "What's wrong?" he asked, his eyes soft with concern.

"This!" she wailed, directing a withering gaze at the paper she clutched in a death grip.

"This what?" Andrew asked.

"This!" my mother said louder, as if the problem was that we couldn't hear her. People in New Jersey could have heard her.

"Sophie," Andrew said in the low, measured tones of a person trying to talk a jumper off a bridge, "why don't you sit down and we can . . . ?"

"Sit?" my mother echoed, as if Andrew had asked her to commit hara-kiri. "This is not the time for sitting! This is the time for action! Sitting around," she cried, thrusting the paper she held at Andrew like a dagger, "is hardly going to get us on *this!*" She returned to shaking the paper like a crazy woman.

"Okay," I said, having had my fill. "Enough with the drama, Mama. We can't even see what you're talking about if you keep waving that around like you're trying to put out a fire. Maybe if you let one of us see it, you could get an answer.

"So, why don't you settle down"—I pointed at the small sofa in Andrew's office—"and we can talk like normal people."

She collapsed into the seat with a resigned plop and sighed heavily.

"Oh my god," she said, no longer loud but with a miserable whine in her voice, "I just threw a diva fit, didn't I?"

"Just a little one," I reassured, rising to join her on the sofa. I took her hand in mine. She squeezed back with the same pressure with which she'd previously throttled the paper into submission. I heard one of my knuckles crack. At least, I hoped that was all it was. A broken finger or two wouldn't have surprised me.

I ignored the pain and soldiered on. "Now, what's all the fuss?"

"This," she repeated. But now she actually handed me the paper, which made the conversation more productive. "Look!"

I looked.

"The nominations for the Daytime Emmys," she moaned. "Someone just showed me. And look—under Best New Talk Show. Notice who *isn't* there?" Her eyes filled with tears. "It's the Jewish thing, isn't it? They always hate the Jews."

The nominations had come out yesterday, but I guess no one thought to tell my mom. Probably an oversight, I reluctantly admitted to myself. Luckily, Andrew and I had discussed them, so I had the words to put her at ease. Andrew and I exchanged relieved glances before I explained.

"It's not you," I explained. "It's the rules. A show has to have been on for six months before it can qualify. We've only been on for four."

The tension drained from my mother in a palpable rush of relief. Her fingers released my hand, which I pulled back and flexed. It seemed like all the digits still worked.

"So it's not," my mother asked, "an anti-Semitic thing? In your opinion?"

My mother blamed the majority of her self-caused problems on anti-Semitism, an issue about which she was very sensitive. Which made it so odd that she'd married my father, a German who looked like the poster child for the Aryan nation. It was from him I'd inherited my blond hair and blue eyes.

"I think it's just the rules, Ma."

My mother turned her face to Andrew. "I'm sorry about that little outburst, darling. I don't know what came over me. Maybe it's this studio—the ghost of Yvonne possessing me."

"Yvonne isn't dead," I reminded her.

"Well," my mother observed, "you can't have everything."

"It's hard," Andrew said, still speaking with the caution of someone defusing a bomb, "to be in the public eye. Sometimes, you just have to let off a little steam."

"It's so nice to have a professional like you on my team," she answered him. "But there's still no excuse for bad manners. Promise me—you'll tell me if I'm becoming too much of a pain in the *tuchus,* won't you?"

Talk about a golden opportunity. "You're already . . ." I began.

My mother cut me off. "I was talking," she said, icily, "to Andrew."

"Oh."

She put her arm around me. "I'm your mother, darling. I'm supposed to be a pain in your ass. It's in the job description." She looked at the list of Emmy nominees again.

"This does get me thinking," she offered.

Andrew and I looked at each other with an unspoken "uh-oh."

"I'm never going to be nominated, let alone win this thing, unless we start doing some more serious shows around here."

"Serious?" I asked.

"Let's face it." My mother sat up on the sofa, her posture eager and determined. "Nobody's getting any awards for shows like we've been doing. Yes, it's all very entertaining to interview transvestite dentists and the women who love them, but it isn't the kind of serious-minded feature that's going to get me recognized by the National Academy of Television Arts and Sciences."

She knew the name of the organization that awarded the Emmys? I was impressed. It must have shown on my face.

"See?" she said, smugly. "I can use the Google."

"Really? I bet Nancy looked that up for you," I asserted, crediting my mother's personal assistant.

"So what if she did?" my mother answered. "I can use the Nancy. The point is: I get things done. And it's all up here," she said smugly, tapping her forehead the same way I had moments before when talking to Andrew. I shivered in the way I always did when noticing any resemblance between us.

"Which is why," she continued, "I think we need to tackle

some bigger stories. If I want to play in the big leagues, I'm going to have to show I have the chops to do investigative reporting like a real journalist. Like a Barbara Walters. Or a Kelly Ripa."

"Don't forget Sherri Shepherd," I offered.

"Exactly!" my mother enthused. "We need to dig deep, team. Find the big stories. Expose injustice. Make some headlines."

Suddenly, my mother was turning into Perry White. For no good reason, I wanted to run around the offices like a lunatic screaming, "Stop the presses!"

"Those are great ideas," Andrew agreed with the patience of a man who'd spent the last two years working with a woman even more deluded than my mother. "We'll get right on it. I see no reason why we can't combine the fun lifestyle advice and entertaining human interest topics we normally cover with some harder-hitting reportage."

I knew my mother would be impressed, if by nothing else, Andrew's use of the word *reportage* in the same sentence as the nonsense we usually aired. Sure enough, she sprang up and pulled the seated producer's head to her in an embrace that threatened to suffocate the poor boy in her ample bosom. "I knew I could count on you," she beamed.

"You too," she told me. "Except, not for anything constructive."

"Nk ooo," Andrew said.

"Sorry," my mother said, releasing him from the deep valley of her breasts. "What was that, sweetheart?"

He gulped in a breath. "Thank you."

"Thank *you,*" my mother gushed. "I can't wait to get something I can really sink my teeth into."

Instinctively, I put my hand over my jugular.

7

Fallen Angel

"Trust me," I'd told Andrew, the minute my mom left his office, "in a few days she'll have lost all interest in becoming the next Diane Sawyer. We just have to provide a distraction. I say we go for an episode where she takes some of her girlfriends to Chippendales. They start all embarrassed and silly, tentatively slipping dollar bills, with the delicacy of vestal virgins, into the dancer's G-strings, and by the end they'll be kneading those boys' buttocks like dough. That'll take her mind off things."

It'd improve Andrew's mood, too, I reckoned. Although maybe the last thing he needed was more testosterone-fueled narcissism.

Andrew drummed his fingers on his desk. "I don't know," he said, a little dreamily. "Have you considered your mother might have a point?"

"Crazy say what now?" I asked.

"Listen." Andrew leaned forward, his eyes a little brighter. "I've spent two years producing hundreds of hours of daytime television that, combined, have had about as much impact on the world as a butterfly's fart. That's a lot of my life to waste on nonsense, Kevin."

"It hasn't all been nonsense," I countered. "You've entertained a lot of people. Touched some, too."

"Not enough," Andrew said. "I think she's right—we should set our sights a little higher. We reach millions of viewers a week, Kevin. We could be educating them. Enlightening them. Instead of being satisfied feeding them . . . drivel."

"You're being too hard on yourself," I argued. "Too hard on the show, too. This isn't the *CBS Evening News*. It's a fun, gossipy talkfest with a wacky hostess who the audience, god help us, seems to love. It's exactly what the people who watch it want it to be."

"Is it? And, even if that's true, is it *enough?*" Andrew ran his hands through his hair. "Maybe I'm stuck on this thing with Brock. He was so focused on giving me what he thought I *wanted,* there was no chance I'd get what I *needed*. By pandering to my expectations, he wound up putting a lot of effort into leaving no real impression whatsoever.

"It was all artifice and no substance—stunts and clown cars. Cotton candy—eat as much as you like and you're still hungry. It's sweet going down, but it dissolves into nothing before it even reaches your stomach. In the end, you feel as empty as you did before. Is that what we're serving?

"Maybe—every once in a while—we can provide something a little more filling."

Great. Andrew was having a midlife crisis in his twenties. He'd bought into my mother's insane idea to disrupt the formula of her inexplicably popular show. Whatever happened to "Don't mess with success"?

Not to mention the absurdity of imagining my mother as some bastion of journalistic truth seeking. Unless you count the TV listings or coupons, I don't think she's ever read a newspaper. As far as general information, if it wasn't covered on *Entertainment Tonight* or in *US Magazine,* she didn't know it happened.

And yet . . . my cynicism wasn't particularly attractive, either. What, exactly, was so threatening about my mother's and Andrew's enthusiasm? Instead of being appalled by their desire to elevate what they did, what if I let it inspire me? Hadn't I just done it with my own life—left the safety of easy money and the freedom to do as I pleased for the chance for a "real" job and a life with Tony?

It was easy to be bitter and sarcastic and predict disaster. Yeah, my mother doing any kind of real investigatory work had the potential of being a total fustercluck. But even a possible train wreck is better than staying parked in the station your whole life. At least it's forward motion. Maybe, just maybe, we could even stay on the tracks and get somewhere. Somewhere better.

Who was I to say otherwise?

"Okay," I began, "if we were going to do this, where would we start? It's not like we have a crack team of reporters to get on the case."

"How hard can it be to find news in New York City, Kevin? *Everything* happens here," Andrew said. "Keep your eyes open. Watch what's going on around you and look for angles no one's seen yet. There isn't a place in the world with more stories, Kevin. We just need to find one."

I went back to my office and thought about what Andrew had said. What stories did my life offer?

"My Boyfriend's a Closeted Cop?" Naw, I didn't think Tony would like that.

"My Best Friend's a Big Old Slut?" Naw, I didn't think Freddy would like that.

"My Mother's Driving Me Crazy and She's the Star of This Very Show?" Naw, someone's mother driving them nuts hardly qualified as news.

What else? In my time as a call boy, I'd serviced more than a few celebrities and politicians whose public personas were vastly different from their private lives. I'd also heard a lot of secrets. The sexual act can establish a sense of intimacy that's way out of proportion to the reality of the relationship. Men who should have known better poured their hearts out to me.

Hadn't someone told me he had a tale to tell? Something potentially explosive? That could blow the lid off an entire industry and even put people in jail?

Who was that? Oh, yeah. Brent Havens. The World's Cutest Porn Star. (And this, mind you, from a guy who normally doesn't go for "cute.")

Brent had been so interested in me that I thought his tease of a "big story" might have been nothing but a way to get some attention. If it wasn't, though, it could be just what I was looking for.

My mind raced through juicy, lurid possibilities of what Brent might know. "Secrets of the Adult Video Industry." What could they be? Boys forced into making films against their will? Payoffs to politicians to ensure legal protections?

Penis sizes enlarged through the use of special effects?

Now *that* would be news.

My mind reeled.

He'd given me his number . . . on the inside of my wrist. I remembered scrubbing it off in a defensive move to avoid any awkward questions from Tony. Damn.

Wait. I'd made a preemptive move, too, and snapped a picture with my iPhone. I opened Evernote and there it was. I dialed Brent's number, practicing in my head a greeting that sounded interested but professional.

No point in leading the boy on. Especially since I didn't completely trust myself to resist his advances.

This, I explained to myself, was all business. Brent hadn't been sure he wanted to tell his story. If he wasn't ready, I wouldn't push.

If he was, though, it could solve a lot of problems. Hopefully, for him, too. There was a part of him that wanted to get out of the business—if he really did have beans to spill, I was pretty sure he'd be persona non grata in the skin biz.

Which might be just what he needed.

I knew from firsthand experience how hard it was to give up the easy money and ego boosting a pretty boy could make in the sex industry. My transition was made easier by the launching of my mother's talk show and the subsequent job offer. It just kind of fell into my lap at exactly the time Tony revealed to me he had a son, a milestone that indicated he was ready to get—somewhat—more serious about our relationship.

I had no idea what Brent planned to do when he stopped

making flesh films. I didn't know if he knew, either. Maybe we could find something here. I was pretty sure Andrew would like him.

Maybe too much, I forced myself to admit. I wasn't sure being chased around the desk would be rewarding work for Brent.

As I pointlessly planned Brent's life for him, I realized, for the second time that morning, I was unconsciously taking on the traits of the woman who'd raised me. Why else would I be Jewish mothering a boy I hardly knew about a situation that might never happen? I thought of them as my Mother's Rules of Parenting: Meddle, Nag, Respect No Boundaries, and Keep 'em Feeling Guilty.

I was only on Rule One, but give me time.

Not today, though. After ten rings, Brent's voice mail picked up. "The voice mailbox of the customer you are trying to reach is full. Please try back later."

Couldn't even leave a message. I switched from my desk phone to my mobile and sent him a text. "This is Kevin from *Sophie's Voice*. We met after Brock's appearance. Please call." I typed in my number.

Waiting isn't my strong suit. I hoped he'd call soon.

Brent seemed like a guy in hot demand. I figured he got a lot of messages and checked them frequently. I'd probably hear from him soon.

Two days later, I sat in my office and concluded Brent either wasn't as diligent at returning calls as I'd hoped, he'd changed numbers, was indisposed, lost his phone, or just didn't want to talk to me.

As long as the last reason wasn't the problem, tracking him down shouldn't be too hard.

I checked my Rolodex (otherwise known as frantically shuffling through the completely disorganized piles of papers that littered my desk) and found the business cards for Kristen LaNue and Mason Jarre of SwordFight Productions.

Kristen was the not-bad-looking, friendly, and seemingly polite director of some of the films in which Brent appeared. Mason was the grossly pushy owner of the company. It wasn't hard to choose which of them to call first to help put me in touch with Brent.

8

Kiss Off

"Of course I remember you," Kristen purred. His sexy Latin accent reminded me that he was more than just "not bad-looking." He was a generous slice of hottie pie. "The beautiful boy who's wasting his life behind the camera. To what do I owe the considerable pleasure of this call? To schedule an audition, I hope?"

Okay, maybe he wasn't *that* much less pushy than Mason. But he was certainly less obnoxious about it. Coming from him, it was actually charming. Complimentary rather than creepy.

Or was it just his swarthy good looks and come-fuck-me honeyed voice that let him get away with it?

I explained the problem I was having getting in touch with Brent.

"Now why would you . . . ?" Kristen began, then paused. "Ah, yes. I suppose a better question would be 'Why *wouldn't* you want to call Brent?' And, since he gave you his number, I assume he was interested in you, too, no? Why wouldn't he be? You two were the loveliest things in the room that day. Your coming together—and I mean that in every sense of the word—is as it should be."

Clearly, Kristen assumed I was calling for a hook-up, which was just as well.

"Of course, if I do help you two lovebirds connect, I must insist you let me film it. If only for my own enjoyment, no?"

I didn't know what to say to that.

"Only teasing," Kristen reassured me. "Although . . . if you wanted a souvenir of your time together, I'd make myself available."

"I'll keep that in mind," I said, smiling.

"And I will pass your message along to Brent when I see him next. *If* I see him, I should say."

Another pause. In this one, I heard background noise. What sounded like grunts and slaps. Someone said something. "Could you make it a little tiger?"

What?

No, not "tiger."

Tighter.

I tried not to be distracted.

Focus, Kevin, focus.

"What do you mean?" I asked.

"He's dropped off the map for a bit," Kristen explained. "Didn't show for the most recent two shoots he'd signed up for. Didn't call, either, at least not as far as I know."

"You wouldn't know?"

"I'm the *creative* on the team. Mason and his people handle the business end of things. Scheduling, booking the boys, finding locations. Brent may have called him to say he couldn't make it, but normally that would have led to Mason arranging for a replacement. Didn't happen either time. We had to do *solo* scenes, as I recall." I heard a shudder in his voice. "They bore the shit out me, to be honest. There's only so many ways you can shoot a guy whacking off. From an artistic perspective, masturbation is not a terribly satisfying subject."

"You take your work seriously."

"Dead seriously," Kristen assured me. "I know people view any movie with explicit sex as pornography, and thus of no artistic merit, but why? Why is it we believe 'serious' cinema can explore any genre, whether it's romance, or comedy, or drama, but only as long as everyone keeps his pants on? What's more real than sex or death? Films are *supposed* to move you. If you laugh, or cry, or find yourself rooting for the hero, the movie is considered successful. But if it turns you on? Somehow, that's wrong. Why the double standard?"

I had to admit, he had a point. But I'd seen some of the movies he'd directed—well, fast-forwarded through most of them—and they were hardly works of genius. Better than most, perhaps, but I didn't remember seeing anything particularly ambitious in them, either.

He answered my question without my even asking it.

"Of course, the work I do for the mainstream companies, like SwordFight, has to follow certain conventions. There isn't much room for artistic expression. But my smaller films, my art movies, are my true passions."

"I don't think I've seen any of the them," I said.

"Well, then, you'll have to come by for a private viewing sometime," he said. The invitation was flirty, but not sleazy.

"Still"—I thought it best to avoid the "private viewing" discussion—"you've been successful even within those limitations, right?"

"It's rude to extol one's accomplishments. But, yes, I have been able to do as much as I can with my studio work. I've been nominated for Best Director every year for the past five by the Gay Video Awards. Won twice, too."

Was everyone obsessed with winning awards? We're all so insecure.

I liked Kristen, but this review of his résumé wasn't going to help me with the job at hand. I switched topics abruptly. "How long has Brent been off the grid?"

"Oh." Kristen thought for a moment. "It's probably been three or four weeks since that first time Brent didn't show."

"No contact at all?" I asked.

He paused again.

"Oh yeah," I heard a voice from somewhere not far from him. "Like that. But harder. And faster. And just a little to the left."

Sounded like someone was topping from the bottom.

"Not that I know," Kristen answered.

"Do you think he's okay?" I asked. "I mean, if Brent's never disappeared like this, maybe something happened to him."

Another thoughtful silence. "Oh, yes!" I heard a shouted cry in the background. "That's it!" There was a snapping noise, like the smack of a cracked whip. "Hurts so good!"

I found it hard to ignore. "Is this a good time to talk? You sound . . . busy."

Kristen chuckled, a warm laugh that made me flush. "Oh, I'm on a shoot. But my assistant can handle the models for a few minutes. Sure you don't want to come down and talk in person? Get a look at what you're missing. It can be quite . . . stimulating."

I bet.

"I'd really like to get in touch with Brent first, actually."

"Of course. And I'm afraid I forgot what you just asked me."

I reminded him of my question: Was it typical for Brent not to show up when expected?

"No, I'd never seen that kind of behavior from him. He was actually one of my more dependable models. He took the work seriously.

"Still, I can't say I'm totally shocked. Boys in this business tend to come and go. They don't all share my commitment to the art. These models tend to be young, self-centered, and easily distracted by the next shiny thing. When they're ready to move on, they just stop showing up. I've learned," he said, his tone mixing weariness with wryness, "not to expect formal letters of resignation.

"It's possible"—Kristen paused, as if he were putting together things he'd seen into a coherent picture—"he was working on putting something together for himself."

"What do you mean?"

"On that last film we were shooting, he kept wandering off set. Every time I'd find him, he was on his cell phone, whispering. The conversations always looked intense, but not in an unpleasant way. He was usually smiling during them, even laughing. When he'd see me approach, he'd hang up before I got close enough to hear."

"Maybe he was just talking to a friend."

"Perhaps. But I don't think so. There was something . . . conspiratorial in the way he was acting. Like he had a secret. One that brought him both joy and guilt. He looked like . . . what's that expression? . . . a boy caught with his hand in the cocaine jar."

I didn't bother to correct him. Given the world in which Kristen operated, the revision was probably more accurate than the standard cliché.

A secret, huh? Kristen started by saying he'd interpreted Brent's clandestine phone calls as being an effort to "put something together for himself." Did he mean a deal with a rival studio? It had come up before as a possibility. I was just about to ask when we were interrupted by a loud shout.

Whoever had minutes ago been screaming in pleasure about being "hurt so good" had something new he wanted to announce to the world. "Hey, wait a minute, is that a—"

"I'm afraid I must go," Kristen interjected loudly. "They're waving me over. The stereotype of the temperamental actor is only too true. Looks like they need me to offer some direction."

"Thanks for your time," I offered.

"No problemo," Kristen said. "Do call Mason, though. He may know something I don't."

"I will."

"And if you get in touch with Brent, tell him to come back. He's more than welcome. He's simply too beautiful not to give another chance."

He disconnected just as the actor he'd been filming screamed with pleasure.

I took Kristen's advice and called Mason Jarre.

"Mr. Jarre's office," a deep-voiced man answered. "Pierce Deepley speaking."

I asked to speak to Mason.

"And what, may I ask, is the nature of the call?" Deepley clipped his words in such a way that he sounded irritated by me already. It usually took longer.

Or, maybe he just didn't like answering phones. In which case, he had the wrong job.

I explained that Mason knew me and I was trying to get in touch with Brent Havens.

"We don't give out personal information about individuals who may or may not be employed by SwordFight Productions or any of its subsidiaries," he answered. "Thank you for calling. Have a . . ."

The creep was going to hang up on me.

"Wait," I said, "I'm not asking for personal information. I'm just trying to see if Mason can help put me in touch with Brent. Brent gave me his number, but—"

"I'm sorry," the officious screener interrupted, "but I'm afraid the details of how you may or may not have met said individual who is possibly known or unknown to us are quite beside the point."

Deepley's legalistic double-talk was making my head spin. Had I taken my medication today? All those qualifiers were hard to follow.

Focus, Kevin, focus.

Deepley monologued on. "We understand many of our customers enjoy our products and imagine they have . . . personal relationships with our models. If, as you say, you met Mr. Haven, and he wishes to . . . encourage your interest, I'm sure he'll return your call at his earliest convenience. If not, well, perhaps it simply wasn't meant to be." Deepley sounded inordinately satisfied at the prospect of Brent not calling me.

Unfortunately, since I didn't know how to get to Mason without going through this asshat, I had to be polite. "I apologize. I haven't been clear. I'm not calling on a personal matter. It's business.

"Mr. Jarre and I met on the set of *Sophie's Voice*. I'm a coproducer. I'm trying to contact Mr. Haven as a follow-up to the successful appearance of another of your models, Brock Peters, on the show. I thought perhaps Mr. Jarre would appreciate the additional exposure for SwordFight. But if he isn't available—"

"*Sophie's Voice*?" Pierce Deepley squealed. "Oh my god, I love her!" His inner queen blazed through his previously icy imperiousness. "She's so funny, so *real,* you know? That episode with Brock was *fabulous!* Hold on, let me see if Mr. Jarre is available. May I have your name?"

He may, and I thanked him as well. It wasn't the first time I'd seen the power of celebrity open a closed door.

A minute later Mason picked up. "Kevin," he said. "Pierce tells me you're thinking of having us on the show again. That's marvelous news. I have a few models I think would make wonderful spokesmen for our company. Are you familiar with Seymour Cox? Or Tag Emnow?"

"Actually," I said, "we were hoping to feature Brent Havens. He and I were talking after Brock's appearance and—"

"Oh," Mason cut me off, "Brent's absolutely adorable, but he's not the brightest bulb on the tree. No, I believe you'd be better served by one of our more . . . articulate performers."

He took a moment before announcing, "Now that I think about it, Hugh Jestman would be an excellent guest. He's actually a classically trained actor who's performed on Broadway. Would you like me to arrange a meeting?"

"No," I answered. I regretted fibbing to Pierce about wanting to schedule another show, but it was the only way I could think of to get through to Mason. Unfortunately, I'm not the greatest liar. I tend to lose track of the details and get easily confused by my own deceits. "That isn't necessary. I'm sure the other guys are great, but we're really interested in Brent."

"That's what I thought," Mason said, his tone no longer quite as accommodating. "There is no show, is there, Kevin?"

"I'm sorry?"

"Cut the shit, sunshine. I saw the way you and Brent looked at each other. The heat between you was enough to set off the fire extinguishers. I'm surprised it's taken this long for you to call. What happened, did you lose his number?"

Okay. I was still going to lie, but this one was easier to manage. "You got me," I said. "But I didn't lose his number. He's just not answering. I hear he hasn't been showing up for his work with you guys, either."

"Yes," Mason answered, "the little brat left us high and dry on two shoots. Unacceptable. Sorry, but you're not the only one he's stiffing. Or, not stiffing, as the case may be." He chuckled at his play on words.

"Are you worried?" I asked.

"Worried? Why would I be worried? Yes, we lose money if we have to cancel a shoot, but in both cases, the director was able to use the sets and crew to shoot solos. Although, that doesn't excuse Brent's unprofessionalism."

Wow. A young man goes missing and the only thing this guy cares about is how it affects his bank account.

"No," I said. "I meant, are you worried about *Brent?*"

"I don't understand."

"Well." I was almost at a loss for words. Did I really have to explain this to him? "My understanding is that Brent was always very responsible. All of a sudden, he drops out of sight and stops answering his phone. Maybe something happened to him."

Mason laughed. "Oh, that's sweet. I'm sure something *did* happen to him, sweetcheeks. He hooked up with a sugar daddy. Or he found religion. Or he met a nice boy—or a nice girl—and he plans to settle down. White picket fence and all. Of course, there's always the more likely possibility he's on a meth binge holed up in a crack house somewhere.

"My point is: Something is *always* happening with these boys. They're not exactly the most stable employees. They come and go. They're young, self-centered, and distracted by whatever shiny thing comes along next. One learns not to worry, Kevin. Well, not about *them*." That also got a little laugh from him. "My business, though, *that* I worry about. I don't think Samuel Goldwyn had to put up with this kind of nonsense when he built MGM."

Parts of what Mason said sounded almost exactly like Kristen LaRue's responses. Did they rehearse these lines? Or was it more likely the case that the "whatever happened to . . ." question had come up in regard to so many men before Brent that the answer became rote?

I knew from my time as an escort that boys dropped in and out of the biz frequently, sometimes for the reasons Mason described. I could see where it would get tiresome for him and Kristen to constantly face questions from fans and press wondering why their favorite performers weren't making new videos.

At least from Kristen, though, I got the sense he thought of Brent as a human being worthy of consideration. Mason's cold assessment made it clear he regarded Brent solely as a product—one that concerned him only to the degree it was no longer profitable.

"Well," I said, "I'd feel better if I knew Brent was okay. All I have is his mobile number. Do you have any others? Or an address? Did he give you contact information in case of an emergency?"

"Come in and we'll talk about it."

"I'd love to," I lied, "but it'll probably take me a few days to get over there. Could I get the info now and call you later in the week for an appointment?"

"No."

"No?"

"Listen, kid, I'm running a business here, not a dating service. Whatever Brent is up to, he isn't making me any money. I need a fresh face to replace him. A studio like SwordFight runs on archetypes. We have the muscle daddy on deck with Brock Peters. We have a popular group of Chelsea gym types like Tag and Atlas. We've got bears, circuit boys, a couple of trannies on call. We've got S&M stars like Pierce Deepley and The Dominator. We . . ."

Pierce Deepley? Where had I heard that name before? "The guy who answered your phone? I thought he was the receptionist."

" 'Pierce Deepley' doesn't sound like a porn name to you?" Mason asked somewhat incredulously. "Five years ago, he was one of the biggest names in the business. But the market for staged S&M has kind of bottomed out, excuse the expression. He makes an occasional film, but he mainly works as my assistant now."

Nothing like an S&M master to run an efficient office, I imagined.

"What we're missing," Mason continued, "is our Boy Next

Door. A fair-haired darling who looks like he should be delivering your morning paper until he winds up spread like butter across your kitchen table.

"It's a place in our lineup you could fill, Kevin. You and Brent are practically twins. If what you're hiding under your clothes is anywhere near as good as it looks like it'll be, you could be pulling a couple of hundred thou a year, working ten hours a week, mostly lying on your back. You seem like a smart boy. Is that something you should walk away from without giving it serious thought?"

Actually, I'd already walked away from similar employment, although there was no way Mason could have known that.

I tried to sound reflective. "Let me think about it," I offered. "Really. In the meantime, if you could just give me—"

"You come in, talk face-to-face, and I'll give you whatever you want. Including five hundred bucks for the audition." I heard another phone ringing.

Pierce called out, "It's Cha-Cha on line three."

"One second," Mason said. He must have held the phone away from his face as his volume decreased even as he shouted. "Tell her to hold on," he instructed his assistant.

His attention returned to me. "I have to take this call. You know Cha-Cha Rivera? She's one crazy dame, but a great director."

"Can't you . . . ?"

"Like I said, if you want to talk, come in. Call Pierce and set up a screen test. You show me what I want to see, and I'll tell you what you want to know. See you soon, babycakes." He hung up the phone.

I listened to the dial tone for a few seconds before pressing the "end" button. Despite having grown up in New York, working as a prostitute, stumbling across more than one murder in my time, and my study of psychology, people still shocked me with how awful they could be. In Mason's case, it was his selfishness and attempted manipulation I found stunning.

Not only didn't he show any concern about Brent's welfare, he was already working to replace him. The fact that I was being considered as the potential successor, despite my repeated disinterest, didn't endear him to me, either.

Meanwhile, it hadn't escaped me how, by the end of our discussion, his offer to meet me for an "interview" turned into an invitation to an "audition."

I'd seen some of the tapes in the SwordFight *Audition* series. They started with an interview and ended with nudity and masturbation. I wasn't interested.

What a creep.

So, why was I considering calling Pierce to set up the appointment? Because I had no other leads. Maybe Mason didn't care about Brent, but, to a probably inappropriate degree, I did.

Was it because Brent reminded me so much of myself? Not only in looks, but in occupation? Kristen and Mason might have been right—maybe Brent decided to walk away. But where to? And why?

For whatever reason, something about Brent's disappearance set off my spider sense. I knew I'd worry until I was sure he was okay. Unfortunately, my best bet for tracking him down required meeting with Mason.

Maybe I could get my questions answered in this "audition" before having to do anything past a PG-13.

I had a feeling this was going to go horribly wrong, but I picked up my phone to call Pierce Deepley and schedule the shoot. I was about to hit "redial" when, at the last minute, I was saved by the bell.

Well, by the ringtone.

I thought I was the only person who cared what happened to Brent.

The incoming call proved me wrong.

9

In Hot Pursuit

"Hello," I answered, not recognizing the number.

"Kevin," the lightly accented voice asked.

"Yeah, this is Kevin." My voice carried a who-did-you-expect-to-answer-my-phone tone of annoyance. After my last conversation, I was a little on edge.

"It's Kristen," the director said. "Kristen LaNue."

"Oh, hey." I tried to sound friendlier. "I'm glad to hear from you. Everything work out on set?"

"How sweet of you to remember." I could hear the smile in his voice. "Yes, I snuffed out the problem and we're on break. Did you call Mason?"

"Uh, yes."

"Was he helpful?"

I wasn't sure how close they were. "He didn't want to talk on the phone," I answered truthfully, without offering the fact that he basically tried to blackmail me into posing nude for him.

Kristen chuckled. "Let me guess—he insisted you see him in person."

"More like he insisted *he* see *me. All* of me. For a screen test," I clarified.

Another laugh. "Well, you can't blame a dirty old man for trying. . . ." Kristen observed.

Actually, given the stakes, I could. "Listen," I said, "I'm flattered you guys think I'd be good at it, but I'm not looking for a job in adult videos—"

"I get it," Kristen interrupted. "Mind you, I'm hoping you change your mind, but I get it. Sadly, I'm not sure Mason will be as understanding. He can be . . . unrelenting when he wants something."

Now I was a "something." This really was a business that turned people into objects.

"On a more positive note," Kristen continued, "I did think of someone you could talk to. He'd probably know how to get in touch with Brent. In fact, Brent might even be with him."

"That's great!" I was excited. Partially because I was looking forward to getting in touch with the boy, partially because Kristen was redeeming my faith in humanity by offering something helpful without requiring me to be naked to get it.

"There's this guy he was seeing. Charlie."

I told Kristen I remembered Brent mentioning him. "Maybe that's who he was talking to while he was on set with you," I offered. "He wouldn't be the first guy to run off and call his boyfriend at every opportunity."

"I thought about that," Kristen said. "But why would he be so secretive about it? Not to mention how guilty he looked when I'd find him."

Good questions.

"So, do you have Charlie's number?" I asked.

"Not even close," Kristen said. "I don't even know his last name."

Great. I had to find a gay "Charlie" in New York City. That shouldn't take too long—a decade or two at the most.

"I *do* know where he works," Kristen continued, to my great relief. "He's a bartender at Intermission. You know the place?"

"I do," I said. "I can probably swing by in the next day or two."

"Really?" Kristen sounded amused again. "Now, how would a nice boy like you know about Intermission, I wonder?" His tone was pointed, but teasing.

I should have feigned ignorance. Intermission was an off-the-radar establishment that catered to wealthy, often closeted men and the working boys who offered their bodies and discretion in fair exchange. It was an exclusive, expensive watering hole, where a bottled water cost a tenner and everything else started at double that. Unless you were a well-heeled buyer or a well-hung seller, the sedate atmosphere, cooly efficient servers, and imposing bouncers made it a particularly uninviting hangout. No, Intermission was a place to conduct a very specific kind of business transaction.

No sign announced Intermission's presence on the first floor of a tony town house on the Upper West Side. I wasn't sure I could even find a listing for it on the Web. Its existence was advertised solely by word of mouth among a select group of elite johns and the high-class hustlers who served them.

Kristen didn't need to be a genius to figure out I didn't belong in the first category.

I'd never peddled my papayas at Intermission, or any other bar for that matter. All my bookings were arranged by the escort agency I worked for, run by my favorite drag queen/possible transexual in the world, the charmingly eccentric Mrs. Cherry.

Although she appeared as dizzy as they come, Mrs. Cherry was a more efficient, protective, and intelligent businesswoman than a season's worth of contestants on *The Apprentice*. She could have run a Fortune 500 company, except for the unpleasant compromises she'd have to accept in not being surrounded by beautiful boys looking to her for guidance and having to squeeze her size 20-something ass into something other than a caftan or housedress. All things considered, she was happier running her own show from her overdecorated apartment, ensuring the income and safety of a never-ending tide of available young men with the looks and breeding to satisfy her sophisticated clientele.

"Kevin?" Kristen asked. I realized I'd been zoning out.

Focus, Kevin, focus.

What had we been talking about? *Intermission*. Right.

Although I'd never gone there looking for work, I did have clients who had wanted to meet me there before proceeding somewhere more private. It was a safe environment for them to check me out in before committing to taking me home.

Although I kind of liked Kristen, I didn't want to reveal any more about myself than I had to. "Intermission isn't exactly an undisclosed location," I answered, although it was. "It's not like that's where they hide the President in case of a terrorist attack."

"No," Kristen answered solemnly, "they secure him, I believe, in Mason Jarre's bedroom. Not because it's so well guarded, mind you, but because no one, not even suicide bombers, would willingly go there."

Now it was my turn to laugh. Kristen was winning me over big-time.

"For the record," Kristen said, dropping his voice in volume and by half an octave, "I never said that. Agreed?"

His deeper, conspiratorial tone was even sexier than his usual Latin lover lilt. I felt a guilty rush of heat.

"Your secret's safe with me," I promised.

"Oh," he said playfully, "I don't have any secrets. But I think *you* do, Kevin. I truly believe you do."

He paused, waiting for me to respond. For once, I was lost for words.

He mistook my awkwardness for strategy. "Smart boy. Keep your cards close to your chest. But someday, you clever thing, I'd like to see the hand you're holding.

"I bet it's a winner. A flush of hearts."

He disconnected without saying good-bye.

A good director knows when to cut a scene.

Why, I wondered, did my conversation with Kristen have my stomach turning in knots?

Was it because I was worried about meeting with Charlie, the boy Brent had been seeing? Remembering my conversation with Brent, I recalled that Charlie had been strongly disapproving of Brent's continued employment in the adult film industry. Maybe he'd convinced Brent to quit the biz. If so, my showing up at Intermission might be misinterpreted as a bid to, excuse the expression, suck Brent back in.

If Charlie took offense at my questions, he'd have no problem getting me out of there. I thought of the bouncers with biceps as wide as my waist and shuddered.

Or was it Kristen's sly insinuations about my "secrets" that were making me skittish? Was I wearing a tramp stamp on my forehead that I thought I'd washed off?

I wanted to leave hustling in the past, but maybe, like Marley in *A Christmas Carol,* my previous deeds dragged behind me like chains, rattling and obvious to anyone who cared enough to look.

Another possibility: Could Kristen be playing with me? It didn't seem out of the question that the sophisticated and worldly filmmaker might have been a client at Intermission. If not as a customer, than as a casting scout? I could think of less fruitful places for someone looking for attractive and sexually open potential models to spend their evenings. The working boys at Intermission had already demonstrated a willingness to walk on the wild side. How much farther down the road would it be for most of them to let their wandering be filmed?

If Kristen had used Intermission as a scouting camp, it wasn't impossible he might have seen me there. Was he trying to tease out a "confession"? If so, it seemed more playful than mean-spirited.

The last reason I could think of for the butterflies in my stomach was the scariest of all. Maybe I was genuinely hot for Kristen.

During the time I've been reunited with Tony, I've had a few flirtations. Hell, I've had out-and-out sex, but only for business and never with anyone for whom I had feelings.

Kristen, however, was different. I thought he was attractive when I met him, but I hadn't really dwelled on it. Two conversations later and I was struck by how much I might *like* him. He seemed smart, funny, and dead sexy.

Like one of the debate assignments from the seventh grade, I found myself comparing and contrasting him with Tony. Yes, I loved Tony, but it was so complicated. I wasn't sure he'd ever be able to get over my career as a prostitute, even if it was a "former" career. Sometimes, in bed, I'd purposely throttle back my performance lest he ask "Where'd you learn that?"

Someday, I feared, he'd call me a whore and I'd never be able to forgive him.

More immediately, there was the problem of trying to build a life in the closet. I may have "secrets," but they're not ones I'm ashamed of. They're just things I'd rather keep private.

But I *was* Tony's secret. The source of his shame. How horrible was that? How could we possibly be happy together if our entire relationship was hidden in the shadows? The only things that grow without light are mushrooms and fungus, neither of which were attractive analogies.

Compare and contrast.

Kristen not only could accept my past as a sex worker, he'd probably be thrilled. It was hard to believe he wouldn't be as sex positive in his private life as he was in his work. If so, I bet he'd be *scorching* in bed.

How different would it be to date a guy who not only wouldn't be afraid to be seen with me, but who would show me off proudly, like a jewel, not hide me like a disfigurement?

Of course, I was getting ahead of myself. It wasn't like Kristen had even made an overt move on me.

Except, I didn't need him to. If there was one thing I knew, it was when a man wanted me.

Kristen LaNue wanted me.

I think I wanted him, too.

The whole thing had me a bit giddy, kind of nervous, and more than a little nauseous. Romance always hit me in the gut and my stomach wouldn't stop churning.

Kristen's attention to me, and my attraction to him, were inconvenient distractions, unwanted temptations.

An excess of alternatives.

A flush of hearts.

10

Hard Cops

I decided to stop thinking about Kristen and instead turn my attention back to the boy this was about.

Brent Havens.

When I'd talked to Brent, he'd complained how his audience often mistook his onscreen persona for his real one. People projected on to him whatever they wanted him to be. Given the movies that comprised his, er, body of work, that person tended to be a youthful, energetic, and available hottie with not much on his mind beyond getting laid and showing his partner a good time. The definition of the best kind of boy toy: one who wants to play with you.

Confusing any actor's performance with how he conducts his life off-camera is obviously absurd. As fun as it would have been to find myself in a Brokeback backbreaking three-way with Jake Gyllenhaal and the late but not forgotten (at least not by me!) Heath Ledger, I wasn't holding my breath.

But we're all guilty of *some* projection. Given the impossibility of ever truly understanding another person, it's only natural we imbue them with traits based on assumptions and prior associations. If you're a healthy person, as you get to know someone better, you replace those presumptions with his or her reality. In my experience, it's at that point when a relationship starts to get into trouble—when the person you've been imagining and hoping for turns out to be the person he or she really is. It's a trap I've tried to avoid.

Yet, wasn't that what I was doing with Brent? I hardly knew the boy. In my mind, though, he was a good kid whose unconventional career choice did nothing to diminish his basic decency. A young man who sold sex not to exploit others but to help them, by making otherwise unattainable fantasies come true. A boy who needed love, understanding, and protection from the Big, Bad World.

Remind you of anyone I am?

Was I projecting myself on to the blank slate of Brent Havens? What did I know about him, really? Who's to say he wasn't some big cokehead on a bender? Or running a scam on some elderly aficionado from which he'd walk away relatively untouched and $50,000 richer? Was my assuming the best about a boy I hardly knew really any more reasonable that the less generous assessments of those who'd actually worked alongside him?

Maybe. Mason's and even Kristen's judgments were clouded by profit. My motives were clean.

Or at least that was what I told myself.

It was a more flattering motivation than the other likely possibility—that my quest to rescue Brent was a subconscious effort to save myself.

I wish I'd gotten to know Brent better before he'd gone missing. Now, there was no way to assess whether he was more likely the victim or perpetrator of whatever happened to him.

Unless . . .

I agreed it was ludicrous to assume a performer's true personality could be assessed in every film role. Still, sometimes the real person showed through. And given the weak plots and emotional nakedness of a sex tape, maybe even more of the star's authentic nature came through.

Maybe I should check out the Brent captured on camera before making any more assumptions.

I could go to the local video shop or the nearest Web site and see what was for sale. Or, I could call the boy voted in his high school yearbook Most Likely to Amass an Astonishingly Large Library of Pornography.

I decided to go the cheap route.

* * *

First, I had to check with Tony to make sure he didn't mind my being out for the evening.

"No problem," he answered, lowering his voice, "baby."

Tony worked in an open cubicle at a police station in midtown. I knew he didn't want his fellow officers wondering who he was calling "baby." As well meaning as his term of affection was, his whispering it made it hurtful.

"I have to work a case tonight, anyway," he said. "We found a guy in the Hudson River. Been there a couple of days. At the least. Water's always tricky—hides a multitude of sins." Tony's tone betrayed his resentment. "Really fucks up time of death."

I found it endearing that, when it came to interfering with one of his investigations, Tony could get mad at water.

"Sorry," I offered.

"Looks like a messy one, too. The victim had been beaten. Whipped, actually. There were also bruises on his wrists that indicated he'd been handcuffed but straining to get out."

I started to get a little worried. "COD?" I asked. You don't live with a detective without learning some of the lingo.

"Too soon to say," Tony answered. "Although we know he was dead before he was dropped in the river. No water in the lungs."

"What do you know about the vic?"

"Not much. We're pretty sure whoever put him there never meant for him to be found. He was nude. There was a rope around his ankle, and we're assuming it was tied to something to anchor him down. But the rope either caught on something or got nibbled through by a cooperative fish or two. The body got free and floated to the surface. Lucky break."

Things weren't going well when that counted as good luck. "So, no ID at all?"

"We know a little. Guy was probably mid-thirties. Dark complexioned. Too much bloating and decomposition to tell much else at this time. Maceration was—hey, are you sure you want to hear this?"

"Yeah," I croaked, unconvincingly. I threw in a "sure, go ahead" to add conviction.

Tony sounded skeptical. Well, more skeptical than usual. Occupational hazard. "You know what maceration is?"

I couldn't help it. "No, but if you let me slip my hands down your shorts, I can try and figure it out."

Tony laughed. "It's not as much fun as that, unfortunately. It's the process of how things soften in liquid. In this case, human skin. After a few days underwater, the skin starts to saturate and peel away in long strips. Every hour, we lose more identifying features. The epidermis detaches and we're left with bone and muscle. After a week—"

"I get it," I interrupted. This was starting to sound more grisly than I wanted to hear. Besides, what few details Tony'd shared dismissed my worst fear—that the victim was Brent.

"Mr. Sensitive," Tony teased.

"Guilty," I admitted. "I am really sensitive. Especially when you run your tongue along my—"

"Gotta go," Tony said, his voice cracking like a teenage boy's. "See you later."

I imagined him sitting at his desk, red-faced and awkwardly turned on. There were many things I loved about Tony, not least of which was how easy it was to get his motor going.

Who's Mr. Sensitive now? I thought, smiling.

A few months ago, if Tony had said he was "working late," I'd have been worried. We'd agreed to an open relationship. In theory, I had no problem with it.

What I didn't like was the lying and evasiveness that accompanied it. There was a stretch back then when he was becoming increasingly unavailable. There were more and more late nights at the office and pretty thin excuses. I was convinced he wasn't just playing the field a bit—something I felt he was entitled to after a long, monogamous marriage and a frighteningly scarce sexual history, but seeing someone in a more serious manner. Having another relationship that *mattered*.

Turned out I was right—but the boy he was seeing was his son, Rafi, whom he'd kept secret from me. When he finally introduced us, it was kind of a breakthrough for our relationship. But it hadn't gone as far as I'd hoped, and I was tired of being known to Rafi as Tony's "friend."

Which brought me back to Kristen LaNue and my fantasies about him. How liberating would it be to be with someone who accepted me as I am, dick and all?

Now I was the one thinking of cheating.

Or was Kristen just another person on whom I was projecting what I wanted? Outside of our brief interactions, I knew nothing about him. Maybe in his private life, he was as deeply closeted as Tony. Or he was a total creep who never picks up the check and leaves the bathroom without washing his hands.

Or, god forbid, he was a plushie.

Could I make a purple dinosaur costume work?

I wouldn't mind finding out. Not if I'd look good in a purple dinosaur costume, mind you. More about Kristen.

Probably not a good idea.

Okay, no more dwelling on the sexy Latino who seemed kind, charming, rich, and into me. Because who'd want to think about him when I could imagine skin dissolving off corpses at the bottom of the river.

Or not. No, I needed to see some skin, but the kind that was attached, and lots of it.

Now that I'd cleared it with Tony, I could place the call that would make that happen.

11

Heatstroke

"You're asking a single gay guy if he has any Brent Haven movies in his collection?" Freddy wondered incredulously when I called. "That's like asking a fat guy if he has ice cream in his freezer."

"Well, I assumed you had the ice cream, chubby," I answered. "I guess I didn't know that Brent's movies were also membership requirements. So, can I come over and watch a few?"

"What's the matter, Tony not putting out for you these days? Bed death *already?* It's only been a few months. What are you two, lesbians?"

"That's a mean stereotype about lesbian relationships petering out on the sex front," I objected. "I know some women who—"

"I was just joshing," Freddy said. "What, I can't joke about lesbos, but you can call me 'chubby'? Double standard much?"

I knew he wasn't really mad. "I'm just trying to get to know Brent better."

"I suppose you could do that by watching him on video getting tag-teamed by Lucas Fisher and Hugh Jestman," Freddy observed. "Or you could, I don't know, call him. Didn't you say he gave you his number?"

"He did, but—"

"I know, why bother talking when you can form the deep emotional connection that only comes from seeing someone anally penetrated by a large vibrating egg? In my opinion, more friendships should start that way."

"Like yours don't," I said. "Besides, I'd prefer talking to him. There's just one problem." I filled Freddy in on Brent's disappearance and my efforts to find him.

"Oh. My. God," Freddy intoned. "That beautiful child. You've done it again."

"What?"

"Gotten another one killed."

"Killed? Who said anything about killed?" I ran through all the other possibilities for Brent's absence, my theories and the ones offered by the guys at SwordFight Productions.

"Yeah, yeah, yeah," Freddy responded. "And maybe he grew wings and flew to the moon, too. Let's be honest, sugar. Boys who go missing around you turn up dead. Terminated. Rubbed out, knocked off, whatever. How many times does this need to happen before you accept that you have the karma of a cadaver dog? You've stumbled across homicides like Angela Lansbury when she played Jessica Fletcher, except without her raw sexuality. I'm calling your biography *Murder, She Wrote. Again.*"

"Okay," I admitted, "maybe I've had some weird flukes in that area. But this is New York. It's bound to happen."

"Oh yeah?" Freddy asked. "Who else does any of this shit happen to?"

"Tony deals with murders all the time."

"He's a *homicide* detective," Freddy said. "People *call* him when there's a victim; he doesn't run into one on every other corner like they're a Starbucks or something."

He had me on that one. Not that I'd admit it.

"Can I come over or what?"

"Sure," Freddy said. "What could be more fun than a movie marathon featuring a probably-dead legend o' porn? We can put on some Amy Winehouse and moon over pictures of a young Patrick Swayze while we're at it."

"Could you stop being so morbid?"

"I don't know. Maybe if you pick up some ice cream on your way over. I just ran out."

"No problem. You want I should pick up some dinner, too?"

"Ice cream *and* dinner?" Freddy asked. "No, darling, the ice cream will *be* dinner. That way, it counts as one course. What are you trying to do, make me fat?"

"Uhhh," Freddy moaned as we watched Brent's movies on his ridiculously large sixty-five-inch screen while lying on his bed. Freddy lived in a studio apartment, and there was no couch, sofa, or other chairs. Given his usual definition of "hosting," there was no reason for such traditional seating. You were either on your way in, out, or in his bed. Why else would he have you over?

"Oh my god, that's good," Freddy groaned. We were watching a particularly sexy scene in a movie called *School Gayz*. Brent played a prospective fraternity member being rushed by the world's hottest pledge master. At the moment, Brent was being asked to prove his loyalty to Alpha Gamma Rimya by seeing just how far up his butt he could accept his co-star's tongue. It didn't seem like a particularly tough hazing, but who was I to judge?

"So sweet. So fucking smooth and good. I gotta have it," Freddy pleaded.

On screen, Brent groaned. "Gimme more, sir," he begged.

Freddy ran a hand over my chest. "Yeah, baby, like he said. 'Gimme more,' " he rasped hungrily, his breath hot against my cheek. "I want more."

"Get it your own damn self," I told him. He was talking about the ice cream I'd brought over. He'd gotten through the first two bowls before the opening credits of the first movie we'd watched were complete. We were now on the third.

The horrible thing about Freddy was that he could eat crap like this and his body somehow managed to turn it into muscle. Whereas I just look at it and need to double my cardio.

"I can't," he whined. "You've killed me. Filled me to the gills with this stuff and now I'm too stuffed to move. You're going to have to feed me in bed for the rest of my life, as I get fatter and fatter until they have to lift me out of here with a crane. Come to think of it, you may want to get me a bedpan, too. This could get messy."

"Okay, that's just gross. I'll make you a deal. I'll get you another bowl if you fast-forward to the next part with dialogue."

"Are you retarded?" Freddy asked incredulously, as I got up to fetch his bowl of frozen crack. "You tell me you want to come over to watch porn, and then you ask me to skip the sex scenes? Isn't this like watching an Arnold Schwarzenegger movie for the acting?"

"No," I said from the kitchen, fifteen feet away. "I didn't say I wanted to watch *porn*. I said I wanted to get a better sense of Brent through his movies. I've already seen him have sex with a fireman, an adoptive uncle, his baseball coach, and a rugby team. Turns out he has a pretty good-sized cock for such a little guy, he's admirably versatile, and, given proper inspiration, he can come twice within fifteen minutes. Not much more to learn on that front."

I didn't add the obvious—that Brent was ridiculously hot. He moved with the grace of a dancer. He had a sexual intensity that singed the screen. His body was flawless. His skin was smooth and almost hairless. He had a quality that made you believe that if you touched the TV, you'd feel real skin. He seemed more *alive,* more *vital,* than anyone else on the set. I wasn't much for tattoos, but he had a two-inch silver star on his right shoulder and a ring of matching, smaller stars around his left ankle that really worked for him.

"You haven't seen the part where he blows himself, yet," Freddy said, watching me with greedy eyes as I returned with another bowl of Rocky Road. "Folds himself in half like he's hinged at the hip."

"Sounds like a cinematic classic," I said, climbing back into bed. "How Spielberg didn't work that into one of the Indiana Jones movies, I'll never know. Still, it's not going to help me figure out where Brent is, is it?"

"It might," Freddy mumbled through a mouthful of frozen delight. "It proves he could be hiding in a very small space."

I took advantage of Freddy's involvement with his dessert—excuse me, dinner—to snatch the remote from him.

"Hey!" Freddy shouted. "That's my job."

I ignored him and fast-forwarded. I sped through a scene in which the school's star quarterback uses skills he probably didn't learn on the football field to persuade his professor to change his D grade to an A minus, and another where the crowded action at the campus library's restroom made me wonder where these boys got any studying done.

Finally, I came to another scene with Brent. After the bacchanalian excess of the previous footage, this encounter was almost romantically sedate. Brent and another freshman were seated across from each other on twin cots in a dorm room. The walls were covered with posters of muscle cars, bikinied pinups, and popular bands. There was an Xbox, stereo, and bong on the desk, but, curiously, not a book in sight. Further testimony that the library was rarely put to its intended use.

The boys were complaining about the various indignities being forced upon them.

"Did he make you, you know, touch it?" Brent asked his costar.

"Yeah," the handsome, shaggy-haired actor answered. He was bigger than Brent, probably about five eleven. More muscular, too. Rounded, plump muscles, like a wrestler's. Despite his size and weight advantage, though, he seemed submissive to the younger Brent.

He ducked his head and looked at Brent through dangling bangs. "He did."

Brent leaned in, placing his elbows on his spread knees. "And . . . ?"

Shaggy shook the hair out of his eyes and regarded Brent with a quizzical shrug. "And . . . what?"

Brent bit his lower lip thoughtfully. "And . . . did you . . . like it?" He idly let his right hand drift halfway up his thigh.

Shaggy's chest rose and fell more rapidly as he started to breath heavier. "Kind of. It was all right." He dropped his hand to his crotch and squeezed.

"Oh, yeah?" Brent scooted forward on his cot, till his knees touched the other boy's. Shaggy was almost panting now.

"Watch this," Freddy said.

The boys touched nowhere other than at the knees, unless you counted the heavy eye contact, a come-fuck-me stare from Brent so intense you wouldn't be surprised if Shaggy spontaneously combusted. They stayed there almost a full minute, silent and motionless, until you wondered why the director was still holding the shot.

Then you knew. Under Brent's unwavering gaze, an expanding, twitchingly jerky elongation grew and snaked down Shaggy's leg. Shaggy was wearing a pair of thin cotton drawstring pants, almost like hospital PJs but white.

Seeing Shaggy's dick stretch and grow was like watching one of those stop-motion shots of a flower blooming, but in real time. Soon, Shaggy's casual confession was betrayed by the untouched but massively throbbing hard-on that now pointed upward, trapped in his pants but with enough room to rise upward and point accusingly at his chin. Shaggy looked at his own lap in surprise—how did that get there?—and Brent's eyes followed.

"Yeah," Shaggy answered, looking at Brent again.

"Looks like you liked it a lot." Brent's tongue flicked across the lip he'd just chewed on. Shaggy's cock gave another leap and, at its tip, a tiny damp spot leaked through the fabric. It was clear whoever chose Shaggy's "costume" for this scene knew what they were doing—the pants were loose and sheer enough to conceal the details but hide nothing.

Shaggy's eyes widened and his jaw went slack as if he was being hypnotized by the irresistible sexual pull of his friend. Although he was probably a foot taller than Brent and had fifty pounds of muscle on him, he appeared completely at the younger student's mercy, spellbound and lost in a fog of thickening lust. The dichotomy of this little Brent so completely dominating the muscular, older stud only made the scene more thrilling.

"Fuck, that's hot," Freddy said. For once, he wasn't talking about the ice cream.

He was right. I've seen the "behind the scenes/making of" extras that come with adult films, and they always show the actors "prepping" for their scenes by getting themselves hard just before the camera starts rolling. Either they're only gay for pay, or they just find it difficult to get excited on the artificial, uncomfortable environment of a movie set. In any case, there's always a cut before the pants come off to reveal an erection.

I couldn't remember ever seeing someone get excited "before your eyes" like this. And it wasn't just the boner, which now pulsed with a steady intensity that matched Shaggy's increasingly loud breathing. It was everything—Shaggy's glazed but somehow alarmed expression, his half-open mouth, the way his body tensed as if about to spring forward or leap away.

Brent reached out and put just the tip of his finger against Shaggy's knee. "Did they make you jerk them off?"

Shaggy nodded.

Brent's finger traced a fraction of an inch higher.

"Did they take off your clothes?"

"Yesss . . ." Shaggy hissed. His cock gave another massive lurch and the spot at its tip spread wider, the stain now the size of a quarter.

Still just teasing with the tip of his finger, Brent slowly ran it up the inside of Shaggy's thigh, stopping midway between knee and balls. He leaned closer, too, his face inches from his friend's, close enough that I imagined Shaggy felt his breath against his cheek.

"Did you get hard?"

Shaggy groaned. "Maybe."

"Maybe?" Brent leaned back an inch.

"Yes!" Shaggy corrected.

Brent smiled and brought his other hand inside Shaggy's legs, too, matching its partner's placement. He laid them both flat against Shaggy's thighs, making small circles with his thumbs.

"Like I'm making you hard?"

"Yesssss," Shaggy panted.

Brent ran his hands higher, up and down, almost touching

Shaggy's balls then sliding back down. Over and over while he made Shaggy talk.

"Tell me what I'm doing to you, buddy."

"You're making me so fucking hard, man," Shaggy moaned.

"Like this?" Brent spread his legs and displayed his own tented shorts.

"Aw, fuck." Shaggy sounded like he was going to cry. His hard-on seemed to stretch almost to his navel as it discharged another round of precome, soaking his white pants to the point of transparency, the pinkness of the head now evident against the see-through cotton.

"You're so sensitive down there," Brent said. "Did they touch you anywhere else?"

Shaggy could only nod.

Brent took his hands and brought them to Shaggy's nipples, which strained against his light blue tee. "Here?" He alternately squeezed and flicked them, playing them expertly. Shaggy's hands gripped the bedspread in an attempt to keep them from doing god-knows-what, while he unconsciously humped his hips into the air, unable to keep them still, causing his clearly overstimulated cock to thrash around in his pants.

"You like that, man?" Brent asked.

Shaggy nodded.

"Tell me."

"I like it."

"What about this?" Brent squeezed Shaggy's nipples harder.

"Oh, fuck," Shaggy cried.

Brent twisted them. Shaggy threw his head back and let out a high keen. His lap jerked upward, desperate for contact, but Brent sat back.

"What do you want?"

"Come on," Shaggy moaned. "Do it."

"Do what?"

"Don't."

Brent kept one hand alternating between Shaggy nipples while bringing the other to Shaggy's lips. He lightly traced them with his index finger.

"Don't what, baby?"

"Don't make me say it."

Shaggy tried to catch Brent's finger in his mouth, but Brent teased him, moving it just out of reach.

"What do you want, baby?" He took the finger not at Shaggy's mouth and returned it to the inside of Shaggy's thigh, this time running it right under his balls. Shaggy humped uncontrollably, spastically, like a man receiving an electric shock.

"Oh," he panted. "Uh-uh-uh."

"Tell me." Brent was insistent.

"Everything," Shaggy shouted. "I want everything."

"Good boy," Brent said. He put one finger against Shaggy's lips, then slipped it inside. Shaggy sucked vigorously, like a man dying of thirst.

Brent stood, his grin triumphant, his own crotch bulging insistently in Shaggy's direction. He removed his hand from Shaggy's crotch and unzipped himself, letting his own oversized hard-on pop free and point at Shaggy's hungry face, an angry crimson sword that had its own dew gathering at the tip.

Shaggy moaned around Brent's finger. Brent stepped closer, straddling his sex-dazed captive. He removed his finger and replaced it with the tip of his cock against Shaggy's now glistening, plumped lips. "Did they make you do this? Did they make you suck their dicks?"

Shaggy nodded again. He lunged forward, but Brent stepped back.

"What are you doing?"

"Come on, man," Shaggy pleaded. "Give it to me."

Brent took his cock in hand and wagged it in small circles. "Give you what, man?" At the same time, he gently, gently cupped Shaggy's balls, eliciting another mewling cry.

"Your cock, man. In my mouth. I gotta have it."

Brent stepped forward and let just the tip of his dick slide between Shaggy's lips. Shaggy's eyes flew open then fluttered ecstatically as he nursed like a baby, trying desperately to swallow more while Brent controlled the pace.

In the meantime, Brent extended a finger again and placed it at the base of Shaggy's long dick, still encased in his pants but now completely visible through the drenched cotton. Slowly, agonizingly, he slid it toward the head.

"Oh god, oh god, oh god," Shaggy cried, his words intelligible but muffled by the mouthful Brent was feeding him.

Brent began a fucking motion, back and forth, in and out, using Shaggy's mouth like a sex toy while teasing him mercilessly.

"Oh! Oh! Oh!" Shaggy humped against Brent's lazy finger like a crazy man, rubbing his ass against the bed and sliding his pants down just enough that his raging hard-on broke free, popping from his pants like a jack-in-the-box, splattering precome all over his T-shirt and Brent's hand.

"Yeah, baby," Brent said, "that's it. Good boy."

Brent drove in deeper while still running his finger up Shaggy's pole, but now skin against slick skin.

"Uuuuh!!!" Shaggy wailed. I was willing to bet he was incapable of speech at that moment. The sound that came from him was primal, animalistic.

Brent slid all the way in, pubes to chin. Shaggy's eyes bugged open as if he couldn't believe what had found its way inside of him. But, if anything, his cock got even harder, stretched beyond what I'd have thought possible.

Brent's finger finally reached just below the tip of that extended member, his finger right in the triangle where head meets base, the most sensitive spot on a man's body. He quickly reached it up to gather the freshest, thickest precome flowing from Shaggy's dick and brought it back to that juncture, circling it once, twice, three times.

Giving one last push into Shaggy's throat, he said, "Come for me, baby," and with a quick flick of his finger against Shaggy's hot spot, he got what he wanted.

Shaggy arched his back and screamed around Brent's cock, shooting a stream of come so strong that it arced over Brent's head and fell on to his own. Subsequent shots were equally massive, drenching Brent's back with a flood of thick white liquid. The whole time, his body jerked spasmodically and his throat clenched out of control. His eyes rolled to the back of his head, and Brent pulled out, stroking his dick for a few seconds before he also shot, grunting lustily, painting Shaggy's face with his own hot juices.

He collapsed on to Shaggy's lap and they kissed voluptuously, rapturously, like two men who, at the least, just had the best sex of their lives. Again, this was the part where a director usually cut away, but in this case, the afterplay was almost as exciting as what had come before.

You wanted to see this, the aftermath of an encounter that in some ways was tamer than the movie's earlier scenes—no orgies, no anal—but in other ways was the most scorching encounter I'd *ever* seen on screen. Their kisses were hungry, then tender, then almost sad.

Shaggy was still trembling, but Brent's weight seemed to relax him. They settled into each other like two parts of a whole. Brent pulled his head back and Shaggy's eyes brimmed with an emotion I hadn't expected to see.

I couldn't imagine a film set was a place you could achieve a real emotional connection. Sure, you could go through the mechanics of sex, and, our bodies being what they are, it might even feel really good. A warm mouth is always a welcome place to be, and being paid to receive even a bad blow job is more fun than painting houses for a living.

But how could it be possible to be truly intimate with all those cameras and crew around? Yeah, you can believe the love scenes in mainstream movies, but those are some of the most talented actors in the world working with great scripts and highly skilled directors. Plus, those actors aren't actually Doing It, which exposes you in ways that makes it hard to maintain the illusion of a character.

Yet, what I'd just witnessed put the lie to my presumptions. Maybe the scene between Brent and Shaggy had started off as a performance, but, by the end, it looked like love.

12

More of a Man

The screen faded to black on the two boys as the credits began to roll. Smart choice. What could have followed that?

"That was very . . . wow," I said.

"The wowest," Freddy agreed. He extended his once-again empty bowl to me. "Only one thing could make it any better. You mind?"

"Don't you have legs?" I asked. Actually, I wouldn't have minded getting him more ice cream, but I didn't want to stand up. There was no way he'd miss the unexpected tenting that had occurred in my pants. I don't usually get hard from watching porn unless I'm playing with myself, but that scene really got me going. I think if Brent ran his finger along me at that moment, as he'd teased it out of Shaggy, just that slight stimulation would have had me hosing down the place, too.

Meanwhile, I tried to ignore that I had an even hunkier specimen lying right next to me who'd be only too happy to relieve my suffering. But Freddy and I agreed long ago that we were better off keeping things platonic, and I wasn't about to blow that.

Okay, that was a bad choice of words to talk myself off the ledge. Don't think about "blowing" anything, Kevin.

"What's his name?" I asked. "The one who wasn't Brent."

"Lucas Fisher," Freddy answered. "Not bad, huh? He's got that whole hot, semi-stoned surfer thing going on, he's ripped to shit and has an ass like two delicious, oversized scoops of ice cream, which I wouldn't mind right now, thank you very much." He passed his bowl to me.

I put it to my side. "It's not just that. He can also . . . act. I mean, he totally sold that scene. He wasn't just going through the motions—he seemed genuinely turned on. Infatuated, even."

"That wasn't acting," Freddy said. "I've seen him in plenty of other movies—he's always snackable, but a little boring. Put him in a scene with Brent, though, and he comes alive. Comes a lot, too."

"They worked together before?"

"After. A couple of movies and, eventually, when the studio realized the chemistry between them, they capitalized on it." Freddy scooted over to the end of the bed and reached into the cabinet under the TV that held his DVDs. Sure, he couldn't be bothered to feed himself, but for this he was Mr. Get Up and Go.

He handed me the case for *Brent & Lucas: More Than Friends*.

What happens when two of the hottest adult video stars realize their feelings extend beyond when the director calls "cut"? When super-cute Brent Havens teams up with fan favorite Lucas Fisher, what starts out as fireworks turns into a nuclear blast of naked desire that can't be contained. Even a steamy bathhouse encounter with mega-hung Pierce Deepley and a jizz-draining three-way with Freshboy *cover model Ashton Pusher aren't enough to keep Brent and Lucas from discovering their true feelings for each other and coming together in an explosive climax that will leave you drenched and begging for more, too.*

"Wanna watch?" Freddy asked.

Yes. "No." There was only so much temptation a boy could take. "Can you tell me what happens?"

Freddy gave me a "duh" face. "They play research scientists who discover a cure for malaria. There's a lot of talk about gene therapy and the ethics of stem-cell research. In the end, they triumph over the evil pharmaceutical companies and distribute the lifesaving vaccine via crop duster over the plains of Africa."

He smacked me on the head. "What do you think happens? They have sex with each other, with a few other people, and then with each other again. Cut, print it."

"No, I meant between them. Are they always that intense?"

"Pretty much. But it's kind of one-sided. They wrote about it on some of the gay porn blogs."

"There are gay porn blogs?"

"There's a blog for everything," Freddy asserted. "I read one the other day for people who like to cook with crickets. As ingredients, mind you, not assistants.

"Anyway, there was a lot of gossip in the industry that Lucas had a big crush on Brent, but his feelings were unrequited. Supposedly, Lucas was the one who got SwordFight to make *More Than Friends* in the hope that more scenes between them would get Brent to fall in love with him."

"Life imitates art," I said.

"Or not. The studio tried to put it out there that the two were really a couple, sending them to industry events and circuit parties together, but the blogs said it was just to build publicity for the movie. There was another rumor, though, that it was Lucas who arranged to be where he thought Brent would show up.

"Probably there was some truth to both versions. SwordFight might have been pushing them together to build excitement for the movie, but it isn't hard to believe Lucas had a bad case of the unrequiteds for your friend Brent. It's there on screen—Brent looks like he's having a good time and all, but Lucas looks like he's found a new religion.

"In any case, a few weeks after *More Than Friends'* release, you never saw them together again. The movie was pretty successful and won some gold at that year's Gay Video Awards. There was talk of a sequel, but it never happened. My guess? After a while, Brent got creeped out by Lucas's affections."

"Or maybe he just didn't want to lead Lucas on," I offered, realizing that I was once again trying to defend Brent by ascribing to him the best possible intentions. Over-identify much?

"Maybe. Whatever happened, that was pretty much the end

of Lucas's career in the industry. He appeared in one or two more films and that was it. In his last one I saw, he wasn't looking too good, either."

"No? What do you think it was? Drugs? Did he get sick?"

"Oh honey." Freddy patted me on the hand and then squeezed it. "He had a terminal case."

Given his line of work, it was tragically probable what had happened to him. "AIDS? I know the studios say they take precautions, but—"

"No, sweetie, not that. It was heartbreak that did him in. You could see it in his eyes. I believe that boy really did love Brent Havens. I think he'd have done anything to have him. He loved that boy to death."

I got back to my apartment around nine. The lights were on and the radio was tuned to a classic rock station. A half-eaten carton of something Chinese was on the kitchen table next to a can of Bud.

Yes, Budweiser beer. Another reminder that no matter how many times Tony plowed me like the fields of Idaho, he'd always be a straight boy at heart.

Speaking of which, where was he? I called his name but got no answer. I turned down the radio and heard the shower running.

Hmmm . . . interesting. I was still kind of worked up from watching Brent's movies, and the thought of a naked, wet Tony twenty feet away brought me back to full salute.

It's amazing how fast you can get naked with the right motivation.

Twenty minutes later, we were drying off together in the bedroom. "That was a nice surprise," Tony said, grinning.

"I figured we might as well get a little more dirty while getting clean," I explained. "You know me. Mr. Efficiency. Screwing in the shower saves time."

"Well, I'm glad you could squeeze me into your busy schedule," Tony teased. He pulled on a pair of sweatpants *sans* underwear. It made me flash back to the scene with Brent and Lucas in the dorm room and I started to swell up again.

"As I recall, you were the one who did the squeezing in."

"Apparently, you liked it." Tony nodded toward the growing proof of my enjoyment. "Again?" he asked.

"What can I say? You bring out the best in me."

Tony sank to his knees and grabbed my ass cheeks. He pulled me toward his face. "Let's see about that."

He took me in his mouth. It had taken a while before our sex was reciprocal in this way. For a time, as long as Tony was the one being done—as opposed to the one doing the doing, so to speak—it helped him maintain his identity as a heterosexual.

Feeling the heavenly warmth of his tongue and throat, I was glad he'd gotten over it.

"God," I said, resting my hands on his shoulders.

For a guy who'd taken to it late in life, Tony gave a pretty good blow job. Maybe not the most technically proficient, but the contradiction with his natural butchness, the incredible interplay of his back and shoulder muscles working in perfect harmony as his head bobbed, and the fact that I loved him more than I should elevated it to an erotic wonder. Despite the fact that I'd deposited about a gallon of come down the shower drain fewer than fifteen minutes ago, I wasn't going to last long.

"Tony, I'm about to . . ."

He pulled back and finished me off with his hand. While he was definitely making progress, swallowing was not on the menu for him.

"Whoa!" he said with boyish enthusiasm as my first shot rocketed past his head and on to the bed five feet away. Subsequent jets were of diminishing, but still impressive, velocity and volume. "Guess I really do bring out the best in you," he said, arching his eyebrows. He looked behind him. "All over the place, apparently."

The sight of Tony, who for so long fought against accepting his feelings toward me, on his knees in front of me, in such a submissive position and covered in my spunk, made me a little dizzy.

"Hey," he said, noticing my unsteadiness. In a flash of naked flesh, he stood up and scooped me into his arms, holding me under my hips. I wrapped my legs around his waist. Tony could hold me like this for hours without tiring. My Big Strong Man. I hugged him, and the semen I contributed to his chest became a shared deposit.

"We're going to need another shower," he said, kissing me. "Not that I mind."

"Or I could do it like a cat." I wiped my tongue over his neck and disentangled from his embrace. I licked him clean from collarbone to navel, stopping only when something very welcome rose to knock against my chin.

I grabbed it possessively. "Looks like I'm not the only one available for another feature," I observed.

Tony looked down at me in the position he'd been in moments earlier. "I don't know," he observed ruefully. "I've got a couple of years on you, Kevvy. I'm not so sure I'm up for another show."

I waved him in my hand. "You look 'up' enough to me."

I believe bad puns are only acceptable in sexual settings, where the mental energy needed to craft more sophisticated repartee takes away too much attention from the main event.

"Guess it depends on how good the show is," he observed. "What's the next movie?"

"Duh," I said, again not bothering to be clever. *"Deep Throat."*

Unlike my still-evolving lover, I had enthusiasm *and* technique. I could pull off that title and had no problem swallowing. A few minutes later, Tony was calling my name in a hoarse and climactic shout and neither of us was any messier than when I started.

Like I said, I'm efficient.

13

Men in Blue

Tony and I walked back to the kitchen, still damp and tingly after our post-shower workout. I looked at the carton he'd left on the table.

"Anything for me?"

His brief pause made me think he was going to go for another oral sex joke, but he resisted the cheap shot. "In the frig. I wasn't sure how late you'd be."

Chicken chow fun. One of my favorites. I brought the carton with a pair of chopsticks over to the table and started going through the mail. Bills, bills, bills. I was tempted to throw them away; after all they'd just send more. Then something more interesting, which Tony had opened.

An engraved invitation.

The Police Officer's Public Service Division Invites You to Join Us for Our Annual Hero Awards Ceremony for Meritorious Service. This Year's Recipients Include . . .

There, along with nine other names, was Detective Tony Rinaldi. He was signaled out for Detective of the Year.

My Tony.

I looked up to see him watching me with a pleased, expectant expression.

I jumped into his lap and smothered him with kisses. "This is incredible! What an honor!" Then I pulled back. I had no idea what these awards were . . . Maybe everyone got one. I regarded him with concern. "This is good news, right?"

Laughing, Tony squeezed me tighter. "Yes, it's great news. They really are very prestigious. Proud of me, baby?"

"So proud," I asserted, squeezing back.

"I could never have done it without you," Tony said.

"That's sweet of you," I said, a little dismissively. "You know what they say, 'Behind every great man is another pretty good one.' "

"No, literally." Tony put his hands on my shoulders and pushed me back until he could meet my eyes. "A major reason I got this was for my work on the Harrington case. But you're really the one who cracked that open."

After having spent years apart, Tony and I were reunited when he was the lead investigator of my friend Allen Harrington's murder. Although it was true I had done a lot of the legwork on the case (and by "legwork" I mean stumbling over my own two feet on my way to accidentally stumbling over the truth), in the end, Tony saved my life when I found out that confronting murderers wasn't quite the cakewalk one might think it would be. Turns out they're not the easiest people to get along with, and their social skills leave a lot to be desired.

Due to many complicating factors, not the least of which was my lack of desire to be exposed to the world as a male prostitute, I worked hard to keep my name out of the story and direct all possible credit to Tony for breaking the case. When the murder turned out to be not just an isolated incident but part of a bigger and deadlier conspiracy, Tony's profile was further elevated.

As far as I was concerned, he deserved all the credit in the world. He was a great cop: caring, hardworking, and unafraid to put his own life on the line in the service of others. Yeah, it just so happened he'd collaborated with me on solving Allen's murder, but there were many other, lower-profile cases that didn't make the papers but which brought justice to those who most needed it.

"Please," I told him, "if you hadn't figured out what I'd got ten myself into, I wouldn't even be alive today. As far as I'm concerned, it's the untold parts of the story that most qualify you as a 'hero.' At least to me."

Tony ran his thumb over my lips. "How do you always manage to say the nicest thing?"

"I follow my heart." I nipped at his finger.

Tony ran his hand through my hair as I scanned the rest of the invitation. The seats ran $500. Not all of them, mind you, just one.

No disparagement to the Police Officer's Public Service Division, but, apparently, I wasn't the only whore in Tony's world. What the hell, I'd like to know, were they serving for $500 a plate? Maybe I should get into the catering business.

Luckily, the card explained, *As a recipient of an Award, you will receive two complimentary tickets. We hope you will share this important evening with the loved one of your choice.*

While a small portion of my attention went toward continuing my discussion with Tony about what a great honor this was and how excited I was for him, the major part of my ADHD-addled, multitasking mind was pondering the question that has preoccupied gay men on occasions like this since time immemorial: What Will I Wear?

The invitation called for "business attire," but that wasn't as clear as it sounded. I wanted to don something tasteful, but not too dull. I had half a closet of conservative Brooks Brothers suits I used to wear to visit some of my escorting clients (either because it was their fantasy to screw a young Republican or because I needed to pass as one to fit in at their apartment/restaurant/hotel), but all of that seemed too boring and generic for Tony's dinner.

I also had some fetish-wear from the old days, but, while I did wear it for work, I was pretty sure it wasn't the kind of "business attire" that'd be appropriate. Disregarding what anyone else thought, I doubted Tony would appreciate my wearing leather chaps, a Catholic schoolboy's uniform, or gold lamé shorts. Well, at least not to his event.

My work attire these days was pretty casual. Consisting mostly of polo shirts in the summer and sweaters in the winter, it also Would Not Do.

Which all led me to one exciting conclusion: I had to go shopping.

I'd have to bring Freddy. He'd enjoy it even more than I would. I'm a bit of a fashionista, but Freddy made me look like someone who'd consider the men's clothing at Walmart the height of haute couture. He could tell the difference between a Giorgio Armani, Hugo Boss, or Ansell Darling suit at five hundred paces. Plus, his taste was impeccable, and he had a way of flirting with salespeople that not only got us the most conceivable attention but the best possible price. For a man who looked his best naked, Freddy knew a lot about how best to cover up.

I was imagining how excited he'd be to paw through the racks of Bloomingdales with me when the part of my brain that was listening to Tony alerted me that I was wasting my time.

". . . especially after all we've been through," Tony was saying, "I think it would be for the best. Don't you? I think it would mean so much for her to be there."

He was talking about his mother. Ever since he'd told her about his divorce, she'd been cold and withdrawn from him. Tony came from a religious family where you stayed married no matter what the problems were. Infidelity, spousal abuse, incarceration: None of these were good enough reasons to put asunder what God had joined together, or some such thing. Even though it was Tony's wife who'd initiated the separation, his mother held it against him.

While a part of me enjoyed knowing it wasn't only Jewish mothers like mine who tortured and manipulated their children with guilt, my heart broke for Tony. He truly loved his mother, and, in his typical good-guy, Boy-Scoutish, has-to-be-perfect, rule-following way, he couldn't deal with disappointing her.

Not that he's ever talked about it. Tony wasn't exactly the type to go on about his feelings.

His bringing her to the awards dinner, I knew, would mean a lot to her. He needed to give her an opportunity to be proud of him. They both needed it.

Tony's decision made perfect sense. His distance from his mother had to be causing him pain, even if he kept it to himself.

Maybe sharing that evening with her would help heal the rift between them.

That would be good for me, too. I wanted Tony to be open with his family about us. Maybe seeing him win this accolade for his professional dedication and achievement would help them understand he was still the same person, with the same high morals and ethical standards, no matter who he loved.

Sure, it would have been nice had Tony chosen me to take to dinner. It would probably be one of the most important nights of his life, and part of me felt I should be the one to share it with him. But, big picture, his decision had the potential to do more good for our relationship than any one evening. If I were mature about it, I had to admit it was a win for me, too.

So, why did I feel like I'd suffered such a loss? Everything Tony said made sense. I even agreed with it.

Yet I couldn't shake the nagging doubt that if I were a *girlfriend*, I'd be there with him. That Tony's bringing his mother as his "date" had less to do with her than with me. It was just another example of my being the Dirty Little Secret.

Was that true? Or just another example of my being self-centered, thinking everything Tony did was a referendum on "us"?

Did it even matter? Supposedly, I'd come to terms that Tony needed time to accept being with a man. So, why was I comparing him to Kristen LaNue earlier and why was I questioning his motives now? I expected him to love me openly and unconditionally, but did he get that from me?

As Tony continued to explain—defend?—his decision, I tried to be encouraging. I said every supportive, self-sacrificing thing I could think of, never letting on I was hurt.

"You and your mom enjoy your five-hundred-dollar dinners," I told him at one point. "Having spent half her life raising a pain in the ass like you, god knows she deserves it."

When it doubt, keep it light. Or a little dirty. "But when you come home," I said, leeringly, "you're mine. And you and I will celebrate your accomplishment in bed. Deal?"

Tony beamed, looking relieved and grateful. He had to have

known I'd expect to be his date. My letting him off the hook so easily probably came as a surprise. A welcome one, at that.

It was a gift I was willing to give him. At least, tonight I was. But tomorrow, or next week, or next year, I was going to need him to start giving back.

If there was one thing I'd learned working the sex trade, it was that love, in any form, comes at a cost. The guys who paid me a couple of hundred dollars to feel cared for got off cheaply. Real love was paid in sacrifice, compromise, and the willingness—no, the desire—to put someone else's happiness above your own.

No matter how hard it was or how far it took you out of your comfort zone.

Would Tony be willing to pay that price?

Would I be willing to wait?

14

Total Corruption

The next day I was in Andrew's office reviewing the week's schedule when my mother burst in waving a piece of paper.

Holy déjà vu, Batman.

"Did you see this?" she shouted.

Andrew looked pained. I could see he was trying to find a polite way to talk her off the ledge.

Happily, I didn't have to be as diplomatic. While I hated to think of myself as the beneficiary of nepotism, there were certain informalities awarded to me by being the star's son. One was being able to do things that would be completely inappropriate for any other staffer.

So, not wanting to play the "Guess What I'm Waving Frantically in Front of Your Face" game again, I just snatched the sheet from her hand.

It was a Xeroxed article from that morning's *New York Times*. My mother actually brought three copies, which was uncharacteristically organized and thoughtful. I credited her assistant. I handed one to Andrew, another back to my mom, and sat down to read the third.

As the story had nothing to do with my mother, I wasn't sure why she'd brought it in. It was a powerful article, though.

We typically think of easily visible child abuse as taking place in lower-class, less-educated communities. Wealthier parents in "better" neighborhoods are subtler in the ways they torture their children. Hence, the thriving psychoanalytic practices on the Upper West Side.

This feature, however, described the case of a couple, the Merrs, in one of the city's most exclusive condominiums, who adopted a child through a private agency two years ago. The infant had never been taken to a doctor or, for that matter, been seen outside of the apartment. His existence was basically unknown until neighbors began complaining about what they thought was a cat screaming for hours on end. The closer ones also contacted the building's management about an objectionable smell they thought was coming from the walls. "I thought a rat died in there," said one.

The Merrs were what you'd call a "power couple." He was the director of the Oncology Unit of one of the city's largest hospitals. He was also an author and highly sought-after speaker on his specialty—the connection between stress and various forms of cancer. It was a popular topic, easily understood in layperson's terms, and Merr dumbed it down further. I'd seen him once or twice and disliked his blame-the-victim approach. His message could have been hopeful and inspiring, but he came across as mean-spirited and blameful. It's your *fault* you're sick. His most consistent claim was that tumors were the result of unexpressed anger, which grew in your body in the form of tumors. More on that later.

Mrs. Merr was the co-anchor of a fluffy morning "news" program on a local station—*Wake Up, New York!* A second—probably trophy—wife, she was in her mid-thirties, a pretty if unremarkable bottle blonde with a sensible haircut and a perky voice perfect for tackling hard-hitting stories like "Finding the Best Manicurist in Your Neighborhood," or "Online Dating: Web of Lies or a Connection to Love?" Ironically enough, the last segment of hers I remember watching (I swear, I was channel surfing at the time) was "Ten Fun Things to Do with Your Kids This Weekend."

Left off that list was her and her husband's favorite activity: Lock him in a cage and raise him like an animal. That's the sight that greeted the police when they paid a surprise visit to the chipper talking head and her equally famous husband.

As far as anyone could tell, Adam had spent his entire life in a large dog enclosure. It was filthy, crusted with uneaten food and human waste. Although most two-year-olds are speaking in full sentences and can understand more, Adam didn't have any usable language. Low muscle tone and a failure to reach physical milestones—he could barely crawl, let alone walk—indicated he hadn't spent much—if any—time out of his crate.

Adam was also covered in a collage of bruises, burns, and scratches that told a story that went beyond neglect into full-blown, systemic abuse.

It was a tale of horror motivated by twisted impulses that would never be understandable by anyone normal. While evil doesn't discriminate, it's still somehow shocking to see this kind of insane abuse perpetuated by such seemingly mainstream, wealthy, successful, and, by conventional measures, intelligent and well-educated people. It spoke to a breathtakingly scary level of sadism.

I can understand a crime of passion—the slap or shot that accompanies a moment of unexpected rage. It's not okay, but it can be human nature to strike out when hurt. But what to make of two people who'd gone to the trouble and expense of adopting a healthy white infant (not a cheap or easy thing to do) for the sole purpose of torturing him? This involved planning, a long process of ongoing deception, and a complete lack of morality or empathy. Was this Dr. Merr's prescription for good health—take out your anger on an innocent child? Raise a kid like a rutabaga and you stay cancer-free?

After his adoption, Adam suffered two years of torment so pronounced as to be literally incomprehensible, both in motive and effect. Those are incredibly important years in a child's development—what would become of this child, who'd learned nothing other than pain and how to endure it?

Besides the Merrs, Adam's birth mother, and the agencies that carried out his adoption, there was no record or report to indicate anyone even knew he existed. It was as if he'd dropped off the earth and directly into hell.

I'd been thinking of Brent metaphorically as a Lost Boy, but Adam was the real thing.

After the article described Adam's horrific living conditions (and I suspected the genteel nature of the *New York Times,* along with the discretion of law enforcement, combined to leave out some of the more graphic details), it explained the Merrs were in custody, held with various charges related to child abuse, endangerment, and neglect, but none that promised a penalty that seemed harsh enough to match the severity of their crimes.

Adam was alive. Unless they actually kill their kid, the law doesn't have that much interest in going after bad parents—even the spectacularly bad ones. Oh, sure, Child Protective Services swooped in, and Adam will receive medical services and a new home. But losing custody of their son hardly seemed like sufficient punishment for the Merrs' deliberate, soul-crushing depravity.

Meanwhile, the Merrs hired some of the best lawyers in the world and weren't talking. I had the sinking feeling that they were going to get off relatively easily.

Given their celebrity status and the nature of the accusations against them, the Merrs were in solitary confinement. Flashing back to my memories of the HBO prison series *Oz,* I found myself hoping a guard "accidentally" released them into the general population, where the criminal code of honor dispensed some rough justice on accused child abusers. I wasn't generally a vindictive person, and I didn't believe in the death penalty, but that only applied to people. The Merrs sounded like monsters. I wouldn't have minded if Buffy dropped by to slay 'em.

Hell, I'd have handed her the crossbow myself.

I shuddered and teared up a little. It wasn't like me to consider violence. Monsters beget monsters.

What would become of little Adam?

* * *

It took me a minute to find my voice.

"This is a terrible story," I said. I looked over at Andrew and saw his eyes were just reaching the end of the article. It wasn't that he was a slow reader—I've always been a fast one. Another thing I credit to my ADHD—typical of the syndrome, I find it hard to focus on one thing at a time. But when I do get interested in something, I hyperfocus. It's like my superpower.

Well, that and the sex stuff. I'm good at that, too.

Andrew looked up. "So, what do you want to do?" he asked my mother. "Try and get the Merrs on the show? Or someone else to talk about the case?"

I took it this was the kind of "hard-hitting" journalism my mother said she was looking for. Although, my guess was everyone was going to be all over this story in the coming weeks, and I wasn't sure my mother's credentials as a professional *yenta* would open any doors CNN couldn't get through first.

Her answer, again, surprised me.

"Everyone's going to be trying to interview the Merrs," she said. "And their friends, families, neighbors. Not to mention every expert on child abuse out there. I don't think we need to go down that road."

Wow. She just made sense.

"Plus, you know what?" she continued. "Who cares what those people have to say? Can you imagine if I actually sat down with one of the Merrs, those *fakakta* pieces of *dreck?*" She was hauling out the Yiddish, once again, a sign she was getting upset. "A *shandeh un a charpeh* like I've never seen," she spat. "*Zol men er vern in a henglayhter, by tog zol er hengen, un bay nakht zol er brenen.*"

My mother's Yiddish wasn't perfect, and mine was worse, but I recognized some catchphrases in there. She was basically calling the Merrs crazy pieces of shit, the likes of which she'd never seen. That last part was a saying that roughly translated to "May they be transformed into a chandelier, to hang by day and burn by night."

Which wasn't so far off from what I'd been wishing upon them.

"No," she continued, "I keep coming back to *him*. The child. Adam." Her voice cracked. "As a mother, I can't help but think of that poor, poor boy. And it makes me so angry.

"Those pigs, the Merrs, they should be put down like dogs. But what about the other people involved?"

"From the article," Andrew observed, "there was no one else. Even their parents didn't know they'd adopted. Their friends, their families and co-workers—the Merrs kept that child a secret from everyone."

"Not from everyone," my mother said. "Someone gave them that child. Placed that boy into their care."

She took another folder from her handbag and passed out some more papers. Holy cow.

"This is from the Web site of the agency that handled the adoption, Families by Design. Listen:

" 'Adoption can be a difficult, time-consuming, and frustrating process. Finding the right child for your kind of lifestyle may seem impossible. But we're here to tell you that families like yours never have to settle for less than a perfect match.

" 'Let us find you the child you're looking for, the one that fits in with your special family. Our exclusive network of social workers, lawyers, and doctors will help connect you with the child of your dreams. He or she is out there. We'll bring him or her home to you.

" 'Our assistance isn't for everyone—only for the privileged few who demand—and deserve—the very best.

" 'This unique combination of one-on-one attention and access to only the crème de la crème of highly trained professionals isn't for everyone. Our premium service is for the elite few willing to make a significant investment in that which we know to be more precious than rubies or gold—the happy, healthy child that looks like your family and that you were *meant* to have.' "

My mother put down the paper and wrinkled her nose in disgust. "Those words. 'Exclusive.' 'Privileged.' 'The elite.' In my days, they meant 'No Jews Allowed.' Today? 'Only the rich need apply.' "

My mother's flaring nostrils, and her eyebrows, which drew toward each other as if trying to meet in the middle, reducing her eyes to lizard-like slits, indicated her genuine outrage. "This isn't an agency for the Angelina and Brads of this world. No Rainbow Coalition going on here. This is for perfect little parents who want perfect little children—or, as I like to call them, stuck-up rich bitches who want white kids with a clean bill of health and a good pedigree.

"These people don't want children." She was practically frothing at the mouth. "They want show dogs. Babies they can wear as accessories before passing them back to the nanny-of-the-month."

"Or locking them in a cage for two years," I muttered.

"Exactly!" my mother exclaimed.

Andrew's eyes widened ever so slightly. "This story means a lot to you, doesn't it?" he asked my mother. His tone was sympathetic and, if I read it right, kind of impressed with her, too. As if he was pleased to see her interested in something that wasn't completely trivial and meaningless.

Or maybe I was just projecting.

"There is no job in life more important than being a good parent," she intoned dramatically. "My children were everything to me. Nothing came before them. All I did was be there for them."

The whole time I was growing up, my mother ran her own business. I couldn't remember her ever going to a school play, attending an assembly, or volunteering in the classroom.

I did have a specific memory of her mockingly referring to the Parent Teacher Association meetings as "that support group for grown-ups who haven't figured out the value of a good cocktail."

Maybe she meant "there for" me in spirit. Which is not to say she was abusive or negligent—she was a great mom. She just wasn't Suzy Homemaker.

Still, I never doubted she loved me. I'm sure my older sister felt loved, too.

It was surprising to me that, in retrospect, my mother felt the need to embellish her maternal involvement. When I was a kid, she was proud to call herself a "career woman," happy to delegate the day-to-day child rearing to a succession of housekeepers and au pairs. Now, she was suddenly Betty Crocker.

I guess everyone has regrets. As we get older, we become aware of how we wished we'd handled things differently and eventually convince ourselves that's what we did.

"Where were the people who were supposed to be there for Adam?" my mother asked.

"Behind bars," I said. "Hopefully, for a very long time."

"No, I mean those stuck-up bastards at Families by Design? Shouldn't they be screening the families who adopt from them? Aren't they supposed to be doing home studies to make sure that the children they place wind up in safe situations? Shouldn't they also do follow-up visits to see how the baby is doing?"

I wasn't sure what the exact requirements were, but most of that sounded right.

"But reading between the lines of that Web page," my mother continued, "I don't think they're 'placing' children at all.

"I think they're selling them."

She let the words sink in.

"Their 'premium service' for the 'elite few' willing to make a 'significant investment.' What does that sound like to you?"

"My brother and his wife adopted," Andrew said, using a yellow marker to highlight the phrases my mother had quoted. "There are fees involved, and I suppose agencies can charge what they want. But there are certain things you can't pay for. For example, you can reimburse the birth mother's health and living expenses during the pregnancy, but you can't give her an out-and-out fee. That would be . . ."

"Selling a child." My mother finished his sentence. "Which would be wrong."

"We don't know that's what they're doing," Andrew said. He'd put down the highlighter and picked up a paper clip, which he toyed with absently.

"No," I offered. "But it does happen." I'd seen a Lifetime movie starring Melissa Joan Hart or some reasonable facsimile of her as a young girl who'd fallen into a baby-selling ring. *Sabrina's Secret Shame: My Womb for Hire,* or something.

"I bet this Families by Design cuts other corners, too," my mother observed. "Whatever preadoption screening they did couldn't have been too careful if they let Adam wind up with two *meshuganas* like the Merrs. What about the follow-up visits? How do you miss that the *baby's in a cage?*" My mother pursed her lips together and pushed out air, miming a spit. "Animals."

"I agree," I said. "But, still. What can we do about it? I doubt we'll get them to come on the show."

"Obviously not," my mother said. "I'm thinking we go undercover. A stink operation."

"A sting," I corrected, although she probably had it right the first time.

"What," Andrew asked her, trying to keep an expression of horror off his face, "do you have in mind?" I noticed he'd half uncurled the paper clip he'd been playing with, bending back the metal with nervous restlessness.

My mother sat up straighter, excited to present her plan. "We pretend to be a couple looking to adopt. A rich couple. But a crazy one—clearly not suitable as adoptive parents. We go in . . . what's that word from *CSI*? Wired. We get them to make some incriminating remarks on tape, and then expose them for the scum they are."

Andrew gave up the pretense of remaining calm. "We?" he croaked.

"Not *we.*" My mother gave a little giggle, wagging her finger between herself and her producer. "I don't think *we'd* make a particularly believable couple, do you?"

"No!" Andrew almost shouted in a combination of relief and agreement. "We wouldn't."

"I meant '*we,*' " my mother explained, indicating with her finger again.

Only this time, it was me on the other end of the wag.

15

Mystery Men

Is there a reverse Oedipus complex? If so, I was pretty sure my mother had one. I instinctively scooted a foot away from her on the couch.

"You want to pretend we're a couple?" I asked, my voice rising on each syllable, until I squeaked out the end of the sentence like a sixteen-year-old girl.

"Why not? You'll be perfect." To Andrew: "He looks so much like his father did at that age."

"Yeah, but now you look *your* age," I pointed out, too appalled to be polite.

"Don't be silly," my mother trilled. "You know I look a lot younger than I am. How often have people told us we look more like brother and sister than mother and son."

Unless the A in ADHD stood for "amnesiac," I was pretty sure the answer to that was "Never."

"Why not have Dad play your husband," I suggested, trying the more diplomatic approach. "He's had more experience."

"Oh, your father's much too old." She dismissed my suggestion. "Who'd ever believe he'd want a child at his stage of life? Besides, you know he'd never go along with the idea."

It was true; my father was much too sensible to get involved with my mother's attention-seeking machinations.

"He's too jealous," she explained. "Of my success." Then, lest she sound immodest, she added, "He's such a sweet man. Wants me all to himself."

What my father wanted most from my mother was to be left alone. My mother saw the skepticism on my face.

"Listen, we have some of the best makeup people in television on this show, right?" She turned her attention toward Andrew. "We have them glam me up a little, take a few years off. At the same time, they throw some gray in Kevin's hair, give him a few wrinkles; he'll look a decade older. He'll appear to be in his mid-thirties, I'll pass for early forties. That's not a huge difference. Remember that episode we did: 'Cougars and the Boys Who Love Them'? Some of those women were twenty years older than their lovers. Kevin and I will look much closer in age than that.

"I mean"—she bestowed upon Andrew her patented imperious expression, which combined the most outrageous possible claim with an implicit dare that you'd better not challenge her—"I really don't look like a woman past her forties even *before* your hair and makeup crew touch me. Given the level of quality I *know* you insist on from the staff, there's no reason we can't make this work, right?"

I could think of at least a dozen reasons, not the least of which was the probability that at least one of the people we'd be meeting with would be sighted. But my mother was studiously, purposefully ignoring me and directing her question at her producer.

Andrew's eyes widened and darted back and forth like a rat caught in a trap. Any sane person would tell my mother her plan was ridiculous. She looked like a woman in her forties only if you took that to mean the decade in which she was born. Plus, I was cursed and blessed with looking far younger than my real age, as proven by the fact that I still got carded at bars. I couldn't imagine a coma patient buying us as a couple, let alone a conscious person.

Added to that, my mother had no experience "going undercover." One of her few undeniable charms was that she was always herself, for better or worse. Her ability to convince anyone that she was genuinely looking to adopt, and to trick them into an admission of unethical practices, was highly doubtful.

Another issue: Who knew how much this wild goose chase would cost? We weren't prepared for this kind of investigation—no hidden camera equipment, no crack research team. As the producer of *Sophie's Voice,* Andrew had to consider the bottom line on things like that.

On the one hand, Andrew had all these arguments and more he could make against my mother's wacky scheme.

On the other hand, he'd like to stay employed.

"No reason at all," he agreed, sounding less believable than Megan Fox in a Michael Bay movie. By now, he's completely unfurled the paper clip he'd been mangling, turning it into a thin, straight, pointed rod. He discreetly pressed it against the skin of his palm while looking at my mother with a, literally, pained smile. "Sounds like a great idea to me."

Back in my office, I stewed for a while. Then I brooded. I followed up this productive activity with some pouting, gnashing of teeth, and an imagined argument with my mother for her harebrained and, on some deeply psychological level, unsettling scheme. That was followed by an interior monologue in which I berated Andrew for agreeing to it.

Unfortunately, in real life, I knew he had no choice but to indulge my mother's folly. It was his job to keep her happy, and if helping her play Girl Reporter was what it took, that's what he had to do.

No, it would be up to me to convince her otherwise. Unfortunately, my mother was like a toddler when it came to being denied something she wanted. You couldn't reason with her. Would you ever try to convince a two-year-old it was genuinely not in her best interest to eat the whole bag of cookies at one time? No. You'd give her one and put the rest somewhere she couldn't reach them.

Taking away my mother's determination to go through with her plan wasn't an option, though. There was no metaphorical cabinet in which I could hide her crazy.

However, as my volunteer work as a teacher at the Sunday school program at my Unitarian church plus my time with Rafi taught me, there are other ways to forestall a child's tantrum when you want to take away something they want that might harm them.

Method number one?

Distraction.

My mother wanted a story she could sink her teeth into. She'd forget about the adoption agency if I could get her interested in something else. Something juicy. Something sexy.

Which brought me back to Brent.

What was that story he'd promised me before he disappeared? Could it even be the *cause* of his disappearance? I had to track him down.

Where had I left things? The owner of SwordFight Productions and its most successful director both claimed they didn't know where he was. To his credit, though, at least the latter had given me a lead.

Brent's boyfriend, Charlie.

What did I know about him? Brent told me he really liked Charlie, but that Charlie hated Brent's working in porn. It had gotten to the point where Brent was feeling so pressured he was considering breaking up with Charlie.

What if things went the other way? Maybe, in the end, Brent decided to keep Charlie and give up the films. It would explain Brent's dropping off the radar.

The too-tasty-by-half Kristen LaNue told me where Charlie worked as a bartender. The place only employed extremely good-looking young men. Charlie was probably quite the looker. He'd have that going for him.

What else did he bring to the table? Was it enough to convince Brent to walk away from the fame and fortune he'd been achieving in adult films? More important, did he know where Brent was and would he be willing to tell me?

Only one way to find out.

If you need to go to the bathroom or grab a snack, you might as well do it now.

It's time for Intermission.

* * *

Memories light the corners of my mind. Misty watercolor memories. Of the whore I was.

The verse repeated itself in my head as I neared Intermission's discreet street-level entrance in an elegant but otherwise typical Upper West Side town house.

I pitied the poor manager who had to hire the bouncers that manned the door. He or she had to find just the right combination of men muscular enough to intimidate, handsome enough not to be a turn-off, but not so good-looking as to get hit on all night. It was a delicate balancing act.

I nodded at the two on duty as I passed by. They nodded back.

I was wearing charcoal-gray Hugo Boss dress slacks, a white button-down Calvin Klein shirt, and a baby-blue cashmere V-neck Versace sweater I'd been told brought out the color of my eyes. I wanted to look good, but not *too* good. Just enough to get me in the door. Not so much that I had to decline offers all night.

Had I been dressed more provocatively or too casually, the bouncers wouldn't have been so friendly. Intermission was what Bogart would have called a "classy joint." It might have been a hustler bar, but it was a tony one. No streetwalkers in short-shorts or too-tight denim need apply. Anyone who gave off the vibe of a reporter, paparazzi, or private detective was similarly discouraged. The buyers here were rich and powerful, the merchandise polished, expensive, and, generally, worth it.

Through the doors, the ambiance was similarly low-key and posh. I'd arrived at seven-thirty, planning my visit for the quietest time of the evening. It was the small window after the "just off from work and looking to pick up some takeout" crowd had left and before the "went home, had dinner, and now it's time for my favorite dessert" customers would arrive.

As I hoped, the place was almost empty. There were men at only two of the twenty or so tables, and another couple in the equal number of booths that lined the walls.

I headed straight for the dark mahogany bar that ran the length of the back. Only one of the brown leather stools there was occupied. An older gentleman was nursing an amber-colored drink in a low tumbler while eyeing two young men at a nearby table. Clearly vexed by analysis paralysis, his glance shifted from blond to brunette and back again. What to choose, what to choose?

The boys, obviously friendly but aware of the competition, chatted amicably while attempting to casually put forward their best faces. They squared their shoulders, sucked in their stomachs, and frequently shared smiles not meant for the other.

"Be a sport," I wanted to tell the indecisive buyer, "spring for them both. They look even cuter as a pair, and I bet two plus one will more than equal three."

So as not to interfere with the emerging deal, I sat at the far end of the bar. There was only one bartender on duty and his back was to me as he sliced lemons by a small utility sink. From behind, he looked good. He was tall, a few inches over six feet. A squarish head with neatly groomed reddish-brown hair sat on a neck thick with muscles. A burly upper body, plump ass, and something about the way he stood, stolidly wide-stanced and confident, as if braced for impact, gave the impression he'd played a lot of football. He'd fill out a uniform nicely.

Probably wouldn't look too bad out of one, either.

Then I noticed behind him a bar-cruiser's best friend: a mirrored panel against the wall that allowed me to observe his front without his noticing. With his chin tucked toward his chest while he worked, I had free rein to study his fine features. His oval eyes, long eyelashes, and full lips would have been pouty on a less masculine man. Rosy, fine-pored skin that suggested at least a little Irish in him. Pronounced pecs stretched out his standard white waiter's shirt, and dome-shaped biceps confirmed my sense he was a high school athlete, or maybe a current school player if he was attending college while not tending bar.

I pictured him with Brent. They'd be a handsome couple by any measure. Smaller, swimmer's-build Brent would fold nicely into this beefy bohunk.

Assuming this *was* Charlie, that is. Finding out was the first order of business. I cleared my throat to get his attention.

The bartender looked up and saw me in the mirror. His face

transformed from an expression of lemon-slicing indifference to a hugely excited and relieved smile in the space of a second. Pivoting gracefully on one foot, he turned around, positively beaming with joy.

Either he was inordinately happy to see another patron, or he'd mistaken me for someone else.

"There you are!" he exclaimed, louder than appropriate in the quiet room. He fast-walked over to me, eyes alight with the eager prospect of reunion. "I'm so glad to see you! I was so . . ."

Charlie, who I was now sure this was, let his voice trail off as he realized his error.

He wasn't the only person who'd noticed how alike Brent and I appeared, but he was the first who looked like the resemblance was going to bring him to tears. His face crumpled like a little boy's who runs downstairs on Christmas morning to find not only no presents under the tree, but no tree. His naturally pink cheeks flushed an alarmingly bright red.

"I'm s-sorry," he stammered, embarrassed both by his miscalculation and his inappropriate outburst. Intermission was a sedate establishment that encouraged a certain level of exaggerated decorum. Shouting, even when joyful, was not expected from the staff.

"It's just—I thought you were someone else," he explained. He'd continued his approach and was now across the bar from me. As if to make up for his earlier gaffe, he spoke in a library whisper.

I gave him a sympathetic smile. "It's okay," I said. "I didn't mean to startle you."

Under normal circumstances, that last part would have made no sense. Nothing I did could have been construed as startling, unless it was generally shocking to see a customer seated at the bar. But a dazed Charlie nodded as if he knew what I meant.

So, now I had two questions answered. One, yes, this was the boy Brent had been dating. Two, it was clear from his reaction that he didn't know where Brent was, either, and probably hadn't for a while.

"So, um, what can I get you?" Charlie still regarded me with a cautious curiosity, as if at any moment his vision might clear and I'd be revealed as his erstwhile lover.

"Information," I said. "I think you and I are looking for the same person. Maybe if we put our heads together, we can find him."

16

Prince Charming

Charlie's rapidly shifting expression now assumed an aspect of suspicion. His full lips narrowed. So did his eyes.

"I don't know what you mean," he said. "But I can get you a drink."

"I'll have a cola," I said. "Then maybe we can talk."

"I'm working," he said, grabbing a glass with one hand while reaching for the soda-dispensing wand.

I looked around the near-empty room. "I think you can spare a few minutes. Bring the lemons over. I'll help." I gave him the reassuring smile I used to give my nervous, first-time clients.

Charlie was recovering some of his cool. "I'm pretty sure that would break a few health code violations. You've already gotten me in enough trouble for the night." He flushed again. While there was definitely a pecking order here, one which allowed Charlie to treat the working boys, which I knew he assumed I was, with more informality than he'd address the older customers, he still had to behave professionally.

"Not that you did anything wrong," he added, plopping my drink down as if it were a live grenade he was glad to be rid of. "It's just, like I said, for a moment . . ."

"You thought I was Brent," I finished. I knew he'd never say it.

Once again, his expression wavered like the surface of a pond with a rock skimming across it. Sadness, confusion, concern.

The suspiciousness was back, too.

I could see he was considering how directly to confront me. He decided discretion was the better part of valor.

"I better get back to those lemons," he said with forced good humor. "You have a, uh, productive night. Good luck."

I was surprised by his reaction. While I didn't expect to be welcomed with a hug, what was the problem with my expressing concern about a mutual friend? If he was truly worried about Brent, why wouldn't he be glad that another person cared about his whereabouts?

Then it came to me—I wasn't a mutual friend. Charlie had no idea who I was or why I was asking about his boyfriend.

Brent had told me about how his fans sometimes confused his public persona with his real one, imagining a connection that didn't exist. Had there been other times Charlie had been approached by overzealous men trying to get to Brent through him? When your lover made his living getting fucked and sucked on film, did it make you overprotective of whatever privacy you could preserve?

"Wait," I called, as he turned to leave.

"It's no problem," he said, already facing away. "The drink's on the house."

"No," I said. "Can we talk? Just for a minute?"

Charlie didn't turn around. But he stopped walking away. "Like I said, I'm working."

"Listen," I said to his back, "I understand why you're being careful. But I also know you're worried. About Brent. So am I. I promise you—I'm not a stalker or anything like that. I really am a friend. I want to help."

It wasn't until I saw Charlie's broad shoulders drop that I realized how tightly he'd been clenching them. He turned around.

"I get off at one," he said, somewhat begrudgingly. "If you're still around, we can talk then."

"I'll come back," I said.

Charlie looked around the bar. "I know it's quiet now, but give it an hour and this place will be bursting. Sure you don't want to stick around and see what you can drum up? I haven't seen you here before, but I can tell you you'll be in the top five percent in terms of looks around here. Fresh meat always does well even when it isn't as cute as you are. You should do well tonight."

"I'm not here for that," I told him. "I just came to talk to you, Charlie."

He cocked his head. "Did I tell you my name?" His guard was back up.

"No," I said. "Brent did. In the same conversation when he told me how much he cared for you."

Another quick shift in character. Charlie's defensive posture shifted to that of a man overcome with unexpected emotion. Then, his face settled into the expression of a man ready to take action. "One minute," he directed me. "Don't move."

He spun on his heels and disappeared into a door hidden behind the bar. A minute later he emerged wearing a black leather jacket over his uniform and followed by another staffer who took his place behind the bar. Charlie took my arm.

"We're getting out of here," he said.

I allowed myself to be dragged behind, suddenly conscious of just how big and imposing a fellow Charlie was.

It occurred to me that if I'd told Tony who I was meeting tonight, which, by the way, I did not, he might have pointed out that when a guy disappears, his disapproving boyfriend, whom he was possibly about to dump, might not be entirely innocent in the matter.

Naw, I thought. Charlie looked genuinely happy to see me. When he thought I was Brent, I mean. If he'd hurt Brent, or, I might as well just say it, killed him, that wouldn't have been his reaction.

Unless he was insane, that is.

He squeezed my arm harder as he hurried me out of the bar. Which he was leaving in the middle of his shift. In what, I supposed, could be called an alarmingly impulsive rush.

After I'd come in and started asking nosy questions about his missing partner.

Had I gotten in over my head again?

At five feet three, that happened to me a lot.

Oh well, it's not like it's ever gotten me killed.

Yet.

"Did you just quit your job?" I asked as Charlie continued to drag me after him. We had just gotten out of earshot of the guys guarding the door, and it seemed like as good a question as any with which to start.

It was a tough economy. If he'd really walked out that suddenly, it would be the surest sign yet that he was crazy. In which case, I was ready to kick him in the balls and run back to the protection of the bouncers posthaste.

Charlie slowed down, as if the sound of my voice reminded him there was a person attached to the other end of his arm. "Naw. It was a slow night. I asked my buddy Cliff to cover for me so we could talk. I should be good for an hour or so."

"I don't want you to get into trouble," I said. "I really could just come back at one. I don't mind." Actually, I kind of did. I couldn't imagine what I'd tell Tony I was doing leaving at that time of night. Or morning, as it were. But I figured I'd deal with that later.

"No," Charlie said. "I couldn't wait—couldn't work all night—thinking that you might know something about where Brent is."

He turned to face me and his eyes were wet. "Do you? Do you know where he is?"

His lips quivered with a boyish vulnerability that made me want to throw my arms around him. If he was a killer, he was the sweetest one ever.

"I don't. I wish I did, though." The night was getting chilly. I rubbed my hands over my arms.

Charlie's eyes widened. "Brent used to do that same thing. You . . . you must know this . . . you look *so* much like him."

"I know," I said. "I'm sorry."

"Sorry?" Charlie was puzzled. "Why would you be sorry?"

It would be totally inappropriate for me to hug him, but I couldn't resist reaching out to rest my arm on his. "I'm sorry because I know that thinking about him is causing you pain. I'm sorry for hurting you."

A single tear formed in the corner of Charlie's right eye. He wiped it away before it fell.

There's something about seeing a big guy like him cry that just breaks my heart. Even more so when he struggles to hold it in.

"There's a coffee shop down that block," Charlie said, resuming his forward march. "We can talk there."

Over a chai tea and an improbably delicious raspberry/white chocolate chip scone, I told Charlie how I'd come to know Brent and what I'd been doing to track him down.

Charlie listened intently, occasionally sipping his black coffee. "It doesn't surprise me those bastards at SwordFight weren't any help," he observed bitterly. "Brent's not a real person to them. He's a thing they made. A product they use and bleed until it runs dry. Then they throw it away."

"You think they threw Brent away?"

"No. I think they drove him away, though."

"What do you mean?"

"Brent wants to leave SwordFight. He's had enough of that life. He wants to be with me, and he knows I can't stand having other men touch him. Not to mention the thousands who are watching. It's . . . obscene.

"I love him. I can't watch him throw himself away like that. He's over it, too. Too many creepy 'fans,' too much exposure to drugs, disease, all kinds of weird shit. It's not exactly the Disney channel over there."

"So, what's the problem?" I asked. "If Brent wants to leave, why doesn't he just quit?"

"He's tried. But they have contracts he's signed and tons of lawyers ready to enforce them. They've spent tens of thousands of dollars creating and promoting the product that is 'Brent Havens.' They're not about to let him just walk away."

"You're saying that Brent ran away because it was the only way he could get out of making more films."

Charlie nodded into his coffee.

"But if Brent . . ."

Charlie's hands tightened around the cup in his hand. I was afraid he'd crush it. "There is no 'Brent.' 'Brent' is the thing they made him into. My boyfriend's name is . . ."

He stopped himself and looked at me again. Appraisingly. What did he know about me? Could he trust me? I knew that must be what he was thinking.

What had Brent told me his real name was again? Oh, shit, this trust-building exercise wasn't going to go well if I couldn't remember. Ralph. Robert.

"Richie," I said. "Richie's the man you love."

Charlie's grip relaxed. "I think you're the only person other than me who's called him that." He was getting choked up again.

I didn't want to be mean, but I couldn't think of a gentler way to put it than this: "If Richie really did leave to be with you, then why isn't he with you? Or, at least tell you where he is?"

This time, Charlie did squeeze the cup hard enough to cause an overflow. The steaming coffee ran hotter than blood over his fingers without his noticing.

"I don't know," he almost wailed. "That's the part I can't stop thinking about. Unless he's afraid they'd send their lawyers after me. That makes sense, doesn't it? I mean, don't they subpoena people in cases like this? I think Richie is protecting me. When their jackals come after me, I'll be able to tell the truth—I really don't know where he is. Then, when this all blows over, Richie can come back."

He looked at me with such need that it was as if he were standing before me naked. "That's it, don't you think?"

Um, no. Nothing about that seemed very likely. For one thing, while it was true that Brent was conflicted about having to choose between Charlie and his job, at least as far as I'd last heard, it wasn't the job he was planning to leave. No, it was big old Charlie who was going to get the heave-ho. Not that I had the heart to tell him that.

Even if Brent had reversed course on that decision, I still

couldn't see why he'd feel the need to disappear—especially from the man he loved. Assuming SwordFight did have enforceable contracts against Brent, what would they sue him *for?* It wasn't like Brent was a millionaire. It would probably cost them more to take him to court than they'd recover. Not to mention all the bad press.

Lastly, there was the question of whatever dirt Brent had on SwordFight. I never got the details as to what it was, but Brent implied the information was so damning it could bring down the company. Which meant they had more to fear from him than he from them. If he really wanted his freedom from SwordFight, why wouldn't he strike a deal? He seemed like a smart kid to me.

More likely, Brent got tired of *everything*. Charlie included. So, he ran away.

Only problem with that theory was that, sitting across from Charlie, it wasn't that easy to believe Brent would do that to him. First, Charlie was terrifically attractive, seemed as sweet as the scone I'd just inhaled at an alarming rate, and was obviously head over heels for Brent. He'd be a hard guy to give up.

Second, even if that were Brent's decision, just disappearing into the night would be an awfully cruel thing to do to a softie like Charlie. Brent had to know that. I did, and I'd only spent an hour with him. Did Brent have a mean streak like that in him?

I didn't know Brent much better than I knew Charlie. But I didn't think so.

Meanwhile, Charlie the gentle giant was looking at me for an answer.

"You could be right," I said. "I mean, everything you say makes a kind of sense. It's certainly . . . plausible." For a moment, I flashed back to Andrew saying something similar to my mother this morning when she presented her nutso plan to investigate the adoption agency. Was this some sort of holiday when you had to humor demented ideas?

Charlie looked so happy to hear me agree with him, despite all my qualifiers, I thought he might cry again—this time from relief.

"Where would he be hiding, though?" I asked Charlie. "Did you know his folks? Have you tried calling them?"

Charlie shook his head. Calmer now, he noticed the cooling coffee on his fingers and absently wiped it away with a napkin while talking. "I wouldn't have a way to contact them even if I thought it would help. But it wouldn't.

"Brent was estranged from his family. He told me his father kicked him out of the house when he found out he was gay. He hadn't had any contact with his parents in years."

This was 2012. It was hard to believe that kind of thing still happened. What was wrong with people? I'd thought of Brent as a Lost Boy; now I realized he'd been driven away. From his family, at least.

"Brothers? Sisters?" I asked.

"He talked about an older sister. I think he had some contact with her, but he never went into details."

"Maybe I should try them anyway."

"Good luck. I don't have their number; and Richie never told me his real last name. He said he wanted to leave all that behind him."

This was going nowhere. Time to face the uglier possibilities.

"I totally see your point about Brent lying low to avoid legal problems," I began. Charlie's lips curled up. I knew how reassured he was that someone else believed that not only was Brent safe, but that he'd gotten out of the porn industry and was willing to go to so much trouble for him. "But we have to consider other scenarios. The . . . less pleasant ones."

Once again, I'd managed to slap the happy right off Charlie's face.

"What do you mean?" he asked, scowling.

"Well, what if something happened to Br . . . Richie? Was there anyone who wanted to hurt him?"

"Physically?"

"Maybe."

Charlie's jaw worked back and forth. "No. Well, I don't know. The guys from SwordFight? I mean, I assume Richie was afraid of them going after him legally, but what if they beat him up or something? On TV, those kinds of businesses are always associated with the mob, right?"

"I don't know much about it. Maybe. What about a fan? Was there someone who showed too much interest? Or made Richie uncomfortable?" I realized I was also describing what sounded like an episode of *CSI*.

"Well, yeah. There were always lots of guys approaching him. A few were creepy, but just in that way like they knew something about him that they didn't, you know? Like, because in a movie he played a kid who liked sex with older men, he must be interested in their ancient ass, right?"

I nodded.

"I mean, just the way they'd look at him was weird. Invasive. It was hard just walking down the street with him sometimes because I'd find myself wondering, Is that man looking at us because we're two guys holding hands? or, Is he cruising Richie? or, Is he cruising me? or, Does he recognize Richie from his movies? It made me kind of paranoid. It must have been one hundred times worse for Richie."

Maybe. Or maybe Brent enjoyed the attention. Wanted people to watch. Some guys like to be looked at.

"The only 'fan' I can think of who seemed a little . . . obsessed . . . wasn't really a fan at all. At least, he wasn't *just* a fan."

I was confused. It had been a long day.

"Come again?"

"Well, when you think of a fan who's a little *too* into someone, you think of all the clichés, right? The guy who shows up at your house with flowers, unexpected. Who sends you gifts you don't want. Who calls twenty times a day. Who sometimes hangs up, but sometimes leaves long, rambling messages about how you're meant to be together?

"Richie had a guy like that in his life. I guess you could say he was a fan, but he wasn't a stranger. Richie knew him."

Charlie's lips did that thing where they narrowed and drew

together. He ground his teeth for a moment, his expression darkening before he said, "When I say *'knew'* him, I mean he had *sex* with him. Not with *Richie,* mind you. With Brent."

I thought it was interesting how Charlie could make that distinction. I wasn't sure if it was healthy or not, but it was interesting.

"They . . . did it together on screen, and I think the dude kind of fell in love with Richie. Or something. It was definitely stalkerish.

"And he wouldn't take no for an answer. Because Richie wasn't interested in him. Richie loved me."

I thought I already knew the answer, but I asked anyway. "What's his name?"

"Lucas Fisher," he said. "At least, that's his stage name. I don't know his real one."

Again, Charlie was making a distinction I wasn't sure mattered much to the people he was describing.

"What about drugs? Did Richie get high?" Crystal meth and other recreational drugs weren't unknown on porn sets. Brent could be on a binge.

"Not even a little," Charlie asserted. I guess I looked skeptical. "Seriously. Have you seen him? He's very serious about his body and staying in shape. He told me he smoked weed once, got the munchies, ate a gallon of ice cream, and decided then and there never to screw with his body's chemistry."

We talked a little more, and then I reminded Charlie he needed to get back to work.

"Thanks," Charlie said. "When you first showed up, I thought you were Richie, and I was so happy. Then, you made me nervous. Now? I'm glad you're looking out for him. For us. Will you let me know what you find out?"

I told him yes and we exchanged numbers.

As he stood to leave, Charlie seemed even taller than he did when we arrived. Not as gentle, either. He clenched his fist and the tendons in his thick neck stood out sharply. "Do you think that maybe Lucas did hurt him? Maybe he made a move on

Richie and when Richie rejected him, he just . . . lost it. It could happen, right?"

"I suppose. It's a little far-fetched."

"Maybe. Maybe not. Love and hate. Two sides of the same coin. Maybe Lucas didn't like how the toss landed."

We said good-bye.

I sat at the table a few more minutes, thinking. Charlie was an interesting case. I wasn't sure what to make of him. Every time I thought him harmless, he'd surprise me with a darker aspect.

He thought in dualities. "Real" people versus "thing" people. Richie versus Brent. Love versus hate. *Everything* was a coin with two sides.

I was pretty sure that Charlie would never hurt Richie.

But he'd kill Brent in a heartbeat.

17

Getting It

When I got home, Tony was sitting at the kitchen table. He'd done takeout for dinner again. This time, pizza.

I was really going to have to be a better wife.

He had papers spread across the table. When he heard the door open, he flipped over two of the pages. As I got nearer, I saw the ones that remained right side up pertained to a case he was working on. A woman who had been found murdered in Central Park. There were witness statements, evidence lists, and some photos of the crime scene. "Hey, babe," he said, standing up to kiss me. "Did you get stuck at the office?"

I didn't necessarily mean not to tell Tony about how I was looking into Brent's disappearance. It's just that it was a long story, and I didn't have the energy to get into it right then. Especially since I suspected Tony would tell me to stay out of it. Which would lead to a fight.

Besides, since the reason I was trying to find Brent was to see if he had a story we could use on *Sophie's Voice,* it wasn't like I was lying or anything when I answered, "Yeah, it was work. Sorry I'm home so late."

"No problem." Tony nibbled my neck. He gestured toward the table. "I brought my work home. It's good you weren't here. Some of this stuff"—he gestured toward the pictures he'd turned over—"you don't need to see." He put the photos in a manila envelope.

"Gruesome?" I asked.

"Not pretty," he answered.

"How do you do it?" I sat at the table and opened the cardboard pizza box. Bacon and pineapple. My favorite. The scone hadn't ruined my appetite so I grabbed a slice.

"What?"

"Work around so much . . . ugliness every day?" Between hearing about that poor kid Adam this morning and then considering all the bad fates that might have befallen Brent, I'd found my day pretty depressing. "Doesn't it get to you? All the garbage, the slime you deal with—after a while, does it ever feel like it's starting to stick?"

"Naw," Tony said. "I may be surrounded by dirt, but I'm the detergent, babe. I get to clean it up."

He tapped on the folder in which he'd placed the photos out of my view. "I'm gonna find the scumbag who did this to her, and I'm gonna make sure he never hurts another girl again."

That's my Tony. Always protecting people. It made me proud. It made me admire him.

It also made me, for some reason, horny.

I decided to skip another slice. Of pizza that is.

"Best dessert ever," Tony said, twenty minutes later when I stood up from between his legs.

"I don't," I said, licking my lips, "remember you eating anything."

"I had a cannoli while you were down there." He grinned. "It was so good I almost didn't even notice what you were doing."

"What?" I heard the whine in my voice and regretted it. "That is just rude. I can't believe—"

"Kidding, babe, kidding." Tony pulled me into his lap for a kiss. "Believe me, not all the baked goods in the world could distract me from those sweet lips of yours." He licked them to reinforce his words.

"You better be telling me the truth, Rinaldi," I said.

"Trust me, the way you get me going? I'd be afraid to try and eat something when you pleasure me. I'd probably choke to death." He ran his hand over my chest. "Speaking of which, do you need me to return the favor? That was a nice surprise, but I don't want to be selfish."

"I, uh, kind of finished already. When I was . . . down there." I blushed a little. "Couldn't help it."

Tony's eyes widened, and he looked down at my crotch. Always the investigator, he wasn't going to let me get away with that claim without checking it out himself. The big wet spot in my pants confirmed my confession.

He grinned wolfishly. He'd never admit it, but the thought that I got off just from getting *him* off made him feel like quite the stud. Which he was.

I grinned back. Nothing made me happier than making him happy. Maybe that made me codependent or too needy, or maybe that was what love was supposed to be about. I didn't care.

"So," he said, "since we can't talk about my case, tell me what you were working on today."

Another opportunity to fill him in on what was happening with Brent. Maybe I'd take it. But first, the more entertaining story.

"You're not doing this," Tony said, stone-faced. We'd moved over to the couch where we cuddled while I told him about the harrowing events of my day. "It's too dangerous."

"It's hardly bungee jumping," I assured him. "I'm just going to ask a few questions."

Tony released me from his embrace and pushed me forward, forcing me to look in his eyes. "Listen, Kevvy. You may have noticed you have a habit of putting yourself into the line of fire. This is the kind of thing that needs to be investigated by professionals. Not you and your loony mother."

This was what I was afraid of. The ironic thing was, I hadn't even mentioned Brent Havens yet. Tony was objecting to my mom's plan to visit Families by Design, the adoption agency used by the Merrs.

"Tony, we're just going to see if they cut corners or suggest anything illegal in their admissions process. At worst, they're an unethical business. It wouldn't make them Murder Incorporated."

"You think they might be implicated in child abuse, Kevvy. That's a crime. You need to report it and let the police do our job."

"There's nothing to report, Tony. That's why we're going."

Tony's sigh was heavy enough to rustle the drapes. "Is it ever possible to talk you out of *anything?*"

"It's not me you'd have to convince," I said. "It's my mother. In which case, no."

"You know what your problem is?" he asked me.

Why is it that the very protectiveness I love about Tony when he applies it to others pisses me off when he pulls it on me?

"No," I said. "Enlighten me."

"That you're a grown man who's still caught up worrying about what mommy will think. Do you see me crying because my mom's PO'ed at me? If she can't accept my divorce, that's on her, not me.

"Trust me: You need to cut the umbilical cord, babe."

"She's not just my 'mommy.' She's also my boss. I kind of have to care what she thinks, Tone. It's not the umbilical cord pulling me into this, it's the paycheck."

He squeezed my shoulder. "Okay, I'll give you that one. But you have to find a balance. Or maybe move on. It might not be the healthiest thing for you to be working for your mother."

"No kidding." I left unsaid the logical question: Would he rather I return to my previous job? That would only escalate the fight.

So, I realized, would bringing up my poking into Brent Haven's disappearance.

For a guy who didn't sit around talking about "feelings," Tony was as sensitive a man as there ever was. It was part of what made him such a great cop—he could read people as well as anyone I'd met. He sensed the rising tension in the room and decided to defuse it.

"Listen, do what you have to do, babe. Just be careful."

"Thanks, Dad."

Tony punched my arm. "Don't push it. I suppose I'd be more worried if I thought your mother's plan was actually going to work. Let me get this straight—she really thinks she looks like she's in her forties? And that you and she could pass as a couple?"

I nodded against his strong chest.

"That is so wrong on so many levels." He sighed again.

"Tell me about it," I muttered.

"Poor baby." He stroked my head, playing with my bangs. "Pretending to be a couple when you're not is always a bad idea. But pretending to be a couple with your own *son?*" He gave a mock shudder. "Ugh."

"Can we talk about something else?" I asked.

He glanced at the cable box. "Actually, I'd like to watch the local news. See if they say anything about the case I'm working on."

I nestled deeper into his arms. "If I can stay here, you can watch anything you want."

He kissed the top of my head while turning on the TV.

While the overly cheery newsreaders chirped away, I couldn't stop my mind from going places I'd really prefer it didn't.

Tony was right—there was nothing admirable about lying about being a couple when you weren't one.

So, how did he justify the reverse?

He still hadn't told anyone in his life that we were together. Wasn't that even worse?

I knew if I confronted him on it, there'd be another fight. In fact, whether it was Brent or Tony's reluctance to be open about us, I felt like half the things I wanted to talk about with him would lead to an explosion.

When did all these land mines get buried between us?

And if his earlier assertion was true—that he really didn't feel the need to justify his divorce to his mother and that it was on her to get over it—why was he taking her and not me to his awards dinner?

Which brought me back to the first question.

"Hey." Tony interrupted my brooding. "You know that guy?" he asked teasingly.

I looked at the TV. There was my boyfriend on the screen, working the crime scene in background footage while the reporter stood in front discussing the latest developments in the case.

"Kind of," I answered.

Tony gave me a little shove. "Always with the joke," he chided playfully. "You know, some people would be proud to see their man on TV."

Who's joking? I wanted to say. But I didn't.

I really didn't want to step on any land mines tonight.

18

Lover Boys

"So, let him take some dirty pictures," an annoyed Freddy said. "Who cares? It's not like you haven't peddled your papayas before."

"Don't pay him any attention," his part-time boyfriend, Cody, chimed in. "I think it's great you have standards. Well, that you have standards *now*. You tell that gross old man to keep his money—you have *morals*."

It was like having a devil and an angel sitting across from me in the greasy downtown diner where we'd met for breakfast. Tony had to leave early to meet with the coroner, and when I called Freddy, Cody had been sleeping over. "We'll both meet you," he said cheerily, seeing no need to check first with his evening's company. Which wasn't wrong—Freddy was Cody's First Big Gay Crush, and he'd have followed Freddy anywhere.

Not that he had any reason to be so clingy. Cody was absolutely adorable, with a young, fresh-scrubbed innocence that was no act. You wanted to grab him by his oversized ears and kiss the down-home country right out of him.

"First of all," I clarified to them both, "I wouldn't be letting Mason film me for the money. I don't *need* the money."

"I'll take the money," Freddy said, raising his hand.

"Then let him take pictures of *your* wiener," I suggested. "The only reason I'm even considering it is because the owner of the company told me the only way he'd talk to me is if I'd film one of his 'auditions.' "

SwordFight put out a highly successful series of these "audition" collections, in which guys were interviewed on film about why they wanted to be in adult movies and then were talked through their first "performance"—which usually consisted of a clumsy disrobing and an even more awkward masturbation. Sometimes, the sessions went disastrously wrong, with the applicant too stoned, nervous, or heterosexual to get it up.

During the whole depressing episode, Mason or one of his associates gave instructions, feedback, and encouragement to the desperate, cash-starved performer.

"I love those videos," Freddy said, dreamy-eyed. "They always have these guys who are so . . . sincere."

Cody blushed. Whether because he was embarrassed by Freddy's love for porn or his own remembered first-time discomfort I wasn't sure.

"Explain," I prompted Freddy with real curiosity, "what is hot about watching someone being awkward? Do you get a woody watching *America's Funniest Home Videos,* too?"

Freddy picked up a French toast stick from his plate and pointed it at me like a dagger. "Because it's *real,*" he instructed. "Most porn is so slick and overproduced. Too choreographed. But those auditions are authentic. When the guys get turned on despite themselves, it's really hot."

"Yeah, but how painful is it when they don't? It's like when you go home with a guy and they're so not into you they don't even get hard."

Freddy looked at me like I was speaking Martian. "That happens to people?"

I rolled my eyes. "It happens to everyone."

"It's happened to me," Cody offered.

"Huh," Freddy said. "Maybe I'm the weird one. Not only have I never had a guy who couldn't bone at my apartment, I can't remember a time when I didn't have them precoming on the way there.

"Maybe," he pondered, "the sample size is too small because I haven't slept with enough guys."

Cody and I smacked him at the same time.

"What?" he asked. "Is it my fault I'm human Viagra?"

"Closer to human ipecac syrup," Cody, who was a nurse, mumbled. To me: "It's a medicine that induces vomiting."

I snorted tea through my nose.

"No, *that* would be the human version of ipecac," Freddy said, referring to my Julia Roberts moment. "So gross."

"Speaking of gross," I said, bringing the conversation back around, "I am not thinking of doing an 'audition' video with that troll Mason Jarre for the money. I'm thinking of . . . putting myself through that humiliation because it's the only way he said he'd be willing to talk to me about Brent Havens and where he might have gone."

"Like that's the most humiliating thing you've ever had to do," Freddy observed. "Weren't you the guy who let someone dress him up like a clown while he pelted you with apple pies?"

There are some stories I wish I'd never shared with that vicious bitch I call my best friend. Which is to say, most stories.

Yes, I worked as a male prostitute and couldn't claim the high ground here. But my objections to being filmed weren't based on some sliding scale of morality. They were practical.

As a hustler, whatever happened between my clients and me was private. There was security in that. I didn't have to worry about my friends, family, or strangers knowing things about me I didn't want them to. Since my clients had even more to lose than I did, my personal choices were kept just that—personal.

Putting yourself on film seemed infinitely more risky to me. Movies lasted forever, especially in digital form. Your image was out there for the rest of your life and beyond, viewable by anyone at any time.

Some guys justified their porn anonymity by the sheer volume of it. With the millions of hours of video available, what were the chances *theirs* would be found?

But already, facial recognition technology has become ubiquitous and easy to use in everything from iPhoto to Facebook. How long before you could search the entire Internet for someone's image—every picture, every video, every Web page? We were entering whatever comes after the Age of Privacy, and if you were counting on keeping any secrets, you'd better keep them *in* your head and *off* the Web.

The work I'd done was different. If I was with a client, and something he said made me uncomfortable or regretful, all I had to do was leave. Had that encounter been filmed, though, I'd have to live with the threat of those images coming out at any time. Where would my presidential bid be then?

Cody almost dropped his coffee. "Someone paid to throw pies at you? Really?"

Okay, maybe my private life wasn't 100 percent safe. Not with a big-mouthed friend like Freddy. Luckily, it was matched by his big heart. He'd tell my secrets only to tease me, not destroy me. He'd never use them to hurt me. He knew I'd already told Cody about my former profession, otherwise he wouldn't have said a word.

What if Brent wasn't so lucky? Could it have been his working in the sex industry that led to his disappearance? Was he being blackmailed? Held prisoner? I had to know.

"I'm going to do it," I announced.

"More clown sex?" Freddy asked, with faux innocence. "Perfect timing since we're at a diner. Shall we order a Boston cream pie to bring home with you?"

"The audition, dummy."

Cody leaned forward. "You sure?"

"It's the only way. Mason Jarre knows something. I have to get him talking."

"You've seen those videos, Kevin," Freddy said. "The 'talking' is mostly along the lines of 'Now, take those shorts off for me,' and 'Yeah, baby, that's hot.' It's not the most rewarding conversation."

"In my experience," I said, a bit haughtily, picking a sausage off his plate and holding it suggestively, "when I get a guy alone, the more clothing I take off, the more I can get him to say."

"Yeah," Freddy said, smirking, "like 'Yuck! Get me the hell out of here!' "

"You're horrible," I scowled.

" 'Please, lord, strike me blind!' " Freddy continued. " 'Where's the rest of it? I ordered a *male* prostitute!' "

I threw the sausage at him.

Freddy put an arm around Cody. "See, honey? He really gets into that whole food-throwing thing."

Cody gave him a half smile and then considered me with concern.

"Are you going to be okay?" he asked me.

"I think I can handle it," I assured him.

"No," Freddy said, pushing away his plate so he could take my hands. "This is serious. You don't know who you're dealing with. You'd better go in ready for the worst. I'm getting you a weapon."

It was sweet that Freddy cared. I could hardly see myself with a gun, though.

"Waiter," Freddy called. "We'll take an apple walnut cake to go."

I pulled my hands away from him.

"*What?*" he asked. "We know you can toss a baked good with the best of them. I figure the nuts will make it even deadlier. Like edible shrapnel."

"Would you stop teasing him?" Cody said.

"Don't worry about it, Codes. I'm used to it."

"Yeah," Freddy said. "It's part of our charming dynamic. Besides, the cake is for me. I'll eat it while I wait."

"Wait for what?" Cody asked.

"For Jerkoff Boy over there," Freddy said, pointing his thumb at me. "What, you think I'd let him go there alone?"

He turned to me. "You call me when you get an appointment. I'll wait outside."

"You'd do that for me?"

"You asshole," Freddy said, helping himself to the croissant I had in front of me. "You know I'd do anything for you."

Cody stroked Freddy's back. I could read in his eyes what he was thinking: *I hope that someday this big, hot man will be there for me like that.*

I was genuinely touched and had to swallow back a lump in my throat. "Thank you," I said, an unexpected huskiness in my voice.

"Except clown sex," Freddy clarified. "That's just sick."

19

Undercover

"I didn't think it would happen this quickly," I said, as an unseen Mason Jarre set up video equipment somewhere to my left.

I'd called his office shortly after breakfast to arrange the meeting. His assistant and former porn star was brusquely efficient. "We can get you in at two."

"Today?" I'd croaked.

"Yes, today," Pierce stated. "Do you still have the address?"

"Yeah, but *today?*" I wasn't looking forward to this. I figured I'd have a few days to prepare, although, thinking about it, I wasn't sure what that would entail. "Can we do it later in the week?"

"We can do it today at two," Pierce agreed with himself.

"Well . . ."

"Mason did explain you'd be paid one thousand dollars for the primary audition, with possible bonuses depending on what you are willing to do."

"Willing to do?"

"Extra acts not including the opening interview with masturbation."

Something about the way he said that last part made it sound like an item on a Chinese menu. *I'll have an Opening Interview with Masturbation. Sauce on the side, so to speak.*

"You know, I'm not totally committed to doing the whole—"

"Mr. Jarre told me about his conversation with you. I'm well aware of your wavering intentions, Mr. Connor. Unlike some people, I don't need the same thing repeated to me a hundred times in order to understand it. But as Mr. Jarre made clear, the only way he'll be able to fit you into his schedule is if you agree to be taped while talking with him. Two birds with one bone, if you will. As is the case with any of our models, you will not be expected to do anything with which you are uncomfortable or that you're unwilling to do. Of course, your remuneration will be commensurate with the acts you're willing to perform."

He paused for dramatic effect.

"So, will we see you at two?"

"I'll be there," I said with obviously forced cheer.

"Very well," he confirmed. "I'm breathless with anticipation."

I wish.

We said good-bye and I made my next call.

"You are not," Freddy growled, trying to sound threatening, "going there alone."

"It's not that I don't appreciate your offer," I told him for the third time. "It's just that I don't want to do anything to put them on guard. I'll be fine. I promise. I've walked into worse situations than this one."

"Yeah," Freddy agreed. "You've also been shot at, beaten, and tied up against your will."

True that.

"The guys at SwordFight might not be model citizens, but it is a legitimate business. I'm glad you'll know where I am, just in case, but I don't think I have anything to worry about."

"It's not that I think they're going to kill you," Freddy said. "But I figured out a way to keep you from having to blow your cover—no pun intended—on film. I go with you. We tell them I'm your boyfriend and that I'm going to wait outside. Then, in twenty minutes, after you've had enough time to ask your questions but before they get you down to your skivvies, I burst into the studio in a jealous rage and drag you out of there."

"That would work," I said, "assuming I could get my questions answered that fast. And assuming they don't call the cops on your ass and get you arrested for trespassing or felony interruption of a jerk-off scene."

I didn't want to inflate Freddy's ego by telling him my more likely concern—that they'd get one look at him and wind up offering him ten times what they'd pay me for an audition.

And that, knowing him, he'd take it.

"So, then how do you get out of there?" he asked. "They're gonna make you sign some kind of waiver or contract, right? You probably can't just walk out in the middle without getting arrested yourself. Or sued."

"No, I think you're right. I also don't want to make enemies of these guys. Even if I don't get the answers I want today, I may need their help later on."

"So, what are you going to do?"

"I have an idea," I said. "Believe it or not, it actually came from something my mother said."

"That's it," Freddy said, more determined than ever. "I'm coming with you. Your solution is based on something *your mother said?* You've obviously lost your mind and need supervision."

"No," I said. "Listen." I told him what I had in mind.

"Huh," he said after I was done. "That's actually not bad."

"See?" I reassured him. "I told you I'd be fine."

"I'm not saying that," he countered. "This is *you* we're talking about, Kevin. You had plans those times you got shot, beaten, and tied up, too. Somehow, you and plans don't get along very well."

"This one, I think I've got."

"Oh, yeah? Well, let me ask you a question—did you remember to take your medication this morning?"

"Of course," I lied, opening my drawer to take out the vial of Adderall I kept there. One pill would help me keep my thoughts more organized as the day went on. I downed it dry.

"You did, huh? Then what was that swallowing sound I just heard."

"That was, uh, practicing. You don't audition for porn without practicing your swallowing."

SwordFight Productions had their own building in New York's trendy Tribeca neighborhood. When I arrived, I was given consent forms to sign and shown to the room where the shooting occurred.

A floor of the building had been converted into one large studio, where industrial video lights hung from the ceiling and various props littered the corners.

The area where I was told to wait was made up to look like a tacky motel room. I was perched on the end of a cheap twin bed. A plywood nightstand next to it supported a plastic table lamp with a dented cardboard shade and a large pump bottle of SwordFight-branded lube. Above the bed hung a painting of a lighthouse so bad it might have been meant as parody. And why a lighthouse? Was it chosen for its phallic symbolism, for the viewer too impatient to wait for the actual phallus that would be making its appearance soon enough?

I was nervous. I was babbling, if only in my own head.

Focus, Kevin, focus.

I was also hot, but not in the good way. I was literally overheating. The studio lights roasted me like a tanning bed in a *Final Destination* movie. Maybe it was intentional—one of Mason's techniques to get first-time models naked as quickly as possible. No pressure. Strip or melt. You decide.

The lights also served to blind me to whatever Mason was doing out there. I heard him puttering around, but he hadn't answered me. I found it unnerving.

"Mason?" I asked.

Long pause. "Yeah?"

"I said, 'I hadn't expected to get in here so quickly.' "

"Huhn," he grunted.

He'd been chatty at the party and on the phone. Here, not so much.

He stepped from behind the lights into my faux hotel room.

I'd been wrong.

"I'm not Mason," Pierce Deepley, former porn star and Mason's current assistant, announced. "He stepped out five minutes ago. He had to take a call. I was just finishing setting up for him."

I didn't like not knowing who was in the room. Maybe there were others there, in the shadows. Unseen viewers hidden by the darkness.

But wasn't that a metaphor for the whole experience of being in porn? You never knew who was watching. That was a level of control you had to sacrifice.

Maybe that was part of the appeal. For a model into exhibitionism, it could be the perfect trifecta: getting paid for getting off by showing off.

For me, not so much.

"Oh, okay," I said to Pierce. "I was thinking it was strange Mason didn't answer me. Now I get it."

"I don't know he would have answered you even if he were here," Pierce said. He always sounded annoyed to be speaking to me, as if I were somehow beneath his attention. "Seeing as how you didn't actually ask anything," he added.

"Sorry, I forgot to phrase my response in the form of a question," I clarified, feeling as if I were being chided by Alex Trebek.

Pierce exhaled noisily through his mouth. "Don't take it personally. It's not as if you're *that* special." I think Pierce would have preferred not responding at all, but he couldn't miss this chance to put me in my place.

"When a potential model calls to schedule an audition, we *always* try to get him in as soon as we can. That day, if possible. All we require are some pictures before we make an appointment. No point in wasting everyone's time if he's a pig.

"If he has the right looks, though, we move fast. The decision to appear on film is generally made on impulse. Often it's out of desperation—money is tight and there are no other options. I can't tell you what a boon the bad economy has been for us. A nine percent unemployment rate is the best recruitment tool we have.

"Still, given a day or two to consider it, an applicant may chicken out. Maybe he'll decide that job at the fast food place isn't so bad after all. Or, he'll swallow his pride and ask Mommy and Daddy for a loan, even though he'd sworn not to. That's why it's imperative we get him on video before he has a chance to identify other options."

"So, basically," I said, unable to stop myself from getting in a dig, "your business model is to take advantage of people at their weakest."

I couldn't make out the features of Pierce's face, but I could hear the smug smile in his voice. "Yes, we're just awful, aren't we? Like those restaurants that feed you when you want to eat. How dare they profit from your hunger?

"Or the credit card companies that are only too happy to extend funds to young people at interest rates so punishing they were previously restricted to the practices of loan sharks and Shakespearean villains.

"How horrid of us," he continued, on a roll, justifying his actions in a controlled but impassioned rant he'd probably given dozens of times before, "to provide these young men with work that pays more than they'd make anywhere else, while protecting their health and safety. No, better they should work for eight dollars an hour in a coal mine getting emphysema than make a hundred times that for suffering the indignity of a well-delivered blow job."

Jeez. I had to admit he made a good case. Not that I'd admit it to *him*.

"It's not like you're doing it out of charity," I pointed out. "You guys are doing pretty well yourselves."

"I'm afraid I don't have the time or the inclination to educate you on the basic tenets of capitalism," he said, dialing his condescension meter to eleven. "Does SwordFight make money from the efforts of its employees? Absolutely. So does every company in the world. I'm simply explaining that, in my opinion, we pay and treat the men who work for us more than fairly. Often, a good deal more."

"So, you don't feel badly about taking advantage of guys at their most desperate?"

"I wouldn't say the majority of our models come to us when they're at their 'most desperate,' as you so charmingly put it. But, even if they did, why would I feel badly about providing employment that I truly believe is in their best interest? Extremely generous compensation for work that is not only safe, but, for those without Puritanical hang-ups, quite fun? The best sex many of them will ever have, in fact.

"And for those who truly are in immediate need of cash? What would be preferable in your world—to offer them nothing? Or to give them a choice?

"We're not holding a gun to their heads, Mr. Connor. Just a camera and a paycheck. Does that really make us bad guys?"

I kind of hated myself for not having a snappy comeback to that. Having been a sex worker myself, I didn't harbor the Puritanical streak Deepley deplored. Nor did I think it was inherently immoral to make or appear in porn. People had a right to use their bodies in any way they wanted. If they could make a living by giving pleasure to others, more power to them.

So, if it wasn't their business I objected to, why was I picking this fight with Pierce?

It was, I realized, because I didn't like *him*. Or Mason. It wasn't their work that made them "bad guys." It was their characters.

From the moment I met them, they struck me as manipulative, uncaring, exploitative assholes. Their callous lack of concern for Brent only reinforced that initial impression.

Maybe I was being naïve, but it seemed to me there was a way they could run their business while remaining human beings.

"Sorry," Mason's voice boomed as he walked back into the studio. "That was the owner of EuroBoys Films. We're forming a partnership with them. Actually, it's more of an acquisition."

By now, Mason had walked over to where Pierce stood. He put his arm around his assistant in a celebratory gesture. *Go team.*

"It would never have happened without Pierce. He's the one who first approached them. The lawyers hammered out the details, but Pierce got the ball rolling."

He was so excited he was mixing his metaphors.

"We're going to be the first *international* M/M video company. Can you imagine what that means to me? I started this company from nothing. *Nothing*. Just a five-hundred-dollar video camera that shot on VHS tape.

"Now, we're weeks away from having a worldwide presence. It's—literally—unbelievable."

The jubilation in Mason's voice was almost manic. His grin was so wide I wouldn't have been surprised to see his jaw completely unhinge, like a snake's.

He squeezed Pierce tighter. There was nothing sexual in the gesture—it was pure pride. All business.

"I'm telling you," he continued, "I'd be lost if anything ever happened to this guy. I'd track him to the ends of the earth if that's what it took."

I didn't doubt it.

As long as Pierce continued to produce, as long as he brought in the money, Mason wasn't about to let him go.

So, why was he so unconcerned about losing Brent?

Something didn't add up.

"But enough about that." Mason released Pierce from his clutches and stood by my side.

"We're here for you today, Kevin. You ready to start making some movie magic for me?"

No, I thought.

"Yes," I said.

"Excellent." Mason clapped his hands together. "Let's get the cameras rolling and see what you've got. Pierce, you ready to start shooting?"

"Oh, I was ready to shoot him before you even arrived," Pierce assured.

If Mason got Pierce's double meaning, he didn't acknowledge it. "I don't blame you," he said, with seeming sincerity. "He's absolutely adorable. I can't wait to see if what's under all that clothing is as delicious as I expect it to be. I'll be surprised if isn't." He winked at me.

Oh, you'll be surprised, I thought.

At least, that was my plan.

Although now, under the blinding, hot lights, the running cameras, and the unexpected presence of Pierce in the room, I was wondering if Freddy was right and I hadn't gotten myself in trouble after all.

Plans and I didn't get along very well.

20

Star Maker

"So," Mason began. He picked up and unfolded a wood-and-canvas contraption that had been leaning against one of the cameras, and I noted with amusement that it was an old-fashioned director's chair. Like something Alfred Hitchcock might have used on set. I wondered if Mason had his last name stenciled on the back. "Even though you've already signed a release, I need to confirm that you're aware that this interaction is being videotaped for possible public viewing at the discretion of Sword-Fight Productions. This distribution may occur online, on DVD, or through other technological means yet to be developed. By appearing in this video, you give full and informed consent. Do you agree to these conditions?"

Mason appeared to have the spiel memorized. I thought of police reading suspects their Miranda rights. They knew those by heart, too.

It didn't usually bode well for the arrested.

Dry-mouthed, I nodded.

"I need you to give your verbal consent, please."

"Yes," I croaked.

"And you are of legal age?"

"Yes."

"You provided a driver's license with your written consent form and contract. Is that accurate?"

"Yes."

"And would you state for the record your date and year of birth."

Considering I'd come here to ask questions, I was giving a lot of answers. I confirmed my birthday.

"Excellent," Mason said. "Tell me what brings you here today."

This was the part where I was supposed to say I was broke and trying to make money to buy my girlfriend an engagement ring. Or, I'd lost my job and the rent was due. Or that my mother had end-stage renal failure and it was up to me to buy her a liver on the black market. Anything to endear myself to the audience, establish my bona fides as a first-timer, and, if at all possible, convince them I was straight and, maybe, just maybe, bi-curious.

Was that what I was supposed to do now? Did getting my questions answered require me to play the role? I looked at Mason for direction.

After all, he had the chair for it.

Mason looked back, a slight smile lying across his face like a dead slug.

Fine. If he wasn't going to do his job, I might as well do what I'd come to accomplish. "I'm here about Brent," I said. "I want to find him."

"All right," he said. "How do you think I can help?"

"Do you have any idea how to contact him?"

"I don't."

"Did you check his application?"

"Pierce?" Mason asked.

His assistant stepped forward and handed Mason a sheet of paper. "Just give it to him," Mason said.

It was Brent's application. He'd used his stage name, not his real one.

There were two emergency contacts. One listed his parents; the other was Charlie.

"The one for his parents was a ruse," Mason said, anticipating my next question. "We tried it. The area code is real; it's for a town in Wisconsin. The number isn't registered, though."

I remembered Brent telling me he came from Queens, New

York. I also recalled Charlie saying that Brent was cut off by his parents.

"You think Brent was from *Wisconsin?*" I asked.

"I think he wrote down the first ten digits that occurred to him," Mason said. "You've met and talked to Brent. Was there anything about him that screamed 'Wisconsin' to you?"

Maybe he liked cheese.

"We have tried to contact Brent," Mason said. "When he didn't show up, we left a message with Charlie."

"Two messages," Pierce corrected from somewhere in the darkness. I'd almost forgotten he was there running the cameras.

"Thank you. *Two* messages. Charlie didn't return either. But, then again, I imagine you know how he felt about Brent's work."

I nodded, scanning the rest of the application for anything useful. Nothing appeared revealing. He left blank the sections for references, experience, and education, but what would you put down for a job in porn?

"That's a copy," Mason said. "You're free to keep it."

I folded it and put it in my pocket.

"So, now that I've given you something, don't you think you should give back?"

"What do you mean?"

Mason looked to his left and I saw he had a monitor there, probably feeding him whatever video Pierce was taping at the time.

"You look as good on screen as I thought you would. It's a rare quality.

"Some people, even pretty ones, come across dead on camera. Flat. The features are pleasing, but you don't *feel* anything when you see them. You might as well be watching animations.

"Think of all the models who've failed to succeed as actors. They're perfectly lovely in still shots, but on film, they're wooden. It's not that they're bad actors, although most of them are. It's that they don't *come alive* on screen.

"On the other hand, you have actors with undeniable screen

presence. Look at someone like Sean Penn. Or Glenn Close. They don't have the most classically beautiful features, but you can't take your eyes off them. It's what makes them stars. That indefinable quality of being amplified by the camera rather than reduced by it.

"Billy Wilder called it 'flesh impact.' He said the first time he saw it was in screen tests with Marilyn Monroe. He described her as radiating sex in every scene, even the comic ones. He said she had 'flesh which photographs like flesh. You feel you can reach out and touch it.' "

I remembered thinking exactly that when I'd watched Brent's movies at Freddy's the other night. That Brent somehow seemed more *alive,* more *present,* than anyone else on the screen.

"Wilder said he'd only worked with a handful of stars who had that quality. Monroe, like I said. Jean Harlow and . . . Rita Hayworth, I think. The man filmed almost every major actress of his time, but he could only name three who had that magical quality.

"So, imagine how rare it is. Look, all of my models are great-looking guys. They wouldn't be in my movies if they weren't. But they'll never have that ineffable *something* that sets them apart. That special quality that makes them the star of any scene they're in, even if the other guy is technically more handsome, or better built, or bigger hung.

"After twenty years in the business, I like to believe I've gotten to the point where I can see as the camera does. That's why I approached you after the taping of that television show. I thought I saw in you the same quality Brent had. Brock Peters has it, too. Flesh impact. Skin the camera reads as *real.*

"Of course, to be sure, I'll have to see more of it." The leer in his voice was subtle but couldn't be missed.

The film history lesson was interesting and flattering. It might even have been enjoyable if I didn't think it was just another ploy to get my pants off.

Something else disturbed me. Mason said "flesh impact" was something Brock "has," but Brent "had." Why was Brent being referred to in the past tense? An innocent slip of the tongue into which I was reading too much? Or maybe Mason just assumed that since Brent had stopped showing up for work, he was done making movies?

Or was there a more sinister reason for Mason's wording? A subconscious slip that indicated he knew more than he was saying?

"I agree," I said. "Brent did have that 'special something.' I didn't know what it was that made him stand out, but you've nailed it. 'Flesh impact.' Wow. You really know your stuff."

A little fawning never hurt.

Mason sat up straighter in his ridiculous director's chair. "My eye for talent is one of the keys to my success."

"Well, yeah, but it's more than that. Anyone can pick out a pretty face," I said. "But you . . . you see deeper, don't you?" I tried to sound sincere with a little awestruck thrown in.

I was sure ambitious and sexy lads hit on Mason all the time. It wasn't that he didn't get his share of flattery. In fact, I bet stroking Mason's ego was in Pierce's job description.

But I've been around boys on the make long enough to know they usually get it wrong. They tell men like Mason how hot he is, that they like the "daddy" type, or they call him a sexy bear, when the truth is he's just overweight. He probably appreciates their efforts, and he may take them up on their offers to exchange sex for a shot in a movie, but he's shrewd enough to know how empty their compliments are.

No, like everyone else, Mason wanted to be appreciated for what *he* thought he did well. For what he was proud of. For his accomplishments.

"Well . . ." Mason stretched it out. I realized for the first time he didn't know what to say. I had him off-script. Finally, he finished his sentence with an awkward "thank you."

"I mean it," I said, sitting forward on the bed. "You have a gift, man. There's no other studio out there that has a roster like SwordFight. It's no surprise you're the first to go international. It's all about picking the right talent and backing them up with production and distribution that's second to none." That last part was actually paraphrased from SwordFight's own Web site. I figured it would resonate with him.

"Exactly!" Mason said with excitement. He sat forward, too, causing his canvas seat to buckle frighteningly low. "That's what I try to tell people. Anyone can throw some hot studs in front of a camera and film them fucking around. Hell, there's thousands of people doing it on the Internet for free."

"But where's the art?" I asked. "Where's the creativity? That has to come from someone with a vision."

"Yes!" Mason agreed.

"Which is why I really hope that Brent didn't leave because he's planning to work with another studio. Even if they pay him three times as much, they'll never make him the star you would have. They'll put him in cheap crap that will make him look like any other boy. Bad scripts, bad photography, bad direction. It'll be the end of him.

"And you know what burns me the most? Your competitors know they can't find talent like Brent. They don't have the eye. But they can *steal* it from you. It must drive you crazy."

"It does," Mason agreed enthusiastically. "It's happened more times than I'd care to remember. But go explain anything of what you just said to a starry-eyed twenty-two-year-old who's being offered more money than he's ever seen before. He doesn't understand that's money that won't be going into good production or promotion. He doesn't see that in a year, he'll be old news, washed up and unwanted. After you appear in enough cheap pieces of crap, the audience isn't going to spend their money on you anymore.

"Whereas, had he stuck with me, he'd be a bigger star than ever at that point, with another decade of work before him. Delayed gratification. It's a concept these kids just don't get."

"So, do you think that's what happened? To Brent? That he's lying low until he announces that he's working for someone else?"

"No," Mason said with no reflection. "I don't."

I wondered what made him so confident. "Well, what *do* you think happened?"

Mason opened his mouth, but it was Pierce's deep bass that responded. "Excuse me. I thought we were here to make an audition tape."

"Aren't you taping?" I asked innocently.

"Please," he replied testily. "Don't bullshit a bullshitter. Mason, weren't you about to propose some quid pro quo?"

"Yes," Mason said, shaking his head as if waking from a daydream. I think he realized he'd given away more than he intended to. "Quite right. Kevin, I've answered some of your questions. Now, you need to answer some of mine. But, not as you."

"Excuse me?"

"You know the way things work, right? The deal is you're an innocent. A first-timer. Usually, a straight boy who's here for the money. Reluctant. The audience likes reluctant."

"I think," Pierce offered from wherever he lurked, "we might want to go the closeted/in-denial gay youth route with Kevin here. I mean, I'm not sure he'd be remotely believable as a straight boy."

Fuck you, too, you creepy son of a bitch.

"Good point," Mason said. "Have you ever done any acting?"

"A little." Actually, my specialty as a hooker had been role-playing. With my adolescent looks and boyish demeanor, I was often asked to play the part of the first-timer or innocent. Judging by the size of the tips I received and my long list of repeat clients, I think I did a pretty good job with it.

"Okay. So, we're going to repeat the first five minutes of our conversation. But this time, you play the part we just described."

"That's not what I agreed to," I said.

"You agreed to do an audition tape," Mason countered. "You know what those are like. Discussing the abominable work ethics of one of my models is hardly the way they begin. No, before we go any farther down that road, I'd like five minutes of usable tape. Just in case you decide you want to . . . go further yourself."

I was dubious. I was here to manipulate Mason, not the other way around. On the other hand, I didn't want to shut down the conversation. Not yet.

Seeing my hesitation, Mason made a concession. "We'll just do up to the part where you start getting undressed, okay? Then we'll stop. I promise."

Sometimes you have to give a little to get a little.

"Fine," I said. "Give me a minute."

I did what I used to do before I saw a client. Closed my eyes and tried to put myself into the character he wanted me to be. Channeled my own insecurity, vulnerability, and virtue to become the wide-eyed virgin just itching to be taken.

I looked up at Mason with new eyes. Nervous, unsure, and more than a little scared.

"I've never done anything like this before," I said, my voice quavering. "I mean, I guess I know I like guys and all, but I've never . . ." I let my voice trail off and took a deep breath.

"Dang, this is harder than I thought. But I could use the money. I've seen the videos on your site, and the DVDs, so I know what I got to do, but . . . man."

I ran a hand absently over my crotch. "It's kind of weird, you know. Like I'm really nervous. But, a little excited, too. So, what do you want to know about me?"

Mason's reply didn't come right away. I could see he was watching the monitor intently, mouth open, eyes wide. He was impressed, I could tell. He didn't know this was an act I'd played hundreds of times before. He must have thought I was either a split personality or the Laurence Olivier of smut. He finally found his voice.

"Let's start with, um, how old you are." He cleared his throat. "And what brings you here today."

I answered those questions and a few more. The more I spoke, the more in character I felt. Even I was hot to see what would happen when this long-repressed twinkie-in-training finally burst loose.

"You've obviously been keeping these feelings bottled up for a long time." Mason's voice was sonorous and calming. "Why don't you take off your shirt for me?"

I was so into the scene I almost did. Then, I remembered.

"Not so fast," I said. "You got your interview. Now, it's my turn to ask a question, right?"

Pierce grunted in the background. Mason moaned. "Fine," he said begrudgingly. "But, Kevin, that was *amazing*. The camera *loves* you. And that performance—are you *sure* you've never professionally acted before?"

What had I said about acting before? I couldn't remember.

Focus, Kevin, focus.

That was what I hated about lying—I was so bad at it.

Better not to answer. "Hey, I'm the one who gets a question now, not you," I said, teasing, but not leaving it open to negotiation.

Mason leaned back and crossed his arms over his chest. Body language experts tell us that's a clear sign of a person guarding himself against giving anything away. A defensive attitude I was determined to break through.

"Ask away," Mason said. "I'm an open book."

His posture said the opposite.

21

Inch by Inch

"I'm worried someone might have hurt Brent," I said. "Or kidnapped him. An obsessive fan or something. Do you have a problem with that kind of thing? Do your models ever get threatened? Or stalked?"

"These boys tend to thrive on attention, not be scared of it." Mason hugged himself tighter.

"Really? That's hard to believe. There are a lot of sickos out there. What about, I don't know, some religious nut who thinks your models are leading the world into sin?"

"Oh, we get letters from time to time. As a company. Nothing serious, though. A few quotes from the Bible, threats of eternal damnation. But nothing that concerns me."

"Really?"

"Really." Mason waved his hands. "Look around. Do you see any guards? Security cameras? Panic buttons? Trust me, I have no desire to be martyred for my work. If I thought we were under serious threat, I'd take whatever precautions I deemed necessary. No, the few people who bother to complain seem harmless enough."

"And the models? Have they *never* felt threatened?"

Mason rubbed his hand over his mouth and left it there. Another body tell—this one indicating a lie. "Not that I remember," he said.

I realized he evaded the question the first time I asked it, too.

"Think back," I said. "I promise I won't say anything. I understand if word gets out that someone is stalking your models, it isn't going to help your casting calls. But if there's a possibility that Brent was stalked by one of his fans . . ."

Mason laughed. Uncrossed his arms and sat relaxed in his chair. "Fans? Believe me, Brent's fans were too busy watching his films to be bothered with stalking. Besides," he said, with a nasty little laugh, "there's only so much harm you can do with one hand. The only person who ever stalked Brent—"

"Ahem," Pierce interrupted. Just like that. As if it were two words. "A hem."

"Thank you," Mason said to him. "You're right. I am giving our young Mr. Connor a lot of information for his one question."

Mason ran his eyes over my body. "Time to hold up your end of the deal, sunshine. Think you could lose that shirt for me?"

"I think," I said icily, sickened by how cavalierly Mason took all this, "if you cared about Brent at all, you wouldn't be playing this game with me."

"Well," Mason sighed, "we're all entitled to our opinions. But I'm afraid you're just too appealing to allow off this set without showing some skin. Take it as a compliment. Besides, it's just your shirt, Kevin. You show more than that at the beach. Don't be such a little prude."

"Brent's life could depend on this," I said, regretting how melodramatic my words sounded even as they left my mouth.

"All the more reason why I can't understand your reluctance to show a little skin. It's just your chest, for god's sake. Are you saying Brent's life isn't worth the shirt off your back?"

What a son of a bitch this guy was.

"Fine," I said through clenched teeth.

"And get back into that character you were doing. That was marvelous."

"Sure thing," I said.

I'd arrived at SwordFight dressed to play the kind of young man who'd find himself auditioning for a porn studio. A plain white Hanes T-shirt, faded Levi's, athletic socks, and white Keds. An anonymous outfit that could have come from anywhere. Nothing top-label or flashy. The jeans and sneakers were distressed in a way that suggested I might be a bit down on my luck.

But it was the custom accessories I wore underneath that I was counting on to get me out of this mess.

"What," Mason asked, looking horrified but trying not to sound too appalled, "is that?"

He pointed to my chest, where a long, red, ugly, and jagged scar ran from just above my left nipple to an inch above my naval.

"Oh, this?" I asked surprised, as if it was something I was so used to that I'd forgotten about it. "It's a scar."

"Yes," Mason snapped, "I can *see* it's a scar. What is it *doing* there?"

I had to suppress a laugh at Mason's indignation. He'd been expecting smooth perfection. The resemblance to Frankenstein's monster did not amuse him.

"Last year, I started getting dizzy spells," I told him. "Lightheadedness, shortness of breath. I thought it was nothing. That I wasn't getting enough sleep or something.

"Then one day at the gym, I just passed out. They took me to the hospital. Turns out I had a congenital heart condition no one had ever noticed. I needed a valve replaced. I was in surgery for eight hours.

"This," I said, pointing to the disfiguring gash that bisected my torso, "is my souvenir. Hey, better than being dead, right?"

From the expression on Mason's face, it wasn't clear he agreed.

The whole story was made up. As was the scar.

After I'd hung up on Pierce earlier today, I knew I was in trouble. There was no way I was going to get to talk to Mason without appearing in an audition video. While I had no intention of actually jacking off on camera for him, I was going to have to show something. At the same time, I had to make sure what I showed was something he wouldn't be able to use.

Then I remembered my mother's crackpot proposal to use

our makeup staff to age me for our visit to the adoption clinic. While the purpose of her idea was wacky, pulling it off wouldn't be impossible. In fact, I had just the man for the job.

As one of the first senior staff hired for *Sophie's Voice,* I did a lot of the initial interviewing of prospective employees. One of my earliest hires was Steven Austen.

A show like ours, with multiple guests on every episode, needs a few people on hand doing makeup and hair. Steven's background for the position wasn't typical. Yeah, he had the basics down and had gone to cosmetology school. He was one of the few straight guys I knew who'd done so.

But for the past few years he'd been employed in the film industry, doing mostly special effects work. A lot of his experience was on horror movies. I thought that sounded about right for working with my mother.

Steven had been successful in Hollywood, but the work was sporadic. He had developed a reputation for his work on slasher films. He created wounds and mutilations so convincing that his participation on a project pretty much guaranteed an R rating.

When Steven's wife had their second baby, she convinced him he needed more steady employment. Movie work paid well, but he often went months between jobs. He was grateful when I hired him, and I knew he liked working on our show, but he also missed using his more specialized skills.

I didn't need Steven to age me. Mason and I had already met—if I showed up looking twenty years older, he'd know right away I was up to something.

But I could use Steven to ugly me up a little. Or, maybe even a lot.

I called him into my office and told him what I needed. I didn't give him all the details. I fibbed, telling him I was playing a trick on my boyfriend. Would he help me?

Steven was thrilled with the opportunity to whip out his prosthetics and liquid latex. "If you want to look really disgusting," he pledged, "I'm your man."

It wasn't a promise I ever thought I'd want to hear, but I was grateful to him for his enthusiasm.

* * *

Mason couldn't have been more uncomfortable. Somewhere inside of him, I believed, was a human being who actually experienced feelings like empathy. Either that, or it was just common sense that led him to say, "I'm sorry you had to go through that."

I never heard a less convincing expression of sympathy. It was further eroded by his subsequent conversation with Pierce.

"So," he asked his assistant, "what do you think?"

Pierce didn't bother to pretend to care. "It looks terrible on screen," he said. "A real turn-off."

"You think we could hide it with makeup?" Mason asked.

I tried not to laugh at the irony.

"Maybe," Pierce replied thoughtfully. "I'd imagine we could cover it up and tone down the redness. You'd still see the ridge, though. It might not be a deal-breaker."

Mason rubbed his chin. "It's really too bad. He's got a great body. If only that scar wasn't so prominent. . . ." The way he talked about me as if I wasn't in the room was so charming and considerate I regretted not bringing a handgun.

It was true I kept in shape. When I worked as an escort, my body was my fortune. I went to the gym nearly daily to maintain my trim but muscular gymnast's form. Since giving up that work, I'd slacked off a bit, but I still tried to maintain what I'd had.

"You know, it could work. Maybe, if we can tone it down a little, some of our viewers will find the scar endearing," Mason offered. "An appealing vulnerability on an otherwise perfect torso."

Pierce snorted.

Mason ignored him. "Let's keep going and see how the rest of it goes. Kevin, could you stand and let us get a look at you from behind? And, in character, please."

These audition videos always followed the same pattern. First, the model took off his shirt. Then he turned around and showed off his back. At this point, Mason usually directed them to flex and show off their muscles.

Then it was time to lose the pants. This also started from the front, with the camera zooming into the cloth-covered crotch. Building suspense. Another pivot as the model removed his underwear, showing off his butt first. Then, the big reveal, when he turned one last time to display his cock, which, through the magic of editing, was always standing at attention and raring to go, as if the very act of disrobing for the viewer was so exciting that it'd brought him to full erection.

I was counting on my video following the same progression. I had my own reveals planned.

First, though, some more negotiation.

"Your turn," I said. "You got my shirt off. I get another question."

Mason stood and looked more closely at the monitor. He spoke to my image there. "Scar aside, Kevin, you look fantastic. You looked like such a kid in that shirt—who'd have known you'd be so ripped when you took it off?" He ran a finger down the screen as if tracing my body with his hand. I felt a chill on my chest as if he was really touching me.

"And I was right. Your skin photographs like silk. So inviting.

"You could be a star, Kevin. I'll even pay for the plastic surgery if there's a way it will diminish that scarring. I'd make that kind of investment in you, Kevin, because I *believe* in you. You can even *act*. You may be the total package.

"So, how about we stop this cat-and-mouse inquiry of yours and just shoot the damn video?"

Mason was getting irritated, and I didn't think he was the kind of man who put up with being put off. The scar had dampened his enthusiasm, as had my questioning. His tone told me I was about to lose him. I had to pull him back.

"If I *did* work with you," I said, feigning interest, "what kind of money are we talking about?"

"For a full feature?" Mason asked.

"Sure."

"Twenty-five K," he said. "To start."

"I make more than that now," I told him.

"I'm sure you do," he said condescendingly. "But we're talking a week's work.

"We wouldn't want to overexpose you, so figure ten films your first year. You do the math."

Multiplication was my Kryptonite, but even I could figure out that came to $250,000.

"Then, of course, there'd be personal appearances and product endorsements. You should be able to pull in another fifty thousand doing those. Maybe some magazine shoots. Some of my models do escort work, too. You'd be amazed what people will pay to . . . date . . . an adult film star.

"Depending on how ambitious you were, and how hard you were willing to work, I'd say you could come close to making half a million dollars your first year with us.

"Not to mention the free plastic surgery," he threw in with a salesman's flourish.

Well, now I understood why someone like Brent was doing adult films. That was an awful lot of money. And while I expect Mason was exaggerating, I didn't think he was out-and-out lying.

Of course, most guys in the industry weren't making that much. But Mason was clearly positioning me as one of Sword-Fight's tentpole performers.

He'd said as much on the phone. I'd be the new Brent Havens.

Which brought me back to the question of what happened to the current one.

22

The Dream Team

"We had a deal," I said.

Mason redirected his attention from the image of me on the screen to the real one sitting right there. I think he was surprised I wasn't jumping on the money right away.

"You said that if I agreed to this audition, you'd answer my questions. I'm doing my part. Now, it's your turn again."

Mason looked flabbergasted that I was persisting with this. Hadn't he just offered me half a million dollars? Just what kind of idiot was I?

"Look," I said. "I can't say I'm not interested. That's a lot of money. A *lot*. I didn't think I'd ever even *consider* something like this, but, I have to say, I never expected it could be so . . . rewarding. And, now that I think about it, the guys who came to the taping that day, Brock, Brent, the others—they didn't seem too unhappy or anything. You've got my attention."

Mason grinned hungrily. Like a shark.

"But if I went into business with SwordFight, I'd have to be able to trust you. Which is why I say: We had a deal. If you don't keep this one, how can I believe you'll keep the others?"

Mason sat back down. "I have to say, you surprise me, Kevin. You're a smart kid. I could see you going places.

"You know, Pierce started here like you. You kind of remind me of him."

Pierce made a strangled noise that sounded like a cross between a gag and a snort. I was also offended by the comparison but hid my feelings better.

"He began his career with SwordFight as a performer but has become much more. He's my right arm. He handles the talent, he knows the business side of things, and he's even directed."

So why do you have him answering the phones? I wondered.

"You have a lot of potential, Kevin. So, I'll answer your questions. Because you're right—we did have a deal. I have a better one for you, mind you, but I'll keep the one we have.

"You can say a lot of things about me, Kevin, but you'll find that I'm quite honest in my business dealings. I don't screw my partners—in *any* way. You'll always be treated like a professional here. So, ask away."

I tried to remember where we'd been. Mason had given me Brent's application, which I had in my pocket. . . . We'd talked about whether someone who'd seen his videos might have gone after him. . . . Oh yeah. I knew what to ask.

"You said Brent never complained to you about an overzealous fan," I said. "But you implied there was someone who might have been stalking him. Who was it?"

"That's such an ugly word," Mason said. He crossed his arms again. "I don't know it went so far that I'd call it *stalking*."

"How far *did* it go?" I asked. "And who was it?"

"One of the other models here. Lucas Fisher," Mason answered the second question.

Lucas Fisher. The boy Freddy and I had seen in that dorm room video with Brent. We both thought Lucas's hunger for his co-star went beyond mere acting.

Brent's boyfriend, Charlie, also talked about Lucas. He said Lucas had asked Brent out several times, and seemed to have trouble taking no for an answer.

Now, his name was coming up for a third time.

I had a feeling it wouldn't be the last time, either.

I was going to have to talk to Lucas Fisher.

"What *did* Lucas do?" I asked.

"Some background first. If you're going to be working with

us, you deserve to hear the kinds of things that sometime come up—and how we handle them."

I decided not to point out that I hadn't agreed to work with him at all. It was clear Mason assumed that even though I expressed some ambivalence, there was no way I'd pass up the opportunity to make the kind of money he'd offered. As far as he was concerned, I was already part of his stable. I resented his arrogance, but if it made him more open to being truthful, I could live with it.

Of course, I knew that if I led him on like this, and then backed out, he'd be even more bitter than if I'd simply rejected him to begin with. But that wasn't my plan.

If things worked out the way I hoped, it'd be *him* rejecting *me*. But that was yet to come.

I scooted back on the bed so that my back was against the headboard, grateful for the opportunity. This was a position I was counting on being able to get into to pull off the rest of my plan.

But to Mason, I must have seemed like an eager eight-year-old ready to hear his favorite story. Good. The more he relaxed his guard, the better for me. "You're right," I said. I gave him my best fake-sincere smile. "I appreciate your understanding my . . . mixed feelings."

"Naturally, I do," Mason said. "It's not like I haven't had them myself at times."

The only feelings I imagined he ever had were pride and greed. I suppose you could mix them, but the result would be bitter.

"You need to understand what it's like to work on the set of an adult film. Especially for the models. But first, you have to understand the audience.

"It's strange—when someone watches a *Die Hard* movie, they don't think Bruce Willis is really getting thrown from buildings and running from explosions. When Julie Andrews sings 'My Favorite Things' to comfort her charges in *The Sound of Music*, the audience doesn't believe she really wants to marry that old man and adopt those adorable little Nazis-in-waiting. Yes, we all swoon when Richard Gere sweeps Julia Roberts off her feet in *Pretty Woman,* but as convincing as those two actors are, we understand they're just pretending. When the director yells cut, we know they go to their separate trailers to complain to their agents or abuse their personal assistants.

"But with all-male porn, everyone wonders 'Is it real? Are the actors really enjoying themselves? Are they even gay?'

"When most people ask me that, I ask, 'Does it matter?' We know Willis isn't really a New York City cop with the most amazing recuperative powers this side of Wolverine, that Andrews isn't really a virginal nun, and that Roberts isn't that dullest of clichés: the whore with a heart of gold."

Hey, what's so unbelievable about that last one?

"Who cares if the actors are having a good time or not?" Mason asked, then answered himself.

"The only question that matters is: Is the *viewer* having a good time?

"That being said, it's a lot easier to pretend that you're suddenly inspired to sing some dumb song about whiskers on kittens or that you find Richard Gere attractive than it is to maintain an erection and ejaculate. I mean, let's face it, there are some things we just can't fake.

"When you see a guy get hard and come, you know, on some level, he's having a pleasurable experience. But Roberts and Gere probably enjoyed kissing each other, too. It's just a physical act.

"And while we haven't yet gotten to the point where digital effects can reliably and believably be used to simulate male sexual performance, there's still a lot of 'movie magic' and editing that goes on behind the scenes. So, while you may see an actor shoot his load across his co-star's back, it's not that ass, no matter how spectacular it may be, that's getting him off. What we don't show you is the ten minutes the top had to spend stroking off to a girlie magazine to get to that stage.

"My point is, what goes on between the actors on an adult movie set isn't love. It isn't really even sex. It's a performance.

Sure, sometimes it becomes something more. 'Real' movie stars sometimes fall in love, too. Look at Elizabeth Taylor's history. But that's the exception, not the rule."

"Lucas," I said, "was an exception, wasn't he?"

"He came to me after the first scene he ever shot with Brent. It was in a movie called . . ." He glanced over at Pierce. "Do you remember?"

"*School Gayz,*" Pierce grumbled, resenting the instruction to be helpful to me in any way.

"*School Gayz,* yes," Mason said slowly. "We filmed that at a real college—between semesters, of course. The dean was a fan of ours.

"I was on set for that shoot. I'd set up a small office in one of the empty dorm rooms there. I hadn't seen the shooting of the scene between Lucas and Brent. I didn't even know it'd been finished. So, when Lucas came in to chat, I wasn't on my guard.

"Lucas was a beautiful boy. The golden-haired surfer type. He'd never be a top-level star, but he was a steady performer with a loyal following. I don't think he was a hundred-percent gay, but he certainly came to enjoy sex with men. There's a lot of gossip on a movie set, mainstream or otherwise, and I'd heard he'd partied with some of his co-stars on the side. He also was hustling.

"In any case, it wasn't unusual for Lucas to hang out with me. He was a huge flirt. Even though he knew I wasn't going to *do* anything with him (as I told you, I never touch a model), it was in his nature to play up to a man he saw as being in a position to help his career. Maybe he even enjoyed talking with me, who knows? He wasn't the brightest bulb on the set, but he was charming and adorable. I was always happy to see him.

"So, on that day, it took a while before I noticed something was up. He was doing his usual shtick of entertaining me with stories and gossip from the set, mixed in with references to surfing and skateboards I never understood, when I realized he was asking more and more questions about one of his co-stars."

"Brent Havens," I supplied.

"Exactly. It began with the kind of conversation he might

make about any of the models on the set. 'So, is this his first movie?' 'Where did you find him?' 'What's his deal in real life—is he into guys or girls?' The usual gossip.

"Then, it got more personal. 'Does he have a boyfriend?' 'Do you know what kind of guy he likes?' 'Where does he live?'

"It took me a while to figure out what was going on. Lucas had fallen for Brent. Like I said, it's not that it never happens. But it's not usually that fast. Or that obvious.

"It was actually," Mason observed, sounding wistful, "kind of sweet. Lucas was like a thirteen-year-old girl meeting Justin Bieber. I answered what questions I could, and dodged the ones I couldn't. Overall, though, I encouraged Lucas. I told him he should tell Brent he was interested.

"Lucas blushed red as a fire truck. He tried to tell me he was 'just curious.' I let him get away with it, but I knew he was lying. I wasn't sure how deep it went, though—whether he was lying to me, or to himself, too. I didn't know much about Lucas. Was he emotionally developed enough to understand how an on-set infatuation burns hot but soon burns out? They're like summer camp romances—you're sure they'll last forever, but once you're back home, you never think of him again.

"In any case, when Lucas left, his usual cocky strut was a little less confident. I called the director, who was just finishing up for the day, and asked him to show me the scene he'd shot with Lucas and Brent.

"I remember him asking, 'So, you heard about that, huh?'

" 'Heard about what?' I asked him. 'What was there to hear? Did something bad happen?' If there was trouble on the set, the director should have come to me. That's why I was there.

"The director heard my concern. 'Nothing bad,' he assured me, 'but something you'll want to see. Something extraordinary. But I'll be there in a few minutes. You can judge for yourself.'

"Of course, at that point, all we had was the raw footage. Usually, watching the films before they're edited is an exercise in the most extreme form of tedium. There are hours of starts and stops, models fluffing themselves, and limp dicks. It's not fun.

"But this scene was different. It was shot in one take. There was no fluffing needed. In fact, I'm lucky the boys held out as long as they did."

Mason gazed up and to the left, as if pulling out memories. "It was . . . magic. Pure sexual chemistry, captured on film. The director told me there wasn't a person on set who didn't almost pop a load themselves just watching it.

"Unfortunately, as so often happens in real life, people can mistake great sex for something more than it is. At least, Lucas did. He came and spoke with me a few days later. He was more open about his feelings this time. He told me he was in love with Brent.

"Who knows what creates the kind of sexual chemistry that occurred between those two? Is it pheromones? Genetic? I can't say. But I did know it wasn't love. It was infatuation, perhaps, but not love.

"I tried to explain that to Lucas. I didn't want to see him get hurt. I told him how easy it is to confuse the rush of endorphins we get from an intense orgasm with something more meaningful. I told him to take things slowly with Brent and not to get his hopes up.

"Lucas listened carefully, and nodded at all the right times, but I don't think he believed me. Why would he? When has anyone ever been able to convince a young person that their romance wasn't real?

"In the meantime, the director of *School Dayz* approached me with an idea. Seeing the incredible energy between the two, he suggested a follow-up movie called *Brent & Lucas: More Than Friends*. He knew the scenes between them in *School Dayz* would be a sensation, and that a movie that put them front and center would be a huge success."

Mason shifted in his sagging seat, uncomfortable. He stood and paced as he told me the rest of his tale.

"Green-lighting that project was one of the few things I've done in my career that I honestly regret. I knew Lucas was in over his head with Brent. I also knew, although only from what Lucas had told me, that the feelings weren't reciprocated. Had I been thinking of Lucas, instead of how much money I'd make, I would have said no. In my heart, I knew that putting Lucas through more weeks of intimate contact with Brent would wind up hurting them both.

"But I said yes. And *More Than Friends* was one of our biggest hits ever.

"But it came at a price.

"Halfway through its taping, Brent came to see me. He told me Lucas was being inappropriate. That he'd told Brent that he loved him.

"Brent said he was kind to Lucas, but he made it clear he wasn't interested. He explained he was already involved with someone.

"But Lucas insisted they were 'meant to be.' He called Brent at all times of the day and night, brought unwanted presents to the set, threatened to hurt himself if Brent wouldn't see him. It got ugly.

"One night, about a week after filming *More Than Friends,* I realized I'd left something in the office that I needed at home. I got there around ten and found Lucas had broken into my office. He was looking for information about Brent. Pictures, Brent's home address and phone number, anything he could find.

"When he saw me, he burst into tears. He knew he was out of control but couldn't stop himself. I called my therapist right then and there. He agreed to talk to Lucas on the phone and they made an appointment for the next day.

"Things seemed to settle down after that. Lucas told me my therapist referred him to another doctor and that he was going weekly. Brent told me the harassment stopped. When the movie came out, we sent them out to do some publicity together and there were no major problems.

"But there were minor ones?" I asked.

"Brent never gave me details. But I could tell something still bothered him about Lucas. For the most part, though, things went well.

"I never put them together in another movie, however. Lucas

asked about it a few times, but I put him off. He lobbied hard for a sequel to *More Than Friends*. So did a lot of people at the company. The movie was a huge success.

"But, believe it or not, money isn't the only thing I care about, Kevin. I cared about those kids, and I thought keeping them separated was best for both of them.

"A few months later, Lucas gave me an ultimatum. He came into my office wild-eyed. He looked like he hadn't slept in days. He'd lost a lot of weight.

"Emotionally, he was all over the map. One minute he was crying, saying Brent broke his heart. Then, he was yelling, blaming me for keeping the two of them apart. He said if I didn't promise him another movie with Brent, I'd 'never see him again.'

"I didn't know what he meant. Was he saying he'd leave SwordFight? Was it a suicide threat? Or, was he implying I'd never see *Brent* again? I tried to get the answer from him, but he ran out of my office in tears.

"I didn't know what to do. So, I called my therapist again. Believing that Lucas might have been making a serious threat to hurt himself—or someone else—I asked my therapist if he could give me the name of the doctor to whom he'd referred Lucas. I thought the only responsible thing to do would be to tell his doctor what Lucas had said.

"My therapist confirmed that he'd given Lucas a referral. But Lucas had refused to take it. Lucas told him that he was fine, that it was Brent who had the problem. To the best of my doctor's knowledge, Lucas never saw anyone for treatment.

"Lucas had lied to me about seeing a therapist. It broke my heart. What else had he deceived me about?

"The next day, I found out. I received a news release that Lucas had signed an exclusive contract with one of my competitors, Hardman Studios. Those kinds of deals take weeks of negotiation, if not longer. Lucas brokered it behind my back.

"But I wasn't upset. I was relieved. At least I knew what he meant when he said I'd 'never see *him* again.' His leaving Sword-

Fight was the least awful of all the possibilities. I felt sorry for him, though. Hardman's a shitty shop, and, sure enough, they never used Lucas properly. He made one or two films with them, then dropped off the radar completely."

"So, he *also* went missing?" I asked, sitting up straighter on the bed. That was two boys from SwordFight gone into the ether. Seemed like a big coincidence.

"Who knows?" Mason said, chuckling. "Maybe they ran off together." He must have seen the distress in my face.

"Oh, Kevin. Don't look so appalled. It's obvious you think there's something . . . sinister going on, but I implore you to use your common sense. Boys who work in adult movies don't submit formal letters of resignation. This is how ninety-nine percent of them leave the business: They just stop. They don't return your calls, they change their numbers, they move on."

I believed most of that. But it didn't explain why Brent hadn't said good-bye to Charlie or let him know where he was. There was something hinky here. I could feel it.

"Trust me, Kevin. No one would rather believe Brent is out there willing to return to the business more than I would. That adorable child brought in *millions*. There's no one at SwordFight who would have wanted to see him hurt."

Hurt was the least of it. Maybe I'd stumbled across one too many murders in my time, but Brent's total disappearance made me seriously wonder if someone might have killed him.

If so, who? One of Tony's rules as a homicide investigator was to follow the money. Most murders that weren't crimes of passion involved either the quest for financial gain or the fear of financial loss. Since it seemed like losing Brent must have cost Mason a lot of money, he made an unlikely killer.

But between Charlie, who hated Brent's double life, and Lucas, who loved him too much, the whole crimes-of-passion angle seemed like a real possibility.

"Do you have any idea where I could find Lucas?" I asked.

"I can answer that question," Mason said. "But it's going to cost you. Ready to start taping again? Turn around and let's check out your back."

This was the last step before I'd have to pull down my pants. And, even if they never used it, I didn't want these creeps having video of me in my underwear.

I may have been a whore, but it was always my decision who got to see me naked. Mason and Pierce weren't about to make the list.

23

Flesh and Blood

I stood up slowly and felt the dripping down my back.

Yuck. So gross.

Good.

I turned around slowly. Now that I'd shown off my chest, this was the next reveal.

"Oh my god," I heard Mason whisper, "that is . . . oh."

While the job Steven Austen did applying the scar to my chest was masterful, the disfigurement he applied to my back was nothing less than horrific. A mess of pimples, boils, and welts scattered across me like the ugliest constellation in the universe. He'd even filled some of them with a viscous white liquid designed to "pop" when pressure was applied—an effect I achieved when I sat down with my back against the headboard.

As I gave Mason a few moments to process the train wreck in front of him, I reached into my pocket and took out what appeared to be a tube of ChapStick. It was actually a tube of Vicks VapoRub, which I applied under each nostril. To Mason and Pierce, though, it should have looked as if I was using lip balm.

I tucked it back into my pants. While my hand was in my pocket, I unscrewed the other vial in there and let the liquid contents seep out.

"Uh, Kevin," Mason said, trying to keep his voice steady. "It looks like you have some kind of . . . rash."

"I do?" I said, aping surprise. I craned my neck trying to see.

"Really? I don't see . . ." I twisted a shoulder as far as it could go. "Aw, crap," I said. "It's back."

"It?" Mason asked. He sounded ready to run screaming out of the room into the nearest decontamination chamber.

"After my operation—the one on my chest that left the big scar," I clarified, just to make sure they remembered how bad I looked from the front, "I had to take some immunosuppressive drugs to keep my body from rejecting the new valve they put in my heart. Annnnyway . . ." I drawled Valley Girl style, "the doctors warned me it could lead to breakouts."

I took a few steps backward, getting closer to Mason. "It happened once before, but it wasn't too bad. How does it look now?"

Mason instinctively backed up, too, the reptile part of his brain directing him to flee in case my condition was catching. "It looks . . ." He stopped, but not because he couldn't find the words. I heard him take a cautious sniff. "What is that *smell?*"

After the third time I'd found a tube of VapoRub in Tony's work pants, I'd asked him why he always carried it when he was working.

"In case I have to attend an autopsy," he'd explained, "or an especially grisly crime scene. A little menthol under the nose blocks out the worst of the stink."

Even through its protective mask, though, I could make out the sickening scent of the ethanethiol I'd poured out a few moments ago.

Steven Austen wasn't the only one of my co-workers who'd assisted me today. Oliver, the maintenance man, helped me figure out how much of the noxious chemical I needed to release to pull off the illusion that my artificial rash smelled even worse than it looked. Ironically, the first time I'd come across ethanethiol was the day I met Brent. Oliver had been transporting to storage a tank of the stuff, which was usually used as an olfactory alarm in case of a gas leak.

Turns out, a quarter teaspoon of the stuff was enough to empty a room faster than a canister of tear gas.

"It might be the pus," I answered Mason, using the grossest word I could think of. "From those weeping sores, I guess."

"Oh my god," Pierce exclaimed. "That is vile!" Unlike his boss, he didn't try to cover his disgust under a veneer of good manners.

"I'm out of here, man. I think I'm going to . . ." Pierce made a retching sound and ran out of the room.

"I, um, I have to go, too," Mason said. I swung around to face him and observed his pallor was a shade of gray I'd never seen on a living person before.

His Adam's apple looked like it was doing jumping jacks in his throat in its efforts to suppress his gag reflex.

"Wait," I said. I grabbed his forearm. His eyes widened in surprise at the strength of my grip. Or, it might have been the nausea making him look like that. Didn't matter.

"You promised to tell me where I might find Lucas," I said.

"I don't know," he said, trying to take the shallowest breaths possible. "But he's still in the city. About two weeks ago, Kristen LaNue says he saw him in a club. By the time he made his way over, though, Lucas was gone."

"Was he sure it was—"

"Yes!" Mason shouted. His complexion had now gone from gray to green. He slapped a hand over his mouth. "I'm sorry," he said, his words muffled. "I really have to . . ."

I made the quick calculation that whatever small chance remained he had anything useful to tell me was outweighed by the increasingly likely possibility he was about to barf on me. I let go of his arm.

"Listen, I'm sorry about the breakout," I called, as Mason headed as quickly as possible to the exit. "Maybe we can try again when it clears up?"

Mason made a strangled sound as he flung open the door. It could have meant, "Sure," or "Are you kidding me?" or "Drop dead."

I didn't care. I'd gotten what I'd come for. A few more answers and a little more insight.

There wasn't anything else I needed from them except . . .

I walked over to the video camera Pierce had been using. Sure enough, it was a model similar to the ones we had at *Sophie's Voice*. I found the "eject" button and removed the digital tape he'd been using. I put it in the pocket that *didn't* have the ethanethiol in it.

I knew from bitter experience that the camcorder could appear to be shooting even if you'd forgotten to load it. I figured Pierce would assume that's what happened.

No reason to leave them with anything with my image on it. Between my luck and Mason's greed, he'd probably find a way to sell it to the three men in the world turned on by open sores.

I put my T-shirt back on and looked around. A fire exit. Most excellent. I was sure everyone would appreciate my leaving without passing through their offices and lobby on my way out. I grabbed my backpack and was out of there.

So much for my film career.

Fade to black, bitches.

A block and a half away, I found an alley between two apartment buildings. I snuck behind a Dumpster and hoped no one came by.

Acutely aware of just how bad I must smell, I took the video I'd grabbed from Pierce's camera and put it on the ground next to me. Everything else, including my pants, sneakers, T-shirt, and socks, I threw into the Dumpster. I opened the package of baby wipes I'd picked up on the way to Mason's office and used them to clean off as much of the ethanethiol as I could.

I bent over to wash off my feet. As I straightened back up, I saw a tall, muscly guy somewhere in his thirties leering hungrily at me.

"Hey, cutie," he called. "Looking good."

Shit. "Um, thanks." I covered my crotch with my hands.

"*Come* here often?" he asked, putting an emphasis on the first word to drive home his double entendre. He chuckled at the cleverness of his own lame joke.

"No, I just had a wardrobe malfunction," I said, reaching for my backpack. Inside, I had clean versions of everything I'd just thrown away. I had no intention of trying to make it home in my ethanethiol-soaked clothing. "I gotta change and get going. Sorry."

"Aw, come on, baby," my alleyway admirer purred. Apparently, the fake scar on my chest didn't bother him. At least, not enough to deter him from attempting a public encounter that might be hot in the kind of videos Mason made, but would probably get us arrested in real life. He cupped his crotch in case I hadn't figured out what he had in mind.

"Really not interested," I told him. "So, if you'll excuse me . . ."

Instead of retreating, he started walking toward me, rubbing himself. "Please. Don't play hard to get, you little tease. Standing out here naked like that. You know you want it, baby."

I've taken down bigger guys than him in my life. Part of me would have enjoyed teaching this asshole a lesson with my martial arts.

But I really was not in the mood.

Better to just give him what he wants and let him go for it. I had a feeling it wouldn't take long.

"You're right," I said, squeezing my own junk as his gaze wandered over my body. "I do want it, man."

Alleyman grinned wolfishly and started unzipping his rapidly expanding slacks. "I'm going to slip it to you so good, sweet cheeks."

Forget the ethanethiol—this guy's rap was going to make me vomit.

"Yeah," I said, "give it to me from behind, lover. It's so hard to find a real man like you"—I turned to show him my still-illustrated back—"who isn't afraid to let a little thing like leprosy come between him and a good time."

His gasp-gag indicated he'd gotten close enough not only to get a good look, but a good whiff, too.

"Uh, look at the time!" he shouted. "I gotta go!"

He almost tripped trying to simultaneously run and zip himself back up.

"Go?" I asked as he recovered from his stumble. "I thought you wanted to *come*."

How clever is that joke now, asshole?

Two minutes later, I was dressed and headed home. While my wipe down and change of clothing helped, I figured I was still too stinky to get into a cab or on the subway. It was a thirty-minute walk back to my apartment, but I could use the time to think.

I had to figure out my next move.

Two blocks later, I realized my next move was to go backward.

Crap.

I'd left the videotape Pierce had shot on the ground by the Dumpster.

Crap.

I ran back. With each footfall, I thought the same thing.

Crap.

Crap.

Crap crap crap crap crap.

I turned the corner and spied the Dumpster. No tape.

Crap!

My best guess was that Alleyman came back. Maybe he'd scored some antibiotics and figured he'd take the plunge after all.

He'd probably enjoy the video, the creep. How long before he uploaded it to YouTube, where the whole world would have the opportunity to see me looking like a kinky leper?

My heart pounding, I ran behind the Dumpster and got on my hands and knees to look underneath. There. *There.*

There it was.

The anxiety flooded out of me like air from a burst balloon. I was deflated with relief.

I must have accidentally kicked the tape out of sight while getting dressed, and then forgotten about it.

It could have fallen into anyone's hands. What was wrong with me? How can someone be so careless with a *sex video* of himself?

Well, I answered myself, *if it's good enough for Paris Hilton,*

Rob Lowe, and at least one Kardashian . . . and those are just the celebrities we know about.

Times like these I reluctantly wondered if maybe the two men who knew me better than anyone in the world weren't right: I had no business playing "Kevin Connor: Boy Detective." I didn't possess the . . . attention to detail the role required.

It wasn't just a matter of flubbing my lines—I was lucky I hadn't gotten myself killed.

Although I *had* come really, really close. At least twice.

But, I thought cheerfully, putting the video into my front pants pocket and patting twice to make sure it was secure, what's life without a few challenges? It'd be boring if we only did the things that came easily, right?

It was either that, or I was an idiot.

I chose to believe the former.

24

Link to Link

On my way home, I had an idea.

Everyone I spoke to about Brent suggested it wasn't atypical for guys in porn to transition into hustling or being set up as a kept boy. If that was what Brent was up to, there was one person I knew who had the connections to track him down.

I called to ask if I could drop by.

"Of course, my sweetest," she cooed. "Just give me ten minutes to shave, shower, and douche myself up a bit, darling. You know Mama likes to look her best for her favorite boy."

I told her I'd be there in a quarter hour. Although one of the reasons ethanethiol was used in commercial settings was because the odor dissipated fairly quickly, and I'd also washed up and changed clothes, I was still worried I might be kind of stinky. I stopped into a pharmacy and grabbed a can of Axe body spray. I applied half of it in the store's restroom and paid for the rest on my way out. I now smelled like something called "Dark Temptation."

Which made me think of Freddy.

I called to let him know I'd survived my encounter at SwordFight.

"Thank god," he said. "I was beginning to worry. You've been there *forever*."

"Actually, I left an hour ago. But I ran into a few problems on the way back."

"Such as . . . ?"

"Nothing major. Just some guy who tried to sexually assault me when I happened to be innocently naked behind a Dumpster. And I had to go a few blocks out of my way to get some cologne to cover the smell of my imaginary pus. Stuff like that."

"If anyone else told me these things," Freddy said, "I'd think they were insane. But, you're right—on the Kevin scale, that qualifies as 'nothing major.' "

"See?" I said. "You had no reason to worry."

"Well, when you have time, I want to hear every detail of what happened."

"Play your cards right," I promised him, "and I might even show you the video."

"My darling, darling boy," Mrs. Cherry gushed as she flung open her door. I was hit by a wave of the Bal à Versailles perfume in which she doused herself, the cloying floral notes fighting each other for attention. It mostly masked the other odors from the apartment—stale marijuana smoke, patchouli incense, garbage that should have been taken out a day ago.

Mrs. Cherry was two hundred pounds and five feet of indeterminate gender. Although she lived as a woman, I was 99 percent sure she'd been born a man. Whether she'd achieved her ample bosom, rounded hips, and other female characteristics through surgery, hormonal supplements, or a wish on a genie's lamp, I had no idea. She had an air of magic and fantasy about her that made any combination of those seem possible.

Mrs. Cherry ran the escort agency I used to work for. She'd been a great boss, looking out for my best interests and screening my clients to ensure I was never in a dangerous or harmful situation. When another guy in her employ was hit by a car a few months ago, Mrs. Cherry paid all of Randy's hospital bills and kept his nursing staff happy with frequent deliveries of food and guest baskets.

After a suffocating hug, she ushered me into her large living space. Years ago, she'd bought several apartments on her floor and combined them into one, creating a labyrinth of mysterious, elaborately decorated rooms. The furniture was overstuffed and buried under mounds of pillows, the walls papered with busy feminine patterns, everything colored various shades of red, purple and pink Tiffany lamps, beaded curtains, and crystal chandeliers further contributed to the illusion you'd been transported to a New Orleans brothel sometime in the 1920s.

I sank into one of her enveloping settees.

"Can I get you something to drink?" Mrs. Cherry offered. "Some champagne? Beer? A Shirley Temple?"

"Water would be great," I replied.

She returned moments later with a silver tray, which held an etched crystal pitcher filled to the top with icy cold water, a matching glass, and a small plate of thinly sliced lemons and mint leaves, all set upon a frilly lace doily. Mrs. Cherry never did anything without embellishment.

"I wish I could delude myself into thinking you're here to tell me you are coming back to work," she said, sitting across from me. "But you look much too happy and successful for me to believe that."

"Well, I don't know about all that, but you're right—that's not why I'm here."

Mrs. Cherry shrugged, then smiled. "I watch your mother's show every day," she gushed. "What a pistol that woman is! Such fun! But my favorite moment is when your name rolls by in the end credits. 'That's my boy,' I think. It's only on screen for a few seconds, but they're some of the best moments of my day."

Her voice cracked on the last few words, and I thought I saw the sparkle of a tear in her right eye. "I'm ever so proud of you, Kevin," she said wistfully. "I always knew you were special."

I thought about the difference between Mrs. Cherry and Mason Jarre. They both were in the business of employing young men for sex work, but Mrs. Cherry genuinely cared about her charges. She didn't use the illicit nature of her enterprise to justify regarding her employees as subhuman commodities. She was proof that, even in the sex trade, you could treat people with kindness and dignity. No, more than that. You could be loving and generous, creating a virtuous cycle of shared loyalty and respect.

Which raised a question. "When your boys leave the business," I asked her, "do they just disappear?"

She looked genuinely puzzled. "Whatever do you mean, sweetness?"

I told her how Mason related his experience with boys dropping out of sight when they wanted to move on, never saying good-bye or staying in touch.

"Oh, that sounds awful," Mrs. Cherry said. "I don't know if I could stand working like that. I'd be so concerned! That man must be out of his mind with worry. If one of my boys just stopped returning my calls or didn't show up for a job, I'd do whatever it took to find him. Just to know he was all right. This is a big city—anything can happen!

"You know as well as anyone, my little angel, when a boy wants to leave the business, I have no problem with him moving on. I wish my boys the best in life. If that man's models are leaving like that, without even a fare-thee-well, there must be a reason. Either they're afraid of him or . . ."

"Or what?" I prompted.

"Or something's happening to them."

"Like what?"

"I don't know." Mrs. Cherry removed a lacy handkerchief from her deep cleavage. She twisted it nervously in her hands. "Nothing good, I'd imagine."

"That's what I need your help with," I said. "Just how 'not good' this situation is."

I explained how I'd met Brent, what happened when I finally got around to calling him, and what everyone had to say about his disappearance.

"How awful," Mrs. Cherry said. "No one seems to care at all about this poor boy." She gave me her warmest smile, the one that makes you feel like she's hugging you even when she's way out of reach.

"Except you," she amended. "But that's your greatest gift, you know. *Caring*. It's what made you such an outstanding escort. It wasn't your good looks—not that you're not absolutely delicious, darling. Nor was it your creativity in bed or, from what my clients have told me, your surprisingly large . . . endowment."

I felt my cheeks redden.

"Darling, you're the only person I know who could sleep with hundreds of men but still blush at even an oblique reference to your penis."

"It's hardly been *hundreds*. . . ." I felt the need to clarify. "And with most of them . . ."

Mrs. Cherry waved her handkerchief at me. "Darling, please. No need to feel defensive. Who would know better than me? I was the onc who arranged those assignments, remember."

I was about to explain that for most of my "career," I'd done more dates that involved role-playing and fantasy than actual sex. Especially after I reunited with Tony, I drew the line at anything that involved oral or anal intercourse. My specialty was safe kink delivered with good humor and a smile.

"My point was"—Mrs. Cherry winked—"your clients raved about you not because you brought them to orgasm—any of my boys could do that. So, for that matter, could their own hands or a laundry machine if you lean against it just right during the 'heavy duty' cycle."

I gave her a WTF look.

"Or so I've heard," she said quickly, anxious to get off that last example. "In any case, it wasn't the *sexual* release they achieved with you that stood out for them. It was the *emotional* connection.

"You made them feel, for that brief time, cared for and understood. That's a gift far greater than merely getting their rocks off."

I remembered my conversation with Freddy and Cody earlier that week about my client who found his deepest satisfaction in clown play. It wasn't easy for him to find someone who wouldn't go running when he told him he wanted him to dress up like Bozo and pelt him with pies. Even paid companions treated him like some kind of freak. They may have gone through with the act, but he could always sense their contempt and disapproval beneath the surface.

But with me, he said, he never felt the nose-holding disdain that his other partners always seemed to have. Which was probably because I didn't feel it. As long as it didn't hurt them or involve hurting someone else, there was no kink with which I couldn't empathize. I didn't *share* the kinks, but I wasn't disgusted by them. Nor did I feel somehow superior or more evolved just because I didn't get a hard-on when I saw a poster for the circus.

Who's to say what determines what turns you on? Why is someone who's excited by a woman in high heels morally better than someone who gets the same rise from oversized jester shoes? As a gay man, 90 percent of the people with whom I shared a gender couldn't understand what I wanted in bed. Who was I to judge someone else?

"It's funny," I said. "I was thinking the same thing about you. How much you care about the boys who work for you. What a difference it makes."

"Darling, no one's life is spared the occasional fall. If we're not here to cushion each other's landings, then what's the *point* of us?"

Suddenly, Mrs. Cherry's overstuffed couches and chairs took on a new meaning for me. I knew she hadn't deliberately planned it, but if you were to trip anywhere in the apartment, there wasn't a piece of furniture you could hit that would hurt you. Every surface was soft, comfortable, and welcoming. I began to wonder if her instinctive drive to cushion life's disappointments also explained why she'd added those enormous breasts to herself, then I decided it was best to return to the business at hand.

Focus, Kevin, focus.

"One thing that came up a few times was the possibility that Brent went into hustling full time. Or hooked up with a sugar daddy. Is that something you could look into?"

"Dear boy, if that boy's turning tricks or being kept in this city, I'll find him. Tell me everything you know about him."

It was depressing how little time it took to do that.

"I'll make some calls," Mrs. Cherry promised, "and let you know the moment I find out something."

"Thanks," I said.

"No," she responded, "thank *you*. For caring enough to look for your friend. For giving me the chance to help you find this lost boy. And for reminding me why I always believed in you."

I could have stayed in Mrs. Cherry's apartment for the rest of the day. I was tired and she was so welcoming. It had been a long day.

But it was about to get longer.

My phone rang.

25

Family Values

"Hey, babe." It was Tony. His voice was hushed. He must have been at his desk.

"Hi, honey."

Mrs. Cherry gave me a saucy wink. "The cop?" she mouthed silently.

I nodded, and she gave me an approving thumbs up. She might have arranged paid assignations for a living, but she also recognized the value of a solid primary relationship. She was glad to hear Tony and I were still together.

"I need a favor," he asked.

"What's that?"

"Can you pick up Rafi from aftercare? I was going to grab him on the way to your place, but I'm stuck. They just brought in a suspect I need to interview."

"Sure," I said. "But, can I do that?"

"I don't know," Tony asked, sounding a little perplexed. "*Can* you?"

"No, I mean will they *let* me?" I couldn't imagine the staff at Rafi's after-school program would allow someone they didn't know to just take him.

"Of course they'll let you," Tony said. "I listed you on his paperwork at the beginning of the year as an authorized guardian."

"You *did*?"

"Why wouldn't I? You've got permission to pick him up, you're an emergency contact, and you can call at any time to see how he's doing." Tony's voice had a "well, duh" quality to it, as if I should have assumed he'd be comfortable giving me that much access to, and responsibility for, his kid.

Wow. I wondered how Tony classified me on the form. As a family member? A friend? *Partner?*

I figured I'd better not push it. It was enough he trusted me with his son's welfare. I was touched he'd thought to include me when filling out those forms. It made me feel like he planned on sticking around.

"Well, then, sure," I said. "I'll be glad to get the Rafster." I knew where the school was, as Tony and I had brought him there together, but I hadn't gone in before.

"Great. Thanks, babe. I'll be home around eight. You don't mind hanging out with him till then?"

"You kidding? He's my second-favorite Rinaldi. Except for when you're cranky. Then, he's my first-favorite."

"I'll call his school and let them know you're coming. Love you," Tony said, whispering the last two words.

"Love you, too," I answered, hanging up.

Mrs. Cherry was smiling with an unabashed mixture of pride and delight. "I couldn't help but overhear. Although I really had to strain to catch his part of the conversation, mind you." She was obviously not embarrassed by her eavesdropping.

"You two are parenting together?"

"Not exactly." I explained how things had been working. By the time I'd finished, her grin had decreased by half.

"It's not ideal," she said, after hearing how I had to sleep in the living room and pretend to be Tony's "roommate" when Rafi came over, "but it's a start. More than a start. A man like Tony, though . . . it's going to take time."

I grimaced. "Tell me something I *don't* know."

Mrs. Cherry was up for the challenge. "I still have a penis." She watched for my reaction.

Whoa. Not expecting that. I should have been more specific with my question.

I tried to keep my face as neutral as possible.

"Okay," I said. "That was something I didn't know." I loved

Mrs. Cherry too much to add the snarky *It was also something I didn't* want *to know.*

"It's not something I ever talk about. . . ." she began.

I can see why, I thought, still with the snark.

". . . But I want you to understand there are things that, even if we want to, are very hard to let go. For me, it's this ridiculous . . . appendage. Every time I see it, it's a painful reminder for me of the mistake God made when I was born. I really wish it were gone.

"For two years, the doctors and counselors have been telling me I'm medically and psychologically prepared to have it removed. But I wasn't quite ready to part with it.

"For Tony, it's his dream of a 'normal life' he can't let go of. One with a wife, a child, and a picket fence. That doesn't mean he doesn't love you. Just like my genitalia doesn't make me any less of a woman. It just means that even when you *want* to change, when you want to let go, it's hard."

I wasn't sure the analogy completely worked for me, but I nodded anyway.

"Is he worth waiting for?" she asked me.

"For now," I answered honestly. "But I don't want to live . . . half a life with him. You know what I mean?"

She looked down at her lap. "More than you know, darling."

"Thank you," I said. "For sharing that. I know it's very personal."

"You're right. It is. And I don't tell many people. But it was the best example I had to help you understand that Tony's . . . reluctance doesn't mean he doesn't want you. Or that he wants what he used to want, either. Any more than I want this . . . thing between my legs.

"You see, there's this . . . in-between space when we exchange one dream for another, where we can't commit to either. We know that moving backward would be terrible, but moving forward is even scarier. It's the muddle in the middle that's the worst part."

Was that where things stood between me and Tony? The muddle in the middle? It sounded right.

"But it doesn't last forever," Mrs. Cherry said. "In three weeks and two days, I have an appointment for the surgery. It took a while, but I'm ready, Kevin. I'm ready to let go of the past."

"That's great," I said, truly happy for her.

"I think so, too." She gave a girlish smile. "And if I can find the—pardon the expression—balls to have my cock cut off, darling, I certainly think Tony should be able to come out of the closet for a prize like you."

For what seemed like the hundredth time that day, I couldn't help but agree with her.

"Kebbin!" Rafi screamed, in an ear-piercing peal of joy. "You nebber picked me up before!" He flung himself at me, wrapping his arms around my waist and nearly knocking me off my feet.

"Let me guess," his teacher said, "you two have met before." She was an uncommonly attractive brunette in her mid-twenties, I'd guess. She had a great body on her, too, which she seemed to be hiding underneath a particularly unflattering and bulky sweater. I wondered how many dads suddenly found themselves uncharacteristically helpful, offering to pick up their kids from her classroom.

Then I thought one of them might be Tony and felt a little queasy.

I shook her hand and introduced myself. The class was seated in a circle in the brightly decorated room. She had been reading them *Where the Wild Things Are* when I'd walked in. It was a book I'd read to Rafi about a hundred and twenty times myself.

"I'm Max," he roared, letting go of me to make monster hands and bare his tiny teeth. "Feah my tewwible fuwy!"

"He knows the book by heart," his teacher, who'd introduced herself as Ms. Sally, said. "That your doing?"

I shuffled my feet. "Guilty as charged." I loved Max from that book. The kid was a badass.

"It's wonderful that you read to him," she said. "You must be a close friend of the family." She arched her eyebrow at me suggestively. "Very close."

"I'd like to think so," I answered, guardedly.

"I'll tell you what," Ms. Sally said to Rafi. "Since you are such a good reader, why don't you finish reading the book to the class while I go talk to Mr. Kevin?"

"*Really?*" Rafi asked. "Can I, Kebbin?"

"Sure," I said.

He ran off excitedly to sit in Ms. Sally's oversized chair and opened the book. "One, two, three," he commanded the class. "Eyes on me."

Damned if all the kids didn't pay attention. Maybe Rafi was going to be a badass, too.

I wish I were. I had no idea why Ms. Sally wanted to talk to me. Had Rafi done something awful? If so, why tell me? Surely, it could wait till a day when Tony or his mother picked him up.

Or, maybe she was interested in Tony and wanted to see if he was available. No, what if they were actually . . . doing it, and she wanted to warn me away from "her" man?

My queasiness was now full-blown nausea. Stomach churning, I let her take my arm and guide me to a quiet corner of the room.

Ms. Sally sat with me on two kid-sized chairs. The seat actually wasn't that small for me, but she was a few inchers taller. Most adults her size would look ridiculous on the tiny perch, but she sat with the straight back and perfect grace of a ballerina. I hated her already.

"Kebbin," she began.

"It's 'Kevin,' " I said.

One of her hands flew to her mouth, getting the message to cover her embarrassing gaffe a few moments too late. "Oh my god, I knew that. I'm sorry, Keb—Kevin! I swear, you spend enough time around these kids and you start to talk like them." She blushed between spread fingers.

Okay, maybe I didn't hate her *so* much. Let's see what she had to say.

"Do you mind if I'm direct?" she asked.

"I'd appreciate it," I said, thinking that seemed like a very grown-up thing to say.

"Three days ago, Rafi asked me if I knew what a 'faggot' was."

My nausea was replaced by a ball of ice in my stomach. "What did . . . how did *that* come up?"

She placed her hands on her knees, forcing herself even more erect. "He said that he heard his mother use the word when on the phone with one of her friends. According to Rafi, he heard her mention 'Tony and that faggot he's living with.' Rafi said she sounded mean and scary."

The thought of Rafi hearing such ugliness, and being hurt by it, broke my heart. Not to mention that I, however blamelessly, was somehow linked to it. I blinked back a tear.

"I don't know who she was talking about," Ms. Sally said, with kindness if not truthfulness, "but . . ."

"I'd be the 'faggot' in question," I said, sparing her the discomfort. She grinned widely. I had the feeling she was probably pretty cool. "What did you say?"

"I asked him what he thought the word meant. He thought for a moment and I knew he was trying to reconcile what he'd overheard with what he's observed and known to be true. Finally, he said, "I think it must mean 'bestest friend.' Because I know my daddy lives with his bestest friend, and that he loves him very much.' "

I was doing a lot of blinking now. I didn't trust myself to say a thing.

"I told him I bet you were his dad's best friend, but that 'faggot' wasn't a polite word to use. Rafi said he could tell it was a 'bad' word from how his mom said it. He said it was the same tone she used when he took a cookie without asking.

"He's a smart kid, you know. You could tell he was really thinking about what I'd said. Finally, he asked, 'But why would my mom think it's bad for my dad to have a special friend? Doesn't she want him to be happy?' "

I didn't envy Ms. Sally for having to come up with a diplomatic, kid-friendly answer to that question. The only one I could think of was "Because your mom's a miserable bitch." That fit neither criteria.

"What did you say?"

Ms. Sally gave a wry smile. "To be truthful, I punted. I told Rafi that it wouldn't be fair for me to guess what his mom was feeling and that he should ask her."

"That seems fair. I think you did a great job," I said.

"I mentioned it to his mom when she picked him up that night." She darted her eyes guiltily to the ground.

"Annndd . . ." I prompted.

"Annndd . . ." she mimicked me, "I really shouldn't say any more."

"I'll bring you chocolate," I offered.

"It's an ethical thing," she said. "Confidentiality."

But she wouldn't have mentioned it if she didn't want to tell me. "Hand to god," I said, raising my right palm. "I won't tell a soul. But it would be helpful—to Rafi—if I knew what he was dealing with."

"Can I have your word *and* the chocolate?"

"I'll throw in a doughnut."

Ms. Sally let out a long sigh. "She said 'I suppose it's just as well. Better he hear about his father from me than on the playground.' "

"Ouch. Now, I'm *totally* withdrawing that Mother of the Year nomination I'd submitted for her."

"So is it true? Are you and Mr. Rinaldi . . . more than roommates?" Her eyes glittered with the zeal of someone excited to hear some especially juicy gossip.

I didn't know if Tony would want me to answer that question truthfully. Actually, that's a lie. I knew he wouldn't.

But, fuck it. He was the one in the closet, not me.

"Yeah," I said, "we're lovers. But Tony's not entirely comfortable with it. I'm the first—well, the only guy he's ever been with. So, please, don't say anything to him about it."

"Are you kidding?" she asked. "Mr. Rinaldi is always very nice, and I can see he's a terrific father, but I'm no idiot. That's a man who could intimidate a Tyrannosaurus rex *and* he carries a gun. I want to live."

I laughed. "I really appreciate your sharing all this with me," I told her. "I'll talk to Tony. He hasn't been open with Rafi about our relationship. I don't think the secrecy is doing anyone any good."

"I've spent most of my waking hours with kids for a few years now," Ms. Sally said. "The thing about keeping secrets from them is that it doesn't work. Most parents who think their children don't know what's *really* going on are deluding themselves. Even if it happens behind closed doors, kids have a way of knowing the truth.

"Plus, lying to children sets a bad precedent. When those kids turn into adolescents and start telling their *own* lies, the parents are always surprised and defensive, asking 'Where did they learn that from? We've always encouraged openness in our home.'

"Yeah, sure. Keep telling yourself that. Better yet, get a mirror, honey."

That settled it. I liked Ms. Sally. A lot. I totally agreed with her whole honesty-is-the-best-policy spiel. But she was right about something else, too: If she talked to Tony like that, he'd shoot her.

"I should let you go," I said, observing that the kids had begun to look a little glazed-over as Rafi tried to read them *Where the Wild Things Are* for the third time. "Again, thank you. I'll talk to both of them. I'd never want to see Rafi get hurt."

Ms. Sally leaned closer to me. Almost nose to nose, she whispered, "Were you really his first guy?"

"Guilty as charged."

"I don't want you to think I'm a homophobe or anything," she said. "It's just . . . I do not get the 'gay' vibe off him at all."

"Don't worry about it," I consoled her. "He doesn't get it, either."

Ms. Sally giggled like a teenage girl seeing a *Playgirl* centerfold. "And what about you? Was he *your* first, too?"

"He was the first I'd been with *that* evening," I answered, winking.

Another naughty-girl giggle. "I'm glad we talked. I think you're going to make a great second dad for Rafi."

I was? I hadn't thought of myself in that role.

I hadn't dared.

26

Daddy's Secret

"Can we go to the park?" Rafi asked, holding my hand as we walked home from his school.

It's kind of a miracle how a kid's hand settles into yours. As if it were made to fit there. When holding a boyfriend's hand, you feel his strength and tenderness matching yours. A union of equals. But a child's hand is so small. Precious. The moment it's in yours, you feel a primal protectiveness that gives you a superhuman sense of power. You imagine there's nothing you wouldn't—couldn't—do to save him from pain.

Yet, I couldn't find any words to open the subject of what he'd heard his mother say. Tony had put boundaries between us. I could break them, but I'd risk losing him.

Is he worth waiting for? Mrs. Cherry had asked me.

Maybe for me, I answered in my head. But suffused with tenderness and caring for the charge by my side, I worried *Is Tony's guilt, confusion, and ambivalence hurting Rafi?*

I could stand getting hurt. But I couldn't be part of hurting a child.

"Sure," I said, giving Rafi what little joy I could, "let's go hit the slides."

Rafi squeezed my fingers. "I love you, Kebbin."

I squeezed back. "Me too, Rafsters."

"That miserable bitch," Tony said later that night.

My thoughts exactly.

Rafi had fallen asleep with Tony ten minutes ago on my bed. Tony'd snuck back out and lay with me on the sofa bed as I snuggled against his rocklike yet still comfortable chest. I'd just filled him in on what Ms. Sally had told me at Rafi's school.

"To let Rafi hear that—what the fuck is wrong with her?"

"I know," I said. "*Faggot* is such an ugly word."

"Still," Tony said, ruffling my hair, "Rafi was right. You are my 'bestest friend,' you know."

I crooked my neck and playfully bit one of his nipples.

"Ouch," he said. "And, uh, yum."

Like many men who'd primarily had sex with women, Tony had no idea his nipples were erogenous zones until I introduced him to their usefulness a few months ago. Now, he was a bit of suckle slut.

"It's not funny," I said. "You have to talk to Raf. And you have to figure out what you're going to say." I told him Ms. Sally's thoughts on kids knowing the score even when their parents thought they didn't.

"I thought we agreed you weren't going to push me on this," Tony growled.

"I'm not saying you have to take out a full page in the *New York Times* announcing your involvement with me," I said. "But you have to think about your son. Eventually, someone is going to tell him about you—about us. Would you rather you be the one to do it, or leave it to his mother or his friends?"

"I don't think I need to tell my five-year-old son about my sexuality," he said icily.

I pulled myself away from him and sat up. "Is that all this is about to you? Sex?"

Tony looked tired. "You know that isn't true. Don't play word games, Kevvy."

"It seems to me," I said, getting up. "You're the one who's playing games. The worst kind, Tony. The kind where no one wins."

"Kevvy, don't be mad at me." I wasn't used to seeing Tony so vulnerable. "I don't know what to do, all right? I don't have a . . . map for this."

"So, trust me. Talk to your son. Tell him how you feel about me. How we feel about each other. Let him know that what he knows to be true, is."

"He's a kid, Kevvy. He doesn't need to know about . . . homosexuality."

Tony had been raised a strict Catholic. I wasn't sure what he'd known about homosexuality himself before I'd sucked his dick at the age of sixteen. Even afterward, I think he thought it was some kind of fluke or wrestling move.

"You don't have to explain the intricacies of anal intercourse to him, Tone. He just needs to know he's in a place with two adults who love each other and who love him, too. That we're both there for him. He's just been through your separation with your wife, Tony. He needs stability. He needs to feel secure.

"He also deserves to know that not everyone thinks it's okay for two men to have that kind of special love. That people might say mean things. Even his mother. But he needs to hear from you that *all* love is good and to be celebrated.

"He's young enough that you still have the chance to shape his moral center. If he senses shame and secretiveness from you, he'll be anxious and think what you're doing is wrong. But if you're open and honest, he'll feel safe and strong."

In my head, Stephen Sondheim's seminal "Children Will Listen" played. As sung by Barbra, natch.

"But that window won't be open forever," I continued. "Eventually, someone is going to define our relationship for him. Wouldn't it be better coming from you?"

Tony rubbed his temples, wincing.

"Let me do that," I said. I sat beside him and dug in, rotating my index fingers in small circles just behind his eyes.

"Mmmm, that's good," Tony moaned. He was quiet for a few minutes while I worked the tension out of his forehead.

"I want to do the right thing," he said eventually.

"I know."

"I do love you."

"I know that, too."

"Let me think about it, okay?"

"Okay."

I massaged deeper, using my thumbs to press the top of the bridge of his nose, another acupressure point for relieving stress.

Tony was quiet, his eyes closed. For ten minutes, he said nothing.

I cherished his silence. In the past, he'd avoided this conversation. I was touched by how much consideration he was giving it now. I knew his stillness meant he was really thinking about what I'd said.

Until he started to snore and I realized he'd fallen asleep. Probably nine minutes ago.

Gently, I cupped his face between my hands.

Why did loving me have to cause this good man so much torment? I wished there was something I could do to take away his pain. To make this all easier for him.

I realized my thoughts walking Rafi to the park earlier today were wrong.

It wasn't children that brought out our protectiveness.

It was love.

On his other visits with Rafi, Tony was always careful to return to my room before he fell asleep, so that his son wouldn't see us in bed together.

I considered waking Tony so he could make his usual retreat but decided against it.

If Rafi saw us together, maybe it would save a lot of discussion. And we could all move on.

Unfortunately, one of us was about to move on a lot sooner than I'd hoped for.

I squinted at the digital clock across the room as if by squeezing my eyes together the numbers would make more sense. 3:15? In the morning?

So why was Tony getting dressed?

"Is the apartment on fire?" I croaked.

"Sorry, babe." He sat on the sofabed and kissed my forehead. Now that he was closer to me in the darkness, I could see he was dressed for work. "We have another floater. I gotta go."

There were downsides to being in love with a cop. "S'okay," I said, already drifting back off to dreamland.

"Listen," he said, apparently unfazed by my looming unconsciousness. "Rafi's only been here a couple of times now. If he wakes up there alone, he's going to be scared. Do you think you could go lie with him in your room?"

"I don't know if I'd get any sleep. Is it like being in bed with you?"

Tony looked mildly scandalized.

"I mean, does he also hog all the blankets, dummy?" I hit him with a pillow.

Tony grinned, his hair mussed by my attack, making him look extra scrumptious. "I'm afraid it's in the Rinaldi genes. Sheet-stealing, chocolate-loving, heartbreaking scoundrels, we are."

I reached out my hand and Tony helped pull me to standing. Then, before I knew it, he swept me into his arms and carried me into my bedroom. He laid me gently next to Rafi. Sure enough, the kid was cocooned in every blanket on the bed. Tony saw me notice and shrugged.

"I'll get you one," Tony whispered, reaching out to unravel his son.

"Just grab one from the sofabed," I whispered back.

"Good idea. And, listen, I hate to take advantage of you, babe, but if I get hung up, can you bring him to school in the morning?"

I didn't know if I should be touched that Tony trusted me with all this parental responsibility, or pissed that I was only entrusted with it when it was convenient for him. "Sure," I said, slurring slightly with sleepiness.

Tony kissed me again. "I'll get the blanket."

I was dead to the world before he returned with it.

27

Sleep Over

I crashed quickly but it was a restless, shallow slumber. Two hours after Tony left, I didn't so much wake as admit defeat. Too wired to go back to sleep, but too tired to bother with the lights, I stumbled from bedroom to bathroom, peed for what felt like three hours, and made my way into the kitchen.

Daylight was just starting to muscle its way through my blinds. Speaking of muscle, when was the last time I'd gone to the gym? True, I no longer depended on a tight body to make a living, but that didn't mean I was willing to let myself go all Kirstie Alley, either. Bleary as I was, I knew a good workout would make me feel better.

I chugged a glass of milk and rinsed out the glass. Invigorated by the prospect of getting my exercise done for the day, I headed to the bedroom to throw on some sweatpants and a T-shirt. My gym was just down the block, so I wouldn't even bother with a jacket. If it was cold, I could walk faster.

I flicked on the light. The gym was one place where I paid no attention to fashion. If my clothes fit and were clean, they'd be good enough for me. I was putting on my tee when I heard a cat mewling from my fire escape. It wouldn't be the first time a stray had found its way up there, only to complain to find itself so unexpectedly far from the ground.

This one was loud, though. He sounded like he was right inside the apartment.

Now that I was paying attention, I realized he was also speaking English.

"Daddy?"

I was pretty sure that ruled out a cat. Or a bird. Or even a parrot.

That was definitely a human being.

Holy shit.

Rafi.

I had totally forgotten Rafi.

Oh. My. God.

Tony wasn't back, and I was about to leave a five-year-old in the apartment alone.

Worst. Parental. Substitute. Ever.

I briefly wondered if I should just strangle myself with my T-shirt right now. It was already conveniently placed around my neck.

"Da—" Rafi began again, his voice rising higher. A slight note of hysteria was creeping into his tone.

Okay, Kevin, stop thinking about yourself. This kid needs you.

"Hey, buddy," I said, moving to sit next to him on the bed. I tousled his hair in the same way Tony did mine.

"Hi, Kebbin!" he said with relief, remembering where he was. "I didn't see my daddy." He didn't have to add how that made him feel.

"He had to go out and help some people who needed him," I said. Rafi's known his daddy as "one of the good guys" his whole life. "But he made sure I was here to keep you company." I lay next to him.

"It's a good thing he did," I added, in a whispery, just-between-us confession. "He knows I get scared being by myself."

Rafi giggled. I looked at the clock. It was just a little after five. Rafi should have slept at least till seven. My guess was he'd have fallen right back into dreamland had Tony been in bed with him. But finding himself alone, Rafi cried out.

"You want to play a game?" I asked. I patted my chest and Rafi settled against me. I put my arm around him.

"I love games," Rafi said, his voice conveying exhaustion and excitement in equal amounts.

"I bet . . ." I said, pausing dramatically as if about to offer a truly thrilling proposal, "I can stay quiet longer than you can. Deal?"

"Deal," Rafi said, thinking himself very grown-up.

"Okay," I said. "You count it down. From three to one. After that, the next one who makes a sound loses."

"Bet I can be quiet longest," Rafi boasted, yawning halfway through.

"We'll see. Okay, start the clock, Rafsters."

"One . . . two . . . twee!" he announced confidently.

All right, he didn't get the whole "counting down" thing quite right, but ending on the adorable "twee" was better idea, anyway.

I clamped my hands comically against my mouth and bulged out my eyes, as if struggling to stay silent. Rafi lifted his head and giggled.

I shot a warning look—no noises! Rafi clamped his lips together and rested his head back on my chest.

I stroked his hair.

Five minutes later, I won. Turns out that not only did Rafi steal the blankets like his dad, but he snored like him, too.

Lucky kid. I felt more awake than ever.

I couldn't believe I'd almost left the apartment while he was in my care. What was I thinking?

I wasn't. But, in my defense, Tony hasn't exactly been making me feel like I was a significant person in Rafi's life. Last night and this morning were the first times he'd given me sole responsibility for his son's welfare. Look how close I came to blowing it.

But I didn't.

There is, I thought, feeling the warm body next to me and the weight of his little head against my heart, a kind of magic in this. A level of trust and unconditional love that you just don't experience from anyone other than a child. A special brand of blessing.

But it's a burden, too. I was *really* looking forward to going to the gym. I felt like I *deserved* it. While I wished I were selfless enough not to resent it, I did feel a little "stuck" here. Literally, as I was afraid to get up and disturb Rafi's sleep.

Sleep. God, that sounded good. Too bad it had deserted me. There'd be no returning to slumber now, not with my feelings of guilt, appreciation, resentment, and happiness running around my head like a bunch of unruly toddlers determined to keep me awake.

Still, it was nice to lie there with this toasty warm little guy nestled against me. He smelled good, like the bubble gum shampoo I'd used on his hair last night with an undertone of that scent unique to loved and happy boys. What was that fragrance? Smooth, new skin, clean sweat, innocence. Even his snoring was sweet, not loud like his dad's but rhythmic in its regularity. Not noisy enough to drown out the sound of his breathing, that relaxing metronome of respiration, in and out, in and out, in and out, in and

"Kebbin!" Rafi called, amused at the reversal of roles that found him waking me up for school. "It's time to get up, sweepyhead!"

I groaned and looked at the clock. 7:37. Enough time to get ready, but we'd have to hustle.

So much for being unable to fall back asleep. Maybe this is why people had kids—for their narcotizing abilities.

He'd rolled on top of me and pressed his nose against mine. "Hewwwooo. . . ." he said. "Is there anybody in there?"

"I'm up, I'm up," I grumbled. Not that I was really mad. I thought Rafi was enjoying playing the bossy parent, though, so I thought it was only fair that I acted the truculent kid.

"On your feet, soldier," he commanded. "We have to go to school." He straightened up and grabbed my hands. "C'mon."

I let him pull me up to sitting and blinked a few times. "All right," I said, "you got me. I'm getting up."

"Good boy," Rafi said, in his manliest voice. "You don't want to be wate for school, do you?"

"No," I said, deciding there was no reason to point out he was the only one going to school. "Have you made breakfast yet?" I asked him skeptically.

"No, Kebbin. I can't make breakfast. That's your job!"

"Fine," I said. "You get dressed and I'll make breakfast for us. But first . . ." I let the tension build.

"What?" Rafi finally asked.

I flipped him off me and on to his back.

"It's attack of the Tickle Monster!" I cried.

Rafi squirmed and laughed with delight as I alternated my attacks between his tummy, underarms, and legs.

"C'mon," he ordered after a few minutes of this. "We have to get weady!"

"All right, boss. You need my help getting dressed?"

"Kebbin," he said with exasperation. "I'm a big boy now. I know how to get dwessed."

Not so big that you can pronounce it, though.

Which I thought was just about perfect.

Ms. Sally gave me a wry smile as she saw me approach with Rafi.

"Is that bed head I see?" she asked wryly.

"On me or him?"

"You," she asserted. "He looks perfect."

It was true. I'd paid a lot more attention to his grooming this morning than mine. The price of being a parental stand-in, I conceded. First I'd skipped the gym, then my shower. Apparently, good child rearing was an exercise in sacrifice.

Her knowing look implied I'd come to this messy end after a night of impassioned lovemaking with Rafi's sexy dad. I would have hated to disappoint her with the dreary truth: Tony and I had a conversation followed by conflict followed by sleep. Then, I helped his son get to sleep and ready for school. Not quite the bawdy man-on-man action she'd been imagining.

Instead, I echoed her observation. "Yeah," I said, "he does

look perfect, doesn't he?" I'd taken extra care getting Rafi ready today, dressing him in a nice outfit he'd left over on a Sunday when Tony'd taken him to church, and slicking his hair back with about fifty dollars' worth of Clinique for Men styling products. He looked like a miniature businessman on his way to close an important deal. He was so cute you could die from him. A fate I wished upon his "faggot"-flinging mother.

"See?" Ms. Sally asked. "Didn't I say you'd make a great second dad?"

"You did at that," I commented. "And if the job opens up, I'll be sure to apply."

Ms. Sally regarded me curiously. "I thought you and Mr. Rinaldi were . . . you know."

"It's complicated," I said. "*He's* complicated."

"Maybe," she said. "But he's not stupid. Hang in there, sweetheart." She gave me a kiss on the cheek.

28

Finding Emo

"It's all set," my mother announced cheerily. "Tomorrow's the big day! Isn't this exciting?"

My mother had a habit of labeling as "exciting" events I found, alternately, embarrassing, horrifying, or deeply traumatic. This was looking to be one of those that managed to be all three at the same time.

We were in Andrew's office again, this time at the oval conference table that fit six. And six we were: Andrew; my mother; myself; Roni, the segment producer; Steven Austen, who'd be handling the makeup; and our cameraman, Laurent. The job before us was to plan the covert taping of the interview Andrew had set up for us at Families by Design, the adoption agency that had placed Adam with the Merrs, the couple who'd caged and brutalized him for the two years he'd been in their custody.

"We're going to expose these chozzers for what they are," my mother practically spat. Well, when I say "almost" I mean "actually." Spittle flew from her lips at the thought of the serial child abusers. The fine spray landed on the left hand of Roni, a somewhat quiet woman in her mid-thirties who commanded respect on the set without ever raising her voice. Roni discreetly wiped the anointed hand against the leg of her jeans.

"We've never done a location shoot like this," Andrew observed. "But we're lucky to have Laurent on our team. He's got the skills to carry the ball on this one."

Andrew had been a jock in high school and it showed.

"Thanks," Laurent answered. Before joining *Sophie's Voice,* he had worked on *60 Minutes* for three years. He was well versed in covert video technology. He explained to the group—sorry, Andrew, *team*—where the cameras and microphones would be concealed on our persons. Laurent was a true geek—passionate about his equipment and oblivious to the mind-numbing boredom settling over the room. My mother suppressed yawns, Andrew started texting on his BlackBerry, Steven appeared to have fallen asleep, and even Roni, whose job was to understand all the details of any given shoot, doodled elaborate designs on her notebook while he droned on for over an hour.

The video would be streamed to monitors in a van that'd be parked on the street, as close to Families by Design as they could get. Andrew, Laurent, Roni, and Steven would be waiting for us in there, observing the proceedings in case something went wrong.

And when I say "in case" I mean "when."

Steven was coming to apply any last touches to our makeup, a process we'd begun hours earlier in the studio.

"How close in age do you think you'll be able to get them to look?" Andrew asked him. I don't think Andrew had anything particularly against Steven, so why he put him in that position I'll never know. My mother had me late in life and was a good forty years older than I was.

Steven's eyes darted nervously around the room, like a man looking for the shooter with the worst aim on the executioner's line.

As he'd just helped me the other day with my SwordFight makeup, I felt compelled to rush to his aid. "I was just talking to Steven about it this morning," I answered brightly. "He says my mother and I will be totally believable as an unmarried couple looking to adopt."

I left out the last part of his warning: "if they're deaf, dumb, and blind. Or just very, very dumb."

"Yes," Andrew said, "but exactly how close can you . . . ow!"

I'd kicked him under the table. Hard.

"Andrew, darling"—my mother slipped into her maternal voice—"are you okay?"

Andrew shot me a dirty look. "I'm fine. Just a cramp."

"Probably from sitting so long," my mother concluded sagely. "I think we've covered everything we need to. Shall we break for now?"

Under the best circumstances, my mother had the attention span of a hyperactive three-year-old. I suspected she'd been looking for a way to wind up the meeting halfway into Laurent's excruciating monologue.

"Good idea!" I sprang to my feet. "It's a wrap!"

On set, that'd be Roni's line, but I felt free to use it here. Steven's grateful nod toward me affirmed I'd been right.

"Kevin, just a minute," Andrew said as I made a beeline for the door. "Could I have a word?"

Andrew's tone implied the word wasn't *thanks*.

"Just one," I said, trying to keep it light. "Choose carefully."

"Is there some reason you kneecapped me just now?"

I explained I was protecting Steven from having to pretend that even with all the makeup in the world, he could get me and my mother looking within a decade of each other.

"Fine," Andrew granted. "But next time you want to change the subject, can you do it without pulling a Tonya Harding on me?"

"Sorry," I said, ducking my head, giving him a look of boyish repentance through my blond bangs. It was a move that worked with most guys. Even the straight ones fell for the contrite choirboy routine. "Forgive me?"

Andrew sat on the edge of his desk and spread his legs. He dropped a hand mid-thigh. "You could," he offered, "kiss it all better."

I should have known that on perennial horn dog Andrew, that look would work *too* well. Lucky I hadn't kicked him in the balls.

"You know Tony carries a gun, right? Even when he's off duty?"

"How is it," Andrew asked, snapping his knees together, "that the mere mention of that man's name is like the anti-Viagra for me?"

"It's a good sign," I encouraged. "It means your desire to remain alive is stronger than your desire for a blow job."

"Oh god," Andrew groaned. "That's a *good* sign? What's a bad one? Male pattern baldness? Early Alzheimer's? Erectile dysfunction?"

"We already covered that last one. You got aging on the mind, old man?" I figured Andrew was around twenty-seven. A little young to be worried about joining AARP.

"It's just everyone I know is settling down. Partnering up. Getting married. Whatever." He hunched over in a defeated slump. "Soon, I'm going to be the last single man in Manhattan."

"Please," I said. "You've got more men nipping at your heels than Joan Rivers has had face-lifts. You've got a pretty deep pool of potential husbands out there. All you have to do is pick one."

"That's just it," he complained. "How do you pick *one*? How will I know?"

"Oh, honey, not even Whitney Houston, god rest her soul, could have answered that question. Although she did hit number one with it."

He looked at me blankly.

"Okay, forget the eighties pop culture reference. Listen, the grass is always greener, right? Half the people I know in relationships wish they were single. Almost all my single friends wish they had a partner. Just enjoy what you have now. The chance for variety. When you meet the right guy, you'll know."

"What," he said, regarding me gravely with a dramatic hoarseness in his voice, "if the one you know is 'the right one' is otherwise engaged? Like, to a jealous cop who could break me in two, for instance?"

Andrew and I met in high school and I think he was still stuck there in his interactions with me. Any day now, I expected him to have Suzy pass me a note in homeroom saying, *I think you're cute. Love, Guess who???*

"You can say that to me because it's easy," I told him, sounding harsh even to myself. "It's safe. You know I'm unavailable."

He looked surprised at my directness.

"The trick," I said, "is being able to say it to someone who *is* available. To make the offer to someone who can say yes."

"You could say yes," he countered. "If you wanted to. There's no ring on your finger, Kevin. At least not yet. Are you really going to wait forever for a man who won't even admit he's gay?"

Was there some reason everyone felt compelled to comment on my personal life? It was starting to piss me off.

"Self-pity isn't a good look for you, Andrew. There's hundreds of guys out there who'd cut off a finger for you. Stop pining for the ones you can't have."

"Hundreds?" he asked. "Not thousands?"

Oh. My. God. "Do you want me to get the other knee? If you can wait a minute, I think I have a baseball bat in my office."

"Fine," he barked, but not without humor. "I hear you. Switching roles for a moment, don't think I haven't noticed how much time you've spent out of the office these past few days. You don't have another job or anything, do you?"

No, but had the audition gone better, I might have.

"Sorry," I said. "I had some personal issues to take care of." Thinking how I'd run out of leads on my quest to find Brent Havens, I felt safe adding, "I think I've taken them as far as I can, though. I shouldn't have to miss any more work."

"Good," he said. "Please don't make me get all 'boss' with you. I'd hate to have my flirting mistaken for sexual harassment."

"No," I assured him, "you were a pig way before I started working for you. Safe as houses there, chief."

"Cute. Just try to cut back on the outside activities a little, okay? At least during working hours."

"Aye-aye, sir," I said, taking this as my opportunity to make an exit. "I promise no more sneaking out during the day."

Although I meant it when I said it, in less than an hour I'd turn that into a pie-crust promise: easily made, easily broken.

"Angel boy," Mrs. Cherry's honeyed voice cooed over my phone. "Is this a good time?"

"Absolutely," I told her, encouraged by her call so soon. It was just yesterday I'd asked her to use her contacts to discover if Brent had escaped into full-time hustling. If she was calling back so soon, she must have found something.

"I found nothing," Mrs. Cherry declared. "I've checked with every contact in the escorting business, as well as those brokers who arrange for . . . more permanent engagements. I even dipped my dainty and perfectly pedicured toes into the tainted waters of the gossip mill to see if he was working off the grid. Nothing's turned up. I'm so sorry."

"It's been less than twenty-four hours," I pointed out. "Maybe someone hasn't gotten back to you yet."

Mrs. Cherry was quiet for a moment. I could swear I felt a chill of cold air coming though the receiver. "*Darling*"—I could tell Mrs. Cherry was trying to contain her inner bitch—"no one 'doesn't get back' to me in this town. If they're smart, they answer my questions before I even finish them. I am, as they say, quite 'connected.' Not to mention"—she dropped her voice to a husky whisper—"I've got a killer rack that no man can resist."

"So, that's it?" I asked dejectedly.

Mrs. Cherry softened her tone. "Not necessarily, darling. He could still turn up. He's just not working in the sex industry. Perhaps he's selling cologne at Bloomingdales, or, I don't know, what do *regular* boys do, darling? Attend trade school? Install cable boxes?"

Yeah, maybe. But it didn't help me find him.

"The frustrating thing," Mrs. Cherry said, "was for a moment I thought I'd found him."

"What do you mean?" I perked up.

"False alarm, darling. Wrong boy."

"How so?"

"Oh, angel, it was so silly. It happened on my very first call. There I was, at my desk—my work desk, darling, not my makeup table—eating a jelly doughnut, with the notes I jotted down after you left. Just as my first contact picked up the phone, I took a bite of my little snack and—wouldn't you know it—just as my friend picked up, half of the doughnut's filling squirted out the back and landed—*splat!*—right on the paper. Covered up *everything. Très* embarrassing.

"Now, I could have wiped it up, but it was *half* the jelly, darling. I couldn't let it go to waste. Not when there are starving dieters right here in my building. That would be wrong.

"But I couldn't very well lick it up while on the phone, either. I have a reputation, darling. God knows what my friend would have thought I was up to!

"I couldn't remember the name you'd given me, but I did the best I could working from memory. I told him I was looking for a young guy who used to work for SwordFight. Early twenties, blond, boyish. I said he might be hustling, working for another studio, or hooked up with a sugar daddy. Did he have any ideas?

"Wouldn't you know, right away he said he knew *exactly* who I was looking for. I was so excited, darling. He gave me the boy's name and told me where he was. Sure enough, the smart kid got himself set up in style. Living with a rich patron in a building known not just for its grandeur but for its security and discretion. I wrote everything down and thanked my friend profusely. I couldn't wait to call you with the good news! I felt like a proper lady detective, I did.

"Then, the moment I hung up, I scooped up the errant doughnut filling to discover—much to my chagrin—that a terrible mistake had been made."

I held my breath, anxious to hear what she'd gotten wrong.

Maybe there was something she'd discovered I could use—even if the connection wasn't clear to her.

"The bakery had given me a *blueberry* jelly doughnut. Blueberry? I'd requested grape! I get a grape doughnut there every day—how could such a thing happen?"

She sounded near tears.

"And . . ." I prompted.

"And?" she asked. "And *what?* I mean, whatever happened to customer service? To loyalty? To . . . oh, you mean about your friend?"

"Yeah," I said. "Not that I don't sympathize with the whole doughnut debacle, but—"

"Quite right," Mrs. Cherry interrupted. "I'm afraid I did lose track for a moment. Yes, well, after I forced myself to choke down that blueberry filling—which, by the way, really wasn't that bad—I looked at my notes from the other day and realized I had the wrong boy! I'd been so sure. A former SwordFight model, the right age and coloring, how many of those could there be? But the names were different, darling. What a disappointment. And none of my subsequent calls turned up a 'Brent Havens,' either."

I wasn't so sure Mrs. Cherry hadn't gotten it right, though. I knew Brent had changed his name at least once for professional reasons. Maybe he'd taken another alias. Or, more likely, now that his work was no longer in the public eye, maybe he was using his real name. My heart beat faster with the sudden conviction I was right.

"The boy you found," I asked, "he wouldn't be 'Richie' something, would he?"

"No," Mrs. Cherry said. "I have a 'Richie' working for me, so I'd remember that."

"You do?" I asked. Could Brent have a second job? "Maybe—"

Mrs. Cherry read my mind. "He's been with me for two years, dearheart. He's a black gentleman in his forties. I don't think he's your boy."

Well, so much for that theory.

I guess I hadn't found Brent. Or made any other progress.

"No," Mrs. Cherry lamented. "I'm afraid I've been no help to you. The boy my friend was talking about was . . . oh, where did I put those notes . . . ?"

She paused and I heard the rustle of paper. I hoped she hadn't eaten them.

"His name was something like Larry. Lucky. No . . . wait. Here it is! Lucas Fisher!" Mrs. Cherry was thrilled to have found her notes, then remembered that wasn't the name I'd given her. "I'm so sorry, my love."

Lucas Fisher. The first boy who'd gone missing from Sword-Fight. I was afraid he'd suffered whatever fate I feared had befallen Brent. That he was another victim of whatever was going on.

I was glad to hear he was okay. In a way, it gave me hope for Brent.

On the other hand, knowing his obsession with Brent had me initially suspicious of him. Now that his whereabouts were accounted for, he'd gone full circle from suspect to victim to suspect again.

"Actually," I told Mrs. Cherry, "I've been looking for Lucas, too. He was a friend of Brent. He might know where he is. This is great. Can you give me the info you got on him?"

"Absolutely," Mrs. Cherry gushed. "So, I was helpful after all?"

"You were amazing," I assured her. "No one else had any idea where to find him. I was just about to give up."

Mrs. Cherry gave me Lucas's address and phone number, sounding quite pleased with herself.

"Now, you will remember to be discreet, won't you, darling? Mr. Fisher's patron pays quite handsomely to keep his dalliance with this young man out of the public eye. I don't know how far he'd go to protect his privacy."

I've seen firsthand how far famous people went to hide their clandestine affairs. No secrets that they were willing to die for, but a few they'd kill someone else to keep. I didn't take Mrs. Cherry's warning lightly.

"I owe you flowers," I told Mrs. Cherry. "Thank you so much."

"No bouquets, please," Mrs. Cherry said. "They just die and depress me. But I'd be happy to give you the number of my local bakery. Just tell them to get the order right, okay?"

29

Bodyguards

And so it was that, less than an hour after I promised Andrew I'd stick around the office, I was sneaking out again.

What else could I do? When I wanted to talk to Brent's boyfriend, Charlie, I had to wait till he went on shift at the bar. My "audition" with SwordFight took even more elaborate planning.

But getting to Lucas should be easier. I knew where he lived. I could call first, but if he were involved in Brent's disappearance, it'd probably be best to take him by surprise. I didn't want to give him time to come up with any excuses, or, worse, make a run for it.

I didn't want to put it off. I had no idea where Brent was. But if there was chance it was somewhere unpleasant, if he were being held against his will—and I couldn't imagine another scenario in which he at least wouldn't have told Charlie where he was—time was of the essence.

BTW: I've always wanted to use the phrase "time was of the essence."

Of course, there was always the risk Lucas wouldn't be home. I mean, what does a kept boy do all day? Go to the gym, I'd imagine. Shop. Play video games. Maybe he was in school.

I remembered Lucas's sexy slacker vibe, though, and struck that last possibility.

Whatever Lucas was up to, and whatever he knew about Brent, I planned to find out soon enough.

* * *

On the way over, I called Freddy. Partly to fill him in, partly to let him know what I was about to do and make my increasingly frequent request of him to call Tony if he didn't hear from me after a few hours.

"I'm coming with you," Freddy said defiantly. "There's no way I'm letting you go into this one alone."

I was touched. Freddy and I had been through a lot together, and the degree to which he wanted to protect me proved what a loyal and true friend he was.

"I'm afraid seeing two of us will scare Lucas off," I said. "And you know I can handle myself if he gets physical. I've taken down bigger guys than him. But I really appreciate your looking out for me."

"Who said anything about looking out for you? We watched him on video together, Kevin, so I know you've seen that world-class ass. There's no way I'm passing up the chance to get into that little hottie's pants."

Okay, I retract all those warm and fuzzies. Freddy was a pig.

"This is not," I said firmly, "about getting into someone's pants. This is about finding a missing friend."

"You want Lucas to talk, right? Well, I've learned," Freddy observed blithely, ignoring the annoyance in my voice, "that with the right kind of boy, a good and thorough plowing has a positive effect on the flow of social . . . intercourse. Loosens him up, so to speak."

"Huh. And you're prepared to make this sacrifice in the interests of helping to locate Brent?"

"No, I'm prepared to make this sacrifice in the interests of burying my dick so deep inside his butt that he feels it against his tonsils. But, if it helps find Brent, then, hey, all the better, right? Never let it be said I'm selfish."

"You're selfish," I said.

"I thought I made it clear never to say that, bitch. Where should I meet you?"

"You shouldn't. But, I'll make you a promise—if I can't get him to talk, we'll try your approach."

"Really?"

"Probably not. But you can dream, which is better than nothing, right?"

"Barely."

"Besides, you've got Cody. What would he think about your shameless pursuit of a retired porn star?"

"As you well know, Cody and I have an open relationship." Freddy affected a haughty disregard.

"On one side."

"Hey, he can screw around if he wants to."

"That's the point. He doesn't want to. He just wants you."

"So do a lot of other people. What am I supposed to do? 'Just say no'? Do I look like Nancy Reagan to you?"

"Only when you wear red," I said. "And, yes, saying no *is* an option, Freddy."

"One minute you're calling me selfish, the next you're saying I shouldn't share this magnificent body god gave me with as many men as I can. Make up your mind, Connor."

Maybe I didn't have ADHD. Maybe my friends were conspiring to make me crazy.

"Whatever. I'm texting you Lucas's address. If I don't call you in two hours, you try me. If I don't answer, call Tony and have him send the cavalry. Okay?"

"Why do I have to be the middleman on this? Wouldn't it be easier if you called Tony now and told him yourself when you might need rescuing? He can watch the clock as well as I can. Probably better."

"Because if he knew what I was sticking my nose into, he'd kill me. Which would make the whole 'rescuing' thing kind of moot."

"Fair enough. Okay, I'd wish you luck, but since your success makes it less likely you'll let me have a go at Lucas, I'll just hope you don't get yourself killed."

"Thanks," I said. "That's very generous of you."

"See?" Freddy pointed out. "*So* not selfish."

* * *

I arrived at the address Mrs. Cherry had given me and immediately recognized the building. It was a tall, skinny sliver of a high-rise condominium that seemed constructed of nothing but glass and steel. It looked more like an oversized piece of jewelry than a place where real people lived. Chic, minimalistic, almost spindly, it was hard to imagine it could withstand a strong breeze, let alone hundreds of people and all their stuff. Yet, despite its seeming fragility, it was considered, in many ways, one of the most secure buildings in the world.

It was called El Santuario. I'd read about it somewhere, the *New York Times,* maybe, or the *New Yorker*. Something with "New York" in it. It was described as the city's most exciting new building, an architectural wonder. As high-tech inside as it looked from the street, every unit was wired for automation and the ultimate in home security. Despite the fact that the walls were almost all floor-to-ceiling windows, you could see out but you couldn't see in. Some kind of special one-way coating gave the residents the best views in the city while also delivering total privacy.

The entrance was set back from the street, flanked by two doormen. You couldn't tell from looking, but I remembered from the article that the doormen were armed. It was also one of the few buildings in the city with an underground garage that allowed residents to pull in and have access to an elevator that would take them straight to the floor on which they lived, bypassing the need to pass through a lobby. This wasn't so much a security design, I'd read, but one instituted to ward off paparazzi, who typically clustered around the city's other high-end developments, hoping for a shot of someone rich and famous.

Given its many protections, El Santuario was home to several celebrities, financiers, and heads of state. People who wanted not only the elegance and status of living in one of New York's most desirable addresses, but the ultimate in protection from prying eyes and the other dangers of city life.

I hadn't asked Mrs. Cherry who Lucas's patron was. I was kind of glad not to know. Whoever it was, he was rich enough to have an apartment here. I had no desire to get on the wrong side of anyone with that much juice.

A man with that kind of money and power . . . now, there's someone who'd kill to keep his secret.

Forget Lucas.

Maybe the real guy I should be worried about was his sugar daddy.

I was glad I had dressed nicely for work today. The armed guards nodded as one opened the door for me. One even smiled.

There are times when being five feet three with boyish features and a slim build are an advantage. I'm not particularly threatening.

Once inside, I faced a long counter, behind which stood a man with the face of friendly bulldog. "May I help you, sir?"

Like most everything else in the lobby, the reception table was silver and glass. I noticed an odd omission of seating. No couches or chairs for visitors. The message was: You're either on your way in, or on your way out. Hanging out was not encouraged at El Santuario. Another reminder that people weren't here to be seen.

"Hi," I answered, in my most disarming manner. "I'm here to see Lucas. In . . ." I forgot the apartment number. "One sec."

I reached into my pocket for the folded sheet in my front pocket and noticed the receptionist's eyes darken. Surely he didn't think I was reaching for a . . .

I'll never know, but suddenly, another guard materialized to my left. He stood a few feet away, but I caught him in my peripheral vision. I heard a slight *whirring* noise and looked up. A video camera, discreetly tucked into a row of track lighting, slightly adjusted its lens. I imagined another guard in an unseen room zooming in on me to see what I was about to withdraw.

Yikes.

I pulled out the paper and opened it, my hands shaking slightly. The receptionist, however, seemed to relax slightly and dropped his shoulders.

"Umm . . . twenty-two F," I said. "Lucas in twenty-two F."

I purposefully didn't give Lucas's last name. I had no idea if he used the same one he used for films, but I bet not. For that matter, he might not have been using the same first name, but it was all I had.

"Of course." The bulldog moved his lips into an approximation of what would have been a smile on a human face. He picked up a phone and pressed some numbers. "Mr. Ford," he said. "There's someone here for your apartment." He paused for a moment, listening. "One moment."

"Mr. Ford wasn't expecting anyone," he said to me. "Your name, please?"

Shit. I hadn't thought of that. Dumb.

If I told him my name, then what? Would he ask the guard to inquire why I was there? What would I say? Anything close to the truth ran the same risk as calling ahead would have. Now that I was here, it seemed even more risky to set off his alarms. Forget being kicked out—I had the probably paranoid but unshakeable feeling that if I said the wrong thing, they'd shoot me.

The few seconds these thoughts ran through my head seemed much longer. I felt a bead of sweat run down my back. I wanted to scratch it, but was afraid any sudden movement would get me thrown to the ground and handcuffed. Unless I was mistaken, the guard to my left was a foot or two closer.

"Brent," I answered, hoping the answer wouldn't get me killed. "Please tell Mr. Ford it's Brent Haven."

The guard relayed my name. He listened again and his brows knitted together. "Of course, Mr. Ford."

He punched some buttons on a keyboard I hadn't noticed under his desk.

"Would you mind looking there, sir?"

He pointed at the lights where I'd seen the video camera hidden. A surveillance system. He must be able to patch the feed into the residents' apartments.

I said Brent Haven was here, and Lucas didn't believe it. He had to see it with his own eyes.

What did that mean?

A number of people who'd known Brent remarked how

much I resembled him. At least, on first glance. By the second one, though, I imagined the differences were clear.

I had a feeling Lucas would be looking very closely.

I'd been in other apartments with video cameras for visitors. The feeds were always grainy and indistinct. But this was the exceedingly high-tech and high-security El Santuario. The video was probably hi-def. Maybe even 3D. Who knew?

I faced the camera, but as slightly as possible. I shifted my weight from one foot to the other and subtly shook my head back and forth. Maybe some movement would make my image blurrier.

The bulldog listened to the voice on the phone. His eyes narrowed.

"Mr. Haven," he said to me.

"Uh-huh?" I didn't turn to face him. I could see him in the corner of my eye and that was enough. I could no longer remember why I'd thought him a friendly bulldog at first. Now, he seemed quite growly. Maybe even rabid. My nerves were out of control. If I had to meet his eyes again I was afraid I'd fall to my knees and confess everything.

That wasn't the only reason I didn't want to turn my head, though. If Lucas was buying me as Brent, I didn't want to chance that seeing me in profile would ruin the illusion.

The bulldog hung up the phone.

The guard to my left was suddenly at my side. Shoulder to shoulder.

Shit.

"If you'd go with Mr. Smith . . ." the bulldog said, nodding toward the guard.

I shifted my weight to the balls of my feet and tried to remember how far behind me the front door was. Should I make a break for it? I didn't know where Mr. Smith intended to take me, but I was pretty sure I didn't want to go there.

". . . He'll call the elevator for you," the bulldog finished.

He looked at the guard. "Floor twenty-two, Matthew."

"Very well, sir. This way, please." For the first time, I saw the guard straight on. He was actually pretty cute, very tall and thin, with a long, horsey face that looked equally dopey and bright. He spoke in a clipped British accent that increased his adorableness by a factor of five.

His eyes twinkled with a manic energy that he struggled to keep hidden. He looked more like a mad scientist than a security guard, but I had no doubt he could handle himself if a situation turned hairy.

Much to my relief, this one didn't.

"Thank you," I said to the bulldog. Now that I was cleared for entry, he smiled again and looked friendly. I resisted the urge to pat his head.

I followed Matthew Smith to the azure-doored elevator, one of the few spots of color in the otherwise neutral entranceway. He called it by punching a six-digit number into the keyboard. No simple "up" and "down" arrows at El Santuario. Another layer of security.

I wondered if the people who paid millions of dollars to live here realized how much their luxurious homes felt like a jail. I felt lucky not to have been strip-searched before gaining entry, although, had Mr. Smith been doing the search, it might have been fun.

"Do enjoy your visit," the mad doctor instructed me as the doors of the blue box he'd called for me opened. He gave me a little wink that made me wonder if he knew more about Mr. Ford than a simple name change could conceal.

"I intend to," I lied.

30

The Porn Identity

For such a new and high-tech building, the elevator seemed to be taking an awfully long time to reach the twenty-second floor. But then again, maybe it was my nerves stretching out the minutes like a prisoner on the rack.

In any case, it was long enough for me to have the increasingly intense suspicion I was walking into a trap. But what? I was probably just being overdramatic.

The doors opened with a ping that made me jump. Nervous much? I pinched my arm. Get over it. I stepped into the chicly stark hallway.

Just as the doors of the elevator closed behind me, it occurred to me what was wrong.

What if I was mistaken about Lucas using a new alias?

Maybe Mr. Ford wasn't Lucas at all.

Maybe it was The Patron who'd allowed the guard to send me up.

The Patron with a secret worth killing for.

I ran through the conversation with the bulldog again.

I said I was here for Lucas and he called upstairs.

Whoever answered, the guard called him "Mr. Ford."

But he hadn't said, "There's someone here to see *you,*" had he?

He'd said, "There's someone for *your apartment.*"

At least, that's what I *thought* he'd said. I wasn't paying that much attention, as I was mostly focused on not wetting myself.

Shit.

Shit shit shit.

Was that why Mr. Ford wanted to see me on the video? Because he knew it *couldn't* be Brent?

So then why let me come upstairs?

Because he'd seen me and determined I wasn't a threat?

Hadn't I just been thinking how lucky I was not to look imposing?

Now, I wished I resembled a more muscular John Cena.

This was crazy. I was crazy. What was I doing here?

Freddy was right.

Tony was right.

I had no business playing Boy Detective.

I turned back to the elevator, relieved to see that on the residential floors there were no secretly coded keypads, just the same two boring buttons you find in every other building.

I was just about to press "down" when two hundred pounds of muscle ran down the hall and grabbed me.

The force of the impact, and subsequent restraint, knocked the wind out of me. I couldn't breath. Or scream. Was I about to "disappear" too?

"Brent!" shouted an excited Lucas Fisher/Ford. He swept me off my feet and twirled me around. "My god, I thought I'd never see you again!"

Already woozy with panic and self-doubt, I was completely disoriented by this sudden embrace and dizzying spin. I didn't even notice he'd gone from turning me to carrying me until we were inside his apartment and he'd kicked the door closed behind him.

"Oh baby, I missed you so much." He pushed me against the door and brought his face around for a kiss. His body pressed against mine with a comfortable intimacy. Well, comfortable for him. For me, it was a little on the awkward side. Although, I suppose I should have been grateful that his initial embrace in the hallway, although overly enthusiastic, was the product of horniness, not hostility.

The tenderness of his touch played in sharp contrast to the hardness of his muscles. His pecs, abs, and quads felt like granite.

The other hardness he pressed against me was equally impressive. Had it been meant for me, I'd have been appreciative. As it was, I felt guilty, like I'd stolen his erection from someone more deserving.

His handsome face, even better-looking than on video, was radiant with joy.

Until a cloud eclipsed its brilliance.

Uh-oh.

There it was.

The second glance.

"Wha . . ." he began. He blinked in confusion. "You're . . . you're not . . ."

Suddenly, the arms that embraced me pushed me roughly against the door.

"You FUCK!" he screamed. "Who the FUCK are you?"

And . . . there's that hostility I was worried about.

He reached down to put his hands around my neck. He didn't tighten them. Not yet, at least. But I wasn't about to take any chances.

Lucas had almost a foot in height and at least sixty pounds on me. I knew from years of self-defense training that wouldn't do him much good.

I swept my arms up between his and quickly spread them apart, removing his hands from my neck. Had I felt truly threatened by Lucas, I'd have probably just kneed him in the balls at that point. It had the advantage of being a move I could pull off quickly and it always worked.

But once I did that, I doubted we could have a friendly discussion.

Instead, I dropped to my knees, darted between his legs before he had time to process what was happening, and was now in position behind him.

I considered pushing him against the door and bending his arm back to keep him in place. That way, he'd be forced to listen. But again, I decided on a more peaceful approach.

Because in the space of a moment, I knew Lucas hadn't hurt

Brent. Whatever his feelings for the boy were, he was unmistakably overjoyed at the thought of a reunion.

And given the confidence of that embrace, there was no way the relationship between them was unrequited. Lucas moved in for that kiss with no hesitation or fear. He knew it'd be returned.

At some point, outside of work and, I bet, behind Charlie's back, Lucas and Brent had become lovers.

I didn't blame him for being incensed to discover I'd lied to him.

I took a few steps backward and assumed a defensive stance. Legs wide for support and arms raised to protect my body and face.

I had a feeling that what I thought was a clever ruse to get myself into Lucas's apartment was, instead, a cruel and heartbreaking deception.

I didn't want to hurt him again.

But Lucas was enraged and built like a linebacker.

He turned and faced me, huffing like a bull facing a matador. His nostrils flared with anger and his eyes blazed. He was flushed with anger, his cheeks scarlet and so hot I could feel their warmth from a foot away.

Even so, I was struck by just how beautiful he was. Too bad whatever came next could get real ugly.

I took another step back, readjusting my arms to a less obviously defensive position. I faced my hands toward him and hoped he could judge body language.

"I can explain," I said.

"Not after I break your jaw," he growled. But he didn't step forward.

"Brent was my friend. I know you cared about him. I'm trying to find him. I came because I thought you'd want to help."

Lucas had one of those broad, open faces that showed everything he felt. His eyes softened a few degrees but his teeth remained clenched.

"Why did you lie? Why did you say you were *him?*"

I could see Lucas was wavering between trust and anger. Hope and betrayal tugged at him in equal measures.

I took another step back. This seemed to make him even angrier. Or more suspicious. What had I done wrong?

I had to play him. But how? What did I know about Lucas Fisher, now Lucas Ford? Nothing.

Except . . . except I'd seen him before. In the first scene he ever taped with Brent. In most porn, by definition, you're going to see a lot of skin. But in Lucas's encounter with Brent, he also revealed what lay underneath.

The desire to be dominated.

From the first moments, it was clear how enraptured Lucas was by his younger partner.

The balance of power between them was striking. Despite Lucas's age and size advantage over Brent, he immediately fell into the compliant role. Whether that was his general nature, or something triggered by the thought of being controlled by a smaller guy, I didn't know.

For whatever reason, though, it seemed like surrendering to a little-brother type flipped a button in Lucas's head. Amend that: flipped buttons on *both* of his heads.

During my years hustling, I learned a lot of lessons. One of the most lucrative was this: If a guy had a button, it always paid to push it.

"That's enough," I barked. I surprised Lucas, and myself, by reversing my slow retreat and briskly striding toward him. I put my hands on his shoulders and pushed him against the door. Not enough to hurt him, just enough to assert authority.

"Cut the crap," I ordered. I got up in his face like a drill sergeant. Like a lover. "I said I was Brent because I had to talk to you. I didn't know how else to get you to let me up.

"I've spoken to everyone else I could think of. No one seems to know where he's gone. You're my last hope, Lucas. You may be Brent's last hope, too."

Lucas was more than big enough to have pushed me away. Instead, he stayed where I put him. An obedient puppy.

For now.

I tried to affect a Christian-Bale-as-Batman deep voice. "So, here's what's going to happen. You're going to calm the fuck down, invite me in, and maybe even offer me something to drink. Like a normal person.

"Then, you and I are going to put our heads together and figure out where Brent is. Are you cool with that? Because, if not, I'm more than happy to leave.

"I came to help you, Lucas, not to get manhandled. So, why don't you stop acting like such a little bitch and maybe we can get to work and find our friend?"

Lucas raised his arms to shove me back. I shifted my weight to my heels. If he came after me too strongly, I was ready to protect myself.

Had I overplayed my hand? Misjudged how hard to push? My natural instincts urged me to back away, but my martial arts training gave me the confidence to remain still until he made his move, so I could use his momentum against him.

I was glad I waited. Lucas surprised me. The arms I expected to attack me instead wrapped themselves around my back. The towering mountain of man meat that fueled the masturbatory fantasies of millions was hugging me with the fervor of a five-year-old reunited with his daddy after getting lost at the supermarket.

Also like a lost little boy who'd just been found, Lucas was crying. Big, gulping sobs that shook the both of us.

"I'm sorry," he said. "I'm sorry, I'm sorry, I'm sorry." He held me tightly enough to be uncomfortable. I felt his strong muscles pressed firmly against me.

Also pressed against me was his hard-on. Just like the first time he hugged me. Only, that one had been meant for Brent. This one popped up just for me.

Apparently, my berating and pushing him around had an even more dramatic effect than I'd expected. Guess I wasn't wrong after all. That button of his was pretty dependable.

Still, as his sobs diminished and I patted his back, telling him it was all going to be fine, the mood shifted from one of confrontation to comfort. As he calmed down, the strength of his embrace and his erection diminished in equal proportions. In a few minutes, both came to an end.

He wiped his face with the back of his sleeve. “You must think I’m a freak,” he said, his voice croaky and breaking. “It’s just, I miss him so much, and I thought you were him. Then, when you weren’t, I wanted to kill you. Not *kill* you, of course. Just make this whole mess . . . go away.”

He looked around for something. My guess was it must have been a tissue, because when he didn’t find it, he untucked his T-shirt and blew his nose into the hem.

“It’s just . . . I haven’t been able to talk to anyone about what happened. Not *anyone*. Not the truth. I couldn’t even tell them he’d gone missing.”

“You can tell me the truth,” I said. “In fact, I’m counting on it.”

“The whole story?” Lucas asked.

“I kind of think you have to,” I answered. “For a whole lot of reasons.”

I didn’t add that his mental health appeared to be one of them.

Lucas nodded, to himself as much as to me. He somehow looked burdened and relieved at the same time.

“Come in,” he said, a little dazed and off his game. He started down the hallway to the living room.

“Can I get you something to drink?” His voice had a robotic quality to it. He was trying to hold it together, but I also noticed he was doing exactly as I’d instructed.

Not quite like a normal person, I concluded. But close enough.

31

The Renegade

"Do you mind if I wash up?" We were passing a bathroom, and I needed a moment to collect myself.

"Go ahead," Lucas said. "You want a drink?"

"Sure. Water's fine."

I closed and locked the door behind me.

The bathroom was chicly high tech. All polished aluminum and glass. The toilet was one of those tricked-out jobs with a built-in bidet, warming seat, and automatic disinfection. It made me wish I had to pee. Across from it, a fifteen-inch LCD screen was built into the wall. I guess reading on the john was passé.

The linen wallpaper, marble floor, and assortment of expensive, hand-shaped soaps spoke to excess wealth. Even the towels were designer, the letters KLN embroidered across their bottom. A play on "clean," I supposed. For what they cost, I thought they could have spelled out the whole word.

I opened the medicine cabinet. No medicine, but as vast an array of cleansing, moisturizing, and toning products as I've ever seen. All of it was labeled as "anti-aging" formulations, or "youth serums." Skin tightening creams, under-eye revitalizers, wrinkle reducers . . . if this stuff didn't work, the only thing left was embalming fluid. I wondered just how old Lucas's patron was.

I could handle myself in a fight, but I was glad I'd avoided one with Lucas. Still, I was flushed with adrenaline and my heart pounded alarmingly. I splashed my face with cold water and took a deep breath. I looked at myself in the mirror. My cheeks were blazing and my nostrils flared.

A few more deep breaths. Better.

Lucas seemed crazy enough for the both of us. I had to stay calm.

"Over here," Lucas called when he heard me close the door as I exited the bathroom. I followed his voice to the impressive living room.

Although it was early afternoon, Lucas had gotten himself a can of beer. He handed me a bottle of Evian.

When Lucas asked if I wanted to hear his "whole story," I didn't know he meant "from birth." Yet, here I was, half an hour into Lucas's recitation and he still hadn't entered his *Degrassi* years. Nor was anything he'd shared—from the town in which he was born to the name of his best friend in the fourth grade—at all relevant. The only mildly interesting thing I'd learned was that he was an army brat, raised by a strict, commanding father of high rank.

I could probably tie that to his fetish for submissiveness, but it wasn't a subject on which I wanted to dwell.

What was going on here? Why this diarrhea of the mouth?

He's lonely, I realized. I looked around the room in which we sat and admired the Scandinavian furniture, the thick carpets, the original Rothkos and Mirós that hung on the walls. All this staggeringly expensive modernity was almost made moot by the floor-to-ceiling glass wall, which opened the room up to the most amazing view of New York City. A constantly changing, living tapestry of life in the world's greatest city. I imagined it must be even more spectacular at night.

It was, I thought, the most beautiful cage I'd ever seen. Coming into the building, I'd been struck by how the redundant security measures made me feel like I was visiting a prison. Sitting with Lucas, I wondered if that's how he felt, only from the perspective of the prisoner.

Here he was, ensconced in luxury, but unable to share it with anyone. I was willing to bet his mysterious sugar daddy didn't encourage Lucas having friends over. Assuming he had any.

I bet Lucas rarely left this apartment. His patron wouldn't be taking him on dates. At least, not anywhere there was a chance they'd be seen together. I had no idea how old Lucas's supporter was, but if Lucas was an anonymous face, he might have been able to explain Lucas as an employee or nephew or something. But Lucas had a face recognizable from hundreds of pornographic movies. I didn't know anything about his patron, but in my experience these men tended to be closeted or even married.

Did Lucas go out on his own, then? Probably not. In my previous line of work, I'd dealt with a lot of very rich men. I learned that most of them got that way partly because they never shared their toys. Whoever was keeping Lucas in this kind of style probably expected not just exclusivity, but for Lucas to be here and available at all times.

Would Lucas even *want* to go out or talk to old friends? He couldn't discuss his work, as he didn't have any. He couldn't share anything about his living arrangement, as that would likely be the end of it.

What did he do all day, every day? Who did he talk to? I assumed no one. Which explained, at least partly, this unendurable outpouring of his heart to me. He was bored, lonely, and taking advantage of the opportunity of an audience.

I'd seen firsthand how much he liked to put on a show.

Was it worth it? I wondered. Sure, it kept him off the streets and surrounded by beautiful things. But was the price Lucas paid for being a rich man's plaything worth the paycheck?

I couldn't stand that Tony didn't shout our love from the rooftops. But at least we could go for pizza together. What must it be like to be not just a secret lover but a hidden one?

These were the questions running through my head as Lucas droned on. I thought of asking them, but Lucas was in the middle of some long story about trying out for his school's seventh-grade production of *West Side Story*. At least we'd made it to junior high school.

Besides, while I felt badly for him, I didn't know that Lucas's job satisfaction—or lack thereof—was of any more relevance to Brent's disappearance than whether or not the thirteen-year-old Lucas wound up cast as a Jet or a Shark. I had to move this along.

At least I didn't have to be subtle about it. Lucas liked it when someone took control.

"Enough." I cut Lucas off just as he was about to launch into a monologue about how his father took the news that his son was joining the Drama Club rather than the football team. "I think we've covered enough of your origin story for one episode. Let's fast-forward, okay? What do you think happened to Brent?"

Lucas slumped in his chair and took a long swig of his beer. He crushed the can in his hand. "I don't know," he admitted. "He said he needed a break. Just for a week or two, he said. But that was two months ago. I haven't heard from him since."

"A break? From what?"

"From me. From us."

What "us" was Lucas talking about? From everything I'd heard, it was over a year ago that Brent had complained to people about Lucas's overeager pursuit of him. He'd cut off all contact. Why would he have been in touch with Lucas as recently as two months ago?

I could have asked a question, but I seemed to get better responses from Lucas when I framed them as commands.

"Tell me what was going on between you and Brent that he wanted to get away from." But even as I said it, I knew what the answer must have been.

"He never said anything? Not even to you? I thought you said you were friends." His voice quavered and his eyes watered again.

I knew what he was thinking. Lucas had no life. Whatever was going on between him and Brent—and what else could it be than the obvious, I realized—was the center of his universe. Lucas didn't know I'd only met Brent once—he probably assumed we were very close. After all, look at all the trouble I was going to to find him. If Brent hadn't told me what was going on, then maybe Lucas wasn't that important to him after all.

At least, that was what I assumed was going through Lucas's mind.

"Of course he did," I gambled. "He told me you and he'd became lovers. It meant a lot to him."

Lucas buried his face in his hands. "Thank god. I was afraid . . . after all this time . . . that he just didn't care."

"I'm sure he did," I fibbed.

"It was hard for him, I know," Lucas said. "He still had . . . feelings for Charlie. He didn't want to hurt him. He also wanted to get away from SwordFight. Like I did. That's what got us talking again."

"Explain."

"There was a time—I'm sure Brent told you—when I was kind of . . . obsessed with him."

"I heard."

Lucas blushed. "I was. But it wasn't just him. There was a lot going on in my life at the time.

"My kid brother. He wasn't like me. I broke away from my father at an early age—I think back when I decided to take the role of Tony rather than join the football team, my dad kind of wrote me off."

Wow. Who'd have thought *that* story would turn out to have been relevant? Maybe I should have been paying more attention. I didn't even remember Lucas mentioning a little brother, although I'm sure he must have during the ten-minute discussion of his family tree.

"I was born a rebel. Never did a goddamn thing I was told to do. Even if it was what I wanted, too, I'd do the opposite just to piss people off.

"But my brother, Colin, was a daddy's boy. Followed orders like a good little soldier. Did everything my father told him to, including enlisting in the army on his eighteenth birthday. Just like dear old Dad."

Lucas lifted his face to me. It was pale and stricken, a mask of tragedy. "He was killed in Iraq within a month of his deployment there. His convoy ran over an IED." Fat tears ran down Lucas's face but he made no sound. He wiped at them like you wave away flies at a campsite—as if they were pests you expected, accepted, and learned to live with. He was quiet for a minute before saying "And that, as they say, was that."

He reached for his can of beer and grimaced when he found it empty and crushed. I thought he might get up for another but instead he just scrunched the corpse he held into a smaller and smaller ball.

"I loved that kid. So much. Despite our differences, we were always thick as thieves. I don't know, but maybe if I wasn't such a fucking hardass, if I'd *listened* more, I'd have gone overseas, too. Joined the army like my father always told me to. Maybe I would have been there with Colin. I could have protected him. Saved him. If only I'd followed orders like a good boy."

Holy Freudian minefield, Batman. I suddenly had a pretty good idea of how Lucas developed his desire to be submissive. Somewhere in his unconscious, he was making up for past sins. He was finally *listening*.

I wondered earlier if Lucas realized he was living like a prisoner. I bet he couldn't have articulated it, but some part of him knew that's *exactly* what he was doing. It led him here, to the most glamorous solitary confinement in the city. Part of him thought he deserved to be punished for his crimes that led to his brother's death.

I wanted to give him a hug. I wanted to carry him out of there and get him on the couch of the best therapist I could find. This boy I thought might have hurt Brent was turning out to be the biggest victim yet. The lostest of the Lost Boys.

"When he died, there was a hole in my heart I was sure could never be filled. For a year, I felt empty inside. I'd come to New York to be a real actor, you know. Only, I didn't have the talent. And I knew it. But I had the looks.

"So, it turned out, did a couple of other thousand guys. Before Colin . . . died, I'd been approached about doing porn. I always turned it down. I had . . . hope I'd make it as a legitimate actor.

"Once he was gone, though, the world was a lot less optimistic. The next time a sleazy guy offered me his card, I called. A month later, I made my first film for SwordFight.

"I liked it. I liked the attention, the sex. I started to feel alive again. When some of my co-stars taught me their tricks, I took their advice.

"I also took their pills. Then, their needles. Turns out I couldn't fill the hole in my heart, but I could numb it out real good.

"And then, I came across the most dangerous drug of them all. Love."

"Brent," I said.

"You got it," he said. "The boy I was meant to love. The boy who'd been made for me."

Lucas's eyes strayed to a framed photo on the grand piano across the room. I hadn't noticed it before. Strange, because I should have—it was one of the only personal items in the whole place. And the only one that obviously belonged to Lucas.

He looked as adorable in the photo as he did in every other. Younger than in the other pictures I'd seen, but unmistakably Brent. I was surprised Lucas had it out like that. I couldn't believe his sugar daddy appreciated having a picture of his boy toy's ex around.

Unless that was part of the appeal. Having not just your own live-in porn star, but one who was connected to another. Acquisition by association.

Brent stood in front of a typical suburban home. It could have been anywhere. The sun settled against his yellow-blond hair like the heavens were kissing him with light. Even though he squinted against the glare, you could see the affection in his eyes for the person taking the picture.

Lucas saw me catch what he was looking at.

"Did you take that picture?" I asked.

Lucas nodded. I suspected it would have been hard for him to talk at that moment.

"That's what makes it so special, then. You can see how much he loved you." As the words left my lips, though, I realized something wasn't adding up. What was it?

I had some part of the story wrong. Okay, maybe Brent had

been sleeping with Lucas on the sly. But love? That deep a connection? When had that developed? Over the year Brent had known Lucas, he was either trying to avoid him or dating Charlie. Unless someone was lying to me, the timeline didn't make any sense.

Lucas nodded again, this time accompanied by the sound of a man trying to swallow the unwanted lump in his throat. From across the room, I could smell his sweat, which had turned sour.

But who was lying? And why? Someone must have misled me, because I had no doubt that the boy in that photo not only loved but *adored* the man who took that picture. There was an innocence about it, too. This was a love that contained no shame nor concealed any secrets. From a boy I'd been led to believe either feared Lucas or was having an illicit affair with him. It made no sense.

"I've seen hundreds of photos of him," I said, "but I don't think I've ever seen Brent more beautiful than he looks there."

Lucas looked at me and, for the first time since I met him, he laughed. But it was a shrill laugh, tinged with a high keen that made me think of breaking glass.

He stood up so suddenly it startled me. He picked up the picture, kissed it, then handed it to me.

"See what I mean?" he said. "Why I believed God sent Brent to me? Why, during one of the worst periods of my life, a time in which I was becoming addicted to four different drugs without even realizing it, I became so obsessed with him?"

I studied the photo he handed me. Yeah, I thought. I can. I'd fall in love with someone who looked at me like that, too.

Then, I peered closer and felt a weird dizziness. Like a kind of double vision as a few details I hadn't seen before emerged like tiny ripples on a puddle from a single drop of rain. A mole on the left cheek. Bigger ears than I remembered. Darker eyes. Differences so small I'd never have noticed them if I hadn't been wondering why Lucas felt the need for me take a closer look.

"I assumed . . . ," I began.

"That's not Brent," Lucas said. "That's my brother. That was Colin."

32

The Lucas Boy

"Well, you know what they say," Freddy mumbled through a mouthful of marble cake. "Incest is best."

"It wasn't like that," I insisted.

I'd called Freddy the minute I'd left Lucas's gilded cage. On the way out, the guard who'd opened the elevator, Matthew Smith, winked at me. "Have fun up there?" he asked.

Something made me think he knew the score between Lucas and his benefactor. I suspected he might have seen a film or two of Lucas's, too. There was a knowingness in his inflection that you only achieve when you've seen a person perform fellatio. It brings people together like that.

Luckily, his goofy smile and foppish hair made his remark more playful than pervy.

I couldn't help flirting back. "The only way it could have been better," I answered, "was if you'd joined us."

Matthew widened his eyes in mock shock and swept back the loose lock of hair that flopped to his forehead. "I don't know if that place could have stood the three of us in there," he teased.

"Don't worry," I assured him, "it's bigger on the inside than it looks from the outside."

Truth was, Matthew's playful banter was a welcome tonic after Lucas's increasingly depressing tale. I shook my shoulders like a puppy shedding a summer rain. I needed to talk through what I'd just heard with someone.

Freddy. I was supposed to call him anyway.

"You're just in time," Freddy answered the phone. "I was about to ring Tony and tell him you'd gotten yourself in the deep shit again, darling."

"No," I said. "Although I do feel like I've taken a swim in the sewers. Wanna grab a bite and I can fill you in?"

"Who could resist an invitation like that?" Freddy asked. "What boy doesn't dream of being invited to dine with someone who's covered in crap?"

"This is New York, Freddy. Everyone's full of crap."

"Yeah," Freddy agreed. "But most of them have the good sense to keep it on the *inside,* darling."

"Okay . . ." Freddy began, scooping up some of the vanilla ice cream he'd ordered as "dessert" for his pound cake. Don't ask.

How Freddy managed to look like he did while chowing down like a starving dog at an all-you-can-eat buffet I'd never understand. Unless what I'd assumed were his biceps and pecs were really fat deposits. Naw, fat never felt that hard and strong. If he were an X-Man, his mutant ability would be to convert junk food into muscle.

I'd skipped dessert—let alone two—and watched him with envy and hatred.

". . . let's say we believe Lucas—that he never fooled around with his real-life brother."

"I *do* believe him," I insisted.

"Okay, Nancy Grace, calm down. I'm giving him that one. But hooking up with Brent because he *reminded* him of his brother is still kind of icky, don't you think?"

"Consider the circumstances," I said. "It's not like he spotted Brent in a bar somewhere and went out of his way to pick him up. The first time he ever saw him was in a pretty unusual situation that forced them together.

"Remember, at that time, he was at one of the lowest points of his life. He was depressed and feeling guilty about his brother's death. He was just getting into the adult film industry and experiencing the excitement of having people constantly telling him how gorgeous, special, and desirable he is. At the same time, he's doing something that goes against every value he's been taught by his conservative army parents. He'd cut off his family—the one he felt he betrayed by allowing his brother to go to Iraq 'in his place,' and he's becoming part of a new community—one that values him only to the extent he stays hot and available. It's all jumbled together in one big mindfuck.

"Meanwhile, he's keeping himself together by self-medicating. Taking every street and prescription pill he can get his hands on.

"One day, he arrives on set tweaked on meth, primed to perform with a hard-on-ensuring Viagra and mellowed out by a Valium chaser. That was pretty much his standard cocktail for filming. He walks into a room crowded with strangers for what he expects will be just another day of shooting. Pardon the pun. That was the dorm room scene we watched.

"There Lucas sees this breathtaking creature who could have been his brother back from the grave. The director introduces them, gives them a simple scenario to act out, and then it's time to fuck.

"Meanwhile, Brent reads Lucas pretty quickly. He doesn't know what Lucas's story is—not yet—but he can tell Lucas is awestruck, almost hypnotized in his presence. Brent, being SwordFight's hottest new property and the happy little narcissist he is, assumes Lucas is reacting to his attractiveness and star-status. He takes charge. He seduces the confused, overwhelmed, and somewhat stoned Lucas right there, on camera, before Lucas has a moment to sort out his feelings."

Knowing that background, the chemistry between the two of them, the impression Freddy and I had watching that scene that whatever was going on between them transcended mere sex, made a lot more sense.

"Are you saying Brent *raped* Lucas? Took advantage of him in some way?" Freddy asked.

"No, of course not. Lucas was a more-than-willing participant. Brent had no way of knowing Lucas was a mixed-up, overmedicated mess deep enough into drugs and depression to fall into a fantasy that confused his feelings toward his brother with Brent. Brent assumed Lucas's reactions were strictly sexual. It turned him on to think he had that kind of power over the big stud."

"It would turn me on, too," Freddy threw in.

"Shocker. In any case, after the scene was over, Lucas got more and more obsessed with Brent. He told me a part of him knew what he was thinking was insane, but another part of him couldn't shake the sense that, somehow, Brent was his salvation. Sent to him by God as a second chance with his brother. But this time, one he could rescue and protect.

"A Lost Boy he could save."

"That," Freddy observed, "is heavy."

"Kind of like your ass is going to be if you eat one more thing," I couldn't resist pointing out.

Freddy stuck his tongue out at me and then used it to lick his bowl of ice cream.

"Could you be any more disgusting?" I asked, wishing I didn't notice how long and flexible that tongue was. I wondered if the sexual tension between Freddy and I would ever totally die out, or if it'd always lurk in the background like a Peeping Tom outside his neighbor's window.

"Absolutely," Freddy promised. "Wanna see?"

"Yeah, no," I assured him. "Today's been depressing enough."

"What I don't understand," Freddy said, "is why Lucas didn't try and track Brent down? If he loved him so much."

"After Lucas left SwordFight, he went to work for lower-rent production companies. He also got into heavier drugs, reckless partying, a real downward spiral. He eventually wound up in rehab and got off all the shit he was putting into his system. He says he also got a lot of counseling and insight into his 'issues.'

"Brent heard through the grapevine about Lucas's troubles and that he'd entered treatment. He was sympathetic. He even felt partly responsible—after all, he was the one who complained to Mason about Lucas's 'stalking' of him.

"Brent wanted to leave SwordFight. I'm not clear why. But he felt the company had a legal hold on him. He was worried they'd sue his ass into oblivion if he didn't continue making movies.

"The only person he knew who'd left the company was Lucas. Having heard that Lucas cleaned up his act, Brent felt there was enough water under the bridge to call him for advice. That part didn't turn out to be too helpful. While Lucas had signed up with a competing production company behind Mason's back, Mason wasn't sorry to see him go. By that point, Lucas was looking strung out from his drug use and his behavior was increasingly bizarre. So, unless Brent was willing to either fake or actually *have* a breakdown, both of them doubted Mason would be as forgiving about his leaving.

"While that wasn't good news, as far as Lucas was concerned, the reunion was a success. Now that he was sober and had some insight into his behavior, he told Brent why he'd acted so weird when they first met. Brent was really touched. He was also relieved—he'd always found Lucas attractive. Now that he knew Lucas wasn't crazy, he felt a lot freer to act on it.

"So, they began an affair. Maybe even fell in love. Certainly, Lucas did. But a week before Brent dropped out of sight, he told Lucas he 'needed a break.' He felt bad seeing Lucas behind Charlie's back. He said he needed time to make a choice. But he couldn't do that *while* he was sleeping with Lucas—he was afraid the guilt he felt was sabotaging any chance they had for building a good relationship.

"Hmm," Freddy observed. "The old 'I have to stop seeing you so I can keep seeing you' line. I may have used that once or a hundred times when I wanted to dump someone."

"Really?" I asked.

"Well, maybe not that much. I mean, you know me. It's not like I ever did the 'dating thing.' More of a 'one night stand' kind of guy. Or, 'one nooner.' Or, 'that morning in a crowded subway car when the lights went out and—' "

"I get it, I get it," I said. We could have been there all night.

"Fine," Freddy said testily. "I'll skip over the hot-air balloon, the opening-night line for the last *Twilight* movie, and the various Jehovah's Witnesses and Mormon missionaries who showed up at my door thinking *they'd* convert *me*."

I circled my hand in the universal gesture for *Get on with it*.

"My point," Freddy said, well, pointedly, "is just because *I* knew I wasn't interested in anything serious didn't mean *they* knew that. So, one learns to be diplomatic, darling."

"Maybe you're right and Brent was trying to let Lucas down easy. But Lucas didn't think so. He thought Brent would choose him."

"Ah," Freddy said wistfully, "they always do, the dear things."

"He was beginning to lose faith, though. Before the 'time-out,' they were constantly in touch. Texting, on the phone. Brent's director, Kristen, told me he'd seen Brent on the set making private phone calls—turns out he was right. Kristen thought the calls were to another production company, though, not another lover.

"When Brent said he needed some space, Lucas assumed it'd be a week or three. As it stretched into months, he became increasingly worried. Not that anything had happened to Brent, mind you. More that maybe Brent hadn't chosen him after all."

"Why didn't Lucas just call him?"

"He promised not to. He'd already made the mistake of pursuing Brent too aggressively the first time around. He even thought Brent's not calling might be some kind of test."

"Lucas could have made the whole thing up," Freddy offered, raising his hand to call over the cute waiter. The dark-haired, dark-eyed Latino was taking an order at an adjacent table. The waiter held up his index finger. One moment.

"Maybe he never did get back together with Brent. It could have been another of his fantasies."

"No, I don't think so. Besides, Lucas knew something about Brent that I'd asked everyone and nobody could answer. Not even Charlie."

"What was that?"

"His *real* last name. *Richie's* last name. Dawson. He even had the phone number and address of Richie's parents in Queens. Look."

I took out from my backpack a picture of Brent's that Lucas had given to me. It showed Brent, a girl a few years older than him, and his parents at Disney World, the four of them smiling like every other family smiles when you point a camera at them in Disney World. Brent looked like he was nine or ten at the time.

On the back, Brent had written his parents' names and all their contact information. He also wrote a note:

> *Dear Mom and Dad,*
> *If you ever get this, know that I*
> *forgive you. I will always love you.*
> *Your son,*
> *Richie*

"Why would Brent have given this to Lucas? Why not just send it to them himself?"

"That part's weird. . . ." I began.

"Yeah," Freddy said. "Thank god the story's finally getting weird. Because the whole porn-star-hooked-on-drugs-and-sleeping-with-a-guy-who-just-happens-to-look-like-his-brother part was so wholesome I was getting bored." He glared at the waiter, who gave an apologetic shrug and repeated his earlier gesture.

"I'm about to give him a finger, too," Fred growled. "But a different one. Sorry, darling. You were saying . . ."

"Lucas said that for a few weeks before Brent's disappearance, Brent seemed distracted. Moody. A little worried. At one point, he told Lucas he had the feeling something—or someone—was after him."

The waiter came over. I got my first good look at him, and I suspected Freddy's motivation for beckoning him over may have gone beyond just wanting to place an order. The server really was kind of spectacular. He had the smoldering looks of an Argentinian soccer player you've never heard of who then winds up modeling for a Versace campaign and dating Miley Cyrus.

"I am sorry to have been detained," he said in a velvety Spanish accent. "How may I be of assistance?" His eye contact with Freddy promised a main course of polite attentiveness with a side order of flirty innuendo.

Little did he know subtlety wasn't on Freddy's menu.

"I hate to bother you," Freddy said. "But my friend thinks this is disgusting. What's your opinion?"

Freddy picked up his bowl and gave it another long, sensuous lick. It was a mortifyingly vulgar display that only he could pull off, and just barely at that. He finished with a final wipe around the rim with his finger, which he sucked into his mouth with the subtly of a voice mail from Mel Gibson.

"I think," the waiter said thoughtfully, taking out his order pad, "you should have this." He wrote ten digits followed by his name.

Freddy tucked the paper into his front pocket. "Bring me another bowl of this and I might call," he said.

"Right away, sir." He scurried off, with a more obvious wiggle to his butt than before.

"*Another?*" I asked incredulously.

"Waiter or dessert?" Freddy asked. "I'm not sure which indulgence you're objecting to."

"I'm talking about what you're going to eat."

"That doesn't narrow it down, honey."

I rolled my eyes and snorted.

"Lovely," Freddy observed. He reached into his pocket and handed me the waiter's number. "Here. Just in case you ever need to piss off Tony."

"You're not going to use it?"

"I have Cody," he said nonchalantly.

Wow. This from the guy who didn't do the "dating thing." I decided to let it pass. This might be a stage in Freddy's evolution that went better unrecognized. At least by him.

"So," Freddy said, "Brent had a bad feeling, huh? He wanted to give Lucas his parents' number in case something happened to him?"

"No," I said. "That's just it. Brent was almost completely estranged from his family. His father wasn't just antigay, he was rabidly homophobic. He kicked Brent out of the house when Brent was still a teen. They had no contact at all.

"A few weeks before he went missing, though, Brent got something in the mail that worried him. Someone sent him an article in the mail. Anonymously. It was clipped from a fundamentalist magazine Brent knew his parents subscribed to at home. It was about an extreme form of reparative therapy."

"Like, for a shoulder injury? 'Cause, if so, I'd like to see it. I was doing flies at the gym the other day and—"

"No, not that kind of therapy. This was for repairing homosexuality."

"Like, making it even *better?*"

"No, you nut, like making it go away."

"Oh," Freddy said. "Like that scam Harrington's son was running."

Freddy and I had come across a similar program when my friend was murdered.

"Kind of," I answered. "But that one, at least, was voluntary. Unethical, sure, but no one was *forced* into it. It was also kind of New Agey and based in psychology.

"The one sent to Brent was worse. It regarded homosexuality not as some kind of undesirable lifestyle but as a cult. It was a deprogramming program. The 'patients' are kidnapped. They're subjected to confinement, mind control, and mental abuse until they conform."

After Lucas told me about the letter Brent had gotten, he showed me some papers from Web sites he'd printed out about these kinds of programs. Deprogramming forces people to abandon their participation in a religious, political, or social group. Since the believer is unlikely to volunteer for this kind of change, deprogramming involves kidnapping and arm-twisting.

Often, deprogramming is arranged for and paid by relatives. Most typically, it's the parents of adult children who foot the bill. They claim they want to help their children, but where do you draw the line? Is it an act of love to take someone against his or her will? Are you saving your child, or is it just another way in which parents seek to control him or her?

On the other hand, some cults *are* dangerous and are manipulative themselves. They prey on the insecure and weak, exploiting their alienation by promising acceptance for allegiance.

It's a dull cliché, but you have to ask yourself: Do two wrongs make a right?

In this case, obviously not. Being gay is natural for some people—it's who we are. No one had to coerce me into liking dick. I had that one covered by myself.

Freddy looked appalled. "Is that even legal?"

"Not as far as I know. It's been challenged in the courts and hasn't fared well. But that doesn't stop some people from trying."

"So, did Brent ever figure out who sent him the article?"

"He figured it was his older sister. The father is very controlling, and he made it clear that no one is supposed to be in touch with Brent—he's exiled until he's willing to change. Anyone who breaks the dad's rules is subject to equal banishment."

"Nice guy," Freddy observed.

"Brent's older sister is the only one who dares to buck her father's edicts. Not too much—Christmas here, birthday call there. She didn't sign the article, but it was postmarked from her town. Brent figures it was her way of warning him without getting in trouble with their dad.

"Bottom line: Brent didn't want Lucas to call his parents if something happened to him. He wanted Lucas to call the police and tell them it was probably his parents who did it. And then he wanted Lucas to send them the picture."

Whether Brent's sentiment of love and forgiveness was sincere, or if he just wanted to make his parents feel remorse for what they'd done, I didn't know. Maybe a little of both.

Guilt: the gift that keeps on giving.

"Oh my god," Freddy said. "That's like, the worst thing ever. And I thought my parents were evil when they wouldn't buy me a pony for my fifteenth birthday."

"You still wanted a pony when you were fifteen?"

"Did I say 'pony'?" Freddy asked. "I meant to say 'subscription to *Playgirl.*' So, now that Lucas knows Brent's gone missing, did he call the cops and rat out Brent's folks?"

"No. Two days after Brent told Lucas about the letter, he told him not to worry about it. He no longer thought his parents would do that to him."

"What happened?"

"Brent never said."

"So, why doesn't Lucas call the cops anyway?"

"Like I said, Brent was sure his parents had abandoned the idea. But if they found out Brent heard they'd looked into it, they'd know the sister was the one who gave him the heads up. He loved her too much to get her into that kind of trouble."

The waiter came over with another dessert for Freddy.

"This one's on me," he purred.

"Maybe later, I really will put some *on* you." Freddy winked. "With some whipped cream, too."

The waiter walked away with a big grin.

"I thought you weren't going to call," I said.

"That doesn't mean I can't flirt," Freddy said. "He did give me free ice cream after all."

"That does look good," I couldn't help admitting. "Think I could score some, too?"

"That depends," he deadpanned. "What are you willing to do for it?"

"Ask nicely?"

Freddy handed me his spoon. "Dig in, baby."

"That's all it took?"

"After tonight's conversation, yeah. Life can be ugly, sometimes. Friendship's like me—it makes the world a little prettier."

33

Top Secret

The next day, I found out what wasn't pretty. Me. At least, me aged and uglied up via the expert application of latex and makeup by Steven Austen.

It was the day I'd been trying to avert but couldn't avoid. In two hours, my mother and I had an appointment at Families by Design, where we'd be posing as the world's worst candidates for adoptive parenthood.

Making me appear older involved adding heavy jowls, deep wrinkles, and an ashy complexion. Steve dulled my natural blondness to a mousy brown, then threw in some gray streaks for good measure.

In the mirror was an unflattering combination of myself, my father, the guy who played the father on *Happy Days* and Gollum from *Lord of the Rings*. It wasn't a good look for me.

Was it convincing? I wasn't sure.

"I couldn't go as heavy on the makeover as I would have if we were working on film," Steven explained. "The camera and lighting can be manipulated to hide a multitude of sins. But this is real life, and you're going to be meeting people face-to-face. So, I had to be more subtle with the appliance work."

"What do *you* think?" I asked Steven.

"I think . . ." Steven paused, searching for a tactful way to put it, "you look more like someone who'd be involved with your mother than you did before."

Which I took to mean that while Steven hadn't managed to

make me look quite as old as my mother, I was at least believable as prey for an energetic cougar.

Speaking of which . . .

"Darling," my mother cried, entering the room. Steven had done what he could with her earlier; now she was emerging from the rest of her makeover.

Steven had done a better job with my mother than he had with me, proving that subtraction is easier than addition. He'd used putty to fill in the lines in her face and a thick foundation to cover all but her deepest wrinkles. A pinker-than-usual tone in her makeup and thick false eyelashes made her look noticeably younger without being so obvious as to cross her over into drag queen territory.

Further enhancing the illusion was the new hairdo. The beautician had covered my mother's hair, which she always wore in her signature beehive, with a red wig shaped in a more youthful bob. It was a convincing, well-done job.

Lastly, the show's stylist, a young straight girl who'd been dying to make my mother look more contemporary since the show's first day, really went to town. She dressed my mother in a chic cream-colored Donna Karan jacket and matching skirt that was slimming and flattering. It wasn't obviously flashy or trying-too-hard, but it was somehow much hipper than my mother's usual matronly pantsuits. It also looked outrageously expensive, which was an impression we were shooting for.

The stylist accessorized my mother's neutral outfit with bold jewelry and a bright gold belt. They attracted attention without being overly ostentatious. It was a smart move, as anything that drew someone's eye away from our faces was bound to help.

One of the problems we had was making sure no one recognized my mother as the star of *Sophie's Voice*. Her image was getting pretty well known. While having someone—anyone—other than her pull off this sting would have made this easier, she insisted on doing it herself.

"They don't," she explained, "give Diane Sawyer an Emmy for someone *else's* investigation."

With her new makeup, hairstyle, and clothing, I had to admit my mother was probably suitably unrecognizable as the Long Island hausfrau hostess. We tried to get her to tone down her distinctive New Yawk manner of speaking, but no matter what we did, she sounded like Madonna after the pop star weirdly acquired an English accent. So, we let that pass.

As for me, I still didn't know what the hell I was doing there. For some reason, my mother had decided I'd be the perfect person to help her pull off this stunt, and whatever Mama wants, Mama gets. At one point, I pulled her aside to ask if she didn't think she'd be better off accompanied by a professional reporter (not to mention one closer to her age).

"Darling," she said, as if my insecurity were the problem, "I *believe* in you. Remember how you helped me that time with Dottie Kubacki?"

My mother was referring to a debacle of an incident where she'd talked me into spying on one of our neighbors she'd become convinced was having an affair with my father. That little stunt had left me with an almost broken tailbone and an equally painful memory of the suspected adulteress in her three hundred pounds of naked glory.

"Who could I possibly trust more than you, darling?" my mother asked. "You're always there for me."

My mother wasn't perfect. But she loved me unconditionally, and that counted for a lot. Plus, she never arranged to have me kidnapped and brainwashed into being straight. You had to add points for that, too.

Sure, she was high maintenance. But most worthwhile things are.

I let myself enjoy what I was pretty sure were likely to be the last nice thoughts I had for her today.

At least I didn't have to worry about my accent—with my mother in the room, I rarely got a word in edgewise. Today, that'd work to my advantage.

My mother gave Steven a hug. "You're a genius, darling. He looks awful."

She grabbed me by the arm. "Get up, old man." She dragged us to a full-length mirror mounted on the wall.

I was already in my costume for the day. A conservative Hugo Boss suit with a red power tie. They had it specially tailored to accommodate the padding they strapped to my belly and shoulders, making me look bulkier and out-of-shape. They also had me in elevator shoes, bringing me to a more respectable height of five feet six, an inch taller than my mother.

"Just look at us!" my mother exclaimed. "Don't we make a gorgeous couple?"

I wouldn't go that far. Nor did I quite get the whole reverse-Oedipal vibe. But, yeah, we did look close enough in age and style that we could pass as something other than mother and son.

At some point, Andrew must have come into the room, because he was the one who answered.

"You know," he said, and I could hear he was being sincere, "I think this could work."

"Of course it's going to work!" my mother assured him. "We're going to be the Jewish Woodward and Bernstein by the time this is done."

I was pretty sure Woodward and Bernstein were the Jewish Woodward and Bernstein. At least, Bernstein must have been. I wasn't sure about Woodward.

My mother gave us one last look in the mirror, squeezed my hand, and grabbed her stylist. "I think," she said, "we'd better go find me a purse. The right purse will be key." They hurried out of the room.

Andrew took her place by my side. Seeing that everyone had pretty much fled the room as soon as they could, he leaned over and whispered hotly into my ear.

"Wanna know how good that Steven is? I can honestly say if I were meeting you for the first time, looking as you do now, I would not, at this moment, want to fuck you."

"Gee," I gushed. "That's the nicest thing you've ever said to me."

"Of course, knowing that's you under all that, I'm kind of turned on in a perverse way. It'd be like making it with you and not making it with you, all at the same time."

"Well, you're going to have to keep that nauseating three-way as a fantasy," I said. "Mustn't smear my makeup and all that."

We reviewed our plan on the ride over to Families by Design. We were in our tricked-out video van, full of equipment rented by our tech guru, Laurent. From this command center, they'd be monitoring and taping every moment of our interview. My mother had a video camera concealed in her brooch and a backup in the temple of the stylishly thick eyeglasses she wore, which she didn't need, but which further altered her appearance.

I was also wired, with my camera hidden in my tiepin.

The small devices wouldn't record more than grainy, heavily pixilated images, but that was adequate for the job. It would give the footage a realistic spy-cam quality. And while it was hard to get good video from this kind of equipment, the sound would be clear and capture everything that was said. That was its most important role in gathering the material we'd need to prove if Families by Design was, in fact, unforgivably lax in assessing its potential parents.

"Now, remember," my mother said to me, "you must turn and look at me frequently. Not just your head, darling, your whole body."

"If we're there adopting a child together," I said, "I assume they'll believe we're a couple. I don't think it's necessary for me to constantly gaze adoringly at you. Wouldn't want to overdo it."

"It's not that, darling. It's just that the cameras I'm wearing aren't going to capture *me*. I need you to get my reaction shots with that clever little one you've got on."

Not for the first time, I concluded that my mother's greatest talent was to make and keep herself the center of attention.

Andrew handed us fake IDs and made us run through our cover story again. He'd already had the production staff prepare the false documents and applications we used to set up the appointment. The most important part of our deception was establishing me as a wealthy investor whose start-up funds helped build three of the five most popular online social networks, making me very rich, indeed.

I'd had input into the planning of our fake identities. What no one knew was that the character I was playing was based on a real customer of mine back in the days I was hustling. Not only was my client fabulously wealthy and a brilliant venture capitalist, but he was also a motormouth. I'd learned enough from him that, if I had to, I could speak believably about how I'd made my fortune through the art and science of angel investing.

Our assumed names were Murray Goldsberry and Zorah Heffelbergen. We decided to pose as an unmarried couple to create the first of many considerations any reasonable adoption agency would want to ask about. Not that unmarried people couldn't adopt, mind you, but it was a point of information worth exploring in a culture where married couples enjoyed certain rights and responsibilities that would affect a child's well-being. But, trust me, being uninterested in tying the knot was the least of the Goldberry/Heffelbergens' problems.

I couldn't wait to see what the folks at Families by Design would make of the others.

34

Covert Missions

"Our goal," the alarmingly well-manicured and groomed owner and chief operating officer of Families by Design, Amanda Peterson, said smiling, waving her arms at us like a spokesmodel demonstrating a particularly valuable prize on *The Price Is Right,* "is to help you build the family of your dreams."

So far, Ms. Peterson said everything with a smile. From "How nice to meet you," to "Can I get you something to drink?" to "So tell me, how did you hear about Families by Design?" was delivered with a Zenlike joyfulness. I wished I had a vest full of explosives so I could open my jacket to see if she announced a bomb scare with that same accommodating merriment.

An attractive, well-poised woman with impeccable diction, Ms. Peterson was probably somewhere in her late forties, although with the right skin care routine and a good surgeon, she may well have been a good deal older. Her skin was tightly stretched against her face, which, like the rest of her, was too thin by half. For all her outward graciousness, you got the sense this was a woman willing to starve herself, or anyone else, for that matter, to get what she wanted.

As generous as she was with her smiles, they never quite reached past her cheeks. It gave them a robotic unnaturalness. The top half of her face was either immobilized by Botox or disinterest; it was too soon to tell.

Her office, like the entire suite, was lavishly decorated in soothing pastels. Mary Cassatt prints of rosy-cheeked mothers and daughters called to the ladies, while Norman Rockwell scenes of fathers and sons playing baseball and reading with their children were hung to bring tears to the eyes of prospective dads. Ms. Peterson sat behind a glass table with no drawers or file cabinets. A sleek silver MacBook Air and our file were the only items on her desk. On a credenza behind her, a tall, single white lotus, in full bloom, arched delicately from a silver bud vase. I remembered reading somewhere that many considered the lotus a symbol of fertility, and I wondered if it was there to inspire or depress.

"Tell me"—Ms. Peterson smiled—"why do you want to adopt?"

"I've always wanted kids," my mother said. The voice that came out of her was a new one. Half New York yenta, half British nanny. She sounded like a character invented by a bad actress in a *Saturday Night Live* skit that would never be heard from again. She threw me an accusatory glance. "But my old man over there only shoots blanks."

She leaned in to give Ms. Peterson a conspiratorial wink. "When he even makes it past the starting flag, that is. Usually, One Minute Murray finishes before he even *enters* the race, if you know what I mean."

If Ms. Peterson ever had nightmares of the kind of woman with whom she'd never want to be in a room, my guess is they featured someone very much like my mother. "I see," she said, the smile still there but trembling.

"Personally," my mother said, "I take it as a compliment. When they finish before they even begin? That's how you know a guy's really into you." She paused for a moment. "If not, literally, *into* you, pardon the pun."

I wondered if it were true that certain ninja masters and Hindu fakirs could, when required, turn themselves invisible. If so, it was a skill I'd have paid anything for at the moment.

Ms. Peterson smiled. "You two have been together long, then?"

I was sure that question had been answered in our application. I wondered if Ms. Peterson was trying to trip us up, or if she hadn't bothered to read it.

"Forever!" my mother exclaimed. She glanced over at me. "Almost eight months, right, honey?"

"Urgh," I answered. Maybe if I appeared incoherent, they'd leave me out of it.

"Eight months?" Ms. Peterson's grin, for one quick moment, fell. "And you're ready for a child?"

"Ready?" my mother asked. "*More* than ready! When you meet the right man, the one you love, the one you want to spend the rest of your life with, the one you know is too smart to marry you without a prenup, which you wouldn't sign with a gun to your head but who you know would never not provide for his beloved child, even if it is just adopted, you know it, don't you, Amy, darling?"

Of all the objectionable, tasteless things my mother had just said, I think calling Ms. Peterson "Amy" was the one that bothered her the most. The smile stayed frozen but the eyes narrowed. I sat forward in my seat, looking forward to being kicked out of there.

"Ah," Ms. Peterson began, "love. To hear you speak of 'love' warms my heart, Ms."—she glanced at the file on her desk—"Heffelbergen?" She said the name as if she couldn't believe it, then quickly recovered. "Isn't that what a family's about? Love? Where there is love, there is life. That's what I always say."

My mother nodded. "But let's face it, Amy. You don't mind if I call you that, do you?"

I was sure my mother noticed how much she did.

"Of course not," said the grinning skeleton across from us.

"I'm not getting any younger. And I hear that these adoptions can take months. Years even. I don't have that kind of time, Amy. When you have a big bass floating near your fishing boat," she darted her eyes at me, "you don't want to waste too much time baiting the hook. You want to reel that sucker in before some other, younger, prettier boat comes along, if you catch my drift." She winked conspiratorially.

"Well." Ms. Peterson smiled, tapping her perfectly rounded nails against the smooth glass of her desk. The clinking noise sounded like coins falling. Pennies from heaven. "These things can take time. There are many, many families looking to adopt. Do you have any conditions? Anything special you're looking for in a child?"

"Oh, no," my mother said. "We'd be happy with any baby, wouldn't we, darling?"

"Rgghtd," I said.

"As long as he's white and healthy, we're fine." My mother continued. "And he should come from good stock. I don't want to be raising some hillbilly trash conceived at the drive-in. I'd like him—oh yes, I'm looking for a boy, thank you—I'd like him to resemble us as much as possible, of course. More me, but that's only because looks are so important, and why not give him every possible advantage in life, no? So, I'd say healthy, white, athletic, good-looking, with birth parents who have at least a college degree. If you could make him tall, that would be great. And, oh yes, green eyes. I love green eyes! Blue in a pinch, though, if supplies are limited."

You'd have thought she was ordering from a catalog.

To me: "Am I forgetting anything?"

I turned toward her, remembering to get at least one shot of her with my camera tie. "Flrkk," I said. "Nrffing."

Ms. Peterson nodded. "I don't see why we can't make that happen." If she had any objection to my mother's list, she didn't betray it. Nor did she seem the least unconfident in her ability to determine, at birth, if a child would grow to be athletic, tall, or handsome.

"But," she said, resuming her fingernail drumbeat, "it is a . . . oh, I hate to make it sound like this . . . a competitive market out there. There are many, many loving couples such as yourself who are looking for the kind of child you describe. You have to find a way to make yourself stand out."

"Anything," my mother said. "My Murray here has been very successful. He's what you call a real 'on top of newer' businessman."

Ms. Peterson looked at me to elaborate. I was pretty sure my mother had been going for "entrepreneur," but I was hardly going to start being helpful now. "Untrependerenter," I said, with great certainty. "Intervestingstan."

Ms. Peterson's eyes stayed on me for another second before blinking twice, rapidly, like an iguana's. Afraid I may have lost her, I slightly more clearly added, "Ova three hundred milzions. Fuzzbok. Twizter. Goggle."

That seemed to ease her mind.

"Now, I can't tell you what to do," Ms. Peterson said playfully, her lilting tone at war with her pulled-back skin, perfect posture, and insincere expression, "but what we like to do here at Families by Design is put you directly in touch with the birth mothers. Through us, of course. You never actually talk to her. In fact, any direct contact is expressly forbidden."

And thus, "directly in touch" took on a whole new meaning.

"On your behalf, we handle all the . . . negotiations. Now, the rules about this kind of thing are very strict. You cannot, under any circumstances, be perceived as trying to 'buy a baby.' " For the first time, Ms. Peterson dropped her smile and looked serious. "That would cause me to lose my license and you to lose your baby. That must never happen. Are we clear on that?"

In the space of a moment, Ms. Peterson had gone from benevolent builder of loving families to mafia hitwoman.

"Who said anything about buying a baby?" my mother asked. "But surely there's some way to . . . reward the mothers, yes?"

Ms. Peterson's smile returned. "I see you're every bit as clever as I thought," she beamed. "Yes, according to state law, all you can do is provide basic support to the birth mother during and immediately following her pregnancy.

"But who's to say what's basic?" she continued. "For some women, 'basic' is a tenement apartment in the South Bronx. Those women require very little support to maintain the lifestyle. Of course, we all know what kind of babies *they* produce."

"What?" my mother asked in a hushed and frightened whisper.

Ms. Peterson answered with cautious alarm, as if the very utterance of the next two words risked raising demons in our midst. *"Puerto. Ricans."*

My mother slapped her hand over her mouth and widened her eyes in mock horror. "No," she gasped, "that would never do."

For the first time, Ms. Peterson's smile appeared sincere. Not friendly or warm, mind you, but sincere. The wide toothy smirk of a shark smelling chum in the water. She moved in for the kill.

"But the kind of woman you're looking for is accustomed to a finer lifestyle. Park Avenue. Maternity clothing from Neiman Marcus. During her pregnancy, she'll require pampering and services to ensure the healthiest baby possible. Massages, spa treatments, nutritional counseling. I'm afraid the costs can be . . . considerable.

"We keep track of everything, though," Ms. Peterson said. "Every dollar passes through us so we can make sure they're spent responsibly. Naturally, for your protection, we retain fifteen percent of the costs you reimburse to the birth mother to ensure proper bookkeeping and accountability."

I bet. Fifteen percent off the top of what I'd expect would be thousands of dollars a week. Not to mention how easy it would be to fake receipts for services never received.

"Nothing," my mother said, her voice heavy with emotion, "is too good for my little boy. Whatever it takes, we can afford it. Right, Murray?"

"Yarghh."

The sawtoothed shark grin broadened. "Then, there are our fees." She reached into our file and withdrew two glossy single-page brochures. She handed one to each of us.

A required Home Study cost $20,000 (I knew from the experiences of friends that they were usually in the $1,500 range). Three mandatory counseling sessions at $1,500 each. Preparation of the Family Profile (a file which is shown to prospective birth mothers) was $25,000 (a service offered free by some agencies; others encourage prospective parents to develop their own). Unspecified processing and administrative fees totaled another $50K.

"This is all so reasonable!" my mother enthused. "If, that is, you can promise us a kid real quick. I can't wait to be a mother! I'm thinking a couple of months." My mother's voice dropped to what I'd always think of as her "pick-up-your-clothes-or-else" tone. *"Tops."*

"We guarantee placement within a year." Ms. Peterson was serene.

My mother picked her purse off the floor and placed it in her lap. "That's not good enough, Amy. You hear that ticking? It's not my biological clock, just the regular one. Always running. Remember what I said before? Fish? Bait? This isn't the time to dawdle, darling."

Ms. Peterson placed her hands faced flat against the table, a poker player about to show a winning hand. "We do offer an . . . expedited process. For the small group of birth mothers who won't be satisfied with anything but the best. They require an even higher level of service." She spun her Aeron Chair around and withdrew two new forms from the top drawer. These were simpler menus of services. Black type on white paper. The agency's name didn't appear on them.

As for the prices, just double what I described earlier. Except for the "processing and administrative forms," which skyrocketed from $50,000 to $250,000.

My mother noticed the same thing. "Listen," she said, "I get it. If I want my dry cleaning back on the same day, it costs an extra buck fifty. I don't see why a baby would be any different. But an extra $200,000 for *paperwork?* What, you go through extra secretaries because they keep breaking their fingers trying to type that fast?"

A patronizing smile this time. "I wish it were that simple. The sad truth is, not everyone is as committed to building happy, healthy families as we are. There are government agencies—faceless bureaucracies, really—whose sole purpose is to interfere in your private affairs. The only way they can maintain their existence is by making things more complicated and intrusive than they need to be. They live to slow things done, erect hurdles, and delay, delay, delay. They say they want to protect the children, but"—she sighed and turned her palms up as if toward God—"all they really want to protect are their jobs.

"Those extra fees help us . . . grease the wheels, if you will. Keep things moving."

My mother looked at her blankly. "Huh?"

"You know." Ms. Peterson arched an eyebrow. "That money . . . incentivizes those state employees not to look so deeply at everything. To accelerate the approval process."

"In what way?" my mother asked.

Ms. Peterson looked frustrated. I knew how she felt. Surely, my mother knew what Ms. Peterson was implying.

Then, I understood. My mother knew *exactly* what Ms. Peterson was implying. What she was trying to do was to get Ms. Peterson to come out and say it. On tape.

Everything Ms. Peterson had done so far was open to interpretation. Sure, she seemed to indulge a lot of my mother's objectionable comments, but she could always later claim that she was just being polite to avoid a confrontation. She could make a credible case that she was merely indulging a crazy woman so she could get her out of her office.

She might even be able to defend her exorbitant costs and Park Avenue birth mothers.

But my mother wasn't as clueless as she seemed. This was her opportunity to get Ms. Peterson to admit to an undeniably illegal act. On tape.

I turned my body to face my mother, aiming my tiepin straight at her. If she could pull this off, she deserved to be captured on video.

Ms. Peterson looked at my mother's mask of confusion, then at my even blanker expression. You could see her thinking *Do I have to spell it out for these idiots?* Every day, she met with couples of considerable wealth who came to her knowing her agency's reputation. They were sophisticated people who knew how to read between the lines. What was wrong with us?

She opened her mouth to say something, then closed it again. "Ms. . . ." Another look at the file. "Heffelbergen. I don't know how to say it clearer. . . ."

"Well, then, I suppose we're done," my mother surprised me by saying. She stood up abruptly. "We're not stupid, Amy. My Murray is a very rich man. He didn't get that way because he's a dummy, did you, darling?"

"Glrff," I replied.

"See? I am not a cheap woman. But if someone wants to sell me something, I expect them to have the decency to tell me what my money is buying." She put the second form Ms. Peterson had given us on her desk, jabbing at the "processing and administrative" line with an angry finger.

"Otherwise, I assume they're ripping me off. Especially if it's two hundred and fifty thousand dollars, Amy. I think I have the right to know where my quarter million is going."

She put her hands on Ms. Peterson's desk and leaned forward, her face inches from the rapidly flushing adoption director's. "I don't think you can blame me for expecting a straight answer."

Ms. Peterson's face was blazing. I suspected the last time she was that red was after her last chemical peel. Her eyes drew together like a snake's about to strike.

"The money goes to the state agencies. To the people whose approval we need—*you* need—to get you your baby. It takes that kind of money to get their stamp of approval with no questions asked."

"Oh, I see!" My mother smiled and sat back down. Ms. Peterson's shoulders relaxed. The heat started to drain from her cheeks.

"So," my mother summarized, "you're saying I need to make a contribution to the agency. Like to a charity. Why didn't you say that in the first place? *That* I understand. I have no problem with that at all. But, why don't I just make it directly so that it's tax-deductible?"

My mother smiled serenely and reached into her purse, extracting a checkbook. "Now, should I just make it out to the New York State Adoption Services, or does it go by another name?"

Ms. Peterson's right eye began to twitch as the left side of her lip slid downward. I wondered if she was about to have a stroke. She once again assumed the scarlet coloring of a freshly steamed lobster.

"No, you . . . you." I could see how much she wanted to insult my mother, but the sight of that checkbook, and my mother's willingness to write a $250,000 check with not a moment's hesitation, made her hold her tongue. She had to be thinking that if she could string her along a little longer, she could probably make a fortune off this silly, careless spender.

Ms. Peterson drew in a deep breath. "The money doesn't exactly go to the agency, Ms. . . ." She didn't bother looking up the name again and just let her voice trail off. "The money goes directly to the official whose signature we need."

"Well, what's his name, then?" my mother asked cheerily, pen in hand.

"We don't give him a check, dear. There can be no trail. It's all . . . off the record."

"Like a . . ."

"Yes!" Ms. Peterson said.

"What's that word?"

"It doesn't matter."

"Murray." My mother turned to me. "What is she trying to say, dear?"

"Klurm?"

"No, that's not it."

"The word doesn't matter, dear." Ms. Peterson's left eye began to twitch in counterpoint with her right, as if they were taking turns winking. "Let's just focus on the results, shall we?"

"It's on the tip of my tongue," my mother said, pretending to be oblivious. "It's a . . . oh, dear, this is going to keep me up all night." My mother bit her lip as if deep in thought. "I give you the two hundred and fifty thousand, and you give it to the person whose signature you need as a . . . bait? Bail? No, that's not it. It's a—"

"It's a bribe!" Ms. Peterson shouted. I ducked, thinking there was a real possibility her head might explode right then and there. "We pay him to stamp your application as approved and get you your goddamn baby. How else do you think a woman like you would be able to adopt? You, or . . . mumble-mouth over there." Rather rudely, she jabbed her finger toward me.

I nodded back, but in a friendly acknowledgment. My obliviousness seemed to upset her even more.

"And in exchange for a quarter million in cold, hard cash," she continued to rant, her voice getting louder and higher-pitched with each clipped word, "he looks the other way and ignores *everything* about you that makes you an unsuitable parent. Although, in your case, we might have to double his payment, as he'd not only have to close his eyes but hold his nose and plug his ears, too." Her entire body shuddered with release, like she was having a particularly strong orgasm.

She was obviously the kind of woman who kept her feelings bottled up. It probably *was* quite gratifying for her to let loose like this. Maybe this experience would do her some good.

"Well," my mother said, standing up again. "I think we're done here. Kevin, let's get out of here."

"Kevin?" Ms. Peterson asked. "Who's Kevin?"

"As for you," my mother said to the director, "any person who would place a child with a woman as obviously unsuitable as I am, is a real piece of, pardon the expression, shit. You already have the blood of at least one little boy on your hands. Tell me, Ms. Fancypants, with your pretty little office and your pretty little pictures on the walls, how does someone like you live with yourself?"

"I-I-I don't know what you're talking about," Ms. Peterson stuttered, rising to stand. She crossed her arms over her flat chest, straightening up to her full height. She remembered who she was—an accomplished businesswoman of good breeding. Whereas the woman challenging her had the class and style of a low-rent streetwalker. "And who are *you* to talk to *me* like that?"

"I'm certainly not Zorah Heffelbergen, you tight-assed, stuck-up baby-seller. Had you done even the slightest bit of due diligence before jumping at the chance to earn a few sheckles by placing an innocent baby into my arms, you'd have discovered

Zorah Heffelbergen doesn't even exist. I'm the woman who's going to expose you to the world as the disgusting pimp you are."

Ms. Peterson lost a bit of her rediscovered confidence and took a step backward. My mother moved in for the kill.

"I'm the ghost of Adam Merr. And I'm going to haunt your ass until you're out of business."

"Adam Merr," Ms. Peterson said, her voice shaking, "isn't dead. Yes, what happened to him was . . . unfortunate. But it wasn't my fault. I'm sure he'll be fine. These things happen. I've devoted my life to helping children find their way to the best possible parents they could have: the select few who can afford our services. The children we place will be raised by families of wealth and privilege. They'll have every advantage in life."

"I suppose it's possible," my mother said, "you're as stupid as you are greedy. That you actually believe a child needs money more than he needs love. Or proper guidance. Or a safe home. Maybe you really are so shallow that it doesn't trouble you that even a *cursory* background check would have revealed the father you placed Adam with had two prior arrests for child endangerment.

"Not to mention that had you done even *one* of the quarterly post-placement home visits your rate list requires, at fifteen hundred dollars a piece, mind you, you might have noticed that *the boy was living in a cage.*"

"Those visits"—Ms. Peterson collapsed into her chair—"can be done by phone."

Thus giving new definition to the term "home visit."

"Yeah," my mother said, "bet you still charge the whole fifteen hundred, though, don't you? Because that would be the most important thing."

Ms. Peterson's eyes glazed over like those of a dying woman watching her life flash before her.

"No," my mother said, "Adam Merr isn't dead. But parts of him were killed. His childhood. His innocence. Maybe any chance he'll ever have to love and be loved, to trust another person, to enjoy a normal life.

"And, you know what, Amy? When I bring what you just admitted to me about bribing state officials to the district attorney's office, and they start looking into your little operation here, I have a feeling that Adam isn't the only child they'll find you've put into an house of horrors to suffer a life of abuse and neglect. I think there's a reason people like the Merrs are willing to pay hundreds of thousands of dollars to get a child with 'no questions asked.'

"When the answers come, I pray to God they're not as bad as I fear they might be.

"Enjoy this pretty office while you can, Amy. Enjoy your pretty home and your pretty clothing and your pretty little bank account, too.

"Because they all came at a price that I'm not sure a woman like you will ever understand. A price paid by innocent babies. A debt you can never repay."

Ms. Peterson burst into sobs.

My mother turned her back and walked away.

At the door, she turned for one last jab. "If I thought even *one* of those tears was for the children," she said, "I might be feeling a little sorry for you right now. As it is, I'm going to enjoy taking you down."

Ms. Peterson raised her tear-streaked face. "Who are you?" she asked again.

"Who am I?" my mother asked. "I'm your worst nightmare. A loudmouth Jewish mother with her own talk show and a burning hatred for anyone who would hurt a child.

"I'm *Sophie,* you despicable bitch.

"Stay tuned."

35

Busted

We entered the van to cheers and applause. Except from Roni, the segment producer, who was weeping. She threw her arms around my mother.

"You did it," she cried. "You got her. That horrible, horrible woman. What she allowed to happen to those children . . ." She couldn't get out any more words.

"That was brilliant," Andrew said. "Getting her to confess to bribery like that. That has to be the final nail in her coffin."

Steven the makeup genius kissed my mother on the cheek. "I knew we were making a *show* today," he said, "but now I see we'll be making a *difference*. You done good, boss."

I stood back, letting the other staffers have their chance.

A fact not unnoticed by the diva herself.

"My own son?" my mother asked. "Nothing to say?"

"What do you think?" I asked. "You did great. You know that. I'm proud of you."

My mother raised a hand and waved me over. "Come here."

I stood to give her a hug but she stopped me. She looked at my face, licked her thumb, and started wiping off my makeup while she talked.

I remembered her doing that when I was kid. Cleaning me with her spittle like that, although generally with a handkerchief or tissue. "That's gross," I'd cry, trying to squirm away.

"You have a little *schmutz* there," she'd say. "Stand still."

"You're rubbing your *spit* into me. That's disgusting."

"A mother's spit isn't disgusting," she'd instruct me. "A mother's spit is love. *Everything* that comes from me to you is love."

She never convinced me of that when I was growing up. Now, I wondered if there was more to it than I knew.

"You asked me why I wanted you there today, baby. You want to know the real reason?"

"Sure."

"Because I was scared. What business do I have being an 'investigative reporter'? What do I know about interviewing someone 'the right way,' to ask the kinds of questions I needed to ask? I was afraid I'd blow it. What the hell qualified me to go in there like that?

"I didn't have what I needed here." She tapped her temple. "I had it here."

She put a hand on her chest. "The instincts of a mother. All I had to do was imagine what I'd do if anyone ever hurt you like they hurt Adam Merr. I knew if I could keep that in mind, the words would come to me. That's why I needed you there. To remind my heart what it needed to say."

Wow.

"Whatever you did, it worked. You nailed her, Mom. You probably saved some kids while you were at it. You even made for some Must-Watch TV. I think you might get that Emmy after all."

I thought I'd seen every expression my mother's face was capable of displaying. But the one she wore now—love, pride, and accomplishment, without the slightest trace of self-consciousness—was new to me.

My mother was always "on." I couldn't remember a time she wasn't calculating how she looked or came across to others.

But not now. Not in this *one* particular moment. She was just *there*. Herself, unguarded, open. In this single instance of selflessness, something shone from her, a light that warmed me even before she pulled me into her arms for an embrace so sincere, so loving, that it felt like I was being hugged for the first time in my life.

"*Bubeleh,*" she whispered in my ear. "Emmy, schmemmy. Who needs an Emmy?"

It was after nine and Tony still wasn't home. I missed him.

Between my amateur sleuthing and his legitimate investigating, I felt like we never saw each other.

I missed him.

It'd been a strange couple of days. Brent. Lucas. Adam. Even Rafi.

All these Lost Boys.

Okay, maybe not all of them were lost. There was still some hope for the first two. People can change. They can be saved or they can save themselves.

But what about the little ones? If the grown-ups in their lives couldn't pull their acts together, what hope did the kids have?

For that matter, Brent and Lucas had been kids at one point, too. Thinking about it, they hadn't been lost as much as thrown away. Rejected by families that hadn't deemed them fit.

My mother's hug earlier today came back to me as a sense memory.

Would anyone hold Adam and Rafi like that?

Would it make a difference?

I love kids. I do. But when I'm with Rafi, there's a part of me that's always holding back. Things are too unsure between me and his father for me to allow myself to get too attached. I don't want him to get hurt, either.

I thought I was being smart. Now, I wasn't so sure. The more time I spent around these Lost Boys, or thinking about them, the more convinced I became that, whatever their problems were, being loved too much wasn't one of them.

Which brought me back to Tony. In his way, he was another Lost Boy. But he wasn't a throwaway—he'd gotten lost by himself when he decided to hide his true self and couldn't find his way back.

I didn't want to hide and I didn't want to be thrown away.

I didn't want to feel like I had to hold back on my affections. As if love were something toxic or rare that needed containment or rationing.

I didn't ever want to be afraid to give someone that hug, the once-in-a-lifetime hug that changes everything.

I didn't want to be a Lost Boy.

And I didn't want to lose any of the ones around me, either.

I'd find Brent.

I'd help Lucas.

I'd convince Tony to come out. I'd give Rafi the unconditional love he deserved.

If it was too late for Adam, who I didn't even know, at least I'd helped expose the people who put him in harm's way. They'd never hurt another child again.

And then I'd . . . cure cancer. End AIDS. Stop global warming, and, uh, invent a really good dessert that doesn't make you fat.

Ugh.

Megalomaniac much?

It was crazy. I couldn't save everyone.

But maybe one?

It started with Brent.

Maybe if I just concentrated on him.

Focus, Kevin, focus.

Think.

What did I know?

Maybe a visual aid.

I went into my bedroom and found an old copy of the *Advocate*. Sure enough, there on the back cover was a full-page shot of Brent's smiling face and bare chest, in an ad for SwordFight Productions.

Hi, Brent. It's me, Kevin. Where are you? What are you up to? Who are you, really?

"That's him!"

The answer came to me.

Wait.

What?

That wasn't coming from my head.

I *heard* that.

There was someone behind me. He put his hands around my neck.

36

Body Search

Tony leaned in and kissed my forehead as he kneaded my tense neck and shoulders. "Hey, babe, how did you find him?"

"Find who?"

"Him. That one on the magazine. I've been trying to put a name to that face for two days now."

"Really?"

"Yeah. I thought you were . . . wait a minute, how could you have known . . . ?" Tony grabbed the magazine, rolled it up, and tucked it under his arm. Then he stood up, took me by the hand, and guided me to the couch. He pulled me onto his lap. "What have you gotten yourself into this time, Kevvy?"

Tony's lap was usually my happy place. Not tonight. Tony didn't like it when I played Boy Detective. Some silly objection to my almost getting myself killed a couple of times.

"I don't know what you're talking about."

"Kevin . . ."

"Let me preface this," I announced, "by pointing out that whatever I've 'gotten myself into' is a good thing." The wrath of an angry Tony was no fun. Especially when he was kind of right.

"I mean, this helps you now, right? I've been looking for Brent, too. So, it's like a, uh, happy coincidence. The best kind. I know *who* he is, and you know *where* he is. Now, we put the name with the face and case solved! You get to talk to him about whatever you need him for, and I get to find out why he disappeared off the face of the earth."

Tony wasn't smiling. Stupidly, I reached the belated realization that if Tony was looking for Brent, it probably meant Brent was in trouble. Or was involved with someone who was. Which might explain why he'd run.

Tony pulled me closer against his chest, resting a hand over my heart. "How well did you know this kid, Kevvy? Was he a close friend?"

"No, not really. He was a guest on the show. When I tried to call to follow up with him, I found out no one had seen him for weeks. I've been curious."

"Babe." Tony held me closer still. He picked up the copy of the *Advocate* that he'd put next to him and pointed at the picture of Brent. "This kid's in the morgue. He's my floater."

I'd gotten increasingly nervous as Tony's tone grew more serious. Now, I let out a sigh of relief.

"No he isn't," I said. I was glad I remembered the details of the case Tony'd shared with me. "You told me the body you found was of a Hispanic guy in his thirties. Brent's in his early twenties, and he's whiter than Wonder Bread."

Tony's voice was one I hadn't heard before. It had a forced calmness to it, a practiced sympathy. I realized it was probably a manner he affected on the job, when he had to give bad news to family members.

"That was the *first* body we found. Three nights later, I got another call, remember? A second body. If we hadn't been down there looking for clues related to the first case, we probably wouldn't have found him for months.

"As it was, we were able to do a pretty accurate facial reconstruction." He tapped the magazine. "It's a match, honey. Believe me, I know. When I saw that first sketch-up, for one terrible moment, I thought it was you. It was crazy—I'd just left you here that morning, so I knew it couldn't *be* you. But the resemblance is so strong. . . ."

"I've heard that before," I said mechanically, part of me still thinking—hoping—he'd made a mistake.

"I saw that picture and thought if something like that ever happened to you . . ." His voice cracked.

We were quiet for a few moments. I was trying to think of something I could say that would prove Tony wrong. Brent couldn't be dead. Could he?

I put my hand over Tony's. "Nothing's going to happen to me."

"It'd better not." Tony ruffled my hair, trying to lighten the mood.

"Are you *sure* the body is Brent's?" I asked. I thought of Lucas's brother. "Apparently, there are a lot more guys who look like me than I knew."

Tony nodded back toward the shirtless image of Brent on the magazine. "That tattoo on his shoulder? Our victim has the same one. And matching ones—"

"Around his ankle." I finished his sentence. I remembered them from the videos Freddy and I had watched.

Tony nodded his agreement, and then froze. "Hey, just how well did you know this guy?"

"I watched a few of his videos." Tony stiffened behind me. Not in the good way.

"What, I'm not enough for you?"

"Research, Tony. For the show."

"Sure, sure."

"So," I asked him, "what happened to Brent? How did he wind up in the river?"

"We don't know. It could have been accidental. Blood tests showed high levels of Ecstasy, Valium, and Viagra. There's some cutting and bruising, but nothing inconsistent with falling into a river and scraping along the bottom. Maybe he was partying and took a tumble on his way home?"

"He wasn't that kind of person."

"He *was* a porn actor, Kevvy."

"So? That doesn't mean he was a drug-abusing sex addict."

"It doesn't make him a model citizen, either."

This wouldn't be the first time we fought about the moral implications of working in the sex industry. Since I was still earning my living as an escort when Tony and I reunited, it wasn't a theoretical discussion, either. Nor was it one I was in the mood to have again tonight.

"Let's talk about something else," I said.

"Probably a good idea," Tony agreed. He scooted me off his lap and pulled a slim reporter's notebook from his pocket. "But let me just get his full name and employer's contact info from you. Anyone else you know who knew him, too."

"Actually, I just got his parents' number. I was going to call and see if they knew where he was, but I guess I won't be needing it now."

Tony frowned. "Catching the bad guys—that's why I became I cop, Kevvy. I still love the feeling that comes with bringing justice. But notifying parents that their child's dead? That part's tough."

I turned around and kissed him. "You'll be very kind, I know. But there are some things you should know. . . ."

I filled Tony in on the broad strokes of what I'd learned about Brent's severed relationship with his parents. I also gave him Charlie's and Lucas's numbers. Not as suspects, but as lovers who needed to be notified. I supposed I could have called them, but I figured it'd be better coming from Tony. He knew how to put things like this. I'd follow with my condolences later.

"Do you need to go now?" I asked when I was done.

"To work on the case? No, it'll wait till morning. It's late. Might as well let his parents have their last good night's sleep for a while."

"I don't know," I said. "From what I heard, his parents won't be too broken up about it. They tossed him aside years ago."

"Maybe," Tony said, "but I bet they never stopped hoping he'd change and come back to them."

"If they wanted him in their lives, they wouldn't have kicked him into the streets because of who he *was*," I snapped, the words coming out with more bitterness than I'd intended. "That's not tough love. That's hate."

Tony knew he'd pushed another button. "I'm not saying they had any right to do what they did," he said, using his calm-the-horses voice. "I'm just saying that, when you have children, it's not that easy to stop caring about what happens to them. Even if you try to. If you were a parent, you'd understand."

If I were a parent, huh? So much for *Rafi Has Two Daddies*.

Who did he think has been spending every other weekend with him and Rafi? Whose apartment was Rafi sleeping in? Who was taking the kid to school? What was I, the nanny? I may have been half-Jewish, but that didn't make me Fran Drescher.

Another conversation I didn't feel like having tonight. More land mines to tiptoe around.

Was it possible Tony and I just weren't meant to be?

Or was I feeling unusually pessimistic having just heard about Brent's death?

"Well," I said, wondering if we could fast-forward to the make-up sex without having to have the fight, "I'm glad you don't have to run out again. I've missed you." I ducked my head and regarded him through my bangs. My patented do-me look.

"Besides," Tony said, ignoring the do-me look for what possibly might have been the first time, "I have to figure out how to ID the vic at the station."

"What do you mean?" I pointed at the *Advocate*. "Just show them this."

"And how would I explain that I was looking at porn ads in a gay magazine?" he asked. "Or should I just say my 'boyfriend' gave it to me?"

Wow. Remember that part about not wanting to step on any land mines? Tony just hit one or two with a hammer.

Boom-fucking-boom.

Only, the mine wasn't filled with explosives. It was like one of those flash bombs that police use to incapacitate suspects with blinding light. And in that moment of searing clarity, a truth I'd buried under the darkness of denial was suddenly revealed.

Tony and I might not make it.

I knew we had our problems. We'd even separated over them.

But I don't think I ever believed they were insurmountable. A part of me was certain we belonged together. Like a couple that meets cute in a romantic comedy but has to endure all the genre obstacles before they finally reach their happy ending.

But, right now, I wasn't feeling the love and I wasn't having any laughs. Maybe we were less *The Main Event* and more *The Way We Were*.

We might not make it to the final reel.

It must have shown on my face.

"What?" Tony asked. He waited.

I couldn't think of a thing to say.

He looked at me being speechless. Another first.

"Kevvy, I didn't mean it like that," he began, assuming I was upset about his ongoing refusal to come out at work. "You know how it is. It's the New York City Police Department, babe. All the 'diversity training' in the world isn't going to—"

I stood up. "I've heard this before, Tony."

Tony rose to meet me. "Babe." He brushed my hair out of my eyes. "You know I . . ." He moved in for a kiss. Sure, now the do-me look was kicking in.

I pushed him away. "I'm just tired, Tone. And sad."

"I know. You just found out that a friend of yours passed away, and I'm playing cop with you. That was a douchebag move on my part, Kevvy. You were right. We should have changed the topic half an hour ago. Come here." He enveloped me in a non-sexual buddy hug.

I didn't mean to and I wished I hadn't, but I started to cry against his strong chest. He just held me, even when I knew he must be uncomfortable, his shirt soaked through with my tears.

"It's okay," he said, "let it out. It's hard when you lose someone." He rubbed my back in circular motions.

I liked Brent. I was sorry to hear what had happened to him. But I wasn't crying for him.

It was the increasingly likely prospect that Tony and I could never be together that was breaking my heart.

Sometimes, when I'm feeling especially sorry for myself, I think in rhyme. Self-indulgent poetry sprung from too many readings of *The Bell Jar* in high school. Worse, with my ADHD, those couplets often stick in my head, repeating themselves in a torturous, self-inflicted loop.

So, as I shuddered and sobbed in Tony's arms, I kept hearing myself think the words I couldn't tell him.

> It isn't Brent's passing that fills me with fears.
> It isn't his sad fate that brings me to tears.
> It's losing the man I thought I'd been born for.
> It's the loss of you, Tony, I weep and I mourn for.

Later, I thought, I'll have to write that down. Then burn it.

As Bette Davis so memorably said in *All About Eve*, "I detest cheap sentiment."

That didn't mean I couldn't wallow in it, though.

37

Dark Places

I sat in my office at work, looking at a long list of people whose calls I needed to return. Every few minutes, I'd pick up the handset, punch in two or three digits (in one notable accomplishment, I even made it past the area code), and then hang up. I was in no mood to talk with anyone.

A week had passed since I'd identified Brent for Tony. In that time, I'd grown increasingly distant. Not just toward him, toward everyone. I felt detached. Maybe a little depressed. I was irritable, distracted, and not at all my usual self. My best moment in the past seven days was the excitement I felt when I heard a radio commercial for a medicine that promised relief from the exact things that were bothering me: the crankiness, the mood swings, the sleeplessness.

Then I realized it was for a medication used to treat PMS.

There wasn't any progress on Brent's case. Tony had talked to everyone whose names I'd given him; nothing turned up.

He told me I was right about one thing, though. Brent's parents really were hateful creeps.

Tony and his partner had gone to their house in Queens to break the news to them. Seconds after he got out the words "I'm afraid I have bad news for you," the father interrupted him with "It was the AIDS, wasn't it?"

Tony said that, no, it wasn't "the AIDS," and managed, barely, to explain about finding Brent's body in the river. By then, the mother had run from the room.

"You've upset my wife," the father said. "I think it best you leave."

"I'm sorry," Tony said, "but your son is dead and I'd think you'd want—"

Brent's father interrupted him. "What I'd want is for you to leave. My son's been dead to us for years now, detective. We didn't need you dragging his corpse back into this home."

Moments later, Tony and his partner were back in their car.

"So," I asked Tony when he told me the story, "are you going to look into them?"

"For what?"

"To see if they had anything to do with Brent's murder," I said, as if it were obvious. "What kind of a parent reacts like that to their son's death?"

"A very, very bad one," Tony said. "But we have no physical evidence. No motive."

"They hated him," I snapped.

"If everyone murdered the people they hated, we'd have a lot more rental properties available in the city," Tony observed. "People kill for money, for sexual jealousy, and, sometimes, for thrills. They don't kill a kid they threw out of the house years ago who they've had no contact with. Besides, given the amount of drugs in Brent's system, I think the ME is going to rule his death an accident, anyway."

"That's another thing," I argued. "Brent's boyfriend Charlie told me Brent never did drugs."

"He said the same thing to us," Tony said.

"See? So why did he have Valium and Ecstasy in his blood?"

"I don't know," Tony said. "Maybe because he was a porn star party boy on the same drugs that every other club kid is taking these days?"

"But Charlie said—"

"Maybe Charlie didn't know Brent as well as he thinks he did," Tony cut in. "He didn't know about that other guy Brent was seeing on the side. Luka?"

"Lucas."

"Right. People keep secrets. They lie. Those guys he made the movies with, the ones from SwordFight, said they weren't surprised to hear Brent had been stoned at the time of his death. They said they'd heard rumors about his drug use. Of course, they said it would *never* be allowed on their set"—Tony rolled his eyes—"but it wasn't uncommon for their 'actors' to get high before a shoot."

The way Tony said "actors," the way he disparaged the whole industry as if it was filled with nothing but the worst kind of scum, really pissed me off.

"And, Kevvy, I gotta tell you: I believe them a lot more than I believe Charlie. We know Brent was cheating on his supposed boyfriend, right? He was found with drugs in his system—drugs that apparently he had a reputation as abusing. He was a flaky, screwed-up kid who had a stupid accident. That kind of thing happens all the time to boys like him."

Boys like *him*. Who were those exactly? Porn stars? Hookers? Pretty little blonds who could be had for the right price?

Boys like me, then.

You can see where I'd be feeling distant.

I waited until after knew Tony had contacted them, and then called Charlie and Lucas.

Since I couldn't tell them about my closeted cop boyfriend, I had to pretend I was just following up, and let them tell me what they'd heard. I hated having to lie like that. It forced them both to go into the details about what they knew about Brent's death, a burden I could have spared them if only I could have been truthful.

But my pain and frustration were nothing next to theirs. They both wept openly on the phone with me. Neither of them had close friends or family in New York, and for a minute, I wondered if I couldn't get them together to support each other. Then I realized that probably would be a bad, bad idea.

Hadn't Tony listed sexual jealousy as one of the reasons people actually *did* kill each other? Brent might not have been murdered, but I could see Charlie and Lucas going at each other like two bulls in a small pen.

I was so angry.

At Tony, for treating our love like it was a dirty secret and for his cluelessness about how his hostility and bias against people who work in the sex industry might make me feel.

At Brent, for not being what I thought he was and for breaking the fragile hearts of two sweet guys who loved him.

At the guys at SwordFight, who, if they knew Brent was using, did nothing to help him. Hell, far as I knew, they encouraged it. The mix of drugs Brent was on was similar to the cocktail Lucas told me he'd use before a shoot. Something to get his mood up (Lucas said he was on crystal meth; Brent had Ecstasy in his system), something to get his cock up, and something to take the edge off (Viagra and Valium for both of them).

Was that suspicious?

What were the other two reasons Tony said people killed for?

Money. Brent made a fair amount, but not enough that I could see someone knocking him off for it. Given his youth and immaturity, I couldn't imagine he'd saved any, so he would have been worth more alive than dead.

Thrills. I assumed Tony was referring to people like serial killers. All I knew about them was from movies and TV, but I'd imagine that if there were any signs of a thrill killing, Tony and his team would have found them.

So, we're back to sexual jealousy. Given the life Brent led, how attractive he was, and how he used sex to get what he wanted (not that I was throwing stones at that one, mind you), that didn't seem impossible.

He'd told Lucas he needed a break from their relationship.

Was the real reason because he was afraid Charlie'd found out about it? If so, was Charlie capable of killing Brent out of jealousy?

Or was it the other way around? Maybe Lucas was lying—Brent had made his decision, and he hadn't chosen Lucas.

Lucas seemed a little unhinged to begin with. It wasn't hard to believe that Brent rejecting him a second time would push him over the edge.

Or, maybe Brent was cheating with a *third* person?

Ugh.

This story could be written any of a hundred ways, but that's all it was: a story.

In my heart, I didn't feel that either Charlie or Lucas seemed capable of killing someone.

Of course, I've been wrong about that kind of thing before.

But I couldn't believe they'd hurt Brent. They both loved him.

Ironically, the only people I knew *had* hurt Brent were the ones who should have loved him most: his parents. They turned on him like milk left in the sun on a hot summer's day. Rejecting him for being born as he was and for having the courage to live his life honestly. Of everyone on my list, I think I was most angry with them. If they hadn't kicked him out of his home, Brent would be alive today.

His father said Brent had been dead to them for years now. Talk about a self-fulfilling prophecy. They may not have thrown him into that river, but their actions set into motion the events that led him there.

Now that their son really was dead, did they even have the decency to feel remorse?

I wondered if there was a way to get through to people who could be so heartless.

Maybe, I thought, remembering something Lucas had given me, there was.

At least it was worth a try.

The door to my office swung open. My mother strode in, not having bothered to knock or otherwise signal her entry. That would have implied she recognized a closed door as being a "boundary," a concept she's never been able to understand.

"I'm going," she announced grandly, throwing her hands in the air like an actress emerging to thunderous applause, "to be a lady of the evening!"

I wasn't sure she knew the meaning of that phrase.

"Say what now?"

"It's true," Andrew said, walking in behind her. They both sat in chairs across from my desk. "We showed the network the rough cut of the footage from Families by Design, along with some background interviews your mother's been doing, and they were knocked out by it. They want to air it as a prime-time special. They think it's going to be huge."

"Can you imagine?" my mother gushed. "I'm going to have a prime-time TV show! Like Barbara Walters!"

"It's great news," Andrew echoed, "but let's not get ahead of ourselves, Sophie. It's just the one episode."

"For now! Wait," she said, pointing a finger at herself, "till they get a load of this!" She shimmied her shoulders like a burlesque dancer. "Bite me, Diane Sawyer."

My mother tended to exaggerate her accomplishments to the point where you had to take them with not just a grain of salt but the full shaker. Still, this was a pretty remarkable achievement.

"I'm proud of you," I told her, walking around my desk to give her a hug. She stood for the embrace.

"I'm proud of me, too," she agreed. "And this guy." She motioned toward Andrew. "It was my idea—my *brilliant* idea, I should say—to go after those bastards at the adoption agency, but he's the one who made it happen. Come here, producer man."

A group hug. Great. Just what I was in the mood for. I removed one arm from around my mother so Andrew could step in.

"You're like another son to me," my mother said to him. "Or a son-in-law. Which I wouldn't mind, if Kevin ever decides to stop waiting around while his idiot boyfriend decides whether or not he's going to poop or get off the pot."

"Mom!"

"I just want you to be happy, baby."

"Me too," Andrew said, taking advantage of the moment to squeeze my ass. "Baby."

"Don't think I didn't see that," my mother said to him.

Andrew blushed. "Sorry."

"Not that I blame you," my mother added. "He does have an adorable little tush."

"Mom!" I broke the hug.

"What?" my mother asked. "I'm not allowed to love every bit of you? My own son?"

I thought of Brent's parents and the Merrs. A parent's love was nothing to take for granted.

"You'd *better* love every little bit of me," I said. "Because I love every big bit of you."

38

Family Secrets

The Dawsons' house was as Tony had described it. A well-maintained, single-family brick home like every other one on the block. The bushes were trimmed, the grass cut, and the garage door painted within the past year.

But there were also three or four newspapers sitting on the porch that no one had bothered to pick up. They matched the overturned garbage can, its trash spreading across the lawn like the world's ugliest confetti. The mailbox had been left open, revealing what looked like a few days' worth of neglected correspondence. In the driveway, a late-model sedan was haphazardly parked at a careless angle. One tire pressed against the grass, having left a deep rut in the lawn on its way there.

Overall, it felt like a place where, very recently, someone had decided it was no longer worth his or her time to Keep Up Appearances.

I knew I should have called first. Unlike my mother, I did understand boundaries. No one wanted an unexpected caller—especially one sure to bring up painful memories. Showing up with no warning or invitation was rude of me.

Good.

I wanted to make this as difficult for the Dawsons as I could. Tony had told me they were both retired, and I was hoping to catch them by surprise.

At least I'd brought a gift.

* * *

The Dawsons' doorbell played the first ten notes of "America the Beautiful." The patriotic call was answered by a man I assumed was Brent's father.

He was of medium height, medium build, and a once-handsome face of no particular character. His thinning hair might once have been as blond as his son's, but now was the most nondescript brown possible. He wore a NY Yankees T-shirt that hung over baggy sweatpants. He was unshaven and his hair hadn't met a comb yet, even though it was well after noon.

I'd been expecting a scowling scarecrow, an obvious villain of a man with the ungenerous features of an Ebenezer Scrooge. Instead, I found myself standing across from a man of stunning blandness. Even his expression was slack, as if his facial muscles couldn't be bothered to reflect any particular mood.

Until he looked at me. Then, I saw the same spark of "Could it be?" in his gaze that I'd gotten from everyone else who knew Brent when they first saw me.

But where Charlie and Lucas were overjoyed that Brent might be back, the same couldn't be said for his dad. His eyes widened in shock, then settled back to their normal size when he realized I was nothing more than a look-alike, then narrowed in suspicion.

"Yeah," he greeted me. "Whaddya want?"

"Hello." I extended my hand. "My name is Kevin Connor. I was a friend of your son's."

I let that sit for a moment.

"And?"

"And . . . I wanted to stop by to offer my condolences."

"Okay, thanks," he said dismissively. "Good-bye." He started to close the door.

I blocked it with my foot.

"Wait," I said.

"What?" he said, his voice close to a snarl.

"Harry?" A woman's voice came from inside the house. "Who is it?"

To her: "It's no one. Don't worry about it."

To me: "Get your foot out from my door, you little fairy."

Lovely.

"I just want to talk," I said.

"I know what you *want,*" he spat. "I know what you *are*. It's because of people like you that my son is dead."

"Right," I said, all at once filled with an anger that surprised me, "because I threw my vulnerable teenaged son out of his home to fend for himself because I was such an ignorant, hateful bigot. Oh, wait, that wasn't me."

It hadn't been my plan for things to get this ugly this quickly. Another one of my schemes gone wrong.

"It can't be 'no one' if you're still talking to him," the woman's voice called. "Who is it?"

"I said don't worry about it, Claudia. Mind your business."

"Her son isn't her business?" I asked.

"She doesn't have a son anymore," he barked. Spittle flew from his mouth in an ugly spray.

I had to hand it to Mr. Dawson—he'd made the transformation from sleepy old dog to rabid pitbull in record time.

"Thanks to you," I prodded.

"Either get the fuck away from this door," Mr. Dawson hissed, making a fist, "or—"

He was interrupted by his wife, who squeezed in beside him. It was closer to dinnertime than breakfast, but she wore a fluffy pink robe with matching slippers. Her hair was pulled into a sloppy, slightly greasy bun, from which stray locks had limply escaped. She wore no makeup. Good bone structure and the same luminous quality to her skin that I'd observed on Brent couldn't hide the bags under her eyes or the deep furrows between her brows.

"Claudia," Mr. Dawson growled. He stepped forward, trying to keep himself between her and me. But she'd already gotten a look at me. With surprising confidence, she pushed him aside and stood before me.

It was her turn. The confused moment of impossible recognition, followed by the reaction that revealed the person's true feelings toward Brent.

What showed on her face was both familiar and unexpected. It hit me like a slap of sunshine.

A flush of hearts.

A mother's love.

Her hand reached out to me instinctively and then pulled back to cover her mouth. She made a tiny, muffled squeak upon realizing her mistake. Her eyes filled with tears.

"I told you, you didn't need to see this." Mr. Dawson grabbed his wife's arm.

Again, she surprised me with the strength with which she moved. She pulled from his grip as if he weren't there, stepping forward and cradling my face in her hands. Her eyes met mine with an intensity and tenderness that I knew weren't meant for me. "Who are you?" she asked in a husky whisper.

"I'm a friend of Richie's," I said. "I just want to talk."

"A faggot friend," Mr. Dawson muttered.

"My god," Mrs. Dawson exclaimed, turning to face her husband with fire in her eyes. "Will it *ever* end? You've already taken my son from me once." She gulped back a sob. "Twice.

"I let it happen," she said, sounding furious and sad at the same time. "Now, it's too late. But if this young man knew our boy, if he can tell me about our son, I want to hear what he came here to say."

She took my hand in hers. "Don't you?" she asked her husband. "After everything that's happened, if there's anything of a father left in you, anything of a man, don't *you?*"

Apparently, the bitter shell of Harry Dawson contained neither father nor man. After giving his wife a disgusted grunt he grabbed his keys off a hook by the door and "accidentally" bumped into me on his way to his car. Real mature, asshole.

He got into his automobile and slammed the door shut for emphasis, just in case we hadn't figured out he was pissed. He peeled out recklessly, swinging in a too-wide arc out of the driveway, leaving new tracks in what was once a nice lawn.

"I'd apologize for him," Mrs. Dawson said to me, "but I don't think I'll be doing that anymore."

She stood up a little straighter and ran her hands down her

robe. "I'm a mess. So's the house. Now, for that, I'm sorry. I usually believe in keeping a neat home."

"Don't be sorry," I said. "It's must have been a difficult week for you."

"It's been a difficult twenty-five years," she said, regarding the damage left in the grass by her husband's hasty departure.

"Maybe it's about to get better," I offered.

She was still looking at the damage to her yard. "Everything grows back," she said, wistfully. Then, remembering what had brought me there, she added, "Except for the things that don't.

"Some things are gone forever."

Mrs. Dawson ushered me into her home. She was right. It was a mess. Dirty dishes everywhere, jackets and shoes carelessly left wherever they'd been taken off, and it smelled: a bitter, rank smell like sweat and old age. Sorrow lived here, sorrow and regret.

All the shades were drawn, and the living room where we sat was dark and depressing. The furniture had been ugly to begin with, and age hadn't done it much good. Thin layers of dust coated everything. Nothing seemed less than twenty years old, except for an incongruously large flat-screen TV that dominated one of the walls. Across from it was the "man chair," Mr. Dawson's hideously oversized brown canvas recliner, which had drink holders built into the armrests. It was hard not to imagine him sitting there self-importantly, watching the Big Game, yelling at his wife to bring him another beer.

I sat on an uncomfortable couch while Mrs. Dawson settled into a club chair to my left.

"Thank you for coming," she began. "You're the only one who did. I know Brent had a life after he left here, but I don't know much about it. Can you tell me . . ." She took a deep breath. Her hands fluttered in the air, looking for a place to land. They settled on her knees, where they clenched and released, clenched and released, like she was kneading.

She was needing. Needing a connection with a son who, through malice or weakness or a combination of both, she'd abandoned when he was at his most vulnerable.

I'd brought the card Lucas had given me from Brent—well, here it was probably better to think of him as Richie—to wound his parents. To pierce their hearts with guilt. Seeing her now, here, I realized she'd hurt herself more than I ever could. In fact, I thought that seeing her son's final words to her might actually bring her some peace.

"He wanted you to have this," I said. "I think he was going to send it himself but never got the chance to." A fib. The first of many, I suspected. There was no way I could tell her the truth about how I'd met her son, or how he made his living. I handed her the note he'd written, telling his parents that no matter what happened, he forgave and loved them.

"You'd think," Mrs. Dawson said, her gaze still directed down at the two-sentence note she'd spent several minutes reading and rereading, "that eventually you'd run out of tears."

She looked up at me, the water running freely from her eyes. "But you don't. It seems like a well that never runs dry." She took a used tissue off a table next to her and blew her nose as discreetly as she could.

"I suppose that's a good thing, too. Because I should cry. I deserve to cry. Every day. For my son. For what I allowed to happen to him."

"You loved him very much."

"Yes." This brought on another wave of sobs.

"Then . . . why?" The obvious question.

"Oh, why? That's the one I ask myself every day. I was raised very traditionally. Conservatively. There was right and there was wrong. Sin and godliness. A man's role was to lead the family and a woman's role was to serve. Blah, blah, blah. I could tell you that I married my husband too young, that I was afraid of him. That he . . . hit me. It would all be true.

"He told me Richie would come back. That we had to be strong and wait out the devil. That the only way to save him was to . . . banish him. To hurt him a little now to save his soul for eternity.

"Every cell in my body knew it was wrong. But I was weak. Weak and afraid. Everything else is just an excuse."

"He never stopped loving you," I told her.

"I know. He told me."

"In the note," I affirmed.

"No." A small smile through her tears. The first time I'd seen her lips curl upward. "On the phone. About a month ago."

"I didn't know."

"I couldn't take it anymore. I've been a stupid, frightened woman, but I was getting stronger. A few months ago, my husband came home with brochures from church. For a 'conversion camp.' "

"I know," I said. "Richie told me about it." Another bending of the truth. It was Lucas who'd relayed that story to me. But you figure out how to describe Lucas's role in all this. Tell me a good way to explain Richie's adulterous relationship with a guy he met while shooting skin flicks. Go ahead. I'll wait.

"I always suspected Ellen—his sister—was in touch with Richie. My husband had warned her not to be, of course, but she's a grown woman now. Living on her own. And she is strong. Stronger than me. She confronted me about the camp. How could I even consider such a thing? she asked. She called it 'torture therapy.'

"She was right. I told my husband the idea was off the table. It was the first time in a long time I'd said no to him. But I insisted. I told him if he even called them, I'd leave and move in with Ellen. I used a word I'd heard on Judge Judy's show. I said it was 'non-negotiable.'

"He spent a few days yelling, slamming doors, and grouching even more than usual. But eventually, he promised me to drop it.

"I got Ellen to give me Richie's number. She'd told me she warned him about the possibility of being abducted by the camp's 'counselors,' and I didn't want him to worry anymore. No, more than that. I wanted to be the one to take that burden off his shoulders."

The tears continued to stream down her face. The front of her robe looked like she'd spilled a glass of water on it, soaked as it was in her sadness. But her voice was even and clear.

"I'd given him so little," she said. "I'd failed him so. Having this one thing to offer him, this tiny piece of good news, was a start, I hoped. A chance for me to begin making it up to him.

"We talked for hours. Hours. He was so happy to hear from me. So happy. As if I weren't to blame. As if he didn't have every reason to hate me.

"But he didn't hate me. I don't know why, or how, but he said he understood. I've never been prouder.

"He told me all about how he was trying to make it as an actor. About the temporary jobs he took to keep himself afloat. The office positions, the sales work. But his dream was to be on screen."

Of course he told her that. I used to tell my parents I made my living as a computer consultant. It seemed easier, and kinder, than telling them I earned my wages as a rent boy.

You can only get away with that for so long, though. Like snow in the city, the lies start out white but get dirtier and uglier over time. Soon, you're standing up to your ankles in nasty slush, your feet wet and cold. What you save in convenience you lose in integrity.

It was a lesson Richie didn't live long enough to learn.

Mrs. Dawson's call to Richie explained why he'd told Lucas he was no longer worried about his parents trying to "deprogram" him. I wondered if it also hadn't been the catalyst in his telling Lucas he needed to take a break from seeing him for a while—at least until he made a decision about Charlie. Nothing like a call from your mother to get the guilt train running down the track. It was also around the time Richie was talking about getting out of the jizz biz. Maybe he was reevaluating everything.

Which, as far as I was concerned, made it even *more* unlikely he'd killed himself while all doped up—whether by accident or on purpose.

Mrs. Dawson encouraged me to talk. How did Richie look? Was he content with his life? Had he found friends? Did he have someone . . . special? Was it me?

I stuck as close to the truth as I could. She accepted any evidence of Richie's happiness with the joy of a person dying of thirst receiving a glass of water.

She brought out pictures. Richie as a baby. Richie in the tub with his sister. Richie dressed like Batman for Halloween. Richie's high school yearbook, where he appeared as a freshman.

Wait.

I looked at the cover of the yearbook.

For a moment, it seemed to come alive, wriggling in my grasp like a magical tome in a Harry Potter novel.

My hands were shaking.

With excitement. With fear. With the shock of discovery.

Tony was right.

People kill for one of three reasons.

Money.

Sexual jealousy.

Thrills.

Now I knew which one got Richie murdered.

"This may seem strange," I told her, "but can I take this?"

"My lord," she said. "After all you've given me? The gift of your coming here? Showing me that Richie had friends who cared enough to reach out like this? You can have them all. Hell, you can have the whole fucking house!"

Her eyes flew open in shock and she made a sound that scared me. A startled, staccato bray than soon turned to laughter. A lovely laugh at that, musical and joyous, which had me laughing, too, although I didn't know why.

"I've never," she said, trying to get the words out between laughs, "used the . . . 'F word' before. In my whole . . . life! It feels . . . it feels like . . ." She couldn't find the word.

I could. Another "F" word. It felt like *freedom.* Freedom to do and speak as she pleased.

But she'd have to figure that one out on her own.

Mrs. Dawson had a lifetime of subservience and suppressing her feelings to put behind her. I had the impression that before the year was over, that god-awful recliner, along with its toxic occupant, would be living somewhere else.

39

The Final Link

In the past, this is when I'd have done something stupid. Namely, gone after the killer myself. That kind of thing has gotten me in trouble before.

It turns out that most murderers aren't particularly friendly when confronted with their crimes. Go know.

This time, though, I wasn't about to make the same mistake. I had a cop living right here with me—one who was already on the case. When the right time came, I'd tell him my theory about who'd killed Brent and why. I might as well let him do the confronting—after all, he got paid for it. Plus, as I may have mentioned before, he carried a gun.

It wasn't the time, though. First, there was another victim I had to get out of harm's way. The poor guy had been through enough, recently. I had to warn him.

"It's good to see you," Lucas said, giving me a warm hug. Unlike the first time we met, though, this hug was meant for me, not Brent. "Thank you for coming."

"Thanks for having me over," I said. "We have to talk."

"Sure," Lucas said, looking a little nervous. "About what?"

"Brent."

"Well, I figured that. Listen, my boyfriend's home. He's in his office here—he won't hear us. But if he comes in, change the subject, okay? I don't think he wants to hear me talking about other guys."

"Sure," I said.

I absently noted his use of the word *boyfriend*. I supposed it made sense. *Sugar daddy* might have been awkward to say. *Employer?* I realized I didn't know the proper etiquette here. I supposed *boyfriend* was as good as anything.

Lucas led me to the living room where we'd talked the first time. After some small talk, I got to the point.

"I don't think Brent's death was an accident."

Lucas paled. "What do you mean?"

"I think he was murdered. Because he had a secret. A secret he was about to reveal. One that would have cost the person I think did this to him a lot of money. It would not only have wrecked the guy's business, it probably would have sent him to jail, too."

"A secret worth killing for . . ." Lucas whispered.

"Yes."

Lucas's coloring went from chalky white to crimson in an instant. "Who? Who do you think did this, Kevin? Because, I swear to god, I'll kill him myself."

I'd forgotten how quickly Lucas lost his temper. "No, I'll go to the police. Don't screw up your life for revenge.

"But I wanted to tell you before I went to the authorities. You may need to take steps to protect yourself when this comes out."

"You think I had something to do with . . . you think I could have *ever* hurt . . . ?" Lucas spoke with unmistakable outrage, the cry of the falsely accused. He looked ready to spring out of his chair.

"No," I interrupted, holding up my hands in the universal gesture for "I surrender."

"I know you wouldn't have hurt him. I'm afraid, though, that *you* might wind up getting hurt before this is all over."

Now Lucas looked confused. I wasn't sure I could blame him. "I don't understand. You think whoever killed Brent would want to kill me, too?"

"No," I said. "Let me tell you what I found out."

But, first, I had to tell Lucas about the conversation I had with Brent after the taping of my mother's show. How he said he had information that could destroy SwordFight and would threaten to use it if he had to.

"You think he told them, right?" Lucas asked. "And they killed him rather than let him go public with whatever they had on him?"

I nodded.

"Who?"

"Mason, probably. It's his business. Although he might have had Pierce do the dirty deed for him."

"But what was the secret?" Lucas asked. "And how does it involve me?"

"I'll show you."

I took from my backpack the high school yearbook I'd gotten from Brent's mother.

"Look," I said. "This is from two years ago. Brent wasn't a senior when his parents kicked him out of the house. He was a freshman."

"So?"

"He wasn't eighteen when he made his first films for SwordFight. He was sixteen."

Lucas fell back into his chair as if he'd been shot. "Fuck."

Fuck was right. Ever since the rise, fall, and semi-rise back up of Traci Lords, it was common knowledge that filming and distributing sexual depictions of minors was a pretty serious crime. I Wiki'ed her after discovering the truth about Brent, and found out that between the ages of fifteen and eighteen, she'd appeared in roughly one hundred adult movies.

The owners of her movie agency were arrested. They and other companies involved in films with her spent millions of dollars defending themselves in court. They also had to go to the expense of making sure that hundreds of thousands of her videos and even magazines in which she appeared were removed from store shelves. My understanding was that they avoided being prosecuted on the more serious charges of child pornography. Perhaps because Traci presented them with a fake ID and they could claim they didn't know her true age.

I didn't think that was the case with Brent.

He'd said something that nagged at me. In the middle of talking about how he had the dirt to ruin SwordFight, he mentioned something about how they'd "helped" him. At the time, it didn't make sense. Isn't helping someone usually a good thing? How did that relate to whatever leverage he had?

Unless, what they'd helped him with was illegal. Like, covering up his real age. Mason was gaga over Brent. All that "flesh impact" and such. I was pretty sure he had the savvy and connections to set up Brent with a fake driver's license, Social Security number, and whatever else he needed to establish a new identity.

I couldn't prove it, but maybe the cops could.

Even if that could never be ascertained, though, just the fact that they'd sold movies of him at all was probably enough to destroy their business and get them imprisoned. Plus, this new information also provided Tony with what he said was missing: motive.

In this case, money.

One of the Big Three.

I hadn't realized how much this all was weighing on me. Laying it all out for Lucas was kind of therapeutic. Somehow, not being the only one to know made me feel better. I felt myself relax into the sofa as I realized I no longer had to carry Brent's secret alone. I hadn't realized how tense I was until I felt myself start to calm down for the first time since I saw that yearbook yesterday.

Unfortunately, my peacefulness didn't last long.

No sooner had I started to feel comfortable when I saw Lucas bound from his chair and come running at me as he swung up his arms.

40

Flashpoint

Damn it. Had I figured wrong? Maybe Lucas *was* involved in Brent's death. How else to explain why he was charging me like a mad bull?

I knew a lot about self-defense. But in the seconds I had before he reached me with almost a hundred pounds of muscle in his favor, I wasn't sure what I could have done. He was hurtling forward and would pin me through sheer momentum and gravity. Fear seized me before he did.

And seize me he did. But not in an attack. In a grateful embrace.

"Thank you," he said, his voice thick with emotion. "Oh, Kevin, thank you. If those bastards hurt him, I want them to suffer. I want them to pay. If it hadn't been for you, they would have gotten away with it."

"You're welcome," I choked out, breathless from his crushing bear hug. Maybe he *was* trying to kill me.

He let go. "Sorry. I didn't mean to crush you."

"No problem," I said. "I'm sure the ribs will heal. But, now, you need to think about yourself, Lucas."

"How do you mean?"

"Well, Mason may have made and sold a film with a sixteen-year-old star, but you screwed around with him onscreen."

"Is that illegal?"

"Honestly? I don't know. But you should. Do you have a lawyer? An agent? Anyone you could ask?"

"I don't." Lucas looked thoughtful and then grinned. "I have something better right here. My boyfriend. He knows *everything* about the industry."

"He does?"

"He'd better. He's one of the biggest directors in the biz."

Really?

"I'll go get him." Lucas trotted down the hallway.

I thought about leaving before Lucas returned. I'd delivered the message I'd come to give. I didn't need to meet the "boyfriend," or whoever he was. I also wasn't interested in getting to know anyone else in the adult film industry. I'd spent enough time swimming in that pool. Maybe it was better to get out before I drowned.

But I didn't want to be rude.

"Kevin," I heard from behind. "I knew we'd meet again."

The voice was honey and silk, warm, sweet, and with a distinctly Latin sensuality.

It was also familiar.

By the time he'd come to face me, I'd almost placed it.

Kristen LaNue.

The last director Brent had worked with.

Of everyone I'd talked with at SwordFight, he was the only one who seemed to regard Brent as anything more than some commodity meant to be used and sold.

How had I not known Lucas was living with him?

I looked around. Other than the picture of Lucas's brother, there were no photos anywhere. No posters of Kristen's films. Not even the Adult Video News Award I'd heard he'd won for Best Director.

No sign of Kristen anywhere except . . .

Oh, yeah, the bathroom. The towels. I'd thought they were designer linens from a line meant to evoke the concept of good hygiene.

But "KLN" wasn't a play on "clean." It was the owner's monogram.

I rose and gave him a hug. We exchanged brief greetings.

"What," Kristen said, sitting next to me, his face drawn with concern, "is this that Lucas is telling me? It's . . . incredible. Can it be true?"

Lucas settled next to him. Close, but not touching. I tried to get the vibe between them, but couldn't. Was this a partnership of convenience or was there real love here? Beat me.

I filled Kristen in as best I could.

"My god," Kristen said when I was done. His pallor was like chalk, his lips tight and trembling. "Lucas was with him on film. I *filmed* it. We thought he was a man, not a boy!"

He drummed his fingers on his knee. "Mason knew. He must have known."

Lucas bobbed his head up and down. "Yeah, I think so, too. He'd do anything for a buck."

Kristen took Lucas's hand in his. "That bastard," Kristen hissed. "He'll get us all thrown in jail."

Lucas moaned and looked ready to cry.

"Sweetheart." Kristen took Lucas's hand and brought it to his lips. He kissed the meaty knuckles. "We'll be fine. I promise. But we need to talk to my lawyer."

I stood. "I have to go to the police," I said. "But I wanted to let you guys know first. Give you a chance to make sure you're covered. You're not the bad guys here."

"We're not," Kristen agreed. "My baby wouldn't hurt a fly. Would you, *mi amor?*"

Lucas put an arm around Kristen. "I'd never hurt Brent," he said. Then, almost as an afterthought, "Or you, Kristen. Ever."

"I know." Kristen patted his shoulder, and Lucas laid his head on it. They looked like they needed time together, alone, to console each other and figure out what to do.

"I have to go," I said. "But will you fill me in on what your lawyer says? I won't talk to the cops until the end of the day. That should give you enough time."

"Thanks for the heads-up," Lucas said. "I owe you twice now, man. We'll call later." He started to stand.

Kristen held him down with a hand on his knee. "Actually, Kevin, can you stay for a bit? It may be helpful for you to talk directly with our lawyer. He might have questions we didn't think to ask."

"Right." Lucas reversed course. "Stay. Please."

I had no idea how Kristen and Lucas got together as a couple, but I'd bet they met for the first time on set. At home, it seemed he still followed Kristen's script.

"Sure," I said.

"I'll get the number," Kristen said. "Lucas, will you help me bring in the speakerphone?"

Lucas nodded and they headed down the hallway, presumably toward the office.

I watched their retreating figures. They looked cute together. Lucas leaned into his older lover. Although bigger and stronger, he was clearly submissive to the worldly LaNue.

They seemed into each other. Why, then, was Lucas so ready to run off with Brent?

For that matter, hadn't Kristen been flirting with me? Or had I imagined that?

I had no problem with people having open relationships, but these two seemed pretty active in their pursuit of others.

Was nothing what it seemed?

Lucas may not have been Laurence Olivier, but he was an actor. Maybe he regarded Kristen as more of a meal ticket than the love of his life.

If so, Kristen would have been an appealing sugar daddy. Rich, handsome, sexy, and I could see he pushed some of Lucas's most obvious buttons. After all, he *was* a director. By definition, he liked to be in control.

And wasn't control what Lucas most craved?

What did Kristen get out of keeping Lucas? Companionship and sex were the obvious answers. Maybe his need for running things at work also extended to his home life. If so, he'd found the perfect puppy to fetch his papers.

Then again, did it even matter? Who was I to be analyzing them? I doubted my relationship with Tony was any healthier.

A loud crash from the door Lucas and Kristen had disappeared behind shocked me out of my reverie.

"Kevin!" LaNue screamed.

I ran down the hall to Kristen's office.

A long desk ran along one wall, littered with papers and eight-by-ten photos. Across from it was tens of thousands of dollars of video and computer equipment. Naked bodies writhed across monitor screens in a silent kaleidoscope of flesh.

Lucas lay unmoving, facedown on the floor. A small pool of blood surrounded his head. It got larger as I watched.

"What happened?" I asked, kneeling next to him.

"I don't know!" Kristen stood in the far corner, hands behind his back, looking frozen. "We just got in and he . . . collapsed. Maybe he . . . fainted or something. He's a sensitive boy, you know. This may have all been too much for him."

"He's bleeding," I said.

"What? Where?"

I pointed at Lucas's head. I had no idea how bad his injury was. Should I turn him over?

"He must have hit the corner of that table." Kristen brought one his hands from behind him and pointed to a corner of the desk. Sure enough, there was a dent and a splash of blood there.

"Should we call an ambulance?" I asked.

I leaned closer to Lucas. A funny smell. Like ozone. Electricity.

"Hey," I said, "is something burning?"

Kristen didn't move. He had a glassy stare that scared me.

Was he in shock?

Why was he was standing so far away?

And, I wondered, what did he have in his other hand?

"Kristen?" I asked louder, trying to rouse him from his stupor. "Lucas is hurt. I think there might be a fire somewhere, too. You think I can get some help here?"

"No, baby." Kristen sounded genuinely regretful. "You probably can't. At least, not in time."

What?

My alarms went off and I started to rise.

"No!" Kristen barked. His sudden authority made me freeze. "Wouldn't want you bruising the merchandise, too."

He brought his hidden hand around.

It wasn't the first time I'd ever seen a stun gun.

Ever the director, Kristen called the scene.

"Lights out, Kevin."

A moment later, they were.

41

Closed Set

From the darkness, light.

If I was dead, at least I'd made it to heaven.

It certainly looked like it. The first thing I was aware of was an infinite whiteness. A blindingly bright flood that filled my vision and obscured everything else. I blinked once, twice, a third time, then left my eyes closed for a bit, fighting off the sting.

I reopened them. Gradually, shapes and shadows formed. Across from me came the second evidence that I'd made it past the pearly gates: an angel. Blond, handsomely shaped, physical perfection. Floating above the ground as if on wings, although none were visible.

I sensed my feet weren't quite planted on terra firma, either. A cloud.

The divine creature facing me appeared to be meditating or asleep. Like you'd imagine, he was beautiful. Pale, golden-haired, and nude, like a vision of God's messenger from a Renaissance painting. His nakedness seemed natural and fitting. We leave the world as we enter it: unclothed.

The only incongruous detail was his impossible-to-ignore erection. It pointed at me accusingly, as if I were to blame for his current predicament. It was large, throbbing, and so red it looked like you could use it as a branding iron. I didn't remember Michelangelo or da Vinci depicting their heavenly representatives as quite so . . . happy to be there.

Seeing the angel's condition made me consider my own. Yup,

pretty much like my cherubic companion's. Hello, hard-on. Who invited you to this party?

But we weren't floating. We are hanging.

I, too, was naked.

And, although I didn't feel particularly happy, I was at full salute, too.

Unless rigor mortis started with your dick, I guessed I wasn't dead after all.

I was dazed, though. My head felt like it was stuffed with mud. Not painful, but numb. My arms were extended above my head. Something that felt like leather looped around my wrists and held me to a beam or pipe I couldn't see. I was standing on what felt like a chair. I moved my legs a little and it rocked under me. Careful. If it tipped over, I'd be hanging free, my full weight pulling on my arms. It wouldn't be comfortable.

My memory of recent events slowly seeped back. I'd gone to see friends. Someone fell. Something sizzled.

Focus, Kevin, focus.

That was no angel.

Hi, Lucas.

Damn, he looked good.

Kristen.

He'd called me in because Lucas had fainted. But he hadn't. I hadn't seen it, but I bet Kristen zapped him like he'd done me.

I was still dizzy and thick-headed. Was I remembering this right? Why would Kristen have done that?

I should have been struggling to get out. Screaming at Lucas. But I couldn't muster the will. All things considered, I was pretty calm. Actually, kind of . . . carefree. Maybe a little turned on, too. Lucas really was adorable hanging there. If I had a free hand, I'd take it and . . .

Wait. If I had a free hand, I should be thinking how it could help me get the hell out of here. Not using it to grope Lucas like he were a cantaloupe I was judging for ripeness.

What was wrong with me? How come I wasn't more freaked out to be here?

Where was *here,* anyway?

I looked around as best I could. It wasn't painful to turn my head, but it wasn't easy, either. The slightest movement took great effort and came with a heaping side dish of nausea.

I hadn't been wrong in my initial impression—it *was* awfully bright in here. But now I saw it came not from celestial grace but from six or seven heavy-duty light stands, like the kind you see on movie sets.

They went along with the cameras, monitors, and other video equipment I eventually discerned in the glare.

Let's see, what did we have here?

Lights, cameras . . . what comes next?

Oh yeah.

Action.

"Well, look who's an early riser." I heard the smooth voice of Kristen LaNue before I saw him walk into the lights. He was dressed in the same jeans and tan, long-sleeved T-shirt I'd seen him in at his home. Could we still be there? No, this space was much too large. Kristen's apartment probably cost well upward of two million dollars, but a setup like this would have been unaffordable by Donald Trump at El Santuario.

Which raised an interesting question: How did a porn director afford a place at El Santuario, anyway? I was sure he was well paid, but nowhere near the kind of money you needed to live there. Kristen must have had another source of income. It probably wasn't selling Girl Scout cookies.

"What's . . . ?" My mouth was dry. I swallowed a few times. "I don't understand."

Not my best line, but, like I said, I wasn't feeling quite myself.

"Ah," Kristen said, stepping up to me. He ran a finger from just under my chin down to just below my belly button. I wish I could tell you my cock didn't give it an expectant little nod, but I'd be lying.

Listen, I'm the first to admit I'm probably oversexed, but this was ridiculous. I'd been accosted, kidnapped, restrained against my will, possibly by a killer, and judging by the red lights on the cameras that circled us, the whole thing was probably being

filmed. How the hell could I be turned on at a time like this? Was I more of a freak than I knew?

Worse, Kristen noticed my reaction. "It looks like 'Little Kevin' wants to play-ay!" he singsonged. He gave Little Kevin a long stroke. I had to bite my lip to keep from moaning with pleasure.

I twisted away as best I could.

More, I thought.

"Stop," I said. "Don't touch me, you sick bastard."

Kristen's smile was dazzling. Confident and cocky. "Your lips say stop—"

"Yeah, yeah." I shut him up. "It's an old line, Kristen. I had you pegged as a little hipper than that."

Kristen's smile didn't waver. In fact, it might have widened. "Listen to you. Considering how high you're flying, you shouldn't be able to form a coherent sentence, let alone be so . . . what's the word? . . . feisty."

How high . . .

"You drugged me with something," I said.

"Oh no." Kristen grimaced with faked offense at my accusation. "I drugged you with a *lot* of things."

A cocktail. I bet I knew what was in it.

"Valium," I said. Which explained why I was feeling so calm under perilous circumstances.

"And Ecstasy," I added, remembering the mild euphoria I'd experienced earlier. Not to mention the yearning to touch and be touched. I'd never used the drug, but I knew it had a reputation of earning its name on a number of levels.

Kristen clapped his hands together in polite golf applause. "Very good. Bunches and bunches of those two. But don't forget 'Little Kevin' here."

The other drug found in Brent's system. "Viagra."

"Impressive. You got three out of four. But the Viagra's just to prime the pump, as it were. More effective is the phentolamine."

"The feenty who now?"

"Phentolamine," Kristen corrected me. "It's a vasodilator. You should be glad I gave it to you while you were still unconscious. It's an injection that goes right"—he put his index finger at the base of my cock—"here. Opens up the flow of blood so you can't help but get hard."

It sounded gross, but I was kind of glad. At least I knew I wasn't to blame for Little Kevin's embarrassing eagerness.

"The Ecstasy's home-grown, too. A special blend that not only increases libido but also confuses the body's nerve response. Everything is experienced as enjoyable. Watch."

He reached out and squeezed one of my nipples. Gently at first, but with a quickly increasing intensity that seemed likely to draw blood. Now, I normally like a little chest play, but he could have cracked a walnut with that grip.

Damn if it didn't feel good, though. My conscious mind registered pain, but somehow, the sensation was indistinguishable from pleasure. Little Kevin agreed, even tearing up a little, and not in sadness.

The whole thing was surreal. The disorienting lights, the physical restraints, the sense of losing all control. I felt apart from myself, detached from my own fate. I had no drive to fight back or resist. So much easier to submit . . .

Last year, when I was looking into the death of my friend Allen Harrington, I'd read a lot about how cults operate. In the first meetings they got you to attend, they'd keep you for longer than they'd promised, using peer and psychological pressure as the restraints. They'd deprive you of food and deny you use of the bathroom. They'd manipulate light and temperature to deny you a sense of physical comfort or any confidence that you'd know what was coming next. Sometimes, they'd even use mild hallucinogens to make you more malleable to their will.

Sound familiar?

These techniques were common because they were so successful. They were the same strategies used by cult leaders, deprogrammers, and Dick Cheney to wear a person down. They combined physical realities with psychological techniques to

break the strongest will. Discomfort and relief, pressure and release, shunning and acceptance, each doled out in measured doses to elicit the desired responses.

There was *some* good news. It didn't work on everyone. One of the best ways to fight off the mind control was to be familiar with the techniques. Like any magic trick, knowing how it was done made it harder to be taken in. I knew what Kristen was trying to do, and that helped.

After tasing and doping me, Kristen expected me to be unconscious longer. I assumed I wasn't the first boy he'd done this to, so I had to assume my recovery was, indeed, faster than most. Why?

Maybe it was my ADHD. I was used to the effects of medication. In fact, I tended to need a pretty high dose, and one that was given more frequently than for most people. My doctor called me a "fast metabolizer." In fact, due to the stress of the day, I'd taken an extra pill before heading over here. My medication was a stimulant—maybe it helped me shake off some of the drugs Kristen administered.

Lastly, Kristen was trying to manipulate me primarily through sex. Well, using my face and body to get guys to do what I wanted them to used to be how I made my living. I was good at it, too. Sure, Kristen had drugs and a physical advantage on me, but I used to be able to control guys *without* those crutches. He was playing on my turf, now. I had to find a way to use that to my benefit.

At the same time, I knew I was thinking best-case scenario. Cult leaders may use subtle mood enhancers, but Kristen had me more doped up than a crack whore. They used peer pressure to keep novitiates in their seats; I was literally all tied up.

It wasn't exactly a fair fight.

But it wasn't one I could walk away from or lose. I had a feeling my life depended on it.

42

Touch Me

"Do it again," I begged. *"Please."* I let my mouth fall slack, licking my lips. I writhed like a cat, arching my back, tightening my abdominal muscles for maximum display. "Touch me."

"In time." Kristen chuckled, fiddling with his cameras. "We have to wait for your co-star to wake up. Then, I promise, we'll get started right away. There won't be a part of you that goes ignored."

I'd said it to make Kristen think I was more out of it than I felt. As long as he thought I was in a sex-crazed delirium, unable to think straight, I had a bit of an advantage.

Sad thing was, it was kind of true. There *was* a part of me on fire. An artificially fueled frenzy that had me *aching* to be touched. My every nerve ending screamed for release.

But I had to find a way past that.

When I worked as a hustler, not every one of my clients was someone I'd have gone home with if I weren't getting good money for it.

Okay, that's an understatement. Most of them weren't particularly appealing at all.

Which isn't to say I didn't have my share of clients who were sevens and above. Good-looking, smooth-talking men too busy or bored or closeted to meet someone in a more traditional manner. Even though those guys could have gotten laid for free, it was easier for them to pay for it and get exactly what they wanted, where and when they wanted it.

They were the minority, however.

There was a trick, though, to appearing—not to mention getting—turned on with someone to whom you're not attracted. You just had to find *something* about him that was appealing. Older men tended to have larger and more sensitive nipples—that was hot. Some guys had ugly mugs but sexy voices, or fat bellies but impressive appendages. Or, maybe they had a sense of humor that made sex fun, or the kind of desperate need that elicited a sympathetic response. Whatever it was, everyone had *something*. It made my job a lot more enjoyable if I could identify and focus on that particular trait.

Now, I had to do it in reverse. Ignore the fact that Kristen was devilishly good-looking. Disregard his deep green eyes and smooth, touch-me-now skin. Try not to think about how soft his trendy buzz cut would feel against my stomach, my thighs. Force myself not to notice his tightly muscled body that moved with a dancer's strength and grace.

Instead, I ran through my head everything about him that was gross and off-putting. When he got close to me, I was struck by his breath, which was sour and yeasty. It matched the smell of his sweat. Not an earthy clean-but-just-worked-out sweat, but an acrid, anxious sweat. The vinegary stench that accompanies nervousness and bad intentions. He had pit stains, too. Ugh.

While he dressed well, it was all too young for him, the clothing of a man ten years his junior. Trendy in a way that just made him look older. I remembered being in his bathroom and seeing a ridiculously large assortment of anti-aging products. It all spoke to a vanity and lack of self-acceptance that went along with the other narcissistic traits he displayed. Not hot.

On closer inspection, I noticed his pretty eyes were a little crossed, making him look kind of dumb. He had crooked teeth with an overbite. His short haircut was contrived to hide early balding. While his hair fled his head, it grew overlong from his nostrils and ears. I was surprised his obsessive self-care regime hadn't caught that. Someone needed to introduce this man to some tweezers, stat.

Oh yeah, and he had no ass. None. Flat as an ironing board back there. Even his too-tight jeans hung where they should have hugged. Coming at him from behind would be like humping a wall.

Plus, he was a sadistic psycho. You had to deduct points for that.

I continued to look for flaws, exaggerating them to the point of ridicule. I did whatever I could to diminish his presence in my mind. To steal his power.

To transfer it to me.

The whole time I played my mental tricks on myself, I continued to moan and writhe. I let my body go on autopilot while I steeled my mind.

Whenever Kristen turned away, I'd try to free myself. Kristen had me bound with some high-quality S&M wrist cuffs. Thick, black leather bands that laced along the slides and locked together at the palms with a steel closure. There'd be no getting out of them.

They were hooked over a pipe that ran across the ceiling. I wrapped my fingers around it—it couldn't have been more than two inches thick. On one of the occasions when Kristen's back was toward me, I lifted my knees to see how much weight the pipe could bear. It bent a little. I put my feet back on the chair and downward with as much strength as I thought I could use without drawing Kristen's attention. Again, there was some give in the pipe. I pulled harder. More movement this time, but not much.

So, I couldn't get my hands free, but with enough force, I might be able to break the bar to which they were attached. I had no idea what that pipe was for—architecture wasn't my strong suit—but it'd been put there for a practical purpose, not as part of a security system. It was the loose link in the chain binding me here.

The problem came to physics. I was strong for my size, but my size was still small. Even if I were free to pull or jerk with all my might, I doubted my 125 pounds would be enough to get the job done.

I was going to have to think my way out of this one.

What did I know about Kristen?

He was vain.

Full of himself.

He thought his work transcended mere pornography.

No, wait.

Not *all* of his work.

I remembered some of what he'd said when we first met.

He made a distinction between his commercial work for studios like SwordFight and his more personal "art" films.

He also lived at a level above what you'd imagine an adult film director could afford.

Had he been born rich? Probably not. Wealthy parents would have fixed his bad teeth and crossed eyes.

A second source of income, then? What?

Was it tied to his "art" films?

What could he be making that would generate so much money? There wasn't much you couldn't see in a typical porno these days.

What was Kristen selling?

When I thought I had it figured out, my stomach seized with a sudden stab of terror. No, it couldn't be.

Except, it could.

I had to know.

My head was a lot clearer now. Funny how fast fear can sober you up.

I had a plan. Well, half a plan. A plan lite.

Lucas's eyes were starting to flutter. He seemed minutes from regaining consciousness. I assumed he'd be as disoriented and dopey as I was when he first opened his eyes.

I was counting on it.

I was sorry, but the only way I could see my way out of this was going to involve hurting him. He was much too big and strong for me to do that when he was fully awake.

I had to work fast.

"Mmmmm . . ." I drawled, sounding a lot more stoned than I

felt. "Are those things turned on?" I nodded toward the cameras.

"They are." Kristen sounded amused. He was busy adjusting one of the lights that hung from the ceiling.

"Me too." I giggled. "Are you going to make me a star?"

"Brighter than the sun," he promised. He was only half-paying attention to me, which was good.

"I'm glad. I was going to call you about it, you know."

"You were?"

"After we met. You told me you made art films. I asked a ground. A found. I mean, *around*." I giggled again. I was faking the flubs.

"Really?" Having done whatever he needed to do with that light, he moved to the next. "And what did they say?" He didn't appear particularly attentive to what I might say, probably having learned from experience that a stoner's conversation is rarely of interest to anyone but himself.

I gave another moan. "Only one of my friends had any idea of what I was talking about. He's a guy who's into Sam."

"Sam?"

"Sam."

"I don't know him."

I laughed drunkenly. "Is not a him, silly. You know—chains and whips and stuff. S.A.M."

"S&M?"

"Thash it!" I gyrated my hips. My still engorged member drew circles in the air. Nothing I could do about that. Whatever Kristen had injected me with down there was apparently impervious to the normally shank-shrinking effect of mortal terror. "Sounds hot."

I was starting to get his attention. "You think so? Your friend, he knew my work?"

"He said there were rumors . . . that you were involved in some heavy stuff."

"Huh."

Why did Kristen seem surprised by that? If he was making films on the side, wouldn't people know? Unless I was right

about the nature of his films. In which case, he might be using a pseudonym. It started to come together.

"Just rumors. The movies are the stuff of legend. Secret." I looked at him bug-eyed. "Don't tell anyone, okay?"

Thinking he was humoring me, Kristen ran his fingers over his chest. "Cross my heart. But tell me more about these films."

"They're real hardcore. The kind of things you can't see in regular movies. They go all the way." I rubbed my thighs together as if trying to get myself off with the friction.

"You can't just get them anywhere." I was making this up as I went along. "You have to know people. People who know people. They're the luckiest people in the world, right?"

Kristen walked toward me. He was definitely intrigued now. I knew he wouldn't be able to resist hearing more about himself. But I was starting to babble. He got closer to keep me focused.

"What else did he say?"

"I do'n 'member." I let my head fall to my shoulder. "Sleepy now."

Kristen shook my shoulders. "Not now, Kevin. Wake up, baby. Tell me what your friend said about those movies."

I darted my eyes toward Lucas. He was blinking rapidly. Another few minutes and he'd back with us.

"Movies . . . oh, yeah. He said he's dying to see them. But very expensive. Only a few people can. People who know people . . ."

"Yes, we covered that part."

"So rare. But beautiful. Are you going to make me beautiful, Kristen?"

I tried to project vulnerability.

"You'll be beautiful forever, Kevin. Preserved on celluloid forever. Just as you are now." He ran a hand across my chest. "The height of youth and allure. Never aging. Cut at the prime of life, like a perfect rose is pruned at the moment of its greatest glory."

He walked out of sight while I let his words sink in. He returned with a silver cart, the kind high-end hotels use for room service.

But the only person who'd be ordering this delivery would be Jack the Ripper. I recognized scalpels and speculums among other spotless, stainless-steel implements. I didn't know what most of them did, but they all ended in sharpened points, vise-like jaws, or curling blades.

A sadist's smorgasbord.

Holy shit.

It was all I could do not to scream. I kept my face as blank as possible. A small sound escaped my lips, but I caught it in time to make it seem like a sexy sigh.

"Anyone can film two boys fucking," Kristen said, his eyes alight with excitement. "It's the easiest thing in the world to make that look good. But to show what lies *beneath* the skin. The muscle. The blood. That's true art, Kevin."

I nodded, but Kristen didn't notice. He was lost in his own vile visions.

"To take what is considered ugly and make it beautiful. To turn pain into pleasure. Showing people what society says they're not allowed to see . . . not even allowed to imagine . . . that's the role of the true artist!

"You'll be part of that, Kevin. Yes, there's risk. Every artist on the cutting-edge faces persecution during his lifetime. That's why I win awards for those insipid factory-made films I oversee but have to put my *real* art out under an assumed identity. Oh, it hurts not to be recognized for one's work.

"But the money helps." He looked at me just as I turned back to him. I was glad he hadn't caught me watching for the first moment I was sure Lucas was awake.

"Your friend was right. My movies *are* expensive. There's an underground network that will pay almost anything to see the forbidden. It's made me quite rich."

"And how do these movies end?" I asked.

"No spoilers," Kristen teased, putting his finger over my lips. "Shhhh."

Although I thought it might make me vomit, I had to be sure. I took his finger into my mouth and sucked, as if it were the most delicious thing in the world.

"Please," I said. "I want to know. It will make it even better, daddy. I'll do anything." I slurped and drooled noisily on his extended digit.

"Oh, you're good," Kristen said huskily. "I knew you would be. I hadn't meant to do this, you know. Usually, I get my talent in ways that can't be traced back to me. But you forced my hand, Kevin. I couldn't have you going to the police.

"I suppose you were your own casting agent," he said. "The role of a lifetime. The *end* of a lifetime. Captured on film. I promise, it won't hurt, my boy. A lot of it will even feel good. You'll be young and beautiful forever."

Snuff films. I'd always thought they were urban legends. Apparently not.

And here I was. *A Star Is Born . . . and then Killed.*

Not today.

Lucas's eyes were finally open, but he hadn't yet found his voice.

It was now or never.

43

A Matter of Size

Would you take a life to save your own?

How about just destroy one?

That was the decision I had to make.

Not about Kristen. I'd blow off his face in a second. Not only would it be self-defense, but I was pretty sure I'd be doing the world a big favor. I had every reason to believe he was guilty of even more crimes than I suspected.

No, it was Lucas I was about to put in harm's way.

Lucas.

He really did look like a heavenly visitor hanging there. But I needed him to be something else. Not just an angel but an *avenging* angel. One I could turn against Kristen, his creator.

The man Lucas called his "boyfriend." The man who made him a star, albeit it in a much different kind of film from the one he was planning to shoot today. The man who'd sheltered him for the past few months after his breakdown.

But what *else* had Kristen been to Lucas? What else had he *done* to him?

At the least, Lucas had strong submissive tendencies and Kristen a natural talent for domination. Had Lucas been involved in some of Kristen's more . . . artistic endeavors? Was he a victim or a willing accomplice? Or somewhere in between?

I had no way of knowing. All I *did* know was that any minute now, Kristen would notice that Lucas was ready for action. At that point, he'd do what he did best.

Direct.

Lucas would be feeling like I did. Euphoric and dazed. In a sexual frenzy. The strapping but easily manipulated man-boy would be under the total thrall of a man he'd come to know and trust. I could try and tell Lucas what was really going on, but would he believe me over Kristen?

Assuming, of course, I had more than a minute to speak. Did I mention that one of the items on Kristen's Cart of Terror was a ball gag? The only reason I wasn't wearing it now was because Kristen thought I was stoned out of my mind. The second I started making sense, I suspected Kristen would shut me up real fast. In that case, the ball gag would probably be the best of my options.

No, I had to make sure Kristen didn't have a chance to exert his control.

I'd have to take advantage of Lucas's fragile psyche to get us out of this. There was no time for anything fancy. Unfortunately, I couldn't think of a quick way to make the boy into a weapon without breaking him first.

If Kristen survived this night, I thought, as I brought my teeth together with every bit of power in my jaw, he was going to be grateful it was only his finger I had in my mouth.

His scream was so loud it brought Lucas completely out of his slumber. "Wha . . . ?" I heard him slur.

I wasn't ready for him yet. I continued to bear down, wondering if I'd wind up actually biting the finger off. Can you bite through bone? My mouth filled with the hot liquid spurting from the veins I was severing, and I felt feral with the sheer animal bloodlust of it all. It was the drugs, I knew, distorting my senses, but I was enjoying it. The searing gush of life flowing from him to me. Watching his eyes bulge with pain and fear.

Kristen might have been planning to make a snuff film, but I was auditioning for the next *Twilight*.

I wasn't the only one with animal instincts, though. Reflexively, Kristen swung at me. Although there was no technique behind his punch, and not much strength, a lucky trajectory brought his fist into my solar plexus. I gasped for breath, giving

him the chance to pull out of my mouth. His finger was still there, but covered in a spurting stream of blood that flew in every direction.

"You . . ." He was gasping and, I saw with great pleasure, crying. "Fuck!" he yelled. He looked up at me. "You're dead now, boy. *Arrgghggh!*" He squeezed the wrist of his injured hand with his other. He was really hurting. "I'm gonna . . ."

He should have shut up and backed away.

I jerked up my right leg with as much speed as I could. My knee connected with his jaw soundly, cutting him off mid-sentence. And when I say "cutting him off," I mean it literally. While I wasn't able to bite off his finger, with some help from me, his teeth made quick work out of slicing through about a quarter inch of his tongue. I watched incredulously as it flew across the room like a worm he'd spit from his mouth.

"*Mmmh!*" he screamed, the sound muffled by his hands, which flew to his face. Wow, between his still-gushing finger and the geyser spurting from his newly severed tongue, there was a *lot* of blood. Whether from the pain or the sight of so much just *pouring* out of him, Kristen's eyes rolled back in his head and he collapsed.

Had he fainted or passed out? Didn't matter. I might have a minute or ten. Either way, unless I acted quickly, Lucas and I would still be tied up and it wouldn't be long before Kristen remembered his Tray of Toys.

No time to waste.

"What's . . . happening?" Lucas asked. "Wha . . . who?"

Lucas looked at the body on the floor. In his stoned state, he couldn't figure out who lay facedown at his feet.

He looked back at me. Despite being tied up and having just seen what happened, he gave me a lazy smile. "Hey, handsome."

I kept my head down, letting my blond hair cover my features. "We have to get of here, Lucas," I said. I started pulling my arms with all my strength, jumping off the chair and using my full weight to hang from the bar. Ouch. That hurt.

The bar bent but didn't break. I wasn't heavy enough.

Lucas was.

"Help me!" I yelled.

"Later," he said. "Let's just chill."

"Lucas!"

His eyes started to close again. Shit.

"Lucas, look at me!"

"Juss a quick nap . . ."

"Lucas, look! It's me!"

Lazily, he raised his head. Squinted his eyes. "Brent?" he asked.

Maybe the thought of helping Brent would be enough to cut him loose from his stupor. But to guarantee results, I had to cut deeper.

"No, Lucas, it's me," I said, pitching my voice half an octave higher than usual. "It's your brother. Colin."

Lucas's eyes sprang open. "Colin? But you're—"

"I'm hurt, Lucas," I whined. "That bad man"—I pointed my chin toward Kristen—"he took us. He tied us up and hurt us. You have to free us, Lucas. I'm not strong enough.

"I need my big brother to save me."

Watching Lucas Hulk-out was a sight. It was obvious how big and built he was, but it was still amazing to see him flex his naked body from the waist up until his muscles stood out like illustrations on an anatomy chart. Unlike me, he didn't attempt to jump and use his weight to break the bar. He just tensed and pulled, like he was using a cable machine at the gym. It took some effort, but in less than a minute Lucas had snapped it in half.

For a moment, I expected steam or some toxic chemical to come surging from the severed pipe. But . . . nothing.

Now free except for the leather restraints around his wrists, Lucas ran and helped me down, too. He looped his bound wrists around my back and pulled me into him. "Colin," he sobbed, "you're safe now. You're safe."

Despite the drugs he'd been given, and the persistent chemically induced (and very impressive) erection he still sported,

there was nothing sexual in the air as Lucas embraced me. Just joy and relief and an innocent affection. A brother's love.

I was afraid that by using the trauma of the loss of his brother to break through Lucas's drug-induced lethargy, I'd somehow break Lucas, too. He was consumed by remorse and guilt and I'd played on those weaknesses to manipulate him into breaking us free.

Maybe I'd been wrong, though. Soon enough, Lucas would come to his senses and understand none of this was real. But I sensed he'd be left, somewhere deep inside, with the memory that, even if it happened in a kind of dream, he'd been able to do the thing he'd spent the last year wishing he could have: He'd saved his brother after all.

I hugged Lucas back, trying to squeeze into him enough love and gratitude to carry him through the days ahead. They weren't going to be easy. But he wouldn't be alone.

I heard a noise from the floor. Moaning. My arms still around Lucas, I looked down and saw Kristen trying to bring himself to all fours. He was a shaky mess. The struggle to rise was complicated by his hand repeatedly slipping out from under him in the pool of blood he'd made.

"Don't bother getting up," I told him. "We'll show ourselves out."

I casually kicked out my leg, catching him in the head. He crashed to the floor again, his skull hitting the concrete with a satisfying *thunk*.

Well, satisfying for me. I'm sure Kristen felt otherwise.

Lucas didn't even seem to notice. He kept hugging me and sobbing with happiness.

Soon, I'd have to rummage through Kristen's pockets for the keys to our wrist restraints. Then, we'd have to get dressed and call the police.

It was going to be a long night.

For now, though, I was content to let Lucas enjoy his fantasy for a while more. No one we love is ever really lost, but it's rare we get the chance to embrace them again. Lucas deserved this. He needed it.

Just because it wasn't real didn't mean it didn't matter. Sometimes, a dream is enough to save a life.

As we got dressed, I told the still-groggy but generally awakened Lucas what had happened. He helped me tie up Kristen—not hard to do given the amount of bondage equipment stored around the studio. Lucas seemed to absorb about half of what I told him, which seemed fine for now. At least he understood I wasn't Colin but Kevin, and if he bore a grudge, he didn't show it.

On our way out to find a phone (Kristen must have dumped or hidden our mobiles somewhere), we heard the heavy tread of footsteps as someone ran into the studio.

"Kristen!" a nasally voice yelled. "Sorry I had to bail on you after we brought the boys over. I had to make the drop to the East Side guys. That is *not* a crew you want to piss off.

"Did our sleeping beauties wake yet? We ready to start shooting?"

I'd wondered how Kristen could have gotten us over here by himself. Turns out he had a production assistant. Who?

Into the light came Pierce Deepley, clad from head to toe in black leather. In one hand, he carried the matching zipper mask that would complete his ensemble. The other held a grande Starbucks cup, from which the sweet smell of syrup wafted enticingly.

A S&M master with a Caramel Macchiato. Not hot.

I *knew* I didn't like that creep.

It took a moment before he realized his intended victims were flanking him.

"Uh, hi," he said, looking nervously from one of us to the other. "I was just, um, walking by and I heard—"

"Please," I interjected. "Shut up. Change of plans. Kristen decided *you* should be on the receiving end for this shoot."

"What?" Pierce panicked. "Me? But . . . I've done nothing wrong!"

"You know too much," I said in my best 1940s-tough-guy detective voice. "Kristen's decided you're worth more dead than alive. Lucas, hold him."

The big lug stepped behind Pierce and pinned his arms back.

"No," Pierce said, "he can't just . . . kill me. He can't!"

"Of course not," I reassured him. "Well, not until we flay you first. That'll come after the whipping and tooth extractions, of course."

Just because I wasn't into S&M like Pierce didn't mean I couldn't enjoy verbally torturing the bad guy for a while. Seemed like the least he deserved.

"What do you think, Lucas? That branding iron hot enough yet?"

If you ever wondered if you could tell through black leather pants if someone's peed himself, I can tell you the answer is yes. The yellow puddle spread to the floor, and I had to step back from getting my shoes wet.

"Okay, that is just gross," I observed. "Lucas, could you, I don't know, knock him out or something?"

He could. We trussed him up to match his partner in crime and headed out.

44

Tailspin

Two weeks later.

Thirteen days since I'd spoken to Tony for more than five minutes at a time. Thirteen days since I'd seen him.

It was over between us.

Snuffed out.

Let me explain.

He was the one I called when Lucas and I found a phone. We weren't at the SwordFight studios. It would come out later that Mason wasn't aware of Kristen's side business. Although he was guilty of knowingly employing the underage Brent, and of helping him create the false documents that made it look legit.

The paper trail wasn't hard to find.

Kristen was guilty of much more.

Turns out the first body that had been found in the river was another victim of the demented director's "art." Videotapes discovered in Kristen's apartment and secret studio promised there were more out there, waiting to be found.

As for Brent? Kristen had killed him, too. The whole thing had been filmed. Not that I ever intended to watch. Tony told me it had nothing to do with Brent's being underage—I was wrong about that. Twisted as Kristen was, he really did have feelings for Lucas. Mind you, those feelings were perverted and had more to do with possessiveness than "love," but they were strong.

When he figured out that Lucas had been seeing Brent on the

side, and that Lucas might be leaving him for his co-star, Kristen had to stop it. Once he made that decision, it only made sense to do it on film. After all, why not make some bank while defending your turf?

That's why Brent was all drugged-up. Knowing there was a chance Brent could be traced back to him (his usual victims were picked up in bars or clubs by a third party), Kristen tortured Brent in a way that didn't leave marks so that the drowning story would be more believable. In fact, that's how he eventually killed Brent, by holding his head in a bucket of water he'd filled at the river, so that the fluid in his lungs would match that from the Hudson.

Tony said that at the moment Brent's body went limp in his arms, Kristen's violent shudder and the ensuing stain in his pants indicated he'd spontaneously ejaculated.

He came when Brent left.

I kind of wish I'd slit his throat when I had the chance.

As it turned out, Kristen had achieved the perfect trifecta.

He'd killed for money, sexual jealousy, *and* thrills.

Every bad motive rolled into one deadly package.

No matter how I protested, Tony wouldn't hear it. After he helped me the night of Kristen's assault, when his fellow officers were done taking our statements and I was safely returned home, he came at me.

"You did it again," he accused. "You almost got yourself killed."

"I *didn't,*" I insisted. "Okay, maybe in the past I kind of ignored your advice, but not this time. I swear. I was going to tell you everything I found out and let you handle it. I just went by Lucas's to give him a heads-up first. I didn't even know Kristen would be there, let alone that he was—"

"Enough!" Tony shouted. "This can't be a coincidence, Kevin. You keep doing this. Putting yourself in harm's way. Lying to me about it. I can't take it."

"I didn't." I tried to explain myself. "I'm not—"

"You say you want to be with me, but you make it impossi-

ble. You're always pressuring me to do more than I can. To make you promises I can't. Because, unlike you, Kevin, if I give my word, I keep it."

That hurt.

"Tony . . ."

"I have a son, Kevin. He needs me. Obviously, you don't. You think you can do it all on your own. Well, I'm not sticking around while you get yourself killed. Rafi doesn't need to lose another adult in his life, either. Maybe it's me. Maybe I'm no good for you. Why else are you so . . . self-destructive? I think we need a break."

That's what Brent said to Lucas before he disappeared. Famous last words.

I didn't try and talk him into staying. I didn't even ask where he was going. Maybe he was returning to his ex-wife.

Tony was right. I had been pressuring him to make a decision. Now, he had.

It just wasn't the one I was hoping for.

I went to work.

I did my job.

Some evenings Freddy came over, more often than not with Cody. We ate takeout and watched movies on my flat screen.

They tried to get me to talk about how I felt about Tony's leaving. I deflected every attempt.

The other evenings, I watched movies alone. Whatever was on, as long as it wasn't a love story. If there wasn't a movie devoid of any possible romantic plot points, I tuned into "reality" shows about people less relatable than Martians, or people screaming at each other on MSNBC's political coverage or, best of all and with alarming frequency, the Home Shopping Network, where the host's enthusiasm for a steam cleaner or plastic jewelry hocked by a C-list celebrity never known for her taste to begin with, blotted out my own emotions, taking my mind almost completely off the Tony-sized hole in my life.

I also spent a lot of time on the phone with Lucas. Almost every other day, for hours at a time. We had the easy intimacy of

two people who'd survived a disaster. Since he'd never met or heard about Tony, it was always a safe conversation. Discussing our near-death experience and torture porn was a lot less upsetting than having people ask how I "felt" about the dissolution of my relationship.

Lucas seemed to be getting better. He was still living in Kristen's place, where he'd found tens of thousands of dollars in cash hidden throughout the apartment. The maintenance fees on the co-op were paid a year in advance, and I agreed with him that until—or if—Kristen's lawyers tried to force him out, he'd be a fool to leave. I also advised him what to do with all that money. Ill-gotten though it might be, Lucas could live off that cash for a long time while he made up his mind what he wanted to do with the rest of his life.

However, as a favor to him and because I really was rooting for the guy, we agreed that, for the short run, the money would go into a safe deposit box for which only I had the key. Lucas knew he was too volatile and immature to be trusted with that much cash. As a recovering addict, he was also too prone to temptation. Part of the deal, though, was that I'd only hold the money for him if he got into therapy. He agreed and I hooked him up with my former psychologist.

In the meantime, he volunteered half-time at Stuff of Life, a nonprofit that made and delivered meals to people living with HIV and AIDS. I used to help there when I was an escort and only had to work ten or fifteen hours a week.

My full-time job on my mom's show made finding time for that a lot harder. I hoped that Lucas filled whatever void I'd left. I know my old friend Vicki, who was the volunteer coordinator there, called to thank me profusely after Lucas's first day.

"Baby," she said, and her deep, throaty voice on the phone made me miss her even more, "he is a *find*. Not only is he enthusiastic and hardworking, but he's so hottified I expect we'll be having men by the hundreds discovering a previously unknown interest in bagging sandwiches signing up. I get a hard-on looking at him, and I don't even have a dick."

"Unless you count the one in the drawer of your nightstand," I joked.

"That's a strap-on," she answered, not joking. "It's more for my girlfriend's pleasure than mine. Not to mention the occasional straight boy I get to deflower. Now, *that's* fun."

Mostly lesbian Vicki had told me before about her love for cherry picking. "You," I said, "are a truly a giver. In every way."

"I try," she answered. I could hear the cocky Elvis-like grin that went with her ebony slicked-back hair and sensual features. "What's going on with you?" she asked. "How's Tony?"

"Oops," I lied. "That's the other line. I gotta go. Good luck with Lucas. And leave his ass alone, okay? He's confused enough as it is."

I disconnected. I was glad to hear Lucas looked like a good fit for Stuff of Life. He needed structure. And some friends, too. I seriously considered giving Charlie his number. They both had some grieving to do. Maybe it would be easier if they did it together. Maybe not. I'd leave it be for now.

Brent's murder haunted us all.

Three times Tony called me with updates about the case. We kept the conversations short and to the point.

Just the facts, man.

I tried to get on with my life.

I tried not to miss Tony.

I tried not to miss Rafi.

Every night, I cried myself to sleep.

Every morning, I woke to a pillow wet with tears. I didn't remember my dreams, only the sadness they inspired.

The days passed.

Once again, I'd come a lot closer to death than I'd planned to.

I was happy to be alive.

But I wasn't *happy*.

One Friday night, three weeks after Tony's departure, two uniformed officers showed up at my door. I hadn't yet changed out of my work clothes. We'd had a meeting with network executives, and I had to dress like a real professional that day—a tie

and everything. For some stupid reason, I was glad the cops hadn't found me in my usual household ensemble of Joe Snyder boxer-briefs and a Hello Kitty T-shirt. It made me feel more grown-up.

"Mr. Connor," they greeted me. They introduced themselves. Officer Payne was an African-American man in his fifties with a graying moustache and a warm, lazy smile that probably was deceptive in its ability to put a suspect at ease. His partner, O'Brien, was maybe in his mid-twenties, a red-haired Irish boy with wide green eyes and a smattering of freckles. His handsome features seemed wasted on him—I had the distinct feeling he had no idea what to do with them. He radiated a sincerity and earnestness that would do him no good either as a player or as a New York City police officer.

He looked like he had a lot to learn, and his partner seemed like the kind of veteran who could teach him.

O'Brien's eyes scanned my apartment. His eyes landed on a copy of the British gay magazine *Attitude* that I'd left open to a particularly provocative underwear ad. He blushed furiously, as if scandalized by the display of rippling abs and padded crotch.

Yeah, he'd have to toughen up if he was going to make it in this city.

It was intimidating to have the law at my door like that, but the armor of my business suit and my immediate ability to imagine these two in the buddy-cop movie version of themselves helped me stay relatively relaxed. I invited them in and they accepted.

It didn't take long before they told me why they were there: Was I available to ride over to the station with them to review some matters related to Brent's case?

"Can't we do it here?" I asked.

With convincing contriteness, they explained there was physical evidence they needed me to review. They made it hard to say no, answering my questions before I had a chance to ask them.

It wouldn't take more than an hour or two of my time. They were sorry to have barged in on me like this, but they didn't want to bother me at work. We could reschedule for a more

convenient time, but they were trying to move the investigation along before people started fleeing town or covering their tracks. The sooner I could help them, the better chance there was for convictions.

I was torn. Was something fishy going on? Did *I* need a lawyer? On the other hand, if this small inconvenience meant I could do more to help bring Brent's killers to justice, I didn't want to delay.

As he had for the past ten minutes, O'Brien glanced at me surreptitiously, making me feel guilty of *something,* although I didn't know what.

Good cop that he was, though, Officer Payne met my eyes steadily and understood my interior struggle.

"We promise," he said, "no hidden agenda. Detective Rinaldi wanted us to give you his personal assurance this is on the up-and-up. He'd have come himself, but he couldn't work tonight. Family thing. But he wanted us to let you know you have nothing to worry about, and he really could use your help."

This unexpected request suddenly made sense. Tony had probably needed some information from me but couldn't figure out a way to get it without our having to see each other. Whatever took him away tonight was the perfect opportunity to get my help without a chance of us crossing paths.

"This 'family thing,' " I couldn't help asking, "is everything okay? His son didn't get hurt or anything, did he?"

Payne's reassuring smile appeared genuine. "No, no, nothing like that. It was more of a family get-together he'd almost forgotten about. Nothing bad."

A "family get-together." For some reason, the first and only possibility that occurred to me was his wedding anniversary. Although he might have been divorced, I couldn't shake my suspicion that after leaving me he would reunite with his ex. He was that desperate to have a "normal" life.

The more generous part of me allowed that some of his motivation might have been to spare Rafi the pain of divorced parents and, possibly, a dad who was in love with another guy.

I thought he was making a mistake. I didn't believe that being

raised in a tense home with parents who despised each other and a father who denied himself happiness was a recipe for a healthy childhood, either.

Plus, I'd have made a *fabulous* second dad.

But, as Tony had made clear, my opinions didn't matter.

Funny. Until he left, I really thought they did. I thought Tony was on the same trip I was. Aware of the potholes on the road to our being together, but committed to reaching the same destination.

I was wrong. I thought we were heading for a happily ever after.

Who knew he'd been looking for the exit ramp?

Still, I trusted Tony wouldn't want to see me hurt. Well, *more* hurt than I already was. If he gave his word through his officers, I believed him.

Even by proxy, I didn't think he'd lie to me.

Turns out, I was wrong about that, too.

45

The Road Home

It was eight-thirty by the time the officers and I headed out to their unmarked car. On the way to the station, I asked what they needed to show me.

"It's better we don't say," Payne responded. He took his eyes off the road for a second to give me another let-me-put-your-mind-at-ease smile. "We're not trying to be mysterious. It's just that anything we tell you may be prejudicial. If we ever have to put you on the stand—and I'm not saying we would—I wouldn't want some smart-ass defense attorney claiming we'd influenced you before you saw the evidence."

It made sense, but didn't make me as comfortable as a more straightforward answer would have. I considered coming at it from a different angle, but Payne distracted me.

"Tell us about you," he encouraged. "What's your day gig?"

"No kidding," O'Brien, the redheaded rookie, said when I'd finished. "*Sophie's Voice*? I love that show."

I thought he was just being polite until he started recapping particular episodes and quoting some of my mother's more outrageous remarks.

I can honestly say that the only thing flaming about O'Brien was his hair. He was as butch as they come, an obviously new but typically tough NYC police officer, displaying nothing that triggered the slightest flicker of my gaydar.

Still, once he'd confessed his fanboy enthusiasm for my mother's

program, I considered it a declaration of homosexuality second only to leading the New York City's Gay Pride Parade.

I suppose there are straight men in the world who genuinely love Oprah. Who subscribe to *Martha Stewart's Living,* and whose preference for watching Rachael Ray over a baseball game is simply an indicator of their varied and enlightened range of interests.

Yeah, right.

I remembered now how red O'Brien turned when he saw the provocative picture in my living room. I'd mistaken arousal for shock. Then, there was the way he kept sneaking sidelong glances at me. He *was* sizing me up, just not in the manner I'd thought.

I didn't know whether to laugh or cry. Here was Tony dumping me because of what he thought his peers would think, while at least one would not only have approved but might have been interested in joining us for a three-way.

Maybe I'd have to get O'Brien's number. Sleeping with one of Tony's subordinates—insert evil cackle here. Not that I was spiteful or anything.

I was distracted enough that when Payne announced, "Here we are," I got out of the car before I even realized we weren't anywhere near the station.

In fact, we were parked in the "No Parking" space in front of the Park Grand, one of New York's ritzier hotels. Payne took my arm while O'Brien flashed his badge and talked with one of the parking attendants.

"This isn't the police sta—" I began.

"Not unless we've moved way up in class," Payne interrupted, leading me forward. "No," he continued, "the evidence you need to see is here.

"I just hope you'll be able to see it for what it is."

As a high-priced call boy, I'd visited clients in a lot of high-end hotels. The Park Grand was one of them.

But in my profession, the goal was to pass through the com-

mon areas as unobtrusively as possible. Don't attract attention from hotel security, press, or an unsuspecting spouse. Head straight for the elevators and casually make your way to your client's room.

So, although I'd passed through the Park Grand dozens of times, I never took notice of the lobby, the meeting rooms, or the restaurants. I kept my head down as if deep in thought and made a beeline for the residential floors.

Therefore, I had no idea of the hotel's geography and where Payne was hustling me with the cool efficiency of a skilled body-guard. Or a hitman. His paternal authority invited no questions, either. It was all "Come-with-me-if-you-want-to-live."

On my other side, O'Brien walked in lockstep. He didn't have Payne's natural aura of control, but he kept me between them, reinforcing the sense that I was better off going along quietly.

We arrived at what appeared to be a meeting room, its twin doors closed. From inside, I heard murmurs over an amplified voice that I couldn't quite make out. As my ears adjusted, I understood the last words of what sounded like an introduction.

The speaker's voice was loud but slightly distorted through the sound system. It was recognizable, but I couldn't quite place it. He had a strong New York accent. An older man, somewhere in his sixties or seventies, I'd guess. ". . . the man of the hour himself. Congratulations on this highest of tributes."

Was I here for some kind of show?

Apparently so.

Payne opened one of the doors and pushed me inside.

"Just stand with me in the back," he whispered. "Looks like we got here just in time."

The man on the stage stood in the center of a bright spotlight. The room had been set up for a dinner. I'd guess about a hundred tables, each of which sat ten, faced the front of the room. A huge panel of LCD monitors, which combined to form a single image, dominated the back wall.

The room was so darkened that it was impossible to make out the audience.

The monitors showed the face of the man who'd just finished

speaking. Now I knew who it was. The city's current mayor, a pretty popular Independent who'd risen to prominence in the business world before entering politics, waited for the next speaker to come to the stage.

The image behind the mayor flickered and was replaced by a blue-and-white logo for the New York City Police Department. A string of letters ran across the bottom of the screen: *The Police Officer's Public Service Division's Detective of the Year: Tony Rinaldi.*

The words were greeted with riotous applause, as was the man who made his way to the stage.

Tony.

My Tony.

Who'd taken his mother to this dinner instead of me.

Who was ashamed of me.

Who'd walked out on me and never looked back.

All of which led to the obvious question: What the hell was I doing here now?

The mayor greeted Tony warmly and handed him a bronze plaque. They posed briefly for a photo together, and the mayor grinned as if they'd been best friends for years. The camera flashed, the mayor's job was done, and he walked off stage with the distracted look of a man thinking about whatever Comes Next.

For the first five minutes of Tony's speech, my heart was pounding so loud it drowned out whatever Tony said. I caught the big themes. It was his privilege to serve. He'd always tried to work on behalf of the public. He thanked his fellow officers who'd awarded him this humbling honor.

Although most of what he said was a drone to me, I couldn't help but be proud of how assured he seemed. What a confident speaker he was. Not to mention how breathtakingly beautiful he looked, bathed in the spotlight's glow like a vision of masculine perfection. I doubted there was ever an actor on Oscar night who looked better onstage.

With his natural charisma and easy charm he held the audience in the palm of his hand.

Having been there myself, in more ways than one, I knew what a nice place that was.

Eventually, my—what? Anxiety? Excitement? Hope? Whatever I was feeling, it began to calm down and I was able to hear what he was saying.

"Part of this plaque," Tony said, referring to the trophy in his hands, "says it's due to my 'outstanding courage in the face of danger.' And I suppose that's true. If there's a situation where I can count on my fellow officers, or my wits, or my training, or, worst come to worst, my gun—to save a life or protect an innocent, I'm prepared to make a stand.

"But tonight, I have to make a confession. Behind this badge, it's easy to be brave. But to be honest, in my personal life, I haven't held myself to the same standards. There I've allowed fear and shame to rule me."

There was a slight quaver in his voice. What he was about to say wasn't easy. That he could say it at all made my heart want to burst.

"But no more. There comes a point where you have to man up. Where you have to take a stand. For me, that time is tonight. Surrounded by my friends. My family. And my *extended* family—the men and women in blue who put their lives on the line every day for this city."

That elicited a hearty round of applause. I don't think anyone suspected where Tony was going with this—at least, where I *hoped* this was going—but he had them on his side.

"For a long time now, I've been in love with someone whom I've kept a secret. A person who I was afraid to acknowledge as the most important thing in the world to me. A true partner. A lover. A soul mate.

"No longer. Tonight, I tell you all the truth."

Tony paused. For a moment, he looked lost. The room was so quiet you could have heard a pubic hair drop.

"Could you . . ." Tony paused for a moment and looked up, toward where I imagined the control booth was. "Do you think you could turn up the house lights a little?"

Whoever was controlling the A/V equipment complied. He slightly increased the ambient lighting.

"Rafi?" Tony asked, squinting against the spotlight. "Could you come up here?"

Rafi? What was he doing there?

The audience burst into laughter and applause as the exuberant five-year-old, looking all kinds of adorable with his curly hair and rented tux, ran to the stage. Tony knelt and held out his arms. He scooped up his boy and held him tightly.

"You remember what we talked about before tonight? About how this was going to go down?"

Rafi nodded enthusiastically. "I do, Dad!"

His pip-squeaked reply brought more laughs and cheers.

I doubt P.T. Barnum could have planned this better.

"You okay with it, buddy? Because if not, you don't have to do it."

"I am!"

"You sure?"

"I want you to do it, Daddy! And just like you told me, I brought the—"

Tony clasped his hand over Rafi's mouth. "Not yet, Rafster. Let's leave *something* as a surprise, okay?"

Mouth covered, Rafi opened his eyes wider in an attempt to communicate. He nodded eagerly. This elicited several "oohs" and "ahhs" from the crowd.

"All right, then," Tony said. "It's time I showed some of the courage I've brought to this job in my personal life." He put his open hand over his eyes as if scanning the back of the room. "Payne, O'Brien, I hope you guys came through for me. . . . Kevin, are you there?"

The crowd suddenly fell silent. The good-natured tittering Rafi's antics elicited stopped dead.

Kevin? What kind of girl was named *Kevin?*

All eyes turned to the back of the room where Tony seemed to peer.

My mouth felt full of cotton. I tried to speak but nothing came out.

"Damn, boy," Payne nudged. "Haven't you been waiting for this? Answer your man!"

I tried again.

There was no air.

"Well, at least get your ass up there!" Payne commanded.

Tried that, too.

Someone had bolted my legs to the ground.

O'Brien let out an exasperated sigh.

"We're on our way!" he called.

O'Brien wasn't subtle. He pushed me forward like a man being thrown in front of a firing squad. Forward momentum kept me moving toward the stage. I found myself standing next to Tony with no memory of how I'd gotten there. I looked at the crowd, but the overwhelming glare of the spotlight prevented me from making out any detail.

So, I turned to Tony, who still held Rafi in his arms. They looked like the two most self-satisfied men in the world.

"Tony," I whispered, "you don't have to do this. This is supposed to be your night to—"

Tony shut me up with a finger on my lips. "Shut up," he whispered back. "I've been a jerk. And a coward. But no longer."

Tony turned back to the crowd. "As an officer and a detective, I've always been responsible for holding up the law. Tonight, I'm going to continue that tradition. But not by arresting someone. Instead, I'm going to exercise my right to a recently enacted statute, one that I couldn't imagine even existing when I first joined the academy.

"Bill number A08354, signed into law by Governor Andrew Cuomo in June 2011. Otherwise, known as the Marriage Equality Act."

Tony took my hand and led me to the side of the podium, where the audience could see as he put Rafi gently on the ground and then lowered himself to one knee in front of me.

"*Now,*" Tony said to his son, "you can give me what I asked you to hold for me."

With great ceremony, Rafi reached into his tuxedo jacket and retrieved a small velvet box that he handed to his dad. Tony

flipped it open to reveal a simple, but gleaming, gold band studded with diamonds.

"Kevin," he said, looking at me with the purest love I'd ever seen, "there's so much I want to say to you. But"—he looked at the crowd hanging on his every word—"maybe we'll save that for later." He winked playfully.

The audience tittered again. They seemed to be recovering from their initial shock and were back on Tony's side.

I followed Tony's gaze to the crowd. There I saw the table closest to the stage, where Tony's mother sat beaming, as if she were truly happy to witness this. Somehow, he'd won her over. My mother and father were there, too, as were, God help us all, Freddy and Cody. How Tony managed all this I'd never know. My mother leaked elegant tears while Freddy sobbed dramatically, clutching Cody for support. What a drama queen.

Then I looked at Tony again. I thought he was . . . shimmering . . . until I realized I was seeing his spotlit form through the filter of my tears.

I'd wept a lot over the past few weeks, but couldn't remember the last time I'd cried from happiness.

"Anyway . . ." Tony continued, his voice suddenly choked up and breaking with emotion, "I have so much I want to tell you. But I don't know if I can find the words. Because it all boils down to this. Something I should have asked you a long time ago."

He removed the ring and held it out to me.

"Kevin Conner," he said, the next four words ones I've longed to hear more than I ever imagined, "will you marry me?"

I fell to my knees beside him. "Yes," I said, although I realized no sound came out. I tried again.

"Yes." My voice was a ghost, blocked by years of waiting and hoping and dreams.

"Yes. Yes, yes, yes!"

I grabbed the ring from him and slid it on my finger before he had a chance to change his mind. It fit perfectly. When and how long had he been planning this?

Maybe he forgot where we were. Maybe he didn't care. All I

know is in an instant Tony's lips were on my mine and I never felt more connected.

Rafi threw his arms around us both.

"I love you, Daddy Kebbin!" he cried.

In the background, as if they were a million miles away, I heard the crowd roar. Maybe there were a few disapprovers who sat this one out, but when I turned my head slightly to look, most of the room was on its feet, cheering, crying, applauding our love.

I felt like Sally Field in *Norma Rae*. All I needed was a handwritten sign with union scrawled on it.

Then, I forced myself to stop thinking in pop culture terms and face the real world.

Tony. This man, this good man, whom I would now share a life with.

Rafi, too. A child who, I swore then and there, would never wind up a Lost Boy.

This was my family. This was my life.

Against the odds, I'd found them.

I'd never be lost again.

If I had it my way, none of us would be.

And, much to my surprise, I had better luck having it my way than I'd ever have imagined.